THE LAST INAUGURATION

THE LAST INAUGURATION

CHARLES LICHTMAN

Lifetime Books, Inc.
Hollywood, Florida

Copyright © 1998 by Charles Lichtman
All rights reserved. Published by Lifetime Books, Inc., 2131 Hollywood Boulevard,
Hollywood, FL 33020. Phone: 1-800-771-3355.
http:www//lifetimebooks.com; e-mail: lifetime@shadow.net

This publication is a work of fiction. While many of the characters in this novel are real
people, most are not. The events and conversations depicted herein did not occur; any
similarities to actual events are purely coincidental.

Library of Congress Cataloging-in Publication Data
Lichtman, Charles H., 1955—
    The last inauguration / Charles H. Lichtman.
        p. cm.
    ISBN 0-8119-0871-2
    I. Title.
    PS3562. I322L37   1998
    813' .54--dc21   97-44989
                                       CIP

10 9 8 7 6 5 4 3 2 1
Interior Design by Vicki Heil
Printed in Canada

ACKNOWLEDGMENTS

To Gayle, my best friend, wife and love. For without her understanding, sacrifice and support, this project would not have been possible.

In no particular order, my thanks to the following persons for their technical expertise or other assistance: Israel Saferstein of the United States Customs Department, Charlotte Woolard and Tikki Davies of The Kennedy Center, Larry Goldman of Restaurant Associates at The Kennedy Center, Gary Baron and the staff at The Holocaust Museum, the security officers at the United Nations Palais des Nations in Geneva, Matt Mehringer, Dr. Alberto Kriger, James Feeney and Robert Lichtman. A special note of appreciation to my friend Charles Katz; to Frank Weimann, my agent; to Callie Rucker for her patience with me, not to mention her hard, excellent work; and to Don Lessne at Lifetime Books for this special opportunity.

PROLOGUE

"DOGTAGS!" bellowed Sam Phillips into the microphone, the order reverberating through the speakers and off the compact metal fuselage of the Whiskey Cobra Attack helicopter. Instantly, a dozen of America's finest marines reached inside their black and green camouflage fatigues, ripping off their ID chains and passing them to the front.

The CIA Middle East bureau chief chomped hard on a three piece wad of Juicy Fruit and continued, "Remember, once you're out there, you're on your own. This mission doesn't exist. If you get caught, we're not coming back for you."

Nobody flinched. These twelve volunteered. They knew the risks and that their destiny that night was either success or death. There was little possibility for anything in between.

Phillips grabbed the night vision binoculars swaying on a hook and examined the skies in all directions through both open side doors and the cockpit window. Surrounding the chopper in formation was an air armada of sixteen Sea Knight transport helicopters and nine other Cobras, all empty except for gunners, ready to provide support if needed. The deafening roar of six fully armed Harrier attack jets blew by overhead to provide advance cover, the sign that their landing was imminent, and, a moment later, the helicopter made a steep dive. This was the eighth straight night the U.S. air convoy crossed the Saudi border and made its illegal entry into Iraqi airspace, testing the recently defeated enemy's fortitude and courage before turning around, working to confuse and lull Saddam Hussein's defenses into a false sense of security. Tonight would be different.

A red bulb over a door started flashing and Phillips grabbed the mike again. "Line up." In perfect synchronization the men rose and formed a column.

He looked them over, took a deep breath and said, "Don't forget men. Get in. Kill him. Get out. Whatever you do, finish the job."

Seconds later the helicopter touched the ground. The moment the red light turned off and a green light glowed, Phillips yelled, "Go!"

The marines had already started jumping out into the waist high brush in an open field situated with an adjacent wooded area not even a hundred yards away. Each man was a walking arsenal, carrying M-16's fitted with infra-red night sights and six thirty round clips, a silenced Ruger pistol, a knife, and a lightweight M203 40mm grenade launcher strapped to his back.

No sooner had the helicopter lifted back up before a bright yellow light flashed on and off three times from the woods. The men dropped flat to the ground, remaining motionless and invisible in the brush, silently counting off thirty seconds to themselves. The light resumed its blinking pattern again, starting exactly on the thirty count. Precisely sixty seconds later the light blinked three more times, followed by a ten second beam. One marine stayed on his knees, aiming his flashlight into the woods, turning it on and off twice, before an identical signal was returned simultaneously. Cautiously the marines rose, spread out and practically squatting, inched their way towards the trees, their M-16's in ready position.

Twenty yards before their destination a tall man in foreign battle dress suddenly appeared from the thicket with two fully armed soldiers flanking him on each side. "Colonel Ronn?" the man questioned in a thick accent.

The marine who flashed his light responded by standing erect, stepping forward and replying, "General Ali?"

The General, chief of Iraq's armed forces nodded and answered, "Time is short. We can talk on the way. Follow me." En masse, without hesitation, the Americans disappeared into the woods with the Iraqis. For half an hour the contingent moved swiftly through the near pitch darkness on a well traveled trail carved from a thousand years of use as a trader's route. When they reached an opening at a dirt road, they stopped.

The Iraqi barked an order into a walkie talkie and within seconds the unmistakable sound of a large truck could be heard starting its engine, then lumbering towards them. Only moments later an Iraqi Army transport truck pulled up, and the entire group scampered into the back, grabbing seats on wooden benches lining each side.

As the truck pulled away, Colonel Ronn asked, "General, you're sure Hussein is at the compound tonight?"

"I spoke with him myself. He's there with some of his family and Captain Sabar of the Mukhabarat."

"We'll try not to hurt them," said Ronn dryly, reciting the official orders provided by Washington.

"No! The family is powerful. And Sabar is an octopus. The influence of the secret police reaches like tentacles in all directions. Kill them all," the General exclaimed emphatically. He then paused and in a low voice, practically begging, added, "Please. Give Iraq its fresh start."

Ronn looked over his men. They knew from his icy stare that their squad leader agreed not just with General Ali, but with their unofficial orders whispered to them only hours before by Sam Phillips. They agreed too. This was war. On tonight's exercise, whoever was in the way would be removed.

"Your men look ready," said Ali, observing the focused and calm demeanors of each man as well as the clear cohesiveness of the group.

"They're professionals. They've been here before. They know the plan," replied Ronn. "But of course we couldn't have done it without you. Getting us the layout of Saddam's retreat was critical."

"To give the credit where it's due, those plans were obtained by Minister Said. He will join me in Baghdad in the morning after the mission is complete -- to make the official statement introducing the new government."

The truck drove for almost an hour, the men totally silent, as they contemplated their need for success in this most covert of missions. When the truck finally stopped, General Ali announced, "We're a mile away. We'll walk from here. The vehicle is too noisy to go further."

As the marines started piling out, Ronn provided one last reminder. "Aim for the head. If you hit his body, do it ten times."

From that point on, nobody spoke a word, for nothing more needed to be said. Each man knew his job and besides, words were noise. Noise was unnecessary.

Moving with cat like stealth and grace, the platoon swiftly glided through the woods on the side of the road for the last mile to Saddam Hussein's favorite family vacation compound. The half-moon provided just enough light to pave the way, allowing the marines to lurk concealed in the shadows, as they traveled to their intended scene of confrontation. When they finally stood together, cloaked in the last bit of natural camouflage brush before the cutaway opening leading to the encampment, Colonel Ronn seized their attention by the simple wave of his hand. He pointed down at his watch. With a strong point of his finger, the soldiers concurrently pushed the stopwatch function on their own timepieces. Having only five minutes to reach their intended destination, they instantly dispersed into an open field, belly crawling in different directions towards the twelve foot tall barbed wire perimeter fence.

Success meant first taking out the guards, and second, gaining entrance into the compound; both needing to be achieved with total silence to avoid alerting the inhabitants of the impending attack. Exactly at the five minute mark the marine assault simultaneously struck all corners of the complex.

Lying on his stomach only ten yards from the south fence, a sharp-shooting marine extended his arms and fired one bullet from his silenced Ruger straight into the head of a German Shepard patrol dog, the gun making no more noise than a soft cough. An instant later, before the canine's master could even figure out what happened, two bullets blew through his chest, knocking him flat on his back, dead.

At virtually the exact same moment eighty yards away on the opposite side of the compound, with identical precision and choice of weaponry, another marine took out Saddam Hussein's second guard dog and companion soldier.

Other marines and General Ali's two soldiers strategically situated outside the main gate, focusing on the handiwork of their colleagues through night vision binoculars. The instant both dog patrols went down, Ali's men, feigning drunkenness and laughing boisterously, stumbled toward the sole sentry guard, standing watch at the gate.

"Who's there?" demanded the guard, pointing his AK-47 at the two soldiers.

One of them fell down practically flat on his face, rolled over and bounced back up laughing. Waving his arms he answered, "If you're going to shoot me, let me have just one more drink so at least I won't feel it." He turned to his partner, grabbed at but missed his arm and said, "Anwar, give me that bottle."

Laughing, Anwar held a quart bottle with a dark liquid in his hand and teasingly raised his arm up and away from his friend. "No, Mustaf. I gave you enough already. Besides, I paid for this, not you," he added as they continued toward the entrance of the compound, the guard within arms distance, separated only by a locked barbed wire gate.

Anwar turned to the guard, held out the bottle and slurring his words said, "Now *you* can have some. *You* didn't get any yet. Do *you* want some scotch? It's right out of Captain Sabar's private stock."

The guard eyed the bottle and then responded, "Are you Mukhabarat? How did you get outside?"

Anwar opened his eyes wide, poked Mustaf in the ribs and said, "Mustaf, how about that! Someone that doesn't know us for once." He then pulled an identification card out of his pants pocket and showed it to the guard, who read it through the fence with the aid of a flashlight.

"Oh, top level Mukhabarat! You really are Sabar's men."

"Yes. And would you *please* let us in because if the 'Prince of Doom' finds Mustaf and me sleeping outside the gate in the morning, he'll have our heads," said Anwar, now swaying as he talked.

Mustaf cracked up laughing again. "And you can have as much of this bottle as you want too."

"Of course," said the guard smiling, first turning a lock and then moving a sliding barrier post out of the way before pushing open the heavy gate. "Get in here. You're both a mess. You owe me for this one."

Anwar walked in, stumbled and fell into the guard's arms. Mustaf slipped behind the guard and instantly put him into a full windpipe crushing choke hold. With the flick of a wrist, Anwar produced a stiletto from inside his shirt sleeve, jabbed the blade into the guard's stomach and yanked it almost a foot across the man's side. By the time the guard fell to the ground, he was already dead.

Seconds later the remaining ten marines sprinted the forty yards from their prone positions in the field to the now open gate. No one paused even for a breath once they reached the compound, and they quickly spread out in all directions.

Two marines moved towards the eighty foot watchtower on the northeast corner which provided the clearest view of the entrance road, as well as the surrounding geography. They bounded up the steps two at a time until the last twenty feet where they slowed down only to lessen the noise of their boots stomping up the steps. When they reached the platform they crouched down on a small ledge to stay below the view of the security booth's window, laying down their M-16s and retrieving their Rugers. They crawled to the door with a marine positioned in a low squat on each side.

Signaling with a nod, one marine opened the door and the other jumped into the booth, his pistol extended. The two Iraqi sentries were caught completely by surprise. As they turned around from hearing the creak of the door, they were met with a flurry of bullets that didn't stop until the first marine's nine round clip was empty. The second reholstered his Ruger, not needing to fire a shot. The marines stepped over the bodies, pulled out their knives and started cutting every cord visible. Less than a minute later they were back down on ground level.

Sixty yards away four marines burst into the three room command post building. Rushing into the front room with their Rugers ready, they sprayed the room with bullets, killing the two guards sitting at a table playing cards. Another Iraqi guard ran towards a back room, diving and narrowly escaping a barrage of bullets. By the time two marines reached the room only a few seconds later the guard was at a microphone trying to call for help, but was cut down instantly, shot in the back repeatedly. He slumped over the electronic panel and the Marines tossed him to the ground. They then removed their knives and started cutting cords, also firing their pistols indiscriminately into every piece of electronic equipment visible.

The two other marines searched the rest of the premises confirming no one was hiding, and laid out four prepackaged C4 plastic explosives, setting the timers for detonation at ten minutes.

Across the great yard of the complex two other marines were at work silently destroying the wiring in the compound's power station with acid, and by cutting wires and planting plastique. By the time they finished, all telephonic and wire communications with the outside world were terminated.

Only four minutes had passed since the front gate opened. The marines were right on schedule, converging from all directions, while the entire group convened outside the soldier's barracks. The lights were out and there was no sign that any of the twenty Iraqi soldiers inside and asleep had a clue about what was going on outside. Every marine checked and readied his M-16. Colonel Ronn stepped to the front, steadying his grenade launcher in front of him. He looked back at his troops and nodded sternly. They knew they had only a few seconds in this building if they were to next sneak into Saddam's residence, before the advantage of the element of surprise was defeated and any defense could be mounted.

Ronn turned around, took a deep breath and nodded again. A marine held open the door while Ronn and eight of the men rushed inside. Not two seconds passed before Ronn fired his grenade launcher into the middle of the ceiling, while two other marines fired theirs into opposite side walls, causing massive explosions and instantaneous fire only thirty yards away. The three stepped back as the remaining marines each showered the room with bullets from their M-16s, firing in the direction of the bunk beds, emptying their thirty round clips and then running back out the door. Ronn dropped a grenade as he left, making sure that if anyone inside the barracks somehow survived, they were trapped without exit.

Without interference, Anwar, Mustaf and the marines sprinted in a group towards Saddam's house fifty yards away, changing their rifle clips as they ran. Half the men charged the back entrance of the home, while the other half rushed through the front. They were inside no more than ten seconds when the building exploded in a blinding bright light and with such force that the ground shook a mile away. A second stronger blast followed and a sea of fire blew apart the walls and roof into shrapnel debris blanketing a 100 yard radius. What was only moments before a building, was now not even a foundation. All at once the marines' locator tracking sensors hidden in each man's boots disappeared off the AWACS plane circling at the nearby Saudi and Iraq border. An instant later the marines C4 explosives detonated, destroying the command post and power station. Fires burned everywhere in the compound.

General Ali stood just outside the woods near the road, his shoulders slumped, his hand over his mouth, the night vision binoculars at his feet. His eyes remained locked on the scarce remains of Saddam's burning home before he buried his hands in his face. He looked up a few seconds later in surprise upon hearing his name. Surrounding him were four Iraqi soldiers and Captain Sabar of the secret police, their pistols pointed in anticipation that he might as much as flinch the wrong way. Standing next to them laughing was Saddam Hussein.

ONE

"So ILICH, WHAT IS SO important that you had to interrupt my day?" Saddam Hussein asked Ilich Ramirez Sanchez, known to the world as the infamous *"Carlos the Jackal."* He rhythmically tapped his fingernails on the oversized desk in his gaudily decorated presidential office that served as a personal living memorial.

"One of my sources has confirmed that the Americans have issued new secret orders to have you killed."

"Again?" Saddam blandly asked, showing no surprise.

Carlos answered by sitting back in his chair, raising his eyebrows and folding his hands on his lap.

Saddam lit a cigarette and took a deep drag. "Haven't they punished me enough for the Gulf War?" he asked angrily. He swiveled his chair so that his back was to Carlos, then turned and calmly, but with frustration asked, "When are they going to quit?"

"As I hear it, not until the mission is accomplished," Carlos answered in a matter of fact tone, speaking perfect Arabic. Part of his genius was picking up not just foreign languages, but their various distinctive dialects as well. He was also fluent in English, Spanish, French, German, Italian, Russian and even passable Hebrew.

"Just to make sure -- your source is reliable?"

"He is the best. Never wrong," Carlos answered. "He's at the top of the government."

"Why would he tell you?" Saddam asked skeptically.

"For as many governments that wish to see me dead, there's as many that wish to have me alive. Apparently, there are people who must feel the same way about you. Even in Washington. Look, I have powerful contacts all over the world that like to do me favors. And I can still return one myself."

"Yes, in some very dark ways," Saddam smirked.

It was true and Carlos would never deny it. Terrorism was his chosen profession. Carlos wore a confident, smug smile. "I know you understand as well as anyone that information is power. They have information. I have information. It's a commodity as tradable as oil and often far more valuable."

Saddam raised his eyebrows. "So my friend, do you know the method of attack?"

"This time I heard it's the Mossad."

"That's no surprise. The U.S. has already proven their best marines could not do the job," said Saddam, a smirk stretched across his face.

Carlos touched his temple and extended his hand outwards as a salute to Saddam's success. "If the Mossad handles this cleanly, Israel has been promised continued funding for their Arrow anti-tactical missile, as well as a financial package to help with its Russian immigrant problem."

"Of course -- I'm sure the Jews would love to kill me," Saddam mused, adding a shrug. "I cannot say this is a surprise. America has tried to kill me for years, so why should they stop now?" Saddam bobbed his head up and down in self congratulations. "But I have survived, and I will survive."

He sighed, stood and stared out of the third story office window of his lavish, palm tree studded palace situated on the muddy Tigris River. Four Soviet T-72 tanks, numerous other armed vehicles and a squad of Republican Guardsmen, the elite of Iraq's army, stood watch below. The president's personal military helicopter was nearby in case he needed to be whisked away at a moment's notice.

Saddam gestured with an open palm to the window. "It is good you came to see me today, because I wanted to talk to you also." He paused and lowered his voice. "I still can't believe the coup attempt by General Ali and Minister Said. In the name of Allah -- conspiring with the Americans!" He pounded his fist on his desk as his face turned flush. "I must take decisive action to end this nonsense! Your report today confirms it! I have to hit them first!"

"And you have to hit them hard," Carlos shot right back. "You have to hit them so hard they'll never try to touch you again!"

"Absolutely right." Saddam leaned over his desk and stared deep into Carlos' eyes. "I've given this a lot of thought. I have a solution."

"Like what?"

"You."

"Me? How can I resolve this?" Carlos asked with a shrug of his shoulders.

"I have a plan. If it works, it will shift the balance of power from Washington to the Middle East, Iraq especially. And, along with this, we will finally drive Israel into the sea."

"You didn't answer my question," Carlos said sharply. "What does this have to do with me?"

"Ilich," Saddam calmly responded. "You're the only person with the intellect and experience to make my plan succeed. I have only asked you to train a few of my men, and for a couple of other minor favors. I have let you stay here. I have protected you. In many countries you would simply be shot on sight," Saddam commented.

"So what do you want?" Carlos retorted impatiently.

Saddam Hussein paused, took a deep breath and said, "They kill me. I kill them. It is only fair."

Carlos didn't even blink. "So you want me to kill the president of the United States?"

"No. No. No," Saddam said, drawing out each "no." "That does nothing. I want more." Saddam looked down as he stubbed out his cigarette, then looked up and said, "I want to take out the whole

U.S. government. Everybody. At once. Then, after you complete your work, I will start mine."

"Which is?" Carlos inquired.

"The final Holy War with Israel. The nuclear bomb we are completing can be dropped on Tel Aviv without killing that many Arabs. Then we invade. Just think of it. The end of America and Israel. Together we will be heroes." Saddam raised his arms in the air in victory.

Carlos leaned back and scratched his head in thoughtful skepticism. "You ask too much. The president is the hardest man in the world to kill, and your goal is far more complex. Besides, aren't you taking this a bit too far? Most Arabs don't even favor using an atomic device on Israel and killing the president may alienate your allies."

In a passionate and fevered voice Saddam responded, "Since the war ended I have longed for revenge against the U.S. It is my enemy. They are imperialists who support anti-Arab policies, and did so even before the theft of Arab land and the founding of that Zionist refuge. And the Jews? Nobody likes them anyway."

Falling back in his chair and planting his elbows on his desk Saddam pointedly asked, "Are you of all people saying the Americans can't be murdered?"

"No. I'm just saying it will be difficult. Very difficult."

"I wasn't suggesting it would be easy. Besides, you just told me to hit them back harder than they hit me."

Carlos rubbed his chin, shook his head and said. "I have nothing to gain by doing this. All I see is the opportunity for me to go to an earlier grave."

"Think, Ilich. If you die tomorrow no one will remember you. The name 'Carlos' will be forgotten. Already, men such as Abu Nidal claim to be greater than you." Saddam's voice increased in intensity as he leaned towards Carlos and pointed at the terrorist. "This is your chance to establish yourself with me as a legend who brought the Arab nations out of the dark ages. We shall not be denied. This is our destiny. Feel it. Grasp it. Make your mark."

Carlos moved from his chair and stood in front of the window gazing out at the horizon. Softly, he said, "It's true. I do miss the action."

Saddam Hussein continued, "I know you're down to less than one million Swiss francs. That will last you two to three more years at best, even living here. But I can assure the permanent security for your family. So tell me. How much do you want?"

Carlos was silent for almost a minute before turning around and looking Saddam Hussein square in the eyes. "Fifty million Swiss francs deposited upon my instructions immediately. Not when I am done, but payment in full now."

"That's ridiculous! Algiers only paid you five million for the OPEC transaction and the Medellin Cartel paid you the same to kill Noriega. And you didn't even succeed there."

Carlos glared at Saddam, not appreciating the dig, but kept his cool. "How can you compare those missions to what you propose now? Wiping out the U.S. government will be an act unprecedented in history. Even you admit no one else but me could even attempt it. If you want a contract, this is my price."

Saddam knew Carlos was both right and unmovable. "Fine. The price is fair, but what assurance do I have you'll perform? That is a lot of money."

"You know my word is my bind. If it was not, I couldn't have survived this long," Carlos snapped. He paused before calmly adding, "Nevertheless, you'll have the best collateral you could want. My family shall remain in Baghdad. I know what their fate will be if I fail to act properly. And, as an added show of my good faith, when the financial transfer is complete, I have my own score to settle in Geneva which is consistent with your goals. After that you'll have no doubt of exactly how serious I am."

"What are you talking about?"

"You'll see. There's something I've wanted to do the past few years, and now is the time. When the event occurs you'll know it was me. If you don't approve of my work, or complications arise so that you wish to cancel the contract, then I'll give back all but two million. But, for personal security, I must make the arrange-ments myself, and keep the plans silent. Even from you."

"Ilich. I do not care about Geneva. I want only for this job in America to be done."

"Trust me. You'll be pleased with the results. Besides, however I figure out this grand scheme against the U.S., important ground-work has to be laid in Geneva. I'd have to go there at some point anyway."

"Fine. So do we have a deal?" Saddam asked.

"No. Not yet. I want a helicopter, fully gassed and maintained, with flying lessons for both me and my wife. Also, I need 250,000 Swiss francs to cover my expenses in Geneva."

"Done!"

"I'm not. You will also pay all expenses of the operation, re-gardless of the cost. And no questions asked. This is my operation, not yours. Finally, no one shall know what we are working on. For both of our protection, it must remain a secret."

"Is that all?" Saddam asked impatiently.

"Yes. For now."

"Then consider it done. When do we start?"

"Today. This moment." Carlos stared at Saddam, having just been the only person in years to order the president around.

Saddam grinned broadly, stood up and hugged Carlos roughly. "My brother, let us celebrate a return to Arab glory," he said buoy-antly.

Carlos put his palms up to stop him and caustically said, "Saddam, we have nothing yet to celebrate."

SITTING IN THE STUDY of his Baghdad villa, his children playing in the next room, Carlos, the most feared and ruthless ter-rorist in modern history, also a family man, prepared to come out of informal retirement. His last acts of documented public violence were bloody attacks against Israel's El Al jets at the Vienna and Rome airports in 1985.

Most of the world associated Carlos with the late December 1975 kidnapping of 11 OPEC oil ministers in Vienna. Ironically, many of the victims of the OPEC affair were the same Arabs that Carlos was now allied with, sharing the same militant anti-American, anti-Zionist view of the world.

Years later, when Carlos sought refuge in Baghdad, few conditions were imposed upon him by Saddam Hussein. Carlos, the purveyor of more governmental secret information than almost any spy worldwide, would share any important secrets he obtained that could benefit Iraq. And, as he had done for years in other radical Arab countries, he would periodically train Iraqi agents in terrorist and intelligence activities.

In return, Carlos was given free use of a villa where he lived with his wife, Magdelena Kopp, a former member of the dreaded West German terrorist group of the seventies, the Baader-Meinhof gang. Saddam also set up telephone and telefax lines so that the terrorist could monitor the globe's sensitive political affairs by maintaining crucial personal contact with his countless well-placed intelligence sources. He was free to come and go across Iraqi borders at will, and Saddam even occasionally facilitated Carlos' travel by authorizing State aircraft to fly him to the Eastern Bloc destination of his choice.

Carlos quickly endeared himself to Saddam, who realized that Carlos had an excellant understanding of world affairs, the economics of oil, and East-West relations. And as much as anything, Carlos possessed natural magnetism which always drew people to him, and Saddam Hussein was captivated by that and Carlos' sheer brilliance.

Today, Carlos was working with Semtex, a devastatingly powerful yet simple to use plastic explosive. It only took seven ounces squeezed into a personal cassette player to blow Pan Am Flight 103 out of the air over Lockerbie, Scotland in 1988. Carlos owned over 200 pounds of it. For his first mission in years, Carlos would meticulously prepare the bombs which upon explosion, would send shock waves throughout the world. The riskiest part of the venture would be slipping through customs and smuggling the Semtex into

Switzerland. Thus, disguising the plastique had to be done with the utmost care, so Swiss customs inspectors would have no idea what they were looking at. One never knew how thoroughly customs agents would search baggage in Geneva's Ferney Aeroport.

Working with Semtex was easy. The yellowish colored explosive had a putty like composition capable of being molded into any shape. Carlos knew how to take advantage of the product's flexibility to suit his purposes.

A new box of toothpaste lay before him. He carefully slipped the blade of his Swiss Army Knife into the bottom of the paper carton to open the cardboard without tearing it. He then wedged open the bottom of the tube until it was fully exposed with a gaping hole, and the toothpaste oozed out by itself. Over the next ten minutes Carlos used his knife and a bent hanger to scrape out practically every last bit of the toothpaste, ensuring the perfect cylindrical integrity of the tube.

Refilling it with Semtex was more tedious; Carlos spent the next half hour working with the knife, the eraser side of a pencil and his fingers to mold the Semtex into the tube, ensuring that it retained its shape. He used thin nosed pliers to reseal the tube's bottom and glued the carton closed. This disguised tube of toothpaste contained no fluoride and would prevent no cavities. Rather, it was now a most potentially deadly 8.4 ounce bomb, which, when ignited with a simple detonator, could knock down a steel reinforced concrete wall.

The next product transformation was much simpler. Carlos carefully unwrapped a new large bar of soap without ripping the paper. After measuring its dimensions with a ruler, he cut off a block of Semtex from a freshly wrapped kilo, and whittled away until its size exactly matched the soap. He rewrapped the Semtex into and sealed the original paper, and put the package into a plastic travel soap box.

The metamorphosis of the third item was even easier. Carlos emptied the contents of a wide neck 16 ounce green plastic shampoo bottle down the kitchen drain, and using the same tools that he made his toothpaste bomb with, painstakingly packed the shampoo bottle full of explosive material.

Carlos next scraped out all of the white goop from Magdelena's cold cream jar, saving much of it on a paper plate. He then placed another 12 ounces of Semtex into the blue glass, leaving about a half an inch of space at the top. Carlos trimmed and inserted aluminum foil to match the inside circumference of the jar, and then filled some of the cold cream back up to the top.

Carlos enjoyed the irony of preparing his final explosive. He needed Saddam's help to acquire his last piece of camouflage, but after calling around Baghdad, a thoroughly Moslem city, a King James Bible was finally located at the eminent Al Rasheed Hotel and delivered to Carlos. He defaced the Book by cutting out a large, deep square from the inside pages, leaving a one inch perimeter intact. Folding aluminum foil inside the cut out opening, he then stuffed another 14 ounces of Semtex into the Holy Scriptures. Carlos knew that the border patrol guard would never consider opening up the bible to question the word of God.

One by one, Carlos carefully examined his work to ensure nothing looked suspicious. He felt secure that even a moderate inspection of his luggage by Swiss customs inspectors would not reveal the four pounds of Semtex secreted into apparently harmless personal effects. If seven ounces of the explosive could knock a jumbo jet out of the sky, he was now prepared with four pounds to destroy something much bigger.

TWO

CARLOS REMAINED WANTED with outstanding arrest warrants against him in almost every European country, including Switzerland. His crimes ranged from murdering two policemen in Paris, to the attempted assassination of a prominent zionist millionaire in London, to planting bombs at the Rome Airport, to plotting to kill Pope John Paul II in Korea. In total, he committed at least sixty notorious acts of terrorism from the early '70s to the mid '80s, many of which were sanctioned by the Iron Curtain or radical Arab countries.

Though one of the most wanted criminals on the globe, hardly any photographs of Carlos existed. His highly refined skill at disguise, relatively plain features, and mastery of languages assured that he could blend into any and everywhere. While the world press frequently called Carlos "the Jackal," he preferred "the Chameleon." It was certainly more accurate to compare him to a cold blooded reptile able to meld into different surroundings, than it was to simply call him a sly wolf.

One thing was certain: Carlos could never be too careful in planning international travel, because his first mistake would be his last. Thus, he always assumed an alias matching one of his 46 expertly forged or stolen passports. Yemen had even provided him diplomatic passport number 001278 under the name Ahmed Fawaz, which under international law authorized Carlos to pass through all customs checkpoints without inspection of any kind.

To avoid the potential customs scrutiny of traveling under the prejudiced auspices of the state owned jets of Iraqi Airways, with a Soviet made AK-47 under his front seat for security, Carlos drove the 570 miles from Baghdad to Riyadh, Saudi Arabia, to fly SwissAir direct to Geneva. Along the route, Carlos successfully passed out countless 500 Saudi riyal bills to soldiers, border control and ticketing agents to smooth his safe passage.

At the King Khalid International Airport, he changed into a gray pinstriped Armani suit to add respectability to his cover. It was pointless, if not suicidal, to bring the automatic weapon with him into the airport. If his self-defense required a gun, a single weapon wouldn't matter. His fate would be death.

The six hour flight from Riyadh to Geneva was expectedly unremarkable, and the plane landed on time at 1:15 p.m. Carlos left the gate and entered a narrow walkway plastered with mini-billboards alternating advertisements between Swiss banks and Swiss watches. He carried only a winter overcoat, a near empty briefcase with a false bottom hiding the 250,000 Swiss francs Saddam had put up for this mission, and a Gucci carry on suitbag stuffed with clothes and Semtex.

The first checkpoint was at the end of the long hall, where at the Passport Control booth, security would inspect his papers. Although deep down he didn't expect any trouble, Carlos knew that getting past this first stop would determine whether he would have safe passage into Switzerland. He looked ahead into the security room. The lines were short and Carlos intuitively headed for the cubicle with the oldest guard, the only one of the four patrolmen on guard smiling. Adrenaline shot through his veins and his natural catlike instincts took over.

"Good afternoon sir. Your passport, please," the guard said.

While handing him the passport, Carlos responded, "It looks slow today. Where are all the skiers?"

The guard's grin told him he was home free. The old man inspected a French passport depicting Carlos in jacket and tie as Jean-Luc Finet, a resident of Paris born in 1949, with port of entry stamps proving visits all over the world.

"Mr. Finet, is the nature of your travel here business or pleasure?"

"Business. I wish it was pleasure."

"How long will you be in Switzerland?"

"Until Wednesday morning." It was Monday.

"And what do you do?"

"I'm a distributor for an international plastics company."

"Where are you staying?"

"The Metropol. I've heard it's very nice. Do you know anything about it?"

"It is one of Geneva's finest hotels," the agent squeaked. "You will be very happy there."

"That's great. I hate to leave my wife and kids, so if I have to travel, at least I want to stay some place comfortable."

"Yes. Of course. Have a nice stay." The guard stamped the passport and handed it back to The Chameleon.

"Thank you," Carlos smiled, thinking, "*Idiot.*" He moved past the security window and through sliding glass doors into the baggage claim area. Carlos took a moment to survey the area amidst the chaos. This was the Ferney Aeroport as he remembered it — without a security guard in sight. He walked through a gate with thirty other people into a bustling modern lobby, then straight outdoors. He smirked as the cold air smacked him in the face, and he hailed the first in a stream of Mercedes taxis.

Twelve minutes later, Carlos pulled up not to the Hotel Metropol, but to the Hotel du Rhone, a block long, six story structure that more resembled a low rent office building in a U.S. suburb more than a modern European luxury hotel. As always, when he stayed here he admired the view of the tree lined boulevards and office buildings of Geneva in front of the hotel, right where Lake Geneva

merged into the Rhone River. A doorman offered to take Carlos'
belongings, but he politely refused. Entering the hotel he instantly
noticed substantial renovations since his last visit. Symmetrical
rich redwood planks covered the lobby walls. A large sitting room
still smelling of fresh paint was off to his left, and a quaint cocktail
lounge was off to his right.

Seconds later an impeccably dressed man behind the counter
smiled and acknowledged his arrival. Carlos approached him and
said, "Good afternoon. Reservation for Finet. Jean-Luc Finet."

"Yes Mr. Finet. Welcome. Please let me check," he said as he
typed into a computer terminal. "We have your reservation listed
for two nights in a master suite with a king size bed. How do you
wish to pay for the room?"

"Here's my credit card," Carlos said, handing the clerk an American Express Platinum card in the name Seltaeb, S.A. "Do I have
any messages?"

"Let me check." The desk clerk ducked away. Twenty seconds
later he reappeared with a slip of paper which he handed to Carlos.
It read, "Call Mr. Miguel Farbero." The clerk then handed Carlos a
bulky steel key marked 612 and offered his full assistance, which
Carlos declined.

As Carlos rode the tiny intricately molded brass lift upstairs, he
thought how well everything was going so far. No problem crossing the border and checking into the du Rhone had been a breeze.
Of course, it helped that the desk clerk was actually Pierre Erne,
Assistant Manager, and Carlos' roommate and fellow terrorist in
Paris in the early '70s, when Carlos started his reign of terror. Though
retired from terrorism, he escaped going to jail only through the
influence of a wealthy family. But to this day, Pierre remained loyal
to his friend and until Carlos left, Pierre would work double shifts
and note any out of place visitors or unusual calls about guests. In
the public lobby of the hotel, Carlos was just another guest to be
treated professionally. In the privacy of room 612, he was a brother.

The message that Miguel Farbero called was Pierre's signal that
he had confirmed Carlos was safe to travel about Geneva. If no

message was waiting, Carlos would have gone to a pay phone where a minute later, Pierre would discretely slip him a note providing Carlos with instructions for his safe and immediate passage out of Switzerland.

Carlos quickly unpacked his bag. He took 150,000 francs from the fake bottom of the briefcase and locked it in the room safe, after first placing 30,000 francs in his wallet and another 30,000 into his money clip. He also wore a money belt hiding an extra 40,000 francs. Years of experience taught Carlos that if he couldn't get what he wanted through violence, he could get it with money.

Five minutes later, Carlos exited the du Rhone into the crisp azure Geneva air. He surveyed the scenery down the river, his eye catching the prominently displayed neon signs that announced UOB Bank, Lloyds Bank, Credit Lyonnais and so on. He would not, could not, conduct his affairs in such public institutions.

Carlos crossed a suspension bridge and briskly continued up the hill of Boulevard Georges-Favon, the gateway to where the real money and power of Switzerland was located: its private banks. He walked past bank after bank, turned up Rue de Hesse and stopped in front of an unnoteworthy building, marked only by a small polished bronze sign engraved, "Banque Privee Ruf, S.A."

Carlos pushed open the heavy baroque door directly into a 20' by 20' lobby with pink marble floors, well furnished with antiques, paintings and plants. Private Swiss banking took place behind closed doors and to get past them, Carlos had to first deal with the receptionist who greeted him with a pleasant but artificial smile.

"May I help you, sir?"

"Please. I'm here to see Mr. Jacques Ruf."

"Do you have an appointment, sir?"

"I'm sorry, no, but I know he'll see me."

"I'm sorry sir, but Mr. Ruf has clients with him this moment, and he has scheduled engagements the rest of the afternoon. Perhaps if you tell me the nature of your business, I can direct you to someone else who can assist you." She followed with a cool smile.

Carlos walked up to the very edge of the desk, leaned over and politely but firmly said, "My business is confidential and no one else will do. Please call Mr. Ruf and tell him that Jean-Luc Finet is here and wishes to see him right now."

The receptionist just as politely but firmly responded, "I'm sorry sir, but I cannot do that. Mr. Ruf is the president of the bank and maintains a very busy schedule. He has standing instructions not to be interrupted when he is with clients. I'm sure that another bank officer can help assist you."

"No" was not a word Carlos accepted. In a soft but direct tone, punctuated with an intense stare he said, "Let me give you a few seconds to think about this. You can pick up the phone right now and tell Mr. Ruf that I am here, or you can refuse. If you don't call him and I leave, I will call him at home tonight on his private line. He will be very upset, not only because he didn't see me right now, but also because he'll have to leave his family to meet with me right then. I can also assure you that within 30 seconds after he hangs up the phone with me, he will also call you at home to tell you not to come to work tomorrow or ever again." In a fury that was pure acting, Carlos slammed his hand on the desk and screamed, "Now pick up the fucking phone and call him!"

Visibly shaken, the receptionist instantly did as she was told. She was shocked again when told to advise the guest that Mr. Ruf would be free momentarily. No more than three minutes later, a wiry, middle aged man with thick glasses and a traditional three piece suit appeared from a side door. He warmly greeted Carlos with a firm handshake and they disappeared down the hall.

They entered Ruf's huge oak panelled office, also decorated with priceless colorful Victorian antiques, paintings and tapestries, many of which were purchased by Jacques' great-grandfather Wilhem Ruf, when he founded the bank 106 years earlier. Ruf motioned Carlos to a chair in a corner, and sat down in the one next to him. A silver tray service with tea and pastries was waiting for them.

"So Jacques, I hope you don't mind me dropping in on you."

"After I saw you received a 50 million franc wire deposit, I figured you'd be paying me a visit."

"What's my balance now? 63 million?"

"You're slipping. You forgot accrued interest." Ruf walked over to his intricately handcarved desk, unlocked a drawer, and pulled out a document. "Actually, 66 million including last week's deposit. I must say, this is very disappointing. You now have more money than me." Ruf shook his head and smiled.

Carlos ignored Ruf's joke. "I need you to take care of some things for me."

"Such as?"

"Move 26 million into my B account and add Magdelena as a signatory."

"Oh. I didn't realize she was with you."

"She's not. I'll sign her name. You'll serve as the witness."

"Yes. Of course."

"Fine. Wire 10 million dollars to Banco de Caracas, Miami, Florida, account 1955621, in the name of Seltaeb, S.A. Send another $10 million to London Royal, account QT43057 in the name of Nileppez, P.L.C. Give me 500,000 francs in cash today, 1000 franc bills, fresh and clean. Take a million francs for your fee and keep the balance waiting for my next instructions."

Ruf wrote down nothing. Though he'd ascended to the top of one of the most prestigious and secretive financial institutions in the world by the good luck of lineage, he kept the job by performing with a level of excellence unmatched elsewhere in Geneva. And sometimes, excellence included bending the law.

"One million for my fee! That's an insult! You've come to me for seventeen years because you know that your affairs remain private here. I sign the Rule 305 clean funds certification so that your transfers avoid the scrutiny of Swiss officials who would otherwise ask for assurances this money is not the proceeds of some criminal enterprise. You couldn't get that warranty so cheap anyplace else in Geneva or Zurich."

"You think not?" Carlos retorted, surprised by Ruf's tone.

"What about all of the countless other items I've taken care of for you over the years? I never ask questions. I know the dirty business you're involved in." Ruf stopped and crossed himself before continuing. "I never pass judgment and I've never hinted to anyone that you're a client. Considering all this, be fair with me. For the risk I'm incurring on these transfers, 2.5 million is fair."

Carlos curled his lips and exhaled slowly, his anger rising. Nevertheless, most of what Jacques said was true, and certainly Carlos could never spend all that money. "You're a pig. You know that?" Carlos paused, looked down and then back up. "I'll give you two million. And don't forget I'm keeping 40 million francs in your Bank, which probably makes me one of your largest depositors."

Ruf beamed. He put his tea down, bent over and patted Carlos twice on the knee. "Your transfers will be taken care of before the day is out." He glanced at his white Roman dial Baume and Mercier watch, banded in tiny 24 karat gold links. It was 2:35 p.m. and the business of banking finished for the day in less than 90 minutes. "Ilich. I hate to ask, but you must excuse me so I can attend to these items for you. It's getting late."

"Yes. Of course. We're done for right now anyway. Just take me down to my safety deposit box. Also, save tomorrow night for me. We'll have a late dinner. Bring receipts showing the transfers were made. I'll call you with details."

Five minutes later Carlos was alone behind locked doors in a morgue-like, brightly lit room which held only 30 safety deposit boxes, each about the size and shape of a casket. Box 21 pulled out from the wall with a locking mechanism preventing it from falling onto the floor. Similar to the arsenals he kept in Paris, London and Prague, the box contained a thin, U.S. made, shoulder held, heat seeking missile launcher, capable of blowing a jet out of the sky or cutting a building in half. Nestled next to it were four shells wrapped in bubble plastic. Jacques had helped him sneak it into the bank five years ago. For a price, of course.

He picked up one of two Uzis and pretended to spray bullets across the room. There were various knives and handguns with over twenty assorted magazine clips stacked neatly. He opened a backpack and counted out a dozen hand grenades. He examined the

American made night vision goggles purchased from an ad in *Soldier of Fortune* magazine.

A knock at the door startled Carlos. It was unimaginable that anyone would ever be interrupted in the privacy of the safety deposit box room. He slammed a clip inside a Glock Model 20/21 10mm Automatic and demanded, "Who's there?"

"Sir. This is Monique. I am Mr. Ruf's assistant."

Carlos slid to the door, clicked the gun ready to fire and pointed the barrel up to the ceiling, opening the door slowly and very slightly. A beautiful young red haired woman in her late twenties stood alone holding a large tape sealed envelope. "Mr. Ruf told me to state his most profound apologies for calling on you here, but he was certain you would want this."

Carlos tucked the gun into the back of his pants and took the package. A second later Monique was gone and the door was relocked. Carlos ripped open the envelope to find 500 crisp 1000 Swiss franc bills. He was satisfied that Ruf was doing the job for which he was paid.

He then picked up one of six matching 9mm Berettas in one hand, a Glock in the other and compared the two guns. While the Glock was a lighter, slightly more powerful weapon with a standard twenty round magazine, Carlos had always been partial to Berettas because of the ease in manipulating the thumb magazine release. This was crucial because a fraction of a second spent changing an empty clip might spell the difference between life and death. Carlos loaded the Beretta, grabbed an extra clip and shoved it and the gun into an ankle holster.

He then counted out 50 of the new bills and folded them into his pants pocket. He put the rest of the money inside a second briefcase that already held huge denominations of Swiss francs, French francs, Deutschmarks and U.S. dollars. He skimmed four false passports and a series of other papers. Emptying the contents of a bag onto the table, the Chameleon picked through various mens and womens wigs, mustaches, sideburns, beards, glass frames and makeup supplies before placing his choices into his briefcase.

Last, Carlos found what he really wanted: an eight pound brick of Semtex. Although the explosive was incapable of detonating in its present state, he gently lay it into his briefcase. He then closed the box and pushed it back into place.

Minutes later, Carlos walked toward the upscale shopping district on Rue du Rhone. The splendid scenery on the avenue provided a cross section of Geneva's diverse architecture, ranging from classical Victorian and Gothic to art deco and ultra modern. The wide sidewalks were spotless, and the street was bustling with shoppers and businessmen. Carlos entered the Grand Passage, one of the best department stores in Geneva, knowing he could indulge in a frivolous shopping spree.

He located the General Manager drinking coffee and smoking a cigarette behind a desk in the Customer Service department. After stuffing a 1000 franc bill into his hand, the manager happily agreed to accompany Carlos through the store with two clerks in tow.

Over the next two hours Carlos walked floor by floor, department by department, frivolously picking up anything that looked remotely interesting. He bought clothes, shoes, toys, books, toiletries, compact discs, cookery, housewares, bedding, hardware and entertainment electronics. By the time he finished, a full furniture crate's worth of items would be filled for shipment back home to Baghdad, where few of the items were available.

To the General Manager's surprise, Carlos paid the 41,237 franc bill with cash, then tipped him another 1000 Swiss francs to ensure everything was packed correctly and delivered that night to Mr. Pierre Erne at the Hotel du Rhone. From there, Pierre would take care of getting the shipment over to his contact at Iraqi Airways, who already knew that a special diplomatic container, exempt from customs declarations and the U.N. embargo rules would be coming.

"I just remembered I forgot a few purchases in the electronics department," Carlos said as soon as the details of his business were arranged.

"Let me take you upstairs to get them," the manager replied.

"No thank you. You've already done enough. Just make sure my purchases make it to the hotel."

"Of course sir."

Once back in the electronics department, Carlos picked out a fully automatic 35mm flash camera, film, standard computer cable and six battery operated household outdoor/indoor lighting timers.

Carlos walked back through drizzle to the hotel on the expansive sidewalk along the Rhone River satisfied with the days events. At the six story Tour de I'lle belltower, he crossed over the river, walked down the post-workday traffic jammed Quai Th. Turrettini and minutes later arrived back in his hotel room.

Exhausted and seeking privacy, Carlos called room service and ordered enough food and drink for three people, intending to take advantage of fine dining while he could; for the kitchen at the du Rhone was renown worldwide.

Pierre joined Carlos for dinner, and they reminisced, drank hard and laughed until Carlos kicked him out, claiming he had work to do.

Carlos opened the Bible and pinched off a marble sized amount of Semtex. Using his Swiss Army Knife, he stripped an inch off of both ends of a short piece of the newly purchased computer cable and threaded one end of the wire through the input jack on one of the timers. Then he stuck the other end into the middle of the Semtex. He chronologized the clock function on the timer for 9:23 p.m. off his Rolex, and set the timer for 9:30. He put on his coat and carefully placed his mini-bomb into the pocket.

He checked his watch repeatedly. The elevator came at 9:25 and by 9:27 he was walking up the steep hill directly behind the du Rhone. At 9:28½ he ducked into an empty alley and removed the bomb from his coat. He placed it on the ground not quite against a wall and moved ten yards away, continually surveying the scene. The alley was black and no one was in sight. At precisely 9:30 a simultaneous intense flash of white light and a loud bang flooded the area.

"Excellent!" Carlos said aloud.

The brick where the Semtex was placed was chiseled out, and the timer was partially burned and cracked in half. Carlos quickly picked up the hot and partly melted timer, scanning the area to confirm the absence of witnesses. Then he walked back to the hotel, crossing the street to the river, where he nonchalantly dropped the timer into the water. He went back upstairs confident everything was falling into place. Just like always.

THREE

A GREY SKY AND COLD STIFF WIND greeted Carlos as he stepped out into a damp fog, the new camera slung around his shoulder. To wake himself up at what he viewed to be an outrageous hour of day, 6:55 a.m., he briskly walked the ten blocks to the Old Town section of Geneva, retracing backwards yesterday's route to the hotel from the Grand Passage.

Carlos effortlessly climbed the ancient steep and uneven brown stone steps and a narrow roadway that led into the Old Town. He wound his way through patternless brick paved streets, passing art galleries, antique shops, coffee houses and trendy stores, none of which showed signs of life in this young and chilly morning. At Rue du Calvin, he turned the corner and stopped.

He stood in front of a four story, 230-year-old, whitewashed, stone building with a brown mansard roof, and a hand painted sign on the window that read "Antiquities." He moved to the right of the window, counted up four large bricks from street level and then over two more. He stuck his Swiss Army Knife blade into an unnoticeable opening at the bottom of the stone and pried it loose. Working quickly, he manipulated the stone out of the wall, took a key from the empty spot where the stone had been, opened the door, and then replaced the key and stone.

After entering the shop, Carlos relocked the door and stepped around the eclectic clutter of knickknacks that the storekeeper called merchandise. He headed to the back office where he sat down in darkness in a bumpy leather chair. He pulled the Beretta out of his ankle holster and placed it on his lap. For the next hour, Carlos sat motionless in near meditation, still wearing his coat.

At about 8:30 the front door opened, signaled by the tone of three flat sounding bells knocking together. In an instant, Carlos was hiding in the shadow behind the office door, gun in hand. He heard shuffling feet, off key whistling and knew that a man was approaching the office. The moment the man stepped into the doorway, Carlos whirled around and locked his neck into a chokehold. He put the gun to his head and clicked off the safety. In a raspy, disguised voice and speaking broken Italian, Carlos said, "Do not speak. Do not move. If you do, you will beg to die before I kill you. And if I don't get the answers I want, I will leave you to suffer forever. If you understand, nod your head."

The man, well over 60, large but weak, shaking and breathing heavily, nodded his head repeatedly.

"Good. Then who's your favorite Venezuelan son?" Carlos said in his normal voice in Russian, completely loosening his grip on the man's throat.

"Carlos! You crazy motherfucker! You son of a bitch! What's wrong with you? You know I hate when you do that shit!"

Carlos was doubled over with laughter.

"You're crazy," the man continued, screaming. "I could have had a heart attack. I still might. What if it wasn't me? Then what?"

"I would have pulled the trigger," Carlos said, still laughing.

"How did you get in? The brick?" the man demanded. Carlos nodded yes. After 30 more seconds of cursing, the incensed man shook his head and sighed, "You're goddamn lucky I'm in a good mood. If I wasn't, I'd kill you." He extended both arms and finally smiled. The men embraced.

Seve Dolchino was no ordinary antiques dealer. From 1961 through 1975, Seve had been Special Instructor at the Patrice

Lumumba University in Moscow, where the KGB trained and politically indoctrinated its special youth in subversionary and guerilla war techniques, terrorism, and sabotage. Seve, purebred Italian, was the grand master of these arts. When he wasn't teaching young right wing Russians methods of death and destruction, he was off somewhere around the world performing sanctioned murders and mayhem for the Soviet government.

Carlos was 17 when his father, a wealthy and avowed Venezuelan communist — who even named his three sons Ilich, Vladimir and Lenin, sent him to Camp Mantzanas in Havana, the Cuban equivalent of Lumumba U. The notorious Col. Victor Siminov of the KGB, who ran the camp spotted Carlos' incredible potential and recommended to Moscow his instruction at the next level, by Seve.

Almost immediately a bond of mentor to prodigy formed between Carlos and Seve, who recognized his pupil's instinctive talents in weapons and explosives, the use of safe houses and aliases, forging of documents and passports, clandestine communications, and something that could not be taught, lying convincingly. Seve also discovered Carlos' taste for blood when he took his young apprentice on a series of assassinations where Carlos also learned the craft of torture.

For over 20 years, Seve had boasted of creating the world's most dangerous man. Having molded a living legendary killing machine, Seve lived vicariously through Carlos' exploits, savoring his terrorist victories as if they were his own.

"So. You need a place to stay, right?" Seve said. "You'll stay with me."

"No. You know me. I keep crazy hours. I come. I go. And you can't cook like the chef at the du Rhone. Besides, I don't want anybody to know I'm in town, and one never knows who's watching you."

"Don't flatter me. I'm an old man now. I can't even remember what I did yesterday. Everybody leaves me alone."

"Yeah right. Tell it to the Pope. I know better. You taught me there's no such thing as being too careful. It's probably your fault I'm paranoid."

"Just thank me for keeping your worthless ass alive," Seve said, smacking his pseudo-son on the arm with a smile.

Carlos looked Seve over. At 17, when he became a hitman for the Italian Mafia, Seve was known as "the Bull" which described not only the shape of his body, but his attitude about life as well. However, now 67, and after a lifetime of abusing vodka and cigarettes, Seve was a shadow of his former self; fat and soft.

"Seve. Go lock the front door. I don't want any visitors right now. Do you mind?"

"Of course not. I don't get busy 'til lunchtime anyway." Seve walked to the front of the store, locked the door, and shut off the main light. "You know, I actually made money here last year," he yelled through the shop.

Carlos muttered under his breath "so what," but loudly responded, "Terrific. What is that, the first time in 10 years?"

"Second. Three years ago I bought a 15th century sword for nothing, and turned it around a month later for about 200,000 francs. That one deal has carried the business, but you know me. I don't give a shit about the money. I've got far more than I can ever spend. This place just gives me something to do. You O.K? You need some cash?"

"I'm fine. I just closed a big deal, but thanks for asking," Carlos said as Seve returned, now standing before him.

"I presume that's what brought you to Geneva?"

"You could say that."

"Well?" Seve asked, his dark eyes gleaming.

Carlos sat silent.

"Aren't you going to share this with me?"

Carlos shook his head no.

"What? Look, if you went to the trouble to sneak in here at whatever time it was this morning, it's because you need me for something. So c'mon. What's going on?"

"Sorry," Carlos said, picking up his coat to leave. "I didn't mean to bother you."

"Alright, alright," Seve said excitedly, running his hands through his full head of shocking white hair. "You're such an asshole. You win. Don't leave. Tell me what you need."

Carlos put down his coat. "How about breakfast, and then we'll talk."

"Fine. There's a brasserie in the neighborhood that delivers."

Ninety minutes later, after a breakfast of breads, cheeses, and strong coffee, Seve changed the discussion from trading war stories about the old days to new business. "So my boy, what are you doing here?"

"Seve. I'm sorry. I don't want to drag you into this. It's too complicated. It's for your protection. I'll have to eliminate anyone who learns even an isolated fact that could lead the authorities back to me."

"You could never kill me," Seve interrupted.

"You don't think so," Carlos said, mostly in jest. "But there's something else. After I finish my work here tomorrow, when Interpol figures out my involvement — and ultimately they will — you'll be the first person they'll want to talk to. Do you really believe that you could withstand a truth serum injection or torture? You'll compromise me."

Seve didn't need to answer. Carlos was right.

"If there's anybody I'd want to share this with, it'd be you. But too much is at stake. You just have to trust me and do as I say?"

Seve nodded.

"Good. Thank you. Then I need you to get me about a dozen blank passport jackets. Try to get as broad a spread of countries as possible, but not Iraq. Can you get them by tomorrow morning? I know it won't be cheap."

"I don't want to promise, but I'm pretty sure it can be done. I have some blanks in stock here and I can make some calls. Whatever's on hand is free. Consider it my contribution to the cause. But third parties are going to be expensive. And on such short notice, they probably won't be blanks."

"What's the going rate here these days?"

"I have one very good diplomatic source who charged me 5000

francs last year for something Andrei Verchenko was doing. Remember him?"

"Yeah, that piece of shit," said Carlos, reaching into his pocket for cash. "Once he started freelancing for the Americans I lost all respect for him. Here's 50,000. This should get it done. If not, cover me and I'll take care of you later."

Seve rolled his eyes. Carlos didn't get it. Seve didn't care about the money. He just wanted to be part of the game.

"Make up some story about why you need the passports, and make sure your friend understands Omerta. Got it?" Carlos symbolically zippered his mouth shut.

"Fuck you," Seve snapped. "Why do you talk to me like that? You've been condescending to me all morning."

Carlos put his hand on Seve's shoulder and looked him in the eyes. "I'm sorry. The last ten years I've dealt with either moronic Eastern European dictators or fucking stupid towel heads. I'm used to spelling out everything in detail. When I don't it gets screwed up. I know you know better. Really, I apologize." Carlos smiled warmly and said, "I'm going to the bathroom."

When he came out three minutes later, Carlos was wearing long full sideburns and a mustache, a pair of glasses, and his wavy hair combed straight back instead of parting it on the side as he usually wore it. Seve didn't say a word to Carlos, but grinned, adding a nod of understanding.

"Seve, I hate to ask you this, but can you also get me a few grams of cocaine or heroin? I don't care which one, or about the quality or the price. I need it for tonight."

After a long pause Seve said, "I have to tell you Carlos. I'm disappointed that you're still using drugs. You've been clean for years. You know you can't do your work on that shit. You'll get yourself killed."

"Thanks for the lecture. I am clean. It's not for me. It's for work."

"Yeah?" Seve asked with a deep frown.

"Yeah. All bullshit aside. It's important. I won't touch it."

Seve felt reassured. "Okay. I don't know what your schedule is, but come back after sundown but before 8:30. I should have your passports ready by then. If the front lights are on that means there's trouble. Just keep going, and if I can, I'll contact you later through Pierre."

"Great," said Carlos as he took a book, notepad and pen off of the desk and put them inside a ratty backpack that was lying in the corner of the office on a two foot high stack of newspapers. He then grabbed the paper bag from the breakfast delivery and placed his Beretta inside it, before adding it to the backpack. "I'm borrowing this stuff. I'll see you later."

Carlos strode out the front door into grey cold skies. He found a taxi and directed the driver to the United Nations complex on the opposite side of Lake Geneva. Fifteen minutes later, he stood about 50 yards away and across the street from the U. N. visitor's gate. He surveyed 360 degrees around him, first noticing on his left the white-walled grandiose headquarters of the International Red Cross. To his right lay the massive grounds of the U.N. complex, dotted with numerous architectural structures which housed the 3000 international civil servants who managed the organization's diplomatic and goodwill affairs.

A steady stream of tourists passed Carlos and walked through a tall iron gate which covered the width of a two lane driveway leading up to a small booth. Four armed guards dressed in blue uniforms stood watch. Each visitor spent about a minute at the checkpoint, but the angle of the booth and the location of the fence prevented Carlos from discerning the entrance procedures.

Carlos opened the backpack and took out the paper bag containing his gun. Not wanting to risk getting searched, he walked up to a public garbage can and discarded the bag, stuffing it deep inside the receptacle. Slowly, he approached the guardhouse. As he shuffled by the guards he saw no evidence they were wearing weapons, but since it was winter, he couldn't be sure what was under their coats. Two guards who clearly wore no waist or shoulder holsters were seated inside the heated stall.

Intentionally jittery and bobbing his head up and down, Carlos loudly asked in French, "Hey. Hey man. Is this where I get public tour tickets?"

A black guard responded, "Yes, sir. The next French tour starts in 45 minutes."

"French tour. You mean you guys do tours in other languages?"

"Yes sir. In English, Spanish, German and Italian."

"Oh. Well how do I sign up?" Carlos twitched his head.

"Right here, sir. The cost is eight francs, but I need to see identification."

"I'm French. I don't have my passport with me. Do I need to go back to my hotel to get it?"

"No sir. Any form of picture identification will do. Your drivers license, perhaps."

"Yeah, I got that." Carlos opened his wallet and pulled out a license with the name Jacques Panko. The picture bore only a slight resemblance to his disguise. He handed the guard a ten franc note.

The guard gave Carlos his change and a ticket but did not compare the picture to the man standing in front of him. He wrote down the name on a guest log and said, "Please wear this tag while you are on the grounds. When you leave, stop back here and exchange the tag for your license. You can walk down the path next to the parking lot in front of you, up to that large building on your left. That's the Palais des Nations. Enter through Door 39."

Carlos slammed his knapsack on the counter of the booth to make sure the guard noticed it, and to test him for a possible search, but the guard merely smiled. "Hey man. I got a question. What am I supposed to do for 45 minutes? Can I just walk around? Take pictures?"

"Whatever you'd like, sir."

For the next ten minutes Carlos sat on a bench twenty yards from the security booth watching tourist after tourist pass through security, confirming the security procedures he had just witnessed were applied to all visitors. He was especially concerned about the guards opening bags and packages, but they consistently failed to do so.

Taking liberties with the freedom to roam the U.N. grounds, Carlos covered the external perimeter of the 80 foot tall evergreen tree lined Palais des Nations, photographing every inch of the building from countless angles. Having never visited the U.N. before, Carlos was particularly intrigued by the backside of the structure which looked out over Lake Geneva. It was constructed on support beams which created a large open deck below the bulk of the ten story structure.

Carlos entered the Palais des Nations as directed at Door 39 and stood in a lobby crowded with people of all nationalities. A young Asian receptionist took Carlos' ticket and confirmed for him that he was allowed to photograph the inside of the building.

To his left was a sitting area with about 60 folding chairs arranged in front of a television. Adjacent to the seating was a bookstore with all four external walls made of floor to ceiling glass. Carlos entered, noting that the store was packed full of tourists purchasing souvenirs and informational reading.

Before the formal walking tour began, the group was forced to sit through a 20 minute videotape describing the various goodwill agencies and the general mission of the U.N. When the tape ended, another young woman appeared and took control over the group. They walked together down a long corridor past the largest cloakroom Carlos had ever seen. At the main lobby, they stopped.

"Ladies and Gentlemen," the tour guide said, "Welcome to the United Nations at Geneva, where over 5000 meetings a year make the Palais des Nations the busiest conference center in the world. Historically, Geneva has served as a haven for the persecuted, a center of religious and intellectual freedom, and a place of decision making among nations, thus serving as a fitting site for a world organization devoted to international peace."

In scoping out the building's security, Carlos observed that the main lobby held a reception desk-command center containing remote television screens and other communications facilities. It was manned by six security officers, again none of whom appeared to be carrying weapons.

The tour moved through the lobby to the back of the great hall, and stopped at a balcony railing directly above the cafeteria. Fifteen feet beyond the rail was a 40' by 80' wall of windows providing the same magnificent view of Lake Geneva that Carlos earlier observed from the back of the building. Carlos, picture hungry, clicked away, turning in a full circle.

"As you can see, the Palais des Nations has a commanding view of both Lake Geneva and Mont Blanc," the guide lectured. "We are located on the Parc Ariana, which covers 25 hectacres bequeathed to the City of Geneva in 1890 by Gustave Reuillod. This was the original site of the League of Nations starting in 1920."

Carlos' concentration was focused elsewhere as he studied the layout and construction of the walls and surrounding internal geography of the Palais des Nations. He estimated that the far end of the balcony overlooking the cafeteria was about 35 feet from the outside support column of the building. He further deduced that there had to be a support beam for the balcony about every twenty feet off of the wall inside the cafeteria. His ears perked up when he heard the tour guide declare, "the cafeteria serves approximately 2500 lunches every day," which he believed, judging by the roar of babble and constantly clanging dishes down below.

The group traveled down a long hallway, up an escalator, and through two amber glass double doors labelled Sabine VII, the visitor's gallery for the General Assembly. The balcony was dimly lit with four rows of chairs set in a semi-circle corresponding to the same seating of the delegates 25 feet below. A glass partition separated the visitors gallery from the oak panelled Assembly Hall.

"The largest of conferences, and occasionally, such as today, the General Assembly meets downstairs in Assembly Hall. Many of the United Nations' activities are discussed here."

A voice from the crowd asked, "What are they meeting about right now?"

The guide replied, "Well, in April 1991, UNIKOM, standing for U.N. Iraq-Kuwait Observer Mission was formed. Its purpose was to restore security with U.N. forces monitoring the demilitarized zone along the Iraq-Kuwait border. Problems in that region have been heating up the last few days as a result of Iraq's noncompliance with required nuclear inspections, and debate on the issue of imposing new sanctions against Iraq is occurring right now."

"How lucky could I get?" Carlos thought.

After ten minutes of watching the proceedings, the guide motioned the group out of the gallery. "We will now enter our library, which houses the largest collection of material on international matters in the world, including original treaties, documents and paraphernalia from numerous wars over the centuries. Please do not talk in here and meet back in ten minutes."

Carlos followed everyone into the main reading room and for twenty minutes aimlessly roamed about, drawing unhappy looks with each flash of his camera. Then, after the group had moved on, in order to get a better feel for crowd conditions and security, he retraced the steps of the tour until he arrived back at Door 39. Security was virtually nonexistent. He walked back up the driveway past the tall pines and stopped at the security station to exchange his visitor's badge for his fake license, and he left the grounds.

Carlos returned to the waste container where he left his gun, and acting as if it was the natural thing to do, picked the untouched bag out of the receptacle and put it back into his backpack. Nobody seemed to notice. Taxis were everywhere and Carlos had his drop him off a block from the du Rhone.

He walked another block into the heart of the retail district. Nestled between a pharmacy and a chocolate specialty shop was a one hour photo lab. He entered and received assurances from the clerk on duty that his four rolls of film would be ready when he came back an hour later.

He strategically parked himself on a circular metal bench built around a tree situated on a small public square directly across from the lab. While he pretended to read a magazine, he unobtrusively peered into the store to see if the clerk made any telephone calls after he viewed the pictures. Just over an hour later, Carlos reentered the store and picked up his pictures confident he had not been compromised.

The moment he walked through the revolving door of the du Rhone, Pierre Erne appeared from the far right side of the lobby. Erne approached his good friend and almost bumped into him. "Oh, excuse me sir. Good afternoon. I trust you had a pleasant day."

"Yes Mr. Erne," Carlos said, looking at the hotel assistant manager's name tag pronouncing his name "Ernie" instead of "Errnay." "It's good that I saw you. I was thinking of having room service tonight and wanted something special off the menu. What can you suggest?"

"I'll be happy to check with the chef and have him recommend your dinner. Would you like me to arrange the meal to be sent up?"

"Please. And tell the chef I'm very hungry," Carlos said, knowing Pierre would pick up the subtle invitation to dinner. "Can you have it delivered promptly at 6:15?"

"Certainly. Please sir, could I have your name again and room number?"

Demonstrating proper etiquette in an upscale hotel such as the du Rhone, Carlos reached into his pocket, pulled out a five franc note and handed it to Pierre, responding, "Yes. Of course. Mr. Finet, room 612. And, I appreciate your effort Mr. Ernie."

FOUR

Carlos ENTERED HIS SUITE, flopped down on a couch, and gazed aimlessly at the wall for a few minutes. Suddenly realizing it was near the end of the banking day and that Jacques Ruf was expecting to have dinner with him, he telephoned the banker apologetically fabricating a story about another important commitment that couldn't be rearranged. Because Carlos told Ruf that he had a proposed business deal that would make them both millions, Ruf agreed to meet Carlos for cocktails at 9:00 at The Globe, a popular disco in Geneva.

Taking advantage of his limited free time before dinner and the evening's events, he filled the bathtub with near scalding water. When the doublesized marble tub was half full, he stepped in, and slowly slunk down in the water up to his neck. After twenty minutes he pulled himself out of the tub and while still soaking wet, ripped off 100 pushups, 100 situps and a series of high intensity martial arts kicks, punches and grabs. He finished with a cool shower and dressed, feeling mentally alert and physically strong.

Room service arrived exactly at 6:15 p.m. and Pierre entered the suite almost the moment the waiter left it. "I took care of getting your crate from the Grand Passage sent over to Iraqi Airways," Pierre said, as he sat down to join Carlos in a full meal of salad, breaded

34

fish, pasta, vegetables, three pastries and the obligatory bottle of French wine.

"Uh, thanks," Carlos said, absently.

After an uneasy silence, Pierre asked, "Did you finish your business today?"

"Like I'm gonna fucking tell you," Carlos snapped.

Ignoring Carlos' mood swing, Pierre said, "C'mon, you've known me for 20 years. We were partners. You know I don't talk. What are you in town for?"

"I ran some errands and paid Seve a visit. I hadn't seen him in two years, and I wanted to say hello. But as long as you're so interested in what I'm doing here, I can use your help with something tomorrow. Can you get away for an hour or so?"

Instantly on guard, Pierre fidgeted in his chair and said, "As long as it doesn't involve anything illegal. Look, now I have a family that I don't want to jeopardize. You can understand that."

Carlos stared at him blankly.

"All right, all right," Pierre said after only a few seconds of the silent treatment. "What kind of shit are you dragging me into?"

"I told you last night I'm retired from the business of violence. I'm in Geneva to close a complicated financial transaction for a special client. All I need is a driver to take me to a meeting, and then to the airport afterwards. Can you handle that?"

Though he didn't dare, Pierre wanted to ask, "*If all you need is a driver, then why don't you rent a limo?*" Instead he said, "Okay. Fine. Nothing crazy, right?"

"I don't lie to you," Carlos lied. "It's a simple business meeting at the U.N. I've got some papers and money to exchange with a diplomat. I don't want to rely on just any cab driver." The story naturally and convincingly flowed from his mouth, and it made sense to Pierre.

"I'll come downstairs to check out right before noon," Carlos continued. "We'll throw my stuff in your car and drive to the U.N. I'll be inside for 15 or 20 minutes. When I'm done you can take me right to the airport for my 2:30 flight. But no matter what," Carlos emphasized, "I have to be on time. O.K.?"

"O.K."

Glancing at his watch, Carlos announced he had to leave. Pierre reconfirmed tomorrow's schedule and Carlos put his arm around Pierre's shoulder and graciously thanked his longtime friend.

Fifteen minutes later Carlos taxied to the edge of the Old Town, getting out a block from his real destination to conceal his business. He walked up to and then past Seve's shop to make sure the lights were out; the signal that it was safe to enter. As a precaution, Carlos bent down as if to tie his shoe, quickly snatched the Beretta from its ankle holster and stuck it in his coat pocket. Keeping his finger on the trigger, he opened the unlocked front door. "Hey old man, it's time for dinner. You ready?"

Seve stumbled out of the dark back office and exclaimed, "You're damn right I'm an old man. I'm tired. I ran all around Geneva for you today."

Carlos relaxed his grip on the Beretta. "Yeah. So what? I made you feel important for the first time in years," Carlos teased. Then turning serious he added, "Does that mean you got everything?"

"You pezzonavante, who do you think you're talking to? Of course I did. Come here and look."

"Then turn on the light so I don't break my fuckin' neck."

"Sure. Don't forget to lock the door," Seve said as he flicked on the lights.

"I presume it's safe for me here?" Carlos asked.

"No one I talked to suggested knowing you were in town, and I sure didn't imply anything."

"Good. Let's keep it that way." Carlos stepped around the clutter and made his way back to the office. "So, show me the goods."

Seve proudly pulled nine passports from his desk drawer, all originating from Middle East countries except one each from France and England. None had been issued, but each showed a few authentic foreign port of entry stamps which made them look used. Since no names, pictures or other vital information was typed onto any of the documents, they could be manipulated to fit anyone.

One by one, Carlos studied each passport closely under the desk lamp. After a few minutes he looked up and announced, "Damn good. These are perfect."

"They should be. They're real."

"Terrific. How much?"

"The guy I got them from wanted 6000 each, but we settled on 50,000 for the lot."

"Fine. Did he ask what or who they were for?"

"No. He's smarter than that."

"Who is this guy?"

Seve lowered his head. "Interpol."

"What?" Carlos exhaled sharply through his nostrils and glared at Dolchino.

"Don't worry," Seve said reassuringly. "Remember, I've been in this business longer than you. Have I ever been wrong? No. This guy is all right. We've done favors for each other since the day I moved here from Moscow. He only cares about one thing... the money. Besides, how many sources do you think there are in Geneva for this kind of merchandise? Especially on short notice?"

"Okay. I guess there's not a hell of a lot I can do about it now," Carlos snapped. "So Seve," he paused, "When's the last time you killed someone?"

"About a year ago. Some asshole in a restaurant pissed me off and I waited for him outside and broke his neck." Seve demonstrated a judo move.

"It's nice to see you still have control over your emotions."

"I just made that up," Dolchino smirked.

Carlos looked up to the sky and shook his head.

"Actually, my last hit was a year ago. A local diplomat paid me 100,000 to take out some guy that was banging his wife. I didn't want to do it at first, but then I decided I could use the practice. Why do you ask?"

"Because when this asshole from Interpol comes around asking you questions after I leave here tomorrow, you're going to have to kill him."

Seve stuck his hands into his pockets and sighed heavily. "Carlos. Earlier today I didn't push you when you didn't want to tell me what you were up to. Now I see you've probably put me in the middle of your shit anyway, so I think I'm entitled to know what's going on."

Carlos took a deep breath and exhaled. "Well...okay. But I can't tell you everything. The U.N. building. Here today, gone tomorrow."

Seve rubbed his chin in thought and nodded his head in approval. "Very impressive. I presume your plans are all set?"

"There's a couple of details I have to finalize tonight, but for the most part, I've worked through the important logistics. The beauty in it is that it's purely a one man job. Have you ever been over to the U.N. complex?"

"Of course."

"Did you notice there's virtually no armed security in the entire Palais des Nations building?"

"Well, no. But I wasn't there to case the place." Seve paused before adding, "Carlos, Geneva is the City of Peace. There's very little violent crime here. Switzerland's not even a member of the U.N. This is neutral territory."

"Not after tomorrow."

Seve fell back into his chair and clasped his hands behind his head in thought. Neither man spoke for a minute. Finally Seve said, "The likelihood that my friend at Interpol will link my purchase of the passports today with the bombing of the U.N. tomorrow is too great. There are certain activities he would overlook, but blowing up the U.N. is not one of them. He may not personally come see me but he'll make sure that somebody does. You're right. He must die."

"I know."

"Tonight. Before he has the opportunity to talk."

"I know."

There was another long silence. Suddenly a metamorphosis seemed to consume Seve. Twenty pounds from his stomach seemed to gravitate upwards to his barrel chest and thick neck. His eyes glowed jet black and he blurted out, "I'll kill the fucker."

Carlos almost responded, "this is not a game," but realized that characteristics such as ruthless, vicious and bloodthirsty never disappear from one's personality; they simply lie dormant until called to the surface. Carlos had seen Seve like this many times before. When he was in this state, nobody would want to get in his way. Carlos stayed focused. "Did you get the drugs?"

"Of course. But Jesus Christ. The element of people you have to deal with to get that stuff is disgusting." Seve reached over to a bookshelf and picked out a volume which he opened upside down. "I've got it here." A two inch square cellophane wrapped packet fell on the desk.

Carlos gave Seve a bewildered look.

Seve explained. "If the police show up here and find stolen passports, I walk. They'll be confiscated, some diplomat will yell at me, and that'll be the end of it. I'm Seve Dolchino. Unspoken immunity. Getting busted for drugs is a different matter. Then I got a problem."

Carlos picked up the narcotic. "What is it?"

"Cocaine. Two grams. Supposed to be grade A."

Carlos unwrapped the packet and put a minute trace on his tongue. "Wow. Excellent stuff." He rewrapped the packet and put it in his pants pocket. "Seve. One more request."

"What?"

"I've got a Beretta," Carlos said, showing Seve the gun hidden in his coat pocket, "but I think I'm going to need another one. Do you have a spare weapon?"

"Yeah, I can get you a couple of guns right away."

"Terrific."

"Open that bottom drawer on the left," Seve said, pointing to the desk.

Carlos broke into a big laugh when he found two Beretta 9 mm's and two extra clips sitting there.

"Lucky guess," Seve said, tapping his temple with his index and forefingers.

Carlos picked up the guns and handed them to Seve. "Hold these." He next looked at his watch and ordered, "Put on your coat. You're coming with me. I don't want to be late for Ruf. I'll tell you about it on the way."

Seven minutes later Carlos walked alone into the Globe. Red smoke smothered lights bounced off the walls and floor. A Michael Jackson song blasted from the line of Bose speakers hanging from the black painted ceiling. A small walk up bar was located in the back of the disco. Carlos instantly picked Jacques Ruf out of the crowd sitting by himself at a table halfway back in the room.

Jacques stood up and greeted Carlos with his traditional firm handshake, and motioned to the chairs. A cocktail waitress appeared, and they each ordered Stolichanaya on the rocks. Knowing Jacques seldom consumed hard alcohol, Carlos told her to make them doubles.

"Jacques, thanks for seeing me. During business hours I don't mind barging in on you. But I'm sure you'd prefer to spend evenings with your family," Carlos said, not sorry at all.

"Not a problem. I'm out of the house two to three nights a week every week. Its been this way forever. Part of the job. Besides, for the money I make off you, I'd meet you on the moon if you said to."

"Don't remind me. I pay you way too much. I bet your wife was happy when you told her about yesterday's commission."

"Are you kidding? She doesn't know a damn thing about my business. As long as she can shop and lunch with her friends, go to parties and drive her Mercedes, she's happy, the bitch. The worst thing I could do is tell her about yesterday. If she had a clue about how much I'm really worth, she'd go crazy."

At the same moment that the waitress brought the drinks, Seve entered the disco. He looked around, asked another waitress a question and went off to the back of the bar, passing Carlos without acknowledging him. Despite Jacques' protestations that he couldn't drink like he had in his youth, Carlos ordered another round before they had even taken a sip off their first drinks.

"Jacques. You've handled a wide range of matters for me over the years. Are you willing to go to the next level and make some real money?"

"I think so," he replied, raising his eyebrows.

"I'm orchestrating a deal that's capable of generating a phenomenal amount of cash. You've been handpicked by me and others for this transaction. It's politically sensitive, dangerous and quite illegal. Me, I don't care about that. You, however, may feel there's too much at stake. If you're not interested tell me now. I won't say anything more and I won't be offended. Once I start though, you're in, and there's no getting out."

"Ilich, I'm flattered, but let me tell you my only concern. I'm a non-violent person. Please don't be offended, but I never approved of your line of work. Frankly, if you ever conducted your operations out of Geneva I wouldn't want to be your banker. But you haven't and I understand everybody is guided by their own set of values. Anyway, if murder or violence is involved, then I'm not interested. If it deals with the flow of money, that's a different story."

Ruf had no idea how serious his insult was. It was bad enough he extorted Carlos yesterday for an extra million francs. This was the final nail in his coffin. Carlos showed no emotion but responded simply, "Violence is not involved, but it will be illegal."

"How much are we talking about?"

"You could make 60 million francs a year."

"I'm interested." Ruf tried hard to hide his glee, but Carlos read it in his eyes.

"You're sure? Once I describe the transaction, that's it. You can't change your mind."

"I'm in."

"Good." Carlos patted him on the hand. "I'm procuring weapons systems for certain Middle Eastern countries and special interest groups. I need a private financial institution to assist with financing purchases, to assure security on large deposits and to launder money through fictitious shell corporations. You get two percent of every purchase, which over the next year should be about

1.2 billion. My couriers will visit you regularly and provide you with everything you need to know. Sound good?"

"Good? It sounds great. And I have experience in these matters. I helped Adnan Khashogi with some of his weapons deals in the '80s. Same thing with the Chinese and the Russians. But never anything on this scale."

For the second time in minutes Carlos felt immediate anger but kept a straight face. Rule number one for a Swiss banker was never to tell anyone the identity of his clients, much less about their business. This slip confirmed that Ruf could not be trusted. The death sentence Carlos imposed in his mind against Ruf was irrevocable. Still, Carlos lied with a show of confidence. "Yes. We knew about Khashogi. It was one of the reasons we picked you." Carlos hoisted his glass, "To our religion. To money. Drink up." Carlos finished his full glass of vodka and motioned for Ruf to do the same.

Ruf clicked glasses with Carlos and consumed his entire drink. His eyes bulged and he exhaled a big "whooh" and a short cough.

"Jacques. Get some paper out of your briefcase. I have some code words for you to keep track of. You better write them down."

"Are you kidding? I don't write anything down. You know that."

"You're writing this down, and that's all there is to it," Carlos said coldly. "We're drinking tonight and this is too important for you to screw up."

Ruf nodded and took out a fresh piece of paper from his briefcase.

"It's critical that you speak only with my messenger. These are the rules. First, you will never meet the same person twice. Second, only women will visit you, and third, it will only be on a Monday. No exceptions. If the same woman shows up, you don't talk with her. If a man shows up, you don't talk with him. If a woman shows up and its Tuesday, you don't talk with her. If a woman on a Monday gives you as much as a syllable out of place from the code, then you stay clear. There are only two people in the world who will know all of this. You and me. Understand?"

Ruf nodded again, and Carlos made him repeat the instructions.

The waitress brought the second round. Ruf gave a hopeless look to both her and Carlos, who took a large gulp from his fresh drink, and again induced Jacques to do the same.

"Now whoever this woman on a Monday is, will have an appointment with you about getting seed money for a new business. Give her your full cooperation if she makes a series of precise comments that are totally inappropriate responses to your statements. If anything at all is out of place act dumb about any arms deal. Got it?"

The banker kept nodding his head and this time, on his own initiative, took another big sip from his drink.

Carlos took out his wallet and removed a piece of paper that contained personal coded phone and bank account numbers. "Write this down. This is the script. Memorize it tomorrow." Carlos acted as if he was reading a list as Jacques wrote, "I'm sorry. I'm sorry. I'm sorry....The time is now.....I must be wrong....It's not worth that much." Carlos put the list back into his wallet.

Ruf looked mystified, a bit suspicious, and also a little woozy from consuming a fair amount of vodka in a short period of time. Still, without comment, he folded the note into quarters and stuffed it into his heavily starched, white dress shirt pocket.

"By the way. I presume you took care of my business yesterday?" Carlos inquired.

"Of course." Jacques handed Carlos an envelope that was stored in his suitcoat. He then yawned widely and shook his head.

Carlos observed Ruf's increasing grogginess and knew that he was ripe for picking. "You look like shit. I can help you. Come with me." Carlos stood up and motioned for Ruf to follow him. They walked to the back of the disco where a sign directed them to the restrooms. Outside the men's room in a short and narrow dark hall, Seve was leaning against the wall talking on the pay phone, his free hand covering his ear to shield it from the music.

"What're we doin'?" Ruf asked loudly, slurring his words.

"We're going to have a party. You'll like this. Trust me," Carlos answered as he pushed the bathroom door open. By good fortune, the room was empty. After Jacques entered, Carlos locked the door behind him. As much as his reflexes had slowed down, Jacques' head spun around quickly. "We need privacy," Carlos said, and Jacques glanced back and forth at the door and Carlos. Seve stood guard outside, ready to advise anyone who might want to enter that his friend inside the bathroom was sick and to come back in five minutes.

Carlos removed the packet of cocaine from his pocket and put it on a metal ledge above the sink. He pulled out a credit card and ten franc note from his wallet and opened his Swiss Army Knife blade, scooping a large portion of the white powder onto the flat dry surface of the ledge, laying it out with the credit card in two long even lines. He rolled the money into a tight cylinder and handed it to Jacques. "You go first. I insist."

"Ilich. I haven't done coke in over five years. I don't want to do this."

"How can you turn me down? I just made you 60 million francs. It's time to celebrate. Besides, you need to wake up."

"These are awfully big lines."

"I know, but the quality isn't that good."

Both the alcohol and Carlos' insistence defeated Ruf's willpower to resist. "Well, what the hell." Jacques blew his nose in his handkerchief, then leaned over and inhaled both lines. Instantly his head jolted back and he grasped his chest. "Oh God, I haven't felt this in ages. Now I remember why I quit," Jacques said fighting through the effect of both the alcohol and cocaine.

"Relax. Give yourself a few minutes. You'll be fine. Now I have a real surprise for you."

"I don't need another surprise."

"Yes you do. Come here. Take down your pants." Carlos tilted his head to the side, opened his mouth wide, tongued his lips, and smiled at Jacques.

"No!" Jacques said, "Not you, I would have never suspected. You know, we can go somewhere else."

"Come sit down," Carlos said, motioning to the stall. Carlos concluded that the confidential sources who fed him information about Ruf had been right about their assessment of his private lifestyle. Ruf would bed anyone.

Jacques pulled his pants and underwear down to his ankles and sat on the toilet caressing his penis. Carlos knelt down in front of Jacques who was clearly physically excited. In one fluid motion, Carlos reached down to his ankle and took the Beretta from its holster. In an instant the gun was pointed at the middle of Jacques' forehead.

The banker's face froze in shock and he gasped for air, unable to speak.

Carlos moved the gun down to Jacques' groin. "Now tell me. Who have you told in the bank or at home that I'm in town?"

Jacques was shaking and pale. "No one. I swear to God. No one. Please don't hurt me."

Carlos smacked Ruf's balls with the gun causing him to double over and yelp. "Shut the fuck up. I don't believe you."

"I swear it. I swear it. Oh my God. Please don't hurt me."

"Who do your assistant and that receptionist think I am?"

"They didn't even ask. They know better. They only know the name Jean-Luc Finet. I swear. Don't hurt me. I'll pay you anything." Jacques started to cry.

Carlos whacked him in the balls again. "I said shut up." A stream of tears ran down Jacques' terrorized face, but he kept quiet despite his fear and the pain in his groin.

"What does your brother know about me? He's second in command isn't he?"

"He knows you're a client but nothing else. He knows the names of all of our clients. He has to in case something happens to me." Jacques put his hands to his face in horror realizing he may have just signed his brother's death warrant. "He doesn't know you're here or anything about yesterday, because I didn't want to share the profit with him. It was my deal."

"You know something you little fucking asshole? You've heard the expression "Pigs get fat, hogs get slaughtered?"

Sobbing, Jacques nodded.

"You're a fucking hog and it's time to get slaughtered." Carlos softened his tone and spoke slowly. "You shouldn't have shaken me down yesterday. Big mistake, you little piece of shit. I am going to kill you but I'll be nice and give you a choice. You can take a bullet in the side of the head which will cause you great pain, and you may linger like a vegetable til you die, or you can take it in the mouth, where death will be instant. Which do you want?" Carlos said cruelly.

"Oh God. Please. You can't be serious. Let me go. I'll give back the money. I'll do anything."

"You have five seconds and then I pick for you. And if it's my choice, you will suffer."

"No. No. In the mouth. No. Please. I beg for mercy," Ruf pleaded. The combination of alcohol, cocaine and fear had effectively paralyzed him, totally fraying his nerves and rendering him completely helpless.

"And just so you know, asshole. I'm not gay. Now open your mouth." Ruf's entire body quivered as he shook his head no. "Okay. Have it your way," Carlos sneered, and he put the gun to Ruf's temple. As soon as Carlos moved the gun, Jacques closed his wet eyes, crossed himself and opened his mouth.

"Good boy."

Carlos put the barrel two inches deep into Ruf's mouth and pointed it upwards. "Now don't worry. This won't hurt." There was a loud bang and the bullet exploded through the top back portion of Ruf's head spraying skull fragments, brain tissue matter and blood in a circular pattern against the wall.

Carlos wedged the body back in an upright position against the toilet. To avoid leaving telltale fingerprints, Carlos had been certain to not touch anything in the bathroom but the door lock. Working quickly, he took out his handkerchief and wiped down the gun handle. Having observed that Ruf used his right hand when drinking his vodka, and holding the barrel of the Beretta in the cloth, Carlos rubbed the gun all over Ruf's right hand and then folded

Ruf's fingers tightly around the handle and trigger. He let the gun drop to the ground and positioned it next to Ruf's feet and pants, so that it was out of sight unless one was standing looking right down on the body. Carlos repeated the same procedure with the cocaine packet and planted it in Jacques' shirt pocket, next to the false code for the false weapons deal.

With great difficulty, Carlos pulled himself out from under the 18 inch opening at the bottom of the toilet stall door. He walked to the door and turned, surveying the scene. Concluding there were no loose ends, he used the handkerchief to wipe and unlock the door. Seve was still there.

"Finished already? I didn't even hear the gun. The music must have drowned it out."

"Good. Did anyone want to come in?"

"Nope."

"How about women?" Carlos motioned with his index finger to the women's room opposite them.

"Nope."

"Then let's pick up his briefcase and get out of here."

"What about the cocktail waitress?"

"She never got a good look at me."

Moments later, Seve and Carlos were outside walking back toward Seve's shop to pick up his car.

"So what did you tell this guy from Interpol?"

"That I just learned the money I gave him was marked and dirty, and that I wanted to exchange fresh cash with him right now, otherwise we both had an immediate serious problem. He was grateful as hell."

"Very creative. I'll have to remember that one."

"Yeah. Well, we're going to have to do him at his home."

"So. That's never been a problem before."

"He's married. Nice lady. I hope I don't have to take her out too."

"You think he tells her his business?"

"How would I know?"

"Hmmm. Tough call. I think you've got a problem."

"You mean we."

"Yeah. Right. Unless she's asleep, I don't think there's a choice. She's gonna have to go."

Seve bit his lip and looked up into the starless, black night. "No question about it." It was a strange quirk to the violent side of Seve. Killing those who had to die for business purposes was acceptable. Innocent bystanders, however, were another story.

A half an hour later Seve pulled his black Mercedes 500 up to the front walk of a small white house with a garden on a middle class street not far from the U.N. complex. He turned the lights off but kept the engine running. "Climb over the console. You'll drive from here. I'll be back in two minutes," Seve instructed. He took the safety off his own Beretta and checked the firing mechanism.

Seve rapped hard on the door. A few seconds later, Hubert Kriger, a professorial looking man in his early fifties with greying short curly hair and round wire frame glasses appeared. Seve was pleased he didn't turn on the outside light and noticed that Kriger was holding what appeared to be the same stack of Swiss franc bills Seve gave him earlier in the day.

"Dolchino, come in," the man smiled.

Kriger closed the door behind Seve. "It's nice to do business with someone with honor and ethics. You know, there's a lot of scum out there who would just as soon either rip me off, or let me go down, and deal with the problem a different way."

"Well, what can I say. I've got your money right here." Seve reached inside his coat and pulled out the Beretta. Before Kriger had time to react, Seve rapidly squeezed off two shots. The first lifted the Interpol agent off his feet, piercing through his eyeglass and right eye, and exiting straight out the other side. The second bullet tore open a gaping hole in the middle of the man's chest. Hubert crumbled to the hardwood floor where a puddle of blood instantly formed.

Almost instantaneous with the gun being fired, Hubert's wife appeared from a kitchen twenty feet beyond the front door screaming hysterically. Seve shook his head and simply said, "Shit." He then motioned to her with both hands as if to say "Sorry," and walked slowly towards her. She backed up towards the kitchen still screaming, "No. Help. No. No."

Seve emptied four bullets into her. The woman's body lurched violently with the impact of each slug as if performing some exotic dance. She finally fell straight on her back, eyes and mouth wide open. Four distinct blood filled holes showed through her robe. Without leaving fingerprints, Seve turned off the lights and exited the house less than a minute after he had entered it.

He got into the car and slammed the door shut. Rather than speeding off, Carlos drove away at a normal pace, but with the lights off for about a block. After a minute of silence, Carlos asked, "Having some fun tonight?"

"Oh yeah. The time of my life," Seve said bitterly.

"I take it you had to do her too." Carlos wondered if Seve had gone soft or if it was just old age. "Did you at least get the money back?"

Seve dropped his somber attitude and cracked up. Both men knew the only proper decision was to leave the 50,000 francs with Kriger. Interpol would find the money on the floor, and based on the security analyst's minuscule salary, would quickly comprehend that one of its agents was involved in something he shouldn't have been. The ensuing investigation would be more for Interpol trying to figure out exactly what Kriger did, rather than a search by the Geneva police for a murderer.

As Carlos drove to the Hotel du Rhone, Seve offered his help for the next days events, now that he was inextricably tied into Carlos' present affairs. Carlos refused, still insisting it was a one man job, and that the success in his scheme was its inherent simplicity. One man walks in. One man walks out. No diversions. Nothing suspicious.

As they pulled up in front of the hotel, Seve jumped out and gave Carlos a bear hug. He then smacked Carlos on the back of his head as he had done a thousand times before. As Carlos stepped into the revolving door, Seve yelled out to him. "Hey, you're right. I had a great time. Let's do this again."

Carlos saluted Seve in military fashion and turned away.

He spent the next two hours in final preparation for the eventful day ahead. Carlos laid out his photographs of the United Nations into groupings of the outside grounds and the inside of the Palais des Nations, calculating the precise points where his bombs would cause the most physical damage to the building. He ran through the entire plan in his mind, perfecting everything from the clothes he would wear, to the false identity he would provide to security, to the route he would walk once inside the building. He then reviewed the plan again, drawing out a rough map of the Palais des Nations, looking for weaknesses in his course of attack until he was absolutely positive there were none.

The easy part remained. Making the bombs. Carlos cut apart the fraudulent toothpaste tube and shampoo bottle, dug out the explosive clay from the Bible, emptied the cold cream jar, and took the brick of Semtex he had brought from his safety deposit box at Banque Ruf, and molded all 12 pounds of Semtex into four pieces. He inserted wires deep into the plastique and attached them to the timers and set each clock. If it was a good day tomorrow, the Palais des Nations, symbol of world peace and goodwill between men, would blow sky high at 12:30 p.m. sharp.

FIVE

CARLOS TUMBLED OUT OF BED at 8:00 from the knock at the door by room service delivering breakfast. Neatly folded next to his tray was the Journal de Geneve. Sipping coffee in the white terrycloth robe provided to all guests of the Hotel du Rhone, he opened the newspaper to find a headline on a front page story that caught his eye.

BANKER RUF FOUND DEAD IN DISCO

Prominent socialite banker Jacques Ruf was found dead late last night in a bizarre public suicide at the trendy disco, The Globe. An employee discovered Ruf's body at closing time perched on a toilet, undressed from the waist down. Ruf apparently shot himself in the mouth, as a gun was located next to the body. Geneva police report that both cocaine and a cryptic suicide note, confirmed by Ruf's wife to be in his handwriting, were also found on the body. Police said no evidence of foul play was present at the scene.

With no reason to read further, Carlos closed the paper, and sat back on his couch contemplating yesterday's successes. Seve had scored his passports, and two potential witnesses were eliminated without incident. It was a good day.

Breakfast was finished and it was only 8:20, with still plenty of time to kill. Although waiting to get started with his mission was mental torture, years of experience taught the master terrorist that a crucial element in the success of any plan was staying on schedule and following the details mapped out. Deviation was unacceptable except for the absolute best of reasons. A terrorist attack was equivalent to war. No army general proceeded blindly into battle; nor would Carlos. He laid back on the bed and thought through the plan, examining his pictures and every physical detail of the U.N. complex for at least the fifth time.

At 9:10 he reinspected the four Semtex bombs, double checking their wire connections and that they were properly set. He wrapped them in separate plastic laundry bags, marking 1, 2, 3 and 4 on the outside, and placed them into the briefcase taken from his Banque Ruf safety deposit box.

He next gathered the innocent containers used to smuggle the Semtex into Geneva, and put them into another bag for public disposal. Each retained evidentiary traces of Semtex.

Carlos spread the new passports obtained from Hubert Kriger across the fake bottom of his regular briefcase. Searching through the attache, the room safe, his money belt and pants pockets, he pooled and counted out over 100,000 Swiss francs.

Next Carlos opened Jacques Ruf's briefcase, shocked to find ten stacks of mint fresh 1000 Swiss franc bills, 100 bills per stack. He laughed out loud realizing that he had stolen back from Ruf a million francs of the commission the banker received for handling his affairs. Carlos put eight stacks of the bills into his briefcase, and left two in Jacques' briefcase.

Anxious to get going, as he had done often to redirect his nervous energy, he moved through an exhausting series of martial arts maneuvers, followed by a long shower. At 11:30, Carlos finally went downstairs to check out.

Pierre was nowhere to be seen and Carlos felt his blood pressure surge with the possibility that Pierre had ducked out on him. An attractive young female desk clerk handled his account, and when she punched the name Jean-Luc Finet into the computer, the screen indicated a message had just been left for the guest. The woman handed Carlos a sealed envelope. He ripped it open and realized everything was on schedule. An unsigned hand printed note simply read, "1145 Church Street." This was a code Carlos and Pierre had used twenty years earlier in Paris. It meant Pierre would be at a church at 11:45. Carlos had to presume it was the Saint Gervais behind the du Rhone. He paid his bill in cash to avoid a credit card trail and left the hotel. As soon as he turned the corner and started walking up the hill to the Saint Gervais, he saw a blue Saab double parked 40 yards away with Pierre standing alongside it, feverously smoking a cigarette.

Right before Carlos reached Pierre's car, he dropped the bag of Semtex residue in a public garbage can. Direct traces of the terrorist Carlos visiting the Hotel du Rhone and the City of Geneva were disappearing piece by piece.

"What's that about?" Pierre asked suspiciously. "You could have left that in your room."

Carlos slapped his forehead with the palm of his hand. "What's wrong with me? I'm such a dope. I knew that."

Pierre, visibly nervous, shook his head, knowing Carlos was lying. Contrary to Pierre's demeanor, Carlos was completely at ease. The men exchanged meaningless chatter on the drive to the U.N. about family and how Carlos would come back to visit Geneva soon. Both knew he was lying. At 12:05 the Saab pulled in front of the Visitors Gate at the U.N. complex. As he exited the car, Carlos instructed, "Be right here precisely at 12:30. If I'm not back by 12:35, then take off. No matter what, do not leave before then."

Pierre nodded affirmatively, now certain that he was in the middle of something very bad. Wearing his grey suit and overcoat, and carrying a leather briefcase, Carlos approached the security booth looking professional and giving the appearance of a person to be taken seriously. Not as an angel of death carrying a message from hell. His first observation was that the lack of security that existed yesterday had not changed overnight.

"Good day. How are you?" Carlos said in a deep Italian accent to the security guard, a different man than the guard from the day before. "I would like to take the next visitor's tour."

"Yes sir. That will be eight francs. And I'll need some form of identification."

"Certainly." Carlos pulled out a ten franc note and handed it, along with a Rome driver's license to the guard. The fake ID showed a recent picture of Carlos wearing a suit jacket and tie, with the pseudonym of Antonio Rostonza. The guard told Carlos the tour would begin at 12:30, and made the same speech Carlos had heard the day before about entering the Palais des Nations through Door 39.

This time, however, instead of scouting the U.N. grounds or waiting to go on tour, Carlos went right to work. He walked briskly straight to Door 39 then to the cloakroom twenty yards up the hall past the bookstore. He put his briefcase on the empty counter, opened it, and took out the bag marked "1".

In planning today's attack on the U.N., Carlos had a difficult time deciding between planting a bomb in the bookstore or the library. There was not enough Semtex to hit both locations effectively. Nor in all likelihood, was there enough time. His goal was to be in and out of the U.N. as quickly as possible. He decided on the bookstore because of its location and the certainty of affecting a larger number of victims. The public shock factor of intentionally marking harmless tourists for death would be enormous.

Briefcase in one hand and the bomb in the other, Carlos entered the store and strolled to a fully stocked bookcase that backed up to a floor-to-ceiling plate glass window, no more than 15 feet from the seating for the tour group. He pulled a thick picture book from the shelf and pretended to leaf through it. Using peripheral vision to assure no one was watching, he placed the wrapped one pound bomb in the slot where the book had been, and turned it flat against the back of the shelf. He pulled the surrounding books out about two inches and replaced the volume he was examining. The bomb was completely hidden from view. It was an extremely remote possibility that someone picking out one of four obscure books would discover Carlos' package.

He left the bookstore, returned to the cloakroom counter, reopened the briefcase and removed the second bomb. Moments later he walked past the circular security booth in the main lobby where unarmed, disinterested guards stood around telling jokes. Much to his chagrin, when he reached the balcony overlooking the full backyard grounds of the Palais des Nations and Lake Geneva, he caught up to an English speaking group which must have started its tour right before Carlos entered. Rather than draw attention to himself by standing around without purpose, Carlos walked into the men's room at the right end of the balcony, and sat down in a stall. He stared at his watch until 90 seconds ticked off.

He exited the bathroom pleased to see that the tour group had moved on and hustled to the enclosed left end of the balcony, out of view of security. After quickly sliding a three foot tall brass ashtray to the front edge of the balcony adjacent to the rail, overlooking the cafeteria down below, he put the bomb on the floor directly to the left of the ashtray and took about ten steps away to inspect the scene. The bag was hidden from sight.

He felt confident that any visitors to the balcony in the next 11 minutes and 45 seconds wouldn't use that ashtray since another was more conveniently located about thirty feet away. In his final survey of the area, Carlos noted the massive 50 foot wall of glass right in front of the explosive and the racket downstairs in the cafeteria, indicating a full lunchtime crowd. He took off to plant his next bomb.

Just as he approached Sabine VII, the General Assembly gallery, the English tour group was entering the room. Lucky enough not to have to waste a minute trying to sneak in with someone else, he nonchalantly joined the tour group and walked in with them.

The Assembly was in full session, and it was clear the diplomats were continuing their debate on the future of Iraq. When Carlos' bomb exploded here in only nine minutes, every nation in the world would take notice. Today many of them would pay dearly for banishing him from their borders years earlier.

He walked to the far end of the gallery's aisle and sat down in the second row. The gallery was lit with only aisle and safety lights, so that the darkness insulated Carlos from being watched by unwanted eyes. Equally important, while the person nearest to him sat only eight seats away, the circular layout of the room precluded that woman from being able to see anything but Carlos' shoulders and head. The room's natural cover didn't even matter as the visitors were engrossed in the proceedings below. Carlos opened the brief-case on his lap and removed Bomb 3.

As quietly as possible, he extracted the gray Semtex and black timer out of the white bag, double checking all connections by touch. He then leaned over and placed the bomb all the way under the seat in front of him. As he sat up, a woman in the first row turned her head and glanced at him, but he was certain she couldn't see what he was doing.

Carlos immediately left the gallery aware that his quick exit might seem unusual. But who could possibly think this aristocrat had just left behind a bomb powerful enough to knock down every wall in the room? So long as no one sat down in the seat Carlos just va-cated and searched under the chair in front, the bomb would not be discovered.

Six and a half minutes left. Carlos walked quickly out of the building. He calculated that he had somehow fallen about a minute behind schedule, tough to make up at this late stage. It was lucky he'd scooted right into Sabine VII. Although he lost a little time having to hide in the bathroom, he had scheduled an extra two min-utes in anticipation of the lockout procedure at Sabine VII. Still, he miscalculated somewhere, and placing the last bomb was the most important of all.

As soon as he hit the outside of Door 39, he picked up the pace even more, continually checking his watch. Less than four minutes to go. He hustled down the sidewalk to the back of the building toward the outside support column. Reaching it, he looked up through the immense back window to view a packed cafeteria and above that, the inside balcony where the second bomb presumably still sat. No time to think about it. He shielded the briefcase with his body before placing it up against the back base of the column, so the civil servants enjoying lunch couldn't see his deposit. Taking a deep breath he turned and walked away. His work was done.

Ten seconds later, Carlos was stunned to hear a man's squeaky voice announce, "Excuse me sir. You left your briefcase." Carlos wheeled around and saw a short, middle-aged Asian maintenance worker standing there holding the valise.

Carlos shook his head and simply responded, "Jesus Christ." After looking in all directions and seeing no other people, he motioned with his index finger for the man to come to him. Carlos smiled pleasantly as he took the briefcase and set it on the ground next to him. In a swift catlike movement, he palmed the man's face across his nose and cheek with his left hand, and correspondingly grabbed the back of his head with his right hand. In one powerful yanking twist he wrung the man's neck, killing him instantly. Carlos looked down at him on the ground and said, "Thank you."

He went back and replaced the case against the column, having lost more of his precious time. Worse, he thought, his reappearance in the back might now draw someone's attention. Fortunately, he saw no other witnesses outside the building.

Only about 1:50 left. All that remained was getting his picture ID back from security. He pulled out his Beretta, stuck it in his coat pocket and broke into a full run towards the front gate. If he didn't get there before the bombs simultaneously exploded, it was unlikely he would be able to retrieve the license which could directly link him to the crime.

Breathing hard, he reached the security booth with 55 seconds to spare. He saw Pierre illegally parked 50 yards beyond. Carlos ripped the visitor's badge off his coat and handed it to the security guard.

"Are you all right, sir?"

"I just remembered a meeting in the Old Town and if I'm late, I'll lose a very big account. It could cost me a fortune. Please, I have to go."

"Oh, certainly sir," the guard said handing Carlos back his drivers license, and logging him out at 12:30 p.m.

"Thank you," Carlos replied, walking away quickly, his hand on the trigger of the gun hidden in his pocket. He exhaled a sigh of relief; there was now no direct hard evidence left tracing the bombs to him. Conjecture, theory and speculation were one thing; proof was another. And, the guard may or may not even think of Carlos as a suspect, much less be able to accurately describe him.

Carlos reached Pierre moments later and opened the door to the car looking at his Rolex as the seconds ticked off...12, 11, 10...

"Right on time. Just like you ordered," Pierre said.

Carlos turned around and looked at the Palais des Nations 150 yards away and said, "Yeah, I think so."

Before either could say another word, two massive explosions rocked the ground like an earthquake, freezing everyone in a 20 square block area right in their tracks. Even through the parking lot full of cars and the tall, thick evergreens which surrounded the front of the Palais des Nations, Carlos could see the blinding white flash of light distinctive to Semtex. Just by seeing, feeling and hearing the raw power of the blasts, he knew his mission was a success.

Moments later total pandemonium broke out on the U.N. grounds. Other explosions were audible from within the Palais des Nations and thick clouds of smoke bellowed from the remnants of the area surrounding Door 39. A bright orange fire with billowing black smoke shot from a window on the third floor. Hysterical screaming people running chaotically in all directions materialized in throngs from every building on the Parc Ariana grounds except the Palais des Nations. Even the U.N. security guards had taken off aimlessly, and Carlos couldn't believe they still apparently carried no weapons. Pierre sat in the car mesmerized.

Carlos' assumption about the bookstore had been correct. The Semtex blew through the bookshelf like a dart through tissue paper. The bookshelf disintegrated into a million pieces of wood and metal shrapnel shattering the plate glass windows in all directions. The explosion instantly ignited the ceiling and electrical system on top of the bookstore, wholly engulfing those present in a fireball sea of flame.

Numerous visitors died in the explosion at Sabine VII, and a 16 foot stretch of the balcony collapsed onto the General Assembly floor below, crushing eighteen other foreign diplomats. To Carlos, the issue of bombing the General Assembly area was not how many people would die from the explosion, but the symbolism of destroying that room; the room of peace.

Three stories below in the back of the building, the scene inside what used to be the cafeteria was chaotic and horrific. The combination of one bomb ripping apart the support column for the overhang outside the cafeteria and the second bomb in the upstairs lobby balcony caused over a 25' x 25' chunk of three foot thick concrete, marble and steel to drop like a meteor on 132 innocent civilians. A hurricane of debris, including over a ton of razor sharp windowpane glass fragments knifed through the air injuring 288 others. Most were trapped in the makeshift torture chamber of a morgue, screaming in fear and pain.

Masses of people continued running toward the front of the burning Palais des Nations where they collected in shocked awe. Carlos stood alone next to Pierre's car observing the surrounding chaos. The Pakistani guard who had left his post upon the explosions a minute earlier, ran back to the security booth and picked up the telephone to call for help.

Carlos recognized an opportunity to close another door which could lead to his identification. He walked back to the booth and opened its door. Standing no more than six feet away, the guard spun around, the phone at his ear. He gave Carlos a puzzled look but before he had the chance to speak, Carlos emptied four shots into his chest. Carlos stepped over the corpse and grabbed the visitor's registry which he stuck inside his coat. The phone swung back and forth off the desk. Carlos drained his clip into the electronics board, watching little red and green lights fade out and he loaded a new clip into his Beretta.

Using his handkerchief he wiped the doorknob clean. Despite the insanity around the Palais des Nations a 100 yards away, nobody seemed to be within 30 yards of the booth, and Carlos felt sure there were no eyewitnesses to the murder despite the presence of a growing mob in the immediate vicinity. He stepped out of the booth, pulled his coat collar up, stooped his shoulders to appear shorter, and walked away with a mild fake limp in his right leg.

The screams of help, horror and pain coming from the burning, smoking building, were clear even from a distance. "Son of a bitch," Carlos said out loud with satisfaction, concluding this had been his most impressive terrorist feat yet.

Carlos kept his head down as he limped back to Pierre's car, climbing into the front seat. Pierre, white-faced, sat behind the wheel in shock. He also prayed he would live through the hour. Carlos was a close friend, but he had killed his friends before if self preservation was in issue. Twenty years ago, Pierre saw Carlos kill a friend on the mere suspicion that he had talked to French counterintelligence agents.

The thought of killing Pierre had crossed Carlos' mind as well. But Carlos knew every major security agency in existence had a file a foot thick on him. Within those files were detailed biographical listings of each of his friends and colleagues. He figured that if his good friend, Pierre Erne, showed up dead in Geneva today of all days, it was possible, perhaps likely, that the authorities would piece the events together and start the investigatory process that could lead to him. The better approach was to instill both a little fear and motivation in Pierre to keep him loyal and quiet.

"Pierre. Let's go. Let's get the hell out of here."

"You know," Carlos said as Pierre drove off in silence, "You probably don't have anything to worry about with the police. I took precautions so that no one can trace anything directly back to me. Look how careful I was to make sure that no one even knew I came to Geneva."

"Right Ilich. I'm sure nobody saw you shoot that guard and jump into my car," Pierre responded sarcastically.

"As a matter of fact," Carlos said, "the guard was the only person who might be able to provide any description of me. And I snatched the visitor's log, which means we're home free." Carlos waved the paper in front of Pierre's face, ripped it into pieces and threw them out of the window. "So buddy, are you mad at me?"

"What do you expect me to say? No matter what you told me, I'd have had little choice in doing this. If I said no, you would have killed me, but because I said yes, this is the position that I'm in. I was fucked either way."

"Wrong. If you didn't want to drive me today, I would not have killed you. I asked for your help because I needed someone completely trustworthy. A good driver. And I remember the job you did at the newspaper office in Lisbon. You were the best. Anyway, you kept asking me what I was doing here. Deep down I think you wanted to get involved."

"You lied. I didn't want to get involved in anything illegal much less something as incredible as blowing up the United Nations."

"Oh well. Too bad. You're in and you've got no defense. If the police show up and start asking questions, I'm sure you'll indicate total ignorance of me even being in Geneva. If you get tied to this in any capacity, you'll spend the rest of your life in prison . . . that is if you're not executed."

Pierre didn't need Carlos to tell him the mess he was in. Even though he unwittingly participated in this plot, first by sheltering Carlos, and second by driving him to and from the crime scene, he technically qualified as a conspirator. Considering his history with Carlos, Pierre knew that no one would ever believe he didn't know of Carlos' plan in advance.

In a cold soft voice, Carlos added, "Pierre, if you ever talk to the police about this, I will kill you. You know I'd find out. You also know I have a very long arm and nobody's ever caught me and nobody ever will. All I have to do is make one call to Seve." He paused and emphasized every syllable to make his point. "He may like you, but make no mistake...he would kill you and your family for me. I don't want that and neither do you."

The terrorist, murderer, extortionist extraordinaire continued with his psychological ploys. Lightening his tone, Carlos continued. "But let's not talk about the negatives. We've been friends too long. Here's a little present for your aggravation." Carlos pulled Jacques Ruf's briefcase from behind him and opened it onto the car seat between him and Pierre.

Pierre's eyes widened when he saw the two stacks of bills. He picked up a packet trying to keep one eye on the road and one eye on the treasure. "How much?"

"200,000."

Pierre snapped up the stacks and stuffed the bounty into his coat pocket. "What was that question about me being mad at you?" Pierre asked with a smile.

"I thought you'd come around. Whatever you do, dispose of the briefcase so no one finds it -- make sure you wipe it down first."

"Fine. You know, maybe I should go into the hotel computer and clear out all references to Jean-Luc Finet. All it takes is the press of a button."

"Good. You should also put another guest in my room right away to get fresh fingerprints to cover mine."

"Done," Pierre answered.

Pierre had said all the right things and Carlos felt confident he'd have no problems with him. He clicked the safety back on the Beretta in his coat pocket. This was good. A live Pierre was definitely better than a dead Pierre.

A moment later the Saab pulled up to the Swiss Air departure gate at Ferney. Carlos unhooked the holster from his calf and placed it, the Beretta and the empty clip into the still open briefcase. "Do what you want to do with this stuff," he said. "I can't take it with me."

"What am I supposed to do with it?" Pierre asked, bewildered.

"I don't care. It's yours now."

"Really?"

"No, you stupid ass. I'm gonna try and sell it at the currency exchange booth in there."

"I think the safest thing is to drop it in the river tonight," said Pierre.

"Good thinking. Thanks for everything. I'll be in touch." Without as much as another word, Carlos got out of the car, grabbed his remaining briefcase and carry-on and slid into the terminal. Pierre hoped he wouldn't hear from his old friend for a long time.

It was now 12:55 p.m. Boarding for Carlos' 2:30 flight wouldn't start for another hour. Because he decided it would be safest to check in at the last possible moment, he walked past the ticket counter, took the escalator up to the coffee shop, bought a newspaper from a vendor and sat at a table in the far back corner. For the next 45 minutes, he pretended to read the paper as his eyes continuously scanned everybody and everything in a 180 degree angle. Nothing seemed even remotely suspicious.

The final crucial element to Carlos' escape was boarding before Swiss authorities would take the investigative measure of closely checking the identity of every single outgoing passenger. Carlos' flight time was the predominant reason he'd timed the bombing for 12:30. He had just enough time to deposit the bombs and then leave the country. When European terrorism was rampant a decade ago, one of the first calls made was to close the airport. Carlos could only hope that he would beat the deadline of that order.

At 1:50 p.m. Carlos stood in line to check in and start the passport control procedures. His heart beat rapidly and his breathing became heavy as everyone around him talked about the explosions at the U.N. So far, details were vague except that damage was extensive and fatalities appeared numerous. He kept telling himself to relax, but to no avail.

The young, pretty reservation agent smiled at "Jean-Luc Finet" as Carlos flirted with her, and issued his boarding pass, checking him in without question. Five minutes later, Carlos had safely cleared through both the Passport Control and the security checkpoints and was down the walkway to his flight back to Riyahd.

The plane took off on time without incident and once the jet lifted off the runway, Carlos knew with finality he was home free. He ordered a triple vodka and finished it in a few gulps. As if he wished it to be so, the alcohol went straight to his brain. He passed out from the week's pressure cooked roller coaster ride and didn't wake up until the flight landed six hours later and a continent away.

SIX

THE DISTINCT REPETITIVE BUZZ of the hot line in the Georgetown home of National Security Advisor Darwin Weisser snapped him out of a deep slumber, as it had countless times before during his service on President Walter Tate's team. The random occurrence of world events meant a call could come at any time. Today it happened to be at 6:50 a.m.; 12:50 p.m. Geneva time. Weisser stumbled across the room to a small desk in the corner and answered the phone with a simple, "Yes."

"Mr. Weisser. This is Tony Pailet, Special Attache to Ambassador Lessne for the U.S. mission at the United Nations here in Geneva. I have Chief of Staff Foler on the line with us."

"Carl?"

"Morning Darwin. We wake you?"

"No. I've been up for half an hour."

"Sure. Listen. We've got a serious problem. Tony, tell Mr. Weisser what just happened."

"Yes sir. Approximately 15 to 20 minutes ago a series of explosions destroyed the U.N. building here in Geneva. I don't have any details yet about damage or fatalities, but it's pretty obvious this was the work of terrorists."

"How do you know?"

"Well, at least two explosions have been verified -- supposedly simultaneously and very powerful. The building's on fire and emergency vehicles are all over the place. It's unbelievable. Total chaos. I'm sorry, but that's all I know."

"Where are you calling from?"

"I'm on the U.N. grounds using one of our mobile security lines. I went out for lunch and came back here about five minutes after the explosions."

"Where's Ambassador Lessne?"

"The General Assembly was in special session, and he's either trapped in the building or he escaped somehow, but I can't say for sure. All electric power and communications facilities are down."

"Carl?" Weisser asked.

"Yeah."

"Have you told the President?"

"Nope. That's why I've got you on the line. I know he'd want to speak with you. And I sure as hell don't want him to hear this on T.V. before he hears it from us. We better call him right now."

"No question. Tony, good job calling this in. Go look for the Ambassador and find out more. Keep this line clear and we'll call you back shortly. Give me the number."

"011-41-22-356-8181."

"Fine. Thanks Tony. Hang up now. Carl, stay on the line. We'll have to track down Secretary Weimann also. I'll ring through to the White House now. I'll do the talking."

ON THE OTHER SIDE OF THE GLOBE, with an eight hour time zone difference, a long flight, and a longer all night drive through the vast and black Arabian desert, at 5:45 a.m. Carlos was pulling up to his home not far from the Tigris River in Baghdad. He entered his rent free, four bedroom, Mediterranean style villa, decorated with the finest of modern furnishings and art from all over the world. As Carlos passed by the den, he noticed a huge crate planted in the room. Looking in, he saw that Magdelena and the kids had already rifled through the crate. Clothes, toys and housewares were strewn all about.

He cursed that somebody draped a sweater across an original, priceless Alexander Calder geometric sculpture.

He tiptoed into the bedroom where Magdelena was curled up in bed asleep, clutching a pillow. He undressed, tossing his rumpled suit across a chaise. He slipped beneath the sheets, dropped his head on the pillow and sighed in comfort. Within seconds Magdelena's hand slid up his thigh and gently massaged his family jewels.

"I see you've still got balls," she whispered in his ear. "That was an incredible piece of work you pulled off in Geneva yesterday," Magdelena cooed.

"I know," Carlos whispered as he exhaled deeply.

"Honey, you forgot about something in your planning though."

Carlos turned his head slightly. "What?"

"That you have two kids and me to take care of, you son of a bitch," Magdelena acerbically said, digging a fingernail a half inch into a very soft and tender spot, and twisting her hand just enough to send a strong message, without damaging the goods. Carlos elevated three inches off the mattress and yelped like a dog kicked in the ass.

"Where the hell's your head? That was the craziest thing you've done in years. What do you have, a death wish? As soon as I heard about the U.N. on the news, I knew it was you. We were worried sick," she ranted, still firmly holding on to Carlos, who wisely didn't move or argue.

Once again, Magdelena established why she was the one person in the world capable of controlling Carlos, even if she had to resort to underhanded methods.

"At least you're back safe," she whispered again, loosening her grip. After about fifteen seconds, she rubbed her breasts against Carlos' chest, nibbled his ear lobe and asked, "Do you want to play?"

"Well, I uh..thought I did."

"Good. I'm going back to sleep. I suggest you do the same. I imagine you've been up all night. And thank you for the presents.

We loved them." Magdelena kissed him lightly on the cheek, turned around and curled back up in the opposite corner of the bed.

"Unfuckingbelievable," Carlos thought staring through the dark at the ceiling. Exhaustion consumed his body and minutes later he was fast asleep.

IT WAS JUST BEFORE 10:00 A.M. when Carlos' children decided he had slept long enough. After they dragged him out of bed and he showered and dressed, drank his coffee and played with the kids, it was time to get back to business. He turned on the large screen television which sat in the corner of his den and tuned the satellite dish control until he found CNN. The bombing of the U.N. complex in Geneva was getting non-stop coverage.

Magdelena sat next to Carlos on a deep cushioned white leather couch absorbing the details of the news report. Carlos was ecstatic by his success. Within minutes of the bombing, electrical fires consumed whole sections of floors...gas main explosions rippled through the building...426 dead, 373 injured, 44 still missing and presumed dead...most of the building and its priceless artwork a total loss... world leaders, including Saddam Hussein, decry this as the most heinous and shocking terrorist act in history and call for the perpetrator to be brought to swift justice...investigators searching for clues...23 extremist political groups ranging from Arabs to Irish to Serbs to Japanese all claiming credit.

Although Carlos' name wasn't mentioned, Saddam's was; most of the world considered him a natural suspect. Curiously, most analysts opined that despite the edicts which Iraq was presently subject to from the U.N., even Saddam Hussein wasn't bold or stupid enough to bomb the Palais des Nations.

After the report, Carlos turned off the set and spent the next two hours telling Magdelena almost every detail of his trip. Magdelena, a terrorist herself, was proud and impressed with Carlos' quick, instinctive and near perfect planning.

"You know, I'm surprised. I thought that when I placed one bomb at the top of the balcony above the cafeteria, and then another on the outside support column, that the building would slip off its foundation and fall into the ravine at the edge of the hill. Now that..."

"Wait a second," Magdelena said. "How much Semtex did you use?"

"About seven pounds."

"Between both locations?"

"Yeah."

"When you tried to level the Radio Free Europe building you used 20 pounds of Semtex, right?"

Carlos nodded.

"And 20 pounds didn't do it there." Magdelena rolled her eyes. "How could you possibly think you would knock a building the size of the U.N. off its foundation with only seven pounds? 120 wouldn't have done it."

"Give me a break. Look what I just pulled off by myself and with just one day of planning. Nobody else in the universe could have done that."

"That's true. So how did you know you could get on the plane back home before the airport closed?"

"Magda, that was my toughest decision. It was a gamble...an educated guess, I knew.."

At that moment, the doorbell rang. Carlos and Magdelena looked at each other. "I'll get that," he said.

Standing at the front door in full military dress were two soldiers, pistols holstered to their side. A black stretch limousine and two army jeeps each holding three guardsmen and a 160mm machine gun were double parked in the street.

"Good afternoon Mr. Sanchez. The president would like you to join him for lunch. We'll come in while you clean up or gather what you need. Please do not take longer than five minutes. We will have you back home in three hours."

"Come in. Give me two minutes." Carlos went back to the den to find Magdelena standing there holding his black leather jacket.

"I figured he'd show up at some point today. You're sure he's going to be happy with you?" Magdelena asked.

"Are you kidding?" Carlos said, fixing his hair in a hall mirror. "But he's crazy. Unpredictable."

"No more than me. Don't worry. If he wanted to kill me, I'd be dead already. I saw his scouts out front last night when I got home. I'm sure they tracked me from the moment I crossed the Saudi border." Carlos leaned over to kiss Magdelena on the cheek and whispered in her ear, "Do another bug sweep."

She kissed him back and answered, "I did it yesterday, plus a phone tap check. Everything's clean."

"Good. I'll see you later." Carlos snapped his Ray Bans out of his jacket pocket and put them on.

The guardsmen escorted Carlos to the limo and as he reached the palm tree lined curb, the door opened. A broadly smiling, casually dressed Saddam Hussein was sitting alone in the back seat, holding an empty champagne glass in his outstretched hand. He got out and hugged Carlos gregariously.

"My brother, what a wild character you are!" Saddam announced through a bellowing laugh. "You know I don't personally use alcohol, but I have learned that sometimes diplomatic protocol requires me to accept the customs of friends or allies. Come join me," Saddam waved with the glass.

The car drove away and the dictator thrust a glass filled with champagne into Carlos' hand. "Congratulations a hundred times over. What a marvelous piece of work!" Saddam laughed again, before raising his glass and solemnly toasting, "To the use of power -- and the abuse of power."

They clicked glasses and Carlos downed the champagne.

Carlos could tell they were leaving the modern Al-Mansur neighborhood and travelling east, which could mean towards the Presidential Palace or the commercial district near the well known Al-Rasheed Hotel. Either way it was a short drive, particularly in a motorcade which stopped for nothing.

Saddam leaned forward and said softly, "Ilich. I presume you know that Minister Shawoof was killed at the U.N. The news reports say that a balcony fell on him."

"I hadn't heard exactly who was killed, just that there were many deaths."

"Hassan was my first cousin. One of my most trusted men. But losing him for revenge against the U.N. isn't so bad. It could have been worse. If you died I'd be out 50 million francs," Saddam smiled at Carlos whose look made it clear he didn't see the humor. Saddam continued, "Anyway, CIA director Richter said Hassan's death convinced him I had nothing to do with the bombing."

"Well, the fact is, you didn't have anything to do with it."

"Tell me. Will this get traced back to you?"

"Anything's possible. After all, even a magazine in the U.S. finally tied together the Lockerbie incident as an assassination of American intelligence agents. And there's a big difference between blowing up a jet and blowing up the U.N. Everyone's going to keep looking until they find answers, and ultimately, they may get it right. But, there's only a handful of extremely trustworthy people who know it was me, and it has to stay that way."

"Yes, I know the ramifications. If this thing is traced to you, then I will be held accountable because I'm the one who's harboring you right now."

"Don't worry," Carlos said. "I don't want the credit and I don't want the blame."

"So why did you do it?"

"Because I'm angry at my past sponsors. I used to be a V.I.P. in about twenty countries. Now I'm ostracized so that travelling anywhere abroad, and even living here in Iraq is dangerous. The Americans saw to it that I became persona non grata, and I hate them as much as you do. This was personal for me."

"I have to say, you made your point."

The car turned onto Abu Nawas Street, a busy commercial boulevard dotted with restaurants and shops not far from the Presidential Palace. Additional security vehicles joined the caravan, and traffic in both directions was moved out of the way for the President. They stopped in front of a small restaurant which appeared to be closed.

Eight armed Republican Guardsmen surrounded the vehicle and Carlos stepped out first, noticing the billboard picture across the street of Saddam in fatigues, mounted on a rearing stallion with a drawn sword slaying the infidels. A flock of men and women wearing traditional black kafiyehs crowded the broken sidewalk applauding as Saddam exited the car. A group of children materialized from a building a few doors down and ran through the guards surrounding Saddam. He laughed, patted them on their heads, and kissed a dark long haired raggedy little girl on the forehead. He went over to the elders and touched some of their outstretched hands. As quickly as the whole public scene began, it ended as Saddam and his entourage entered the restaurant.

The place was empty as was always the case when Saddam went out in public. The two men sat alone at a large table in the corner, facing the room and the front window. Within seconds, a tall, fiftyish, thin man with large sparkling black eyes and a full beard wearing a bright purple headcloth and flowing royal blue caftan appeared, holding a silver and turquoise pitcher.

"Good day, Mr. President. I think you will be pleased with the special meal I have prepared for you and your guest," the man said as he poured large cups of cardamon, the Iraqi spiced coffee.

"I'm sure it will be excellent, Hosnu. As always."

The man respectfully bowed his head and backed away.

Both men simultaneously picked up and sipped the cardamon, and sat in an awkward and unusual moment of silence. Finally, Saddam placed his hand on top of Carlos' and spoke, "Look, I know you've been busy, but have you given any thought yet on your plan for the United States?"

Saddam sighed and shook his head. "I don't have a clue on the specifics of the plot. I just know I personally can't be the one to pull it off."

Saddam sat straight up and brusquely said, "What do you mean you're not going to do it? Why did I just pay you all this money?"

Carlos stuck both palms up to Saddam. "Calm down and listen."

Saddam grunted. Before Carlos had a chance to continue the

discussion, Hosnu and a waiter brought out trays of fish, chicken and rice, and in almost a motherly fashion, served both men. Carlos waited for them to leave.

"For me to take out President Tate and everyone else that you want dead, an incredible amount of planning will be necessary. This is not like anything I've ever done. I know I can get in the U.S. for a few days at a time to make plans if I keep a very low profile, but I can't stay too long, particularly in Washington, because the FBI is just too good. What I can do is set up things there for someone else to carry out my plan. But I'll need a fresh face...someone with no record or tie to terrorists or you, whose identity is beyond scrutiny."

"So tell me. Exactly who is this fresh face?"

"I only know a good place to start looking."

"Where?"

"The Republican Guards."

"I have a 150,000 to pick from. I don't understand," Saddam said.

"The Guards are the best of your troops, aren't they?"

"Of course."

"I want the best of the best. Someone smart and educated, athletic and loyal. Out of 150,000 men, I'm sure you can put together a group of ten or so for me to pick from."

"Yes. This can be done."

"I'll spend whatever time is needed teaching him everything I know. This won't be easy and it'll take a while. But believe me Saddam, I will create my clone, and then together, we can take down the U.S. After that, this man will be yours forever."

Saddam sat pensively before exclaiming, "My God, it's brilliant. Between the Republican Guardsmen and the Mukhabarat, we can find you some excellent candidates. You'll have a list right away."

"No. Leave the Mukhabarat out of this. They're nothing but a bunch of thugs. I trust Captain Sabar and I know he's faithful to you, but the Mukhabarat still has their own hidden agenda and they talk among themselves too much. If any of Sabar's men disappear to train with me, too many people will ask questions, and we can't have questions. A single soldier pulled from the Guards is easy for us to handle."

Saddam nodded in agreement.

"It is critical that no one except you and me know our final mission. If I learn that anybody has found out about our plan, I'll give you back the money and the deal's off. Tell Minister Hakim to do the preliminary search himself. Tell him I'll be training this man to be your personal bodyguard. He knows my experience in weapons, communications, surveillance and self-defense. It will make sense to him, especially with all of the recent attempts on your life."

Saddam responded, "Of course."

Carlos was in complete control, and as he often did once he asserted himself, he sat silently as a display of his power.

Looking around the empty restaurant, Carlos suddenly noticed that of the four Republican Guardsmen who entered the restaurant with him and Saddam almost an hour earlier, only one remained, a stranger, as Carlos knew the faces of Saddam's personal guards. This man also had a machine gun slung around his back, while Saddam's guards usually only wore sidearms.

It also seemed odd that Hosnu had disappeared from his station only 15 feet away. No longer listening to Saddam, Carlos peered through the window and saw a few Guardsmen sitting in the jeep and four others standing with their backs to the window. His senses jumped to full alert as he whispered to Saddam and motioned with a tilt of his head, "Who is this Guardsman?"

Saddam was taken aback. "I don't remember his name. He just started with me a week ago. He was designated for assignment by General Yassin."

"I think there's trouble. Take out your gun and keep it on your lap under the tablecloth. Do not move." Carlos crossed his left leg on top of his right and removed a knife from a sheath attached to his shin. In seconds he slipped it up his shirt sleeve with most of the cold blade in his hand, next to his fingertips.

Carlos rose from the table and slowly walked towards the Guardsman, subtly glancing behind him for Hosnu and the waiter.

"Excuse me soldier, do you have a cigarette?"

"Yes. Certainly."

As soon as the guard reached into his jacket pocket, Carlos snapped his wrist and grasped the knife handle. He plunged the instrument deep into the fleshy part of the guard's throat, and the man could only gurgle and gasp in response. Saddam's eyes instantly widened. Carlos barked out a silent order to Saddam by pressing two fingers to his lips. He then put his arm around the shoulder of the stumbling, aspirating guard and dragged him to the booth, blood gushing from his throat, seating him next to Saddam. "Put your arm around him and smile. Act like you're talking to him. Ignore the blood. Don't let him fall over," Carlos whispered.

Aware of the silence of the dining room, Carlos realized there was an unnatural lack of noise from the kitchen. He took the guard's sidearm, noting it was a nonregulation, Ruger Super Redhawk pistol, chambering a full round of .44 magnums, capable of stopping deer-sized game at close range. Carlos then slammed his knife into the side of the man twice more, then pulled him to the ground where he was hidden by the floor length tablecloth.

He grabbed the machine gun and softly but firmly directed Saddam. "This is serious. Shoot everyone. No matter who. Don't ask questions. We're going out the back door and then coming back through the restaurant to your car. Follow my lead. Don't waste bullets."

Carlos slid around the left of the table keeping one eye on the front window and one eye on the back room. No more than 45 seconds had passed since Carlos had approached the guard, and the soldiers on the sidewalk still had not turned around. He pointed with his index finger to Saddam, and then to the kitchen. Saddam understood the message and slid over to the wall next to the kitchen's entrance. Carlos put his hand up to stop him, leveled the machine gun at his waist, and opened up the automatic weapon. Bullets crashed through the glass and into the backs of the four unsuspecting assassin traitors. At the sound of the gunfire, two men holding machine guns dressed in black barged through the swiveled kitchen door. Saddam was on one knee waiting for them, and he emptied his entire clip into them. Gunfire broke loose outside on the front sidewalk as well.

Carlos yelled to Saddam, "Pick up their guns and go to the back door. Don't go out."

Saddam did as he was told and Carlos ran to one of the men in black and dragged him to the back exit. "Help me stand him up."

Carlos held the dead man around the chest. Intense gunfire continued outside, and bullets started flying around the restaurant. "Now open the door but don't go out."

Saddam kicked it open and Carlos shoved the corpse as hard as he could into a filthy rat infested alley. No gunfire came from beyond the door.

"Follow me. Be alert."

Carlos jumped out into the alley ready to shoot, with Saddam right behind him. Garbage cans, junk, two old cars and back doorways to other buildings filled the decrepit narrow alley. Carlos took one of the machine guns from Saddam, now holding one in each hand. He pointed to a beat up, burned out Ford, 30 feet away. "Get behind the car and shoot at whoever comes through this door or down the alley." Carlos perched himself into a large deep set doorway, sheltered by the shadows of the sun hitting the building. He pulled the strap of one of the machine guns over his shoulder.

Five seconds later two Republican Guardsmen came running through the door. They didn't take two steps before the hidden crossfire from Carlos and Saddam killed them both. A moment later another guard bolted through the door and met the same fate.

Eighty feet away, through the backlit end of the alley that opened up onto another crosstreet, Carlos saw yet another guard crouching and walking down the alley towards him. The soldier apparently saw the mound of bodies and cautiously inched along with his back flat to the wall, machine gun ready to fire. Carlos and Hussein remained out of the enemy's sight. All other gunfire had stopped, and the silence made the scene even more eerie. Knowing the general long range inaccuracy of machine guns, Carlos waited until he was sure the enemy was close enough that one succession of rapid fire bullets would not miss the mark. He took out his knife and held it low in the palm of his hand. When the guardsmen was within thirty feet, Carlos pitched the knife out into the street, hitting the wall twenty feet down. The instant the Guardsman whirled towards it, Carlos spun out of the doorway and emptied three seconds worth of bullets into him.

He slipped back into the alcove and noticed a thumbs up gesture from Saddam from behind the Ford. Neither moved for almost three minutes until Carlos finally crept out of the dark, cautiously turning in reconnaissance in a circular pattern. Saddam took Carlos' cue and did the same. They congregated over the various bodies and Carlos worked quickly to strip away every spare machine gun clip of bullets, which he divided between himself and Saddam. To be safe, Carlos reloaded the machine gun he had fired, although its clip was still half full.

Saddam stood with his back against one side of the door, and Carlos stood on the other. "Don't go in until I say." Carlos opened the door wide, but stayed behind it. Again, more silence. Both men entered the back of the restaurant to find it empty. Carlos pushed open the kitchen door and saw both Hosnu and the waiter lying dead.

The men walked warily through the bullet riddled, completely trashed restaurant, past seven more dead soldiers and out on to Abu Nawas Street. A large quiet crowd of about 100 civilians already surrounded the grisly scene of over a dozen dead Guardsmen — loyal and traitor — crumbled on the front sidewalk and street. Upon seeing Saddam Hussein emerge from the restaurant, a ring of cheers and applause rose from the people. Saddam smiled and thrust his arm and machine gun into the air, invoking yet more cheers.

Saddam's chauffeur also lay dead on the ground next to the Presidential limousine. "He should have stayed in the car. It's bullet-proof," Saddam dryly commented.

"I would hope so," Carlos responded.

As other security vehicles started pulling up to the scene of the attempted coup d'etat Carlos said, "Let's get out of here. Somebody else can clean up this mess."

Knowing his every move was being watched, Saddam kneeled down and kissed his driver on the forehead before he walked around the limo and got in the front seat. Carlos walked up to a man taking pictures and grabbed his camera. He pulled out the film and threw the camera to the ground. He walked back to the car; the keys were still in the ignition. Carlos took the drivers seat.

"Head to the Defense Ministry, Ilich."

"Fine."

As they drove away, Saddam seemed calm considering how close he'd come to death. After a couple of minutes of reflection, Saddam finally spoke, "Thank you for saving my life. This is the first time I've seen you at work. How did you know?"

"Training, instinct and paranoia," Carlos responded.

"Hmmm." After a few seconds Saddam spoke again. "There are too many forces at work in my path. This was the closest I've come to being killed. In Allah's name there is nothing more important to me than seeing you complete your mission in the U.S., so I can fulfill my destiny and lead the attack that will be the end of Israel. What happens if next time I'm not so lucky, and next time happens to fall before you take care of the Americans. What will you do? It won't change anything, but tell me the truth."

Carlos answered truthfully. "I'm a businessman and I consider myself a man of honor. I have a contract to complete. Only one person can cancel it. You. Your death does not terminate the agreement. And besides, remember, I hate the U.S. as much as you."

SEVEN

AT 8:35 A.M. PRESIDENT WALTER TATE entered the Oval Office with his arm draped around the shoulder of Deputy Undersecretary of State for Iraqi Affairs, James Yarmuth. Protocol required everyone rise when the president entered the room. "Please gentlemen, keep your seats," the president said, motioning with both hands, palms down. "I see we have Senator Dervishi with us this morning." The President gave the slightly built, preppy looking elderly man a gentle pat on the arm. "Thanks for coming on such short notice."

"Yes sir. Duty calls," answered Senate Majority Leader Bruno Dervishi with an outstretched hand. "You know that I'm always at your service."

"Hmm. Let's see what you say in an hour," Tate said with a big smile, causing everybody to laugh, albeit Dervishi did so uncomfortably.

National Security Adviser Darwin Weisser nudged forward asking, "Senator, have you met Jim Yarmuth before?"

"No sir." The two men nodded at each other and shook hands.

"Well now you have," Tate quickly interjected. "Let's get started. I've got a busy day planned, and I'd like to try and stay on schedule for once."

His aides smiled since the president was hardly ever on time.

"Brendan, have we learned anything new about who was responsible for the U.N. bombing?" Tate asked.

The head of the CIA sat up straight from his outstretched half slump and took a deep drag on a cigarette. As smoke poured from his mouth and nose, Brendan Richter said, "No sir. We're still at square one. We know the bombs were made with Semtex, a Czechoslovakian made plastic explosive. Unfortunately, Semtex is as popular with Middle East terrorists as it is with the Provisional IRA. There's an unlimited supply of this stuff, and virtually anyone with underground contacts can purchase it. I don't think we'll ever be able to trace its source."

"Are you saying there are no leads yet?" the president harshly queried.

"We believe that because of the complexity of the scheme, and the number of targeted locations in the U.N. building, that at least four terrorists were involved in planting the bombs. We've interviewed witnesses, checked the limited videotape that exists and gone through every other record imaginable, but so far everything comes up a blank."

"How can that be?" the president asked, frowning deeply. "What kind of security did they have there in Geneva?"

Richter raised his eyebrows, made a clicking sound off the roof of his mouth, and responded, "Basically, none. And that's why these terrorists were so damn successful. I hate to say it, but it was a brilliant operation," Richter shrugged. "They must have planned it for months. Real pros."

The Oval Office door opened and Chief of Staff Carl Foler entered. "Mr. President. Gentlemen," he said, smiling an acknowledgement at each person. "Sorry I'm late." He looked back at Walter Tate and said, "I had that breakfast meeting with Governor Levine."

The president nodded in understanding. "Brendan was just reporting on the status of the U.N. bombing investigation. Brendan, please continue."

Foler took the empty seat always reserved for the Chief of Staff on the president's right side. "Interpol has also recovered fragments of a suitcase that carried the bomb at the back of the Palais des Nations, but so far, we haven't traced the make, much less the country where the bag was purchased," Richter said. "It looks like that'll probably also be a dead end."

The president shook his head in disgust and the others showed various expressions of frustration and anger.

Richter continued, "They also used standard household timers to ignite the Semtex."

"Mr. Richter, how about going store by store through Geneva to track the purchase of those timers?" Dervishi asked as he cleaned his oval gold wire frame glasses.

"That's easier said than done. We suffer a serious manpower shortage, and besides, as I just said, the timer could be purchased almost anywhere. Bruno, you have to understand. This was obviously a meticulously planned operation by a well funded terrorist group, and I have to believe that the Semtex and timers were smuggled into Switzerland. We simply just can't waste resources asking 10,000 Geneva shopkeepers and all their employees if they remember selling a bunch of timers to one person."

"What about your so called worldwide web of informants? Haven't you gotten any leads from them?" Yarmuth asked.

Richter looked down and smiled tightly. "It's strange. Nobody's heard a thing. I would have expected that by now we'd have had five to ten solid tips, but so far...nothing. The only thing our sources have done is help us rule out certain suspects."

"Such as?" the President asked.

"Strangely enough, most of the well established terrorist groups including the PLO, the IRA, the Red Army, and what's left of Baader-Meinhof. Even the Libyans and Abdul Abbas' hands appear to be clean. We don't know about Abu Nidal. And Carlos is in retirement, if he's even still alive."

The analytical mind of Weisser dissected the problem. "Well Brendan, that tells me that you should focus in on who has the greatest motive for destroying the United Nations, or the most to lose if discovered, or perhaps both."

"I agree, but it's still a guessing game."

"I still think it was Saddam Hussein," the president asserted, taking the same private stance as he had since the day of the bombing. Publicly the president reserved comment on who was to blame, simply making a strong and repeated demand that the villains be caught and brought to face swift and severe justice.

"I'm sorry sir, but I respectfully disagree," the country's top spy responded. "First, Hussein has way too much to lose and he's smart enough to know he can't keep something like this secret. He also knows if we found out that he ordered the attack we'd blow him away. Even the Israelis can't trace the bombing to anyone in the Mid East, including Iraq. And the Mossad knows the region better than anyone."

"I think it was the Iranians or some Islamic fundamentalist group," Weisser answered.

"You could be right. Those people are total lunatics," Richter said.

"In fact gentlemen, that's one of the reasons I asked James to come to the meeting," the president said. "I know he believes it was either Saddam or the Iranians, and I wanted him to share his thoughts with you. I thought that Bruno particularly could benefit from James' insight into the region."

Yarmuth self-assuredly began, "It's an unequivocal fact that Iran is recruiting, training and financing terrorists in two training camps set up within their borders. They call this part of their "liberation movement," but make no mistake, this is state sponsored terrorism."

"You mean government sanctioned?" Dervishi asked.

"For the most part. The Moro National Liberation Front is literally located in an office building in downtown Tehran. The Iranian government has boasted of its successes in arranging terrorist activity. There's also the more well-known Islamic Jihad, which was known for supplying men to Ayatollah Khomeini. Of course, you've also heard of Hezbollah, the radical Shi'ite party of God. And I think the most intriguing group is Al Dawa, which is made up of Iraqi Shi'ites funded by Iran to overthrow Saddam Hussein. Its leader, Mohammed Bakr Hakim could become the ruler of Iraq. He's as crazy as Saddam."

"Can you explain exactly what this Islamic fundamentalist movement is?" Dervishi asked.

"Simple. It's fanatical extremism in the name of the Shi'ite Islamic religion, with martyrdom as the guiding light into heaven. The fundamentalists believe that the interests of Islam are paramount to the interests of the state, although the government is heavily influenced and almost run by the religion," said Yarmuth. He looked down and leafed through a few papers he brought with him until he found what he wanted. "So you know what you're dealing with on this martyr issue, Khomeini, who was considered the messiah, wrote: *'The more people, especially young ones who die for our cause, the stronger we will become. Muslims everywhere must conquer the fear of death so that they can conquer the world.'* Senator, during the Iran-Iraq war, volunteers literally came to the front carrying their own coffins. Some carried signs that read: *"The Ayatollah has given me permission to enter Heaven.'"*

"Jesus Fuckin' Christ," Dervishi muttered, rubbing the back of his neck. He looked over to Walter Tate and said, "Excuse me sir."

The president smiled, nodding his head slightly.

"And I take it that the United States and Israel are part of this holy war?" Dervishi asked.

"In their eyes, we go hand in hand. They feel Israel exists on land that belongs to them and that Israel is an agent for American imperialism," asnwered Yarmuth. "Therefore, in order to defeat Israel, the fundamentalists have to defeat the U.S. As they grow stronger in the Mid East -- and there's no question that they will -- I think we're going to see a rise in terrorist acts here."

"It sounds to me like there's no real hope for a permanent Mid East peace as long as the fundamentalists have a voice in the region," opined Dervishi, wearing a deep frown and with his eyebrows pointed.

"That's our analysis, but of course, we don't publicize it. Especially with the Arabs and Israel working so hard for peace," said Foler while toking hard on the pipe he was lighting.

"We don't expect these fanatics to disappear either," said Yarmuth. "The Shi'ites have been a sect of Islam since the 7th century, and its always been the faith of the poor and dispossessed, a perfect profile for a martyr." He paused, opened his hands and added, "These people have nothing to lose, so they live and die for Allah."

Dervishi shook his head and looked at Weisser. "Darwin, does anyone else in the State Department know as much about the region as James?"

"Nope," Weisser responded. "He's our expert."

"Well then, James, I presume you'll consider coming up to Capitol Hill one day and explaining this to some of my colleagues in the Senate that just don't have the full background on this mess in the Mideast. Behind closed doors, of course."

"If the president or Mr. Weisser have no objection, I'd be honored," Yarmuth answered, clearly pleased by the opportunity.

"Not a problem," President Tate answered.

Weisser nodded, naturally agreeing with the president.

"But let's move on," said Tate. "Bruno, I also asked you here this morning to brief you on a joint allied military exercise in Iraq that will begin in just a few hours. Darwin." The president looked to his National Security Advisor for a report.

Weisser glanced at notes from a legal pad, scratched his cheek and began, "At 10:45 this morning, 6:45 p.m. Baghdad time, a squadron of 110 U.S., British and French aircraft, mostly stationed in Saudi Arabia, are scheduled to attack air defense targets in Southern Iraq. We're targeting four command centers which hold communications and radar equipment and four mobile surface to air missile sites. We think this action is appropriate in light of last week's proof that Saddam Hussein has continued to build a nuclear weapon, despite the U.N. Gulf War directives. We also think this will send a strong message to those religious lunatics you just heard about."

Seeing Dervishi was about to speak, President Tate seized the floor. "Look Bruno. I won't deny there's a deep personal animosity between me and Saddam Hussein. But the United States has a duty to make sure this dictator understands who's boss, and that he's going to comply with the U.N. resolutions, one way or the other. And also don't forget he gassed our men. We hope the Congress will support us on this action and approve our use of force against Iraq. You control your party. This is an issue that transcends party politics."

Dervishi looked straight at President Tate, saying slowly and softly, "Mr. President, with all due respect, we're only a couple of hours away from this raid on Iraq, and my camp is finding out about it at the same time that your staff is probably out leaking the story to the press." Dervishi's lips tightened and his nostrils flared. "You've put us in a very difficult position. In only a few minutes a hundred reporters are going to ask me about this attack, without my having the slightest opportunity to be properly briefed and to talk with my colleagues. And you want us to tow the line?" he added sarcastically.

"What's your point Mr. Dervishi?" Foler asked. "This isn't that big a deal. It's a no brainer."

"Bombing a foreign country is a no brainer?" asked Dervishi, shaking his head, clearly astonished. "Even though it's just Iraq and you're probably right, you should have told us about this earlier. Like when the idea first crossed your mind. I talk with you people every day about something, and now, at the last moment, you dump this surprise in our laps. Now my people can deal with it," Dervishi continued, "and I'll make sure it looks like there's that real spirit of cooperation that you keep telling the press about, but in exchange, I want a firm committment right now that my amendment to the labor bill won't get vetoed. Tell me. Right now." One by one, Dervishi looked right into the eyes of the president and each of his top aides. He added, "If you don't, I'm going to tell the press how deeply disappointed I am about not being consulted about this little military foray of yours."

"Bruno, tell me, what does a labor bill have to do with foreign affairs?" questioned Chief of Staff Foler, rubbing his chin.

"Nothing. Absolutely nothing."

In an exasperated slow drawl, Foler asked, "Well what kind of horse trading is that? Get real."

In a cold voice, Dervishi responded. "It's what I want. So listen closely. I would think that if the Senate and key members of my party in the House don't support you, the attack could have a very detrimental impact on public opinion of the White House." He looked at each of the men again and added with a nod, "Fair statement?"

Walter Tate stared icily right back at Dervishi, but remained silent. Weisser raised his eyebrows and leaned back. Yarmuth didn't even blink, not knowing how to react. Richter looked away with a grimace.

Foler finally burst out laughing and leaned over, slapping Dervishi on the knee. "Goddam, boy. You're good. Damn good. I heard you never lose a poker game and now I know why. What the hell. I guess you're right. We should have told you about this sooner. Sorry." President Tate's master of damage control took a long puff on his pipe. "Mr. President, I think we should make that deal."

The president looked at his watch, stood up and announced sharply, "Fine. Gentlemen, I have to move on." And with that executive order, he quickly exited the room.

EIGHT

Outside Baqaa, Jordan

Norman Richards approached the small dirty white broken building that at one time someone called home. It wasn't difficult to conclude that the building's demise resulted from one hell of a battle, evidenced by over a hundred bullet holes just on the front wall of the structure alone, and the triangular shards of glass sticking out from the shuttered windows. Somehow, faded yellow and brown flower print curtains survived and still flapped around the window frames from the outside breeze lightly blowing in. Nothing else was remarkable about the building, largely because numerous others just like it dotted the landscape. There was no sign of life anywhere on the surrounding half brown, half green, cascading rocky hills, although Richards' sixth sense felt the many sets of eyes undoubtedly closely watching his every move.

Ten feet before reaching the front door Richards stopped and glanced back, double checking that his dusty and dented red Jeep was still there -- as if somehow it wouldn't be. He then checked his watch to confirm he was on schedule at 2:30 p.m. as requested, and ran his hand through his greased back thick brown hair. At a deliberately slow pace he moved up the gravel and weed-filled path toward the door and knocked loudly three times. Five seconds later the door creaked open and a deep resonant voice instructed in Arabic, "Ahlan wa sahlan. Please come in Mr. Norman."

Richards had taken only two steps inside the house when his peripheral vision picked up the unmistakable shape of a pistol held no more than three feet from his head. The door closed behind him in a loud thud, almost with a sense of permanency.

"You know our procedures Mr. Norman. Turn over your weapons, take off your shirt and loosen your pants. And thank you for being on time for once." A middle aged man with large black eyes set in a weather beaten leathery face, partly hidden by a salt and pepper mustache and goatee, stepped before Norman Richards. Abu Nasir, cloaked in a white thobe, the traditional Arab floor length shirt-dress with its black and white checkered matching gutra, the head scarf, commanded instant respect by his physical presence.

Richards reached inside his decade old blue jean jacket and retrieved a Smith & Wesson Model 29 Classic .44 Magnum, and handed it over to Nasir. Richards next removed his jacket deadpanning, "There's some extra bullets in the side pockets, but can I at least keep the hand grenade?"

Nasir showed no emotion in response to Richard's wisecrack as he examined the silver plated 8 3/8" long barrel gun. Extending his arm, closing an eye and peering through the sight, Nasir pointed the weapon across the room at an imaginary target and asked, "Do you still carry a knife?"

Richards peered upwards at the slightly taller Arab. "I was getting to it."

"I'm sure you were."

Richards lifted up his right pant leg, unbuckled a strap and pulled a nine inch Legionnaire's double edged stainless steel blade from its sheath. He handed it over to Nasir correctly by holding the tip of the blade. He then completely unbuttoned his red plaid shirt, pulled it off his shoulder, turned around and lifted it upwards revealing his highly defined musculature, sculpted from years of rigorous bodybuilding. Nasir nodded in acknowledgment that no weapon or recording device was hidden. Richards next undid his blue jeans and dropped them to his knees. The guard checked inside Richards' alligator cowboy boots and pants pockets, then did a quick and insensitive lower body pat down. Richards faked both a cough in the guard's face, and the obligatory apology afterwards. When the guard finished his inspection and stood up, Richards quickly redressed himself.

The semi-strip search was a precautionary security measure undertaken whenever Nasir did business with any non-Palestinian. If you didn't like it, you didn't have to do business with him. Nasir also didn't hold it against Richards that he traveled with weapons. It was a prudent practice in hostile territory such as Baqaa. Nasir might actually have thought less of him if he didn't come armed.

Nasir barked out an order in incomprehensible Arabic slang and within seconds, four more Arabs appeared from a back room and stood at near attention in front of Richards. Nasir, regal and elegant in his thobe, stood in the midst of his smaller and poorly dressed companions. Following proper Arab etiquette starting with Nasir, Richards greeted each man with "as-salaamo alaykum," a handshake, and a touch to his heart with the open palm of his right hand.

Nasir smiled in approval at the gesture. "As always, Mr. Norman, your weapons will be returned when you leave. Now, I presume you brought the shipment?"

"Some of it. I've got six dozen grenades, a dozen of the Glock pistols with extra clips and a couple thousand rounds, and six of the new NVG 500 night vision goggles."

"Where's the rest?" Nasir demanded. "That's not even half of the order. I was expecting a full delivery today."

"Sorry. Circumstances beyond my control."

"You assured me there would be no problem."

"I said sorry. You don't think I like making extra trips out to this hell hole, do you?"

Nasir glared at Richards. "Watch your mouth. You're well paid, so don't complain. Now tell me. And no lies. When will you have the rest? We wanted the Stinger missiles today."

"I know, I know. I've been promised they'll be here in two days. All the other pistols and machine guns should be here in a week. The whole shipment won't fit in my Jeep though, so I have to arrange alternate transportation. And as you know, slipping this stuff past the Israelis is never easy."

"That is not my concern, Mr. Norman. Transportation is your responsibility. You get one week. I will accept no more excuses."

During his twelve resident years in the Middle East, Richards never got used to Nasir or any other Arab calling him "Mr. Norman." However, having learned that a frequent common form of address through the Arab world was to attach the person's first name to "Mr.," he learned to tolerate and occasionally participate in the custom. Particularly with Nasir and power brokers like him who served as funding sources for his weapons deals. He also recognized that accepting the cultural practices of the Arabs made it easier for them to accept and do business with him, since it was presumed that Richards, like all Americans, was untrustworthy.

Abu Nasir, 51, had lived most of his life in the Palestinian refugee camp at Baqaa. He was an intelligent man, and recognized the inequity which resulted from the establishment of the State of Israel for the Jews in 1948 by the U.N., while his people, the Palestinians, were stripped of both basic liberties and a homeland. One day his people would have their own homeland. Nasir would kill or die for this, and if need be, he would do both.

While never formally a member of the Palestine Liberation Organization or any of its factions, he had always been an ardent supporter of anyone whose mission involved the destruction of Israel. Over the past two decades Nasir had gained the respect of the prominent Arab militants for his skill in many areas: gun smuggling, providing an assassin, establishing a safehouse, or perhaps just simply obtaining and sharing strategical information on the enemy. Always a different but valuable service.

Then, five years ago, through his involvement with Hamas, the radical Palestinian Islamic fundamentalist group, Nasir helped found, organize and lead the Jericho *intifada*, the violent Palestinian uprising and resistance to Israel's occupation of the West Bank of the Jordan River. The next year, the PLO rewarded Nasir's loyalty and achievements by unofficially authorizing him to serve as its middleman in orchestrating weapons deals, such as the pending transaction with Richards.

To many he became a hero. His flowing white thobe and gutra were a gift from his fellow Baqaa refugees, and he wore them with pride and as a symbol of his leadership. As a result of his high profile activities, however, the Israeli Mossad targeted him high on its "watch" list. When Nasir's outlaw status with the Zionist state became publicized, it only heightened Nasir's stature in the eyes of his Arab brethren.

"Mr. Abu, this is the third shipment I've delivered to you in a year. Where's all this stuff going?" Richards asked, the inflection in his voice evidencing natural curiosity.

"How dare you ask my business?" Nasir answered harshly.

"Sorry. Sometimes I just like to see whose death I have a hand in," Richards sarcastically grinned. "And to tell you the truth, I thought perhaps there might be some other merchandise I could provide for you or whoever you're doing business with. I *am* a salesman after all."

"Mr. Norman. Let me remind you that you have yet to complete this contract. Prove yourself worthy by delivering the Stingers and we will talk about the future. A word of caution. Do not ask questions about my business. Men sometimes get killed over misunderstandings on private matters." There was a hard bite to Nasir's tone, and he stared icily at Richards.

"Look Nasir," Richards said, "I asked a harmless question. You don't have to make veiled threats. I mean no disrespect, but as you know, I've been in this business more than a few years. Longer than you in fact, and my credentials and record are impeccable. How do you think I've survived this long? I know you checked me out thoroughly."

"That we did."

"I'm sure you also recall that last time, when you told me that two dozen of the grenades were dead, I replaced them, no questions asked."

"You should have. They were defective."

Richards shook his head. "They weren't," he said emphatically. "But that's okay. I know you weren't the end user, and you just passed along whatever story you were told."

"Perhaps. Anything is possible."

"Look, I'm just trying to make another deal. I can get you 60 of the NATO M249 Squad Automatic Weapons, and its just gone through modifications. There's a new ventilated heat shield that clips over the barrel, an articulated carrying handle, a hydraulic buffer and a redesigned buttstock assembly." Richards moved his hands around an invisible submachine gun like a mime, illustrating the product improvements. "I've got one with me in the Jeep if you want to see it. I don't have a price yet, but if you're interested you'll have to let me know right away. If you don't want them, somebody else will." Richards smiled and added, "Don't forget, I'm a capitalist. First come, first serve."

"We're well aware of your economic philosophy, and that is exactly why our business relationship will continue to proceed slowly. If there's any interest in this weapon you mention, I'll tell you next week when you make final delivery. I have nothing against you personally, I just do not like or trust Americans."

"Whatever's happened with your people isn't my fault. Mr. Abu, consider me a supporter of your cause. My effort, my business, plays an important role in helping you fight your war. I just want to help. These guns will be gone in days."

"So be it. But I also know exactly what your past and present politics are Mr. Norman, and I do not think it will benefit either of us to discuss this any longer." Nasir smiled coldly, paused and continued, "However, as long as you like to help my people, then please give my friends a hand carrying the weapons in from your Jeep."

"Sure. But don't forget one thing."

"What?"

Richards clicked his fingers twice and held out his open palm.

Nasir nodded slightly and reached inside his robe retrieving a beaten tan leather pouch. He counted out fifty U.S. $100 bills and handed them to Richards, demonstrably putting an additional large stack of American money back into the pouch. "As you can see there is plenty more. You would have been paid in full today if you had done your job properly."

Richards felt his blood pressure rise. "Five thousand? Are you kidding? This doesn't even cover the cost of today's delivery. This isn't right. You gotta be fair with me."

"Mr. Norman. I am not interested in what is right or fair. *Right* would have been delivery of my entire order today. In my view, *fair* is that I paid you at all. Be happy I don't cut the price as a penalty. I will not steal the balance of your money. It is safe. I, too, have a reputation. I presume, however, that you will certainly now be more motivated to assure that the rest of the shipment is forthcoming, and quickly."

Knowing he could not change the situation, Richards exhaled deeply and spit on the concrete floor, a gesture he knew the Arabs hated. "I guess that's business, huh?"

Nasir smiled, ignoring Richards' insult, and motioned to the door with a sweep of his arm.

With Richards help, it took only one trip for the seven men to carry the munitions inside the building.

"Mr. Norman, please excuse our manners," Nasir said after everything from Richard's Jeep was unloaded. "We have no coffee or Siddiki to offer you today. From what I know of you, I'm sure you find the absence of alcohol particularly bothersome. But I promise you -- next time -- when you deliver the rest of the shipment, we will celebrate together."

Suddenly everyone in the room looked up to the sky in unison as if they could see through the ceiling and roof. The distinct sound of whirling helicopter blades came from nowhere and appeared to be headed directly towards the house at an alarmingly fast rate. Nasir knew it was unusual for helicopters to be in the skies in this territory, particularly traveling west from Israel to east. He motioned strongly with his index finger at two of his men and then to the door, silently ordering them to go outside and investigate what was happening. Over the next few seconds as the roar of the blades got closer and closer, everyone froze as if they knew what might be next, yet with that degree of uncertainty that prevented decisive action.

The group's paralysis ceased the moment the unmistakable rapid cracks of machine gun fire erupted over the thunder of the helicopter, now hovering directly on top of the house. Nasir's two guards were instantly cut down. The men scattered in all directions inside the house, frantically scrambling for their weapons. Richards instantly grasped the extreme prejudice he faced having had his handgun and knife confiscated only 15 minutes earlier. He turned toward the back of the safehouse where he saw the guard move his gun and knife.

Richards took no more than four steps when the front door was blown open, and a group of eight Israeli commandos wearing green fatigues and an array of protective head and body gear stormed into the room spraying machine gun bullets in all directions. Richards dove and hit the floor hard, curling up into a fetal position facing the attackers not even 15 feet away. He watched wide eyed while the Israelis systematically took out everyone who moved.

The Arab who helped Nasir search Richards at the front door was the first to go. He had barely lifted his arm to fire his gun when a sequence of about ten Uzi bullets ripped him apart. Two unprepared, unarmed Palestinians running for their weapons were shot in the back and fell lifeless to the floor. The sole Arab who pulled a gun and got off a couple of wild shots was smashed six feet back into a wall from the force of the countless bullets which immediately smothered him. At that same moment, Richards felt the hammer like impact of a series of projectiles hitting his body and looked down to see blood flowing freely from his chest. The last thing Norman Richards witnessed before he drifted away was Nasir taking a bullet in the leg, a bullet in the chest, and slumping to the ground.

NINE

AT THE SAME MOMENT that Israeli bullets ripped through a broken down not so safehouse outside Baqaa, Jordan, some 500 miles to the East, Carlos sat in a dark cubby hole of a room inside Saddam's secret underground fortress, known as "the Cave," spying through a peephole at six young nervous Iraqi soldiers, brought together for reasons unknown to them.

Much was at stake on this complex future enterprise and Carlos concluded that training a few additional new terrorists would not only provide extra support for this mission, but perhaps others down the road as well. Naturally, Saddam enthusiastically ratified the idea, believing it would also give him the wherewithal to expand Iraqi terrorism across the globe, as he had envisioned even before the Gulf War.

Over the past month, Carlos had spent countless hours pouring through the dossiers of Republican Guardsmen searching for the best and brightest stars within Saddam's elite troops. He had now pared down to a short list the men sitting on just the other side of the wall. At least on paper, each candidate had the potential to be selected as the protege Carlos would train to kill President Walter Tate and annihilate the U.S. government.

These men stood out over thousands of others because of their documented history of superior intellectual, physical and leadership capabilities. Nevertheless, a dossier told only so much about a person's character. Determining who was truly qualified to enter his terrorism grad school could only be accomplished by face to face personal interviews. There was no place better to do this than the privacy of the Cave.

The existence of the Cave was public knowledge, but very few knew exactly where it was located. Access was limited solely to one elevator, remotely hidden away in the Ministry of Defense. Only six people held keys to operate the elevator, protected every minute of the day by one of Iraq's elite soldiers, a Republican Guardsman, hand picked by Saddam. If one somehow found the elevator without a key and touched any button, his instant death by nerve gas was guaranteed. If a keyholder punched in the wrong five digit numeric code which changed every other day, it was the same result. Even for Saddam.

The Cave remains one of the largest underground buildings in the world, with two levels each the size of three football fields. Constructed with 12 foot thick concrete and lead walls to provide insulation from nuclear attack, it includes dormitory type housing for 1800, with kitchens, water filtration plant, a six month food supply, backup generator and oxygenation systems, a full service hospital, an armory, radio and television studios, and of course, a military command center that even the Pentagon would be proud of.

Carlos intentionally controlled the environment in the tiny room so that simply sitting still was a test. The heat was raised nearly to sauna level, the lights were turned bright, and the men were seated in undersized wooden slatted chairs. When each soldier was picked up without prior warning by Saddam's military police, he was directed not to ask questions or even speak. The men sat together for thirty minutes, again with strict instructions not to move from their chairs or to talk. Carlos studied them behind the peephole, pleased to see that no one disobeyed orders.

After Carlos finally entered the room and sat down in a chair placed in the center, he stared intently at the group as a whole and each man singularly. Five minutes passed without sound except for the low hum of the bright and hot halogen light fixtures.

One soldier's eyes anxiously bounced about the small room like pinballs and he shifted positions in his chair repeatedly. His apprehension was to be understood, since for all these men knew, they could be here for disciplinary reasons, which in the Iraqi army often meant execution. Still, without a word having been said, the man's demeanor didn't fit the profile of what Carlos needed.

"Do any of you know me?" Carlos finally said. Each man shook his head no. "My name is Ilich Ramirez Sanchez. I am known by many as Carlos, which is what I want you to call me. Do any of you know that name?" Two men raised their hands, pleasantly surprising Carlos, though he showed no expression.

The two soldiers who claimed to know him were the nearly identical twin brothers, Ahmed and Khalil al-Sharif. When Carlos found the twins, progeny of a famous Baghdad police captain, and lifelong friend and ally to Saddam, he knew he had struck gold. Carlos theorized that if he could actually use the brothers together, placing two of the "same person" into the middle of a terrorist attack provided intriguing possibilities; enemy governments would call it frightening. And even if they couldn't be teamed together it didn't matter; separately they qualified to be taken under his wing.

Carlos addressed the group in a strong and passionate voice. "I am a terrorist. I am in Iraq to help your president fulfill an important mission. That is, to train you as terrorists. There are only a handful of men across the world who can teach the things I know. After your instruction is finished you could be sent anywhere in the world on missions necessary to advance the interests of the State. It is likely you will become rich. It is just as likely you will die violently. But if you do, it will be a death with honor, in the service of your country. So if any of you don't want to participate in this assignment, this is your only opportunity to leave. If you go, it won't be held against you in any way. But if you do leave, you must maintain complete secrecy."

Two men raised their arms.

Carlos smiled pleasantly and gestured at one, "Yes?"

A tall, lanky soldier stood up straightening his dark green army suitcoat. "Carlos, I'm honored to be selected for this program. Thank you. But for the past two years I have been training with the Air Force, and in only two months I will be certified to fly fighter jets. Can I finish my program and then come back to join your group?"

"No. You are Hafez Abbed, correct?"

The Guardsman nodded.

"I'm sorry, but you'd be too far behind the others in training. No one here needs a reason to be excused, but yours is a good one, and we suspected you would make this request. Perhaps there will be another opportunity in the future, and we will keep you in mind. You're excused. Gentlemen, I'll be back."

Carlos left and personally escorted Hafez Abbed safely up the elevator exiting the Cave.

Carlos had barely sat back down when the soldier who Carlos earlier perceived as being nervous raised his hand. He announced the man's surname as an authorization to speak, "Shaheed."

"I've served Iraq with great distinction and have the battle scars to prove it." Shaheed patted his chest and thigh. "But I am married with two young children, and it sounds as if your training and missions will often take me far from home. I will never refuse to give my life for Iraq, but I would prefer to continue in the army. My service will be complete soon and I hope to then begin engineering school. Are you sure this won't affect my record?"

"I'm quite sure," Carlos replied. "Mr. Shaheed, come with me. I'll see you out." They walked down the hallway in silence, and when they reached the elevator, Carlos explained, "As you saw earlier, there's a special code needed to get the elevator moving."

Carlos leaned inside the door and randomly punched numbers on a keypad, winking at Shaheed as the door closed. A clear, odorless gas instantly hissed from the control panel and filled the elevator. Within five seconds the man's eyes were bulging and he was gasping desperately as if knifed in the throat. Five more seconds passed and Shaheed was sprawled dead. By the time the elevator reached the ground floor ten seconds later an exhaust fan had sucked out all of the poison, and when the door opened, the Republican Guardsman sentry found the corpse.

Hafez Abbed lived because Carlos liked him. Shaheed died simply because he rubbed Carlos the wrong way.

Carlos returned to the room and stood behind his chair, planting both hands firmly on the chairback, staring coldly at the remaining four men. In a commanding voice he said, "You are under my control now. You belong to me. There will be complete secrecy about your training. If you violate this covenant, only one punishment will be imposed -- your instant death. If you speak to anyone, that person will die as well. Although you will each receive the same training, President Hussein and I expect that ultimately, you will handle separate projects. There is one critical mission that one of you -- the best of you -- will work on with me. I will demand and obtain complete perfection from you, because there is no room for error in what we do.

"As we train you will give me everything you have and more. When I have finished your instruction, you will be ready for any thing. You will be experts in weapons, self-defense, communications, surveillance, disguise, sabotage and murder. You will understand the complexities of politics and world affairs. You will learn to speak foreign languages. You will learn the psychology of fear and power, and you will conquer fear yourself. And this much I promise you," Carlos looked down and then back up, slowly and softly enunciating each of his next words, "Men will fear you. Then you will know real power." He paused again and raised his voice. "Are there questions?"

A physically immense recruit rose from his chair. "Carlos. I thank you and President Hussein for this opportunity. I will not let you down. I'm sorry I do not know you, but would you please tell us about your background?"

This was a fair question and Carlos appreciated Omar Rafsani's nerve and candor. Moreover, this was a perfect opportunity for

Carlos to instill fear in their minds, a necessary means in gaining their respect. And their fear and respect was critical to make them open the yet to be discovered cold and black side of their hearts which only Carlos could mold.

Carlos sat down crossing one leg over the other. "You are Omar Rafsani?"

Rafsani nodded.

Carlos spoke softly, allowing his deeds to speak for themselves. "About 20 years ago I went to Cuba where I began my socialist political indoctrination and terrorist training. I then moved to the Soviet Union where I was instructed by the legendary Seve Dolchino of the KGB, and I freelanced for them until recently. I have lived and conducted operations in Paris, London, Vienna, Rome, Prague, Bonn, Budapest and cities throughout Asia and the Middle East."

Carlos proudly continued, "It was I who kidnapped the OPEC oil ministers in Vienna and planned the raid against the Israelis on the Olympic Village in Munich. I've hijacked airplanes and bombed airports and public buildings, and I've assassinated at least 200 people. I know that violence is the only method to bring about social and political change, and to publicize the causes I support. Unfortunately I now remain wanted in many countries, and most of them have imposed shoot to kill orders if I am merely spotted. So — I've told you enough about me so that if I even suspect you disclose to anyone I'm here, I would kill you and whoever you told without hesitation. Even if I might be wrong. And just so you know, I could kill any of you with one hand, and all of you at once if I had to. One last item. I've been authorized by President Hussein to do whatever I wish to you while you're under my charge to protect State or my personal security."

Carlos learned from Seve that the student must first believe in the teacher as a person, before the student would fully accept the instruction of the teacher. Carlos felt confident his talk had relayed the appropriate message.

Khalil al-Sharif raised his hand. "When will our training start and how long will it take?"

"It started the moment you learned my identity. It will last until you learn everything I can teach you. Tomorrow you will be moved to a secret location outside of Baghdad. You will be excused in a few minutes to go pack one suitcase of clothes, and one box of whatever personal items will entertain you in the few free moments I'll give you. Nothing else."

Khalil rose from his chair, "Carlos, what should we say to friends and family who are bound to ask where we're going?"

"Tell them you've been selected for a special training program to become a personal bodyguard to President Hussein. You'll be gone for six months to a year, and you'll telephone from time to time. Nothing else."

Ahmed al-Sharif took the floor. "Carlos, you said that the best one of us will be chosen to go on a special mission with you. I volunteer. In the name of my family and for Islam, if it is necessary, I would be proud to die for the honor of Iraq."

Carlos wanted to say, *"Sit down you asshole. Nobody should be proud to die for any reason,"* but he recognized the youthful good intents of Ahmed, combined with the martyr spirit of true Islamics. Instead he replied, "Why are you the best?"

"I am the strongest and the most brave. My convictions against our enemies run deep through my blood. I am not afraid to kill. I already have no fear."

"Hmmm. What do the rest of you say about this?"

Resounding cries of disagreement filled the room. Omar Rafsani, an incredible physical specimen at 6'4" and 235 rock solid pounds with brute animal instincts jumped up. "His boasts are lies," Rafsani shouted. "This man doesn't know me. I challenge him to a fight right now to prove who's better."

"It couldn't possibly be that these men are the best of Saddam's soldiers," Carlos thought. But before he could respond, Khalil stood up again and announced, "Carlos, I can't believe that you will determine who's the best of us based upon who's the strongest. I am strong and agile. But my best traits are my mind and determination. I've heard you're the greatest terrorist alive. If that is true, it's be-

cause you have instincts and intelligence, not just raw strength."

Khalil was right. It was all about brainpower, not horsepower. Although Carlos was impressed with Khalil's response, he wouldn't give him the benefit of acknowledging it in front of the others. Right now they all had to be developed and to accomplish this Carlos had planned his own creative psychological tests to determine who really had the most potential. He decided to start testing the candidate he thought least likely to succeed, Siddig Saleh.

Siddig was there only because he was Saddam's nephew. His record was unexceptional, though like almost all Republican Guardsmen he was a fierce and faithful warrior.

Carlos glanced down at the folder he'd brought into the room containing reports, vital information and an analysis on each man. "Siddig Saleh, please step forward."

A younger version of Saddam Hussein rose from his chair and confidently strutted towards Carlos. Standing over six feet tall, Siddig had his uncle's dark curly hair, thick mustache and wide sparkling black eyes. He extended his hand to Carlos, who just looked down at it and then up at the young man with contempt.

"You've had everything handed to you all your life. You were placed into the Republican Guard only because your uncle is the president. Isn't that true?"

Without waiting for an answer, Carlos moved into Siddig's face saying loudly and sarcastically, "I don't think you're qualified for this line of work and I didn't want you here. I let you visit with us today as a favor to your uncle. I reviewed your record. You're not man enough to handle our training." Carlos slapped Siddig hard across the face. The man flinched and bit his bottom lip, but remained silent. The others were shocked as Carlos proceeded to make an example of Siddig.

"You are a worthless human being. I heard your mother made you enlist in the army," Carlos lied, spraying spit in Siddig's face.

The young man was fighting to keep his composure. Staring straight ahead he softly responded, "That's not true, sir."

"And you repeatedly disobeyed orders from your commanding officers, claiming some sort of privilege because of your uncle," Carlos lied again, still yelling.

"No sir," Siddig said a little louder.

"And during the war with the Americans, while these other men were out on the front risking their lives, you had special jobs behind the lines so that your privileged ass would be safe."

"False. You must have reviewed someone else's record, sir. I was cited for valor and have always been prepared to die for my country. I still am."

"Oh yeah?" Carlos asked in a deep and sinister tone.

"Yes, sir."

"Let me cut off your finger right now as proof of your commitment."

Siddig paused but responded, "If that's what will convince you."

"It would be a sign that you're not the little girl I think you are."

"Fine," Siddig said.

Carlos reached into his pocket and pulled out his Swiss Army Knife, opening its largest blade and flaunting it for all to see. "Put your hand flat on the table, and extend your little finger out by itself."

Siddig gave Carlos a bewildered look, trying to figure a way out of the dilemna he was so quickly and artfully manipulated into.

"I'm waiting," said Carlos.

Finally, Siddig rubbed his hands together and grimaced as he lay his left hand flat on the table. Carlos flipped his knife about three feet in the air, catching it neatly by the handle and jamming it into the table, placing the blade between Siddig's outstretched fingers with butcherlike precision. Siddig flinched his hand back.

"Are you ready?" Carlos asked. Breathing hard, Siddig slowly nodded his sweat beaded head and put his hand back in place.

Carlos firmly grasped Siddig's wrist. "Here goes," he announced loudly to all, staring deep into Siddig's frightened eyes.

Upon hearing this final warning and seeing the knife rise a few inches above his finger, Siddig yanked his hand back at the last second, shouting, "No." He began to hyperventilate as the color drained from his face. A collective sigh came from the others in the room.

"I didn't think you could do it," Carlos said. "Now get out of here. I can't use you. You're not like these other men."

A downtrodden Siddig left the room. Carlos followed behind him, understanding the necessity to assure Siddig's safe departure up and out of the elevator.

As he punched in the correct code, Carlos smiled and said, "Don't feel too bad, son. I know I was hard on you. Don't take it personally." Carlos patted him on the shoulder and stepped back as the elevator door closed. He turned around and bumped into Saddam Hussein.

"You knew I was watching. Did you have to humiliate him like that?"

"Yes. He wasn't qualified for this."

"You didn't have to do it that way. I mean, c'mon Ilich... cutting off a finger?"

"You've done worse to your men. Now you see I was right about him. He's soft. I tried to tell you this before."

"The others wouldn't have given a finger either."

"Maybe. Maybe not. But guess what, that's tough. Now please excuse me. We can finish this later."

Carlos left Saddam standing alone in disappointment and returned to the room. Upon seeing Carlos, the three remaining men promptly stopped their animated discussion. Carlos picked the knife off the table and whipped it across the room to the back wall where it lodged into the plasterboard. He walked past them, extracted the blade, and with his back to the men he asked, "Who's next?"

Omar Rafsani and Ahmed al-Sharif both spoke almost in unison, asserting their manhood and willingness to give a finger for the cause. Carlos hoped Saddam was watching again. He nodded at them both and looked at Khalil, "What about you?"

"I may be brave but I'm not stupid. I hope this doesn't keep me out of your program, but I see no point in sacrificing a finger. If you can logically justify a benefit to it, then I'll consider it."

Carlos smiled and replied, "Khalil, while your brother and Omar are not wrong, and I believe they're firm in their convictions, you are right."

Khalil al-Sharif just passed a major test in becoming the protege to Carlos.

TEN

The West Bank, Israel

"I'M TIRED OF SITTING AROUND waiting for this asshole to wake up," said Sam Phillips, Mid East bureau chief for the Central Intelligence Agency.

"Get him up," replied Dudi Bareket, Chief of the Anti-Terrorist Unit of the Israeli Mossad. "I've got better things to do than waste time here with you. If it was my choice I'd just as soon shoot him for all the aggravation he's caused me."

"He's been out almost a day. He looks dead. What did you use on him?" asked Phillips.

"Dioxide-methophenaline."

"Never heard of it."

"It's used mostly to sedate large wild animals before they're transported long distances. It also works as a truth serum on humans, that is, if you can wake them up for questioning."

"At least now I know why we didn't get access to him for four hours, huh?"

"Think what you want."

Phillips leaned over an unconscious Norman Richards and slapped him hard across the face. Bareket laughed when Richards failed to budge. Richards looked like a corpse lying on the unsheeted cot in a back room of a kibbutz, in the dangerous occupied territories in the Promised Land. Phillips exhaled, angry that Richards didn't just snap to attention when slapped. He grabbed Richards by the hair and shook his head repeatedly, whacking backhands against his face while the rest of his body remained limp. Richards' eyelids fluttered and he moaned softly, but remained unconscious.

James Yarmuth shook his head, incredulous over what he was witnessing. "Sam, stop it. This is terrible. I said stop it," Yarmuth demanded.

"Shut up," Phillips replied.

"Don't tell me to shut up. I'm here as a representative of the president of the —"

"I don't care who you are," Phillips interrupted. "I said shut the fuck up. If you don't, I'll kick your wimpy ass right back to Washington. And you know what'll happen if you report this? Nothing. Because we're not supposed to be here. So shut up."

Yarmuth was silent.

"Hand me that pitcher of water," Phillips said, pointing at a small dented tin pitcher sitting on a wood desk stationed in a corner of the room.

Phillips pried Richards' mouth open and poured the liquid down his throat. Richards bolted awake, his eyes bugging out of his head in a five minute long convulsive fit of coughing. Phillips and Bareket failed to offer any assistance to Richards, and in fact seemed amused by his peril. Finally, when Richards caught his breath, he fell back on the cot, rubbing his bloodshot eyes and massaging his temples, as if it would kill the pain that radiated through his skull.

Slowly he lifted his heavy head and squinted up at the three men. In a hoarse whisper he groaned, "Shit. Please tell me this is a nightmare. Or better yet, that I'm dead." He closed his eyes again, then added, "I thought I was never gonna have to see your fuckin' face again, Phillips."

"Always the diplomat, huh Normie. Not even a kiss or a hello."

"Yeah, you're right. Sorry." Norman Richards opened his eyes again. "Hello you two bit cocksucker. Kiss my ass. Now what the fuck am I doing here and who are these jerk offs next to you?"

Yarmuth tapped Phillips on the shoulder. "You didn't say you knew him."

"You didn't ask," Phillips said, glancing at Yarmuth. Turning back to Richards he continued, "Boomer. Come on now. You're not being very polite."

"Don't call me Boomer. Do it again and I'll knock your fuckin' head off. Only my friends, and I mean my *friends* get to call me Boomer." In a better moment, he would and could have flattened Phillips. The nickname "Boomer" was bestowed upon Richards during his boxing days in the Marines where he was known for his prodigious right hook.

"By the way, nice hair," Richards added. Phillips was cueball bald, and highly sensitive about it. Phillips twitched and Richards laughed.

Richards sat up, quickly realizing he had no energy and slumped back down. This time Phillips laughed.

"I told you he was a total asshole," Phillips said to Bareket, who nodded in understanding. "This, Boomer, is David Bareket. I get to call him Dudi. He gets to call you Boomer, and you get to call him Sir. Mr. Bareket runs the anti-terrorism unit of the Mossad."

"Dudi. Nice fuckin' name. You'd never survive in the States with a pussy name like that," Richards said, fluttering his fingers like butterflies.

Phillips reached over and locked onto Richards' throat with a claw grip. "Look big mouth. Show some fucking respect and open your ears. I'm not gonna put up with your crap."

"Alright. Alright," Richards gasped. "Let go, goddammit."

Smiling through his dark beady eyes, Phillips knew that enough was enough, and he released his grip.

Richards took a couple of deep breaths. "Can I get some water and aspirin? Some food too?"

"I just gave you water and you spit it out. C'mon, look at the mess you made on your shirt," Phillips replied. "Dudi, have your man outside get him something, will you?"

Bareket opened the door a crack and gave brief instructions to a soldier with an Uzi slung around his shoulder standing guard.

Richards pointed at Yarmuth and asked Phillips, "O.K., so who's this twerp?"

In his most important voice, Yarmuth replied, "Department of State. I've been sent by President Tate to assist Mr. Phillips and Mr. Bareket in fact gathering --"

Richards put up his right palm, silencing Yarmuth. "Oh man. I've got a CIA bureau chief, a top level Mossad agent and the State Department all holding me hostage in the middle of God knows where for God knows what. I've got a big fuckin' mess here."

He exhaled deeply, sat up again, swiveled his legs, and planted his feet firmly on the grey concrete floor. He continued to rub the side of his head when his face suddenly contorted. "Wait a second! What the fuck! I was shot!" Richards frantically pulled up his shirt looking for the expected bullet wounds and blood. While there was something that appeared to be dried blood on the front of his shirt, he found no holes either in his clothing or his flesh. He looked up and leaned his head forward, opening his eyes wide, waiting for the explanation.

"Not with bullets, only drugs," Phillips replied.

Richards anxiously ran his hand through his greasy, disheveled hair. "Phillips. I don't want any bullshit lies. What did you drag me into?"

"We didn't drag you into anything. You got yourself into trouble. How long did you think you could go on running guns without having problems with either us or the Israelis?"

"Come on. Not this shit again," Richards said, shaking his head and curling his lips together. "What's the game?"

"You've been rehired by the Agency."

"I didn't re-apply."

"Doesn't matter. It's only a temporary job, because we know you can't hold one full time."

"I'm not interested."

Phillips shrugged. "Oh well. Too bad."

Richards paced back and forth from wall to wall, clearly distressed. "Let me take a guess," he snorted. "One way or the other you won't let me walk away from this. Whatever *this* is."

"Right."

"So explain to me the blackmail aspect of this deal first, so I know how bad I'm being fucked."

"You've been selling weapons and training Arab terrorists for what, ten years now?"

"Bullshit," Richards interrupted, "I didn't train anybody."

Phillips continued in a rhythmic voice, "In the course of engaging in this illicit weapons trading, you've disclosed secret information to the Arabs that you learned while employed by Langley. The U.S. Attorney tells me that makes you a traitor. What do you think, James? That a federal felony? Must be worth 20 years to life in Leavenworth."

"Absolutely," Yarmuth said with confidence.

"Hey punk. Absolutely this." Richards made an obscene gesture at Yarmuth.

Phillips continued, "Let's see, what else do we have?" He pulled a multi-folded paper from his back pocket and read, "Ohh yeahhh. You've helped broker some impressive heroin and hashish deals out of Lebanon. And how many people is it you assassinated? Five? Six?"

"Two. And I was on payroll then and Richter personally approved both."

"C'mon Boomer, how can you make up such a story?" he said facetiously. "He wouldn't have sanctioned anything like that."

"This is all bullshit and you know it. I sell weapons and that's it. And I know you don't give a flying fuck about it."

"We do now," Phillips looked over to Yarmuth, who nodded in agreement. "So Boomer, if you don't go along with us, my Israeli friend here will sign papers extraditing your ass right back to the states where you get the honor of either pleading guilty, or spending every cent you have defending yourself."

"You forgot something, Sam," interjected Yarmuth. "He won't have the money to hire a lawyer because we'll use the RICO statute to seize his assets. One phone call to Zurich will freeze your accounts in Switzerland." He turned to face Richards. "But we'll get you a great young public defender."

"You guys are such assholes."

"Norman. Be fair. Even if all you do is sell guns to Arabs, you're still breaking the law. And not paying taxes either, according to what the IRS told me a couple days ago. Another crime. Just what do you do with all that money?"

"What do you think? I spend about 90% on stuff like women and booze and I blow the rest."

Phillips didn't think it was funny that he made $50,000 a year while Richards had stashed away over $4 million in Zurich. And that was just what the CIA was able to find.

"By the way, how did you track me into Jordan?" Richards asked.

"We put a homing device in the axle of your jeep about a month ago. We've been watching you ever since."

Richards cursed under his breath.

"Norman, under the circumstances, I don't think it's wrong of us to call in a little favor every so often. Especially considering the shit you get away with. We'll leave you alone after this."

"I've heard that before. Richter begged me to help Ollie North out. After I did, you extorted me the same way you're doing now. I ended up locating those Libyan terrorist training camps because you couldn't get the job done yourself. Your word isn't worth shit. Go take that back to Brendan."

"That was the past and a different administration," Yarmuth responded. "President Tate gives his personal word that the CIA won't bother you again if you help us out here."

"What's your name again?"

"James Yarmuth."

"Look Yarmuth. I'm not naive. Either you are which makes you stupid, and considering your apparent standing with the president, dangerous as well, or you're just another lying bureaucrat. Either way you're full of shit."

"Based upon past promises and the way we brought you into this thing, I understand your attitude," Yarmuth said placatingly. "But we really didn't have much of a choice. You wouldn't have helped if we asked you nicely, and this is critical to national security."

"It's *always* national security," Richards said.

"You tell me. What do you want?" Yarmuth asked.

Sam Phillips' blood pressure exploded and his face turned red at hearing the exchange between Norman Richards and James Yarmuth. He turned and poked Yarmuth in the chest with his index finger. "He gets nothing. This is my operation. My territory. My show. We do it my way." Phillips then moved right into Richards' face and in his most acerbic voice said, "You're doing it and that's all there is to it."

Yarmuth snapped at Phillips, "I've had it with your fucking attitude and your big mouth. You work for me and I've got orders from the top. If you want, we'll call Langley right now and see who's running this show."

Yarmuth and Phillips glared at each other intently. Bareket looked at the floor, embarrassed by the untimely and inappropriate confrontation.

Richards grinned broadly. "You dickheads really should have worked out your good cop bad cop routine better before you came to strong arm me."

Yarmuth and Phillips turned their heads in unison and gave Richards the same "shut up" look, but Richards seized the moment, smacking Phillips on the side of the arm. "Sorry, Sam. Now that I know who's boss, here's what you've got to do for me."

"What?" Yarmuth asked tersely.

"A full Presidential pardon for everything I've ever done or you *think* I've done, including Iran-Contra and taxes. Get me two originals, both sealed and I'm not doin' nothin' til I get 'em. Send a third original to my brother Bill in Boston. I'm sure you can find him, and I'll confirm by telephone that he's received it."

"I have to talk to Washington before I can give that commitment," Yarmuth said. "Even if the president approves this, it may need clearance from the Attorney General, and I doubt he'll go for it."

"Listen Mr. Bigshot, get me the fucking pardon. I know how these things work. It's an executive decision, and I'm telling you, I'm not on duty until the pardon is in my hands. You want to motivate me to do your dirty work correctly, right?"

Richards was right about the simplicity of obtaining the pardon, but there was no way that Yarmuth would let him control the situation. "Now you listen Mr. Bigshot. You're gonna do what we ask or we will prosecute you. And just imagine what your prison cellmates and showers will be like. Or try this. We'll just drive you back to Baqaa right now and you can figure out how to get out of there yourself. Would you like that?" Yarmuth looked at Richards smugly adding, "That's the end of it. Don't fuck with me."

Richards shrugged his shoulders, opened both of his palms towards Yarmuth and Phillips then dropped them to his side, and smiled. "I think I understand what you're getting at."

Yarmuth continued. "Because this administration is trying to show it conducts business differently than its predecessors, I'll do the best I can to get your pardon. And our word is good."

"So, tell me what I have to do," Richards said, not really believing Yarmuth.

Phillips leaned over and patted Richards on the leg. "You're gonna love this. All of our intelligence analysts predict an increase in terrorist violence against the West along the lines of the U.N. incident, perhaps growing out of it."

"Are you surprised?" Richards answered. "Think about it guys, the U.S. acts like it owns the planet. Probably four out of five countries hate America, and the Arabs...they despise us."

"Mister Richards," Yarmuth angrily replied, "the United States has a responsibility to assure that all people in this world obtain their fundamental right to personal liberty. I didn't come all this way to discuss geopolitical theory with you. I've read your file and I know your viewpoints. I want you to obtain information about what happened to the U.N. in Geneva, and to prevent future terrorist attacks on U.S. soil."

"You jerkoffs from the State Department are all the same. You just don't get it, do you? What I said was fact, not theory." Richards shook his head, cynically remembering again why he'd quit the CIA a few years earlier. During the late seventies and through the eighties Norman Richards had been the best covert field operative the Central Intelligence Agency controlled. He left the Company after concluding that its primary goal was to pillage the globe in the guise of democratic sanctity. When he quit, shock waves reverberated through all levels of the intelligence community and the CIA's top brass took a lot of grief for Richards' so called defection. And Sam Phillips, Richards' direct supervisor, bore the brunt of it. The hard feelings between the men never disappeared, and seemingly elevated.

"Fine. What do you know? What do the reports say?" Richards asked.

At that moment, the door swung open and an Israeli soldier entered the room carrying a tray stacked with bread, mixed cold cuts, cheeses, fruit and a bottle of mineral water, and placed it on a nightstand next to the cot. Yarmuth said, "Food. As you requested."

"Thanks." Richards spotted a bottle of rubbing alcohol on a shelf in an open medicine cabinet on the other side of the room, and stumbled across the floor to get it. Sitting back down on the bed, he soaked a piece of rye bread with the isopropyl and stuffed it in his mouth. Yarmuth was aghast. Phillips doubled over in laughter. Bareket seemed strangely impressed. "You were saying?" Richards mumbled through a full mouth, oblivious to the others' reactions.

"You are really sick," Yarmuth pronounced.

"Nah, he's a drunk," reminded Phillips.

"Yeah. That's true," Richards replied. "C'mon, go on."

Shaking his head, Yarmuth continued. "First, we still haven't found out who did the U.N. job in Geneva and we don't have a lot of time to figure it out. We think that whoever hit Geneva will strike again. We can't afford another disaster. There's virtually no evidence leading us in any direction, and we know as little today as we did two months ago. Most terrorists claim their attacks, but we haven't heard from anybody. Even our informants have come up empty."

"That spells big trouble because it means that whoever's responsible has gone to great lengths to keep it quiet," Phillips added. "Our top experts say the silence is their cover to pop in and out again on another attack. The likelihood is that whoever did this is in the Mid East. The bomb was made from Semtex."

"So what. Almost anybody can get Semtex. Shit, you can buy it in New York. It's not like the old days."

"Right. But since the two largest stockpiles of it are in Czechoslovakia and Libya that means we have to first start looking behind the old Iron Curtain and here. Do you remember Matthew Hellman and Greg Kalt?" Phillips asked.

"Sure."

"They're leading the team that's combing Europe right now."

"And you've got me to cover over here?"

"Not just you, of course. There are others involved but you're not on a need to know basis as to who they are."

Richards understood there was no good reason for him to know the identity of the other spies. If he was ever discovered by hostile parties, and it was a possibility because nobody walked a tighter rope than he, the other men's lives could be jeopardized because their names could be drugged or tortured out of him.

"Let me make sure I understand this joke of yours," Richards said, stuffing a piece of meat into his mouth. "You want me to casually ask around to an incredibly dangerous bunch of crazy militant Arabs to see if they know who blew up the U.N., and where the next target is going to be?"

"I wouldn't have phrased it quite like that, but I guess that's about right," Yarmuth answered.

"Do you at least have a starting point for me?" Richards asked, puckering his lips in anger.

Phillips raised his hand as a sign that he wanted to answer. "There are a few possibilities and I believe you have contacts with them all.

First, the Israeli and PLO peace talks are back on track. Arafat seems to have a better handle on Hamas. We think it's possible that by the late summer, more self rule and land concessions will be granted by the Israelis."

Bareket felt compelled to take over. "Norman. The implications of Israel making the final peace with the PLO are staggering and will trickle down through other Arab countries. Think of it. A true Middle East peace. Not just on paper, like they signed a few years ago. Unfortunately, as we all know too well, there are certain Palestinian factions that oppose peace. You know people we've never been able to get close to -- George Habash, Carlos, Abul Abbas and Abu Nidal. These men are extremists and can be expected to use their influence and manpower to disrupt the peace process, and that's why we've kept the talks out of the news. But even putting the negotiations aside, your contacts might know who did the U.N. job, and since we fear there could be more problems, you've got to find out who's doing what."

"Let me complicate it further," Phillips interrupted. "You can't rule out the threat from the Islamic fundamentalists in Iran, Syria and Egypt. Also, both Abbas and Nidal are close to Saddam Hussein and Gaddafi. Jesus Christ, I don't have to tell you, those lunatics are capable of anything."

"So what do you expect me to do? Just drive around Jordan, Syria and Lebanon and ask every Arab I know if he blew up the U.N.?"

"Can't you be serious for a moment?"

"I am serious. Shit," said Richards shaking his head in disgust. "All you've said is that you've got no clue who destroyed the U.N., and that a bunch of terrorists want to stop peace between the PLO and Israel. Based on that, I'm supposed to solve your crime and tell you the future." Richards yelled, "Wake the fuck up! This is impossible! Especially considering I was supposedly killed!"

"Maybe," Phillips calmly replied. "But as long as you try, we'll leave you alone. If you don't, you can call your parents in Long Island once a month from Leavenworth."

"Sam, you're missing the point. I only have to hear extortion once to understand it. C'mon, where do you think Nasir's money comes from? Where do you think the guns were headed? You know he's just the front. When Nasir shows up dead and I show up missing, that's gonna raise some eyebrows. And those eyebrows are gonna be looking for me. Don't you see it? You put me out of business. I'm fucking history." Richards fell into a chair and threw his legs out in frustration.

"Give us *some* credit. We laid the groundwork for you to go right back in."

"Here we go. More bullshit. You know where my apartment is. You could have picked me up there. You didn't have to take out Nasir when I was with him."

"That was my decision," Bareket injected. "We've wanted Nasir dead for a long time. We think our plan gives you even more credibility with the Palestinians when you go back in now."

"You're out of your fucking mind! All of you!" Richards screamed. With a sweep of his arm he slashed the bottle of mineral water to the floor, shattering the glass and creating a puddle.

Nobody commented on Richards tantrum or moved to clean up the mess.

"As far as the Arabs are concerned, I should have been shot dead with Nasir. But look at me. I don't have a goddamn scratch. There's no way they can think I wasn't involved in your raid."

"You're wrong," Bareket responded. "There were no survivors, no witnesses. When we burst through the doors we had one man assigned to shoot you with drugs and a paintball to simulate blood. You always wear that blue jean jacket so it was easy to single you out. Then one of our soldiers switched his clothes with yours and we painted him to simulate wounds. We carried you out in his clothes so it looked like we suffered a casualty. A few minutes after we left he staggered out of the house leaving a trail of blood and drove off in your jeep. See, we know that Nasir always has lookouts posted with cameras and binoculars somewhere in the hills. Our man kept his face down, but there's no doubt the Palestinians saw him -- and think they saw you -- escape, though wounded. We even left your weapons delivery behind, against my better judgment. When you show up again in Baqaa with more weapons, they're not going to think you set up Nasir."

"You people forgot one major item. How do I explain the lack of wounds? Nasir's people do strip searches every time I meet with them. They're bound to notice that I wasn't *really* shot."

"Don't worry about that." Bareket looked down at his watch. "In a few minutes you'll be meeting with our plastic surgeon. You'll be a little sore, but your new grafted chest wounds will look like the real thing."

Norman Richards' mouth dropped open and his face froze in a blank stare.

"An hour with a scalpel beats the alternative of actually getting shot." Bareket said.

"It's not too late," Phillips added. "I'd be happy to shoot you."

Richards remained silent but knew there was no other alternative. At some point he would have to show someone scars to substantiate his cover and stay alive.

"Oh, I almost forgot something," Phillips added, reaching inside a brown bag and pulling out Richards' blue jean jacket. "We saved this piece of shit for you. But we had to shoot a couple holes through it to correspond to your new wounds." Phillips stuck his index finger through the middle of the cloth.

"You fuckers. You shot my jacket?" Richards kicked the cot and covered his eyes with an open palm.

"Tell us when your next contact was supposed to be with Nasir," Bareket said. "We'll facilitate your travel and place you safely back in his camp so you can pick up where you left off."

"Right. Something else for you to screw up."

"Uh-uh," said Phillips. "We're trying to help you. Otherwise, we don't get what we want."

Bareket added, "We've got to help you set a cover before you travel outside Israel. If you don't share your plans with us, then we can't help you, and you *will* be dead. It's as simple as that. Like you said, news of Nasir's death has traveled to all corners of the region."

Bareket's matter-of-fact businesslike tone was logical and convincing, and Richards knew he was right.

"Alright, but I want assurances that once I walk out of here, I don't have any interference from you guys. You simply can't go out on any more search and destroy missions busting up my deals. I'll check in with you if and when I learn anything, and only when I feel its completely safe."

"Oh come on Norman," Phillips replied. "We know that if we show up on your heels again your cover is blown. But at the same time, we can't let you just go out on your own wild west show."

"You've got no choice," Richards replied. "Like you said, the Arabs have to see me conducting business as usual or I might as well move to Kansas. We're running this job my way. It's my ass on the line if there's a problem, not yours." Richards then looked at Yarmuth. "Look it up twerp. Nobody in the Agency was better than me at this kind of stuff, and I know that's why you keep dragging me back in every time you've got a problem. Phillips may not like me, but he'll tell you it's true."

Yarmuth's nod served as his tacit acknowledgment of the truth and was affirmed by Phillips silence.

"Fine. We'll leave you alone. But tell us what's next," Phillips said.

"I've got a shipment of Stingers and some other small arms due in a few days. Actually, they were supposed to be in last week and delivered to Nasir yesterday. If I'm to reestablish credibility, I have to deliver. That's all there is to it."

Bareket's nostril's immediately flared. He bit his bottom lip and announced, "Forget it, Sam. No deal. There's no way I'm going to let missiles go to the Arabs. Handguns and ammunition are bad enough. Figure out something else."

Moving closer to Bareket, Richards poked him hard in the chest with his index finger and yelled, "Fuck you. I've been selling you and the Arabs weapons for years without objection. If anything,

I've probably been an intelligence gold mine for you. Now you put me in this position and this is my only way of getting out. Take it or leave it." Richards turned his head to Yarmuth and Phillips. "And one last thing. If you assholes try dragging me back to the states for prosecution I'll embarrass you more than you can ever imagine."

Phillips stepped between the two men, separating them. "Cool down, both of you. Dudi, what if the U.S. increased loan guarantees for additional housing for the new Soviet immigrants? Would that help your problem?"

"I fail to see your bribe serving as a fair trade off for sacrificing Israel's security," Bareket snapped.

"Okay. Try this," Phillips replied. "What if we put a transmitter inside each missile to track their location by satellite? If they're moved into an offensive position, you can step in and intervene. Or perhaps we could partially disable the missiles so that their aiming and tracking systems are off, or so they prematurely explode. There are options here that protect both of you."

"I can live with that," Richards said.

"I suppose we can too," Bareket added begrudgingly. "I want to start our talks about those loan guarantees today, though."

"Wait Sam, there's no authority for this," the straight-laced Yarmuth interjected. "Iran-Contra started the same way. I don't want a scandal out of this thing."

There was a long silence in the room, then Phillips broke into a broad, almost corrupt grin. "You're right James. This would be illegal. We'll call the whole thing off. You go back and tell the White House we couldn't put the deal together and to just let Interpol do their job. Then go talk to Richter about the problems Norman will incite one way or the other now that we put his life in jeopardy. You can also explain the whole mess to the *New York Times*, the *Washington Post* and ultimately some Senate subcommittee and grand jury." After a few moments he added, "Now wake up, your ass is already in this as deep as shit can get. We're going forward."

After a moment's pause Yarmuth said in a whisper, "Right."

"Good. Then let's go. Boomer we'll be in touch. Have fun with the plastic surgeon," Phillips sneered as he turned his back and walked to the door.

"Sam. Wait a second," Richards said.

Phillips turned around and was met with a thunderous right uppercut square on the chin. Phillips crumbled backwards falling against the wall, his legs giving way from underneath until he was sitting on his butt.

"Never mind," Norman Richards said with a big smile, shaking the sting out of his fist.

ELEVEN

Near Ba'iji, Iraq

"RUN HARDER. PUSH IT. Three hundred meters to go. Don't quit," screamed a ranting Republican Guard drill instructor as he ran behind Omar Rafsani and Ahmed and Khalil al-Sharif. It was easy for him to say. The instructor was clad only in a T-shirt, shorts and jogging shoes. But despite soggy 80 degree heat, Rafsani and the al-Sharifs were clothed in full Iraqi military battle garb, lugging 90 pounds of gear with AK-47's strapped to their backs.

It had been an hellacious 49 day revisit through Iraqi basic training. Omar, Ahmed and Khalil all thought they'd been selected by the infamous Carlos for some special terrorist project, yet they hadn't seen their new leader a single time since they'd first met in the Cave almost two months before. Instead, they were prisoners trapped in a 24 hour a day demanding obstacle course of exercise, sleep deprivation and weapons training. Mixed in was a wilderness survival course that took the men through Iraq's diverse geography of the Zagros Mountains in the North, the Syrian Desert in the West and a river filled valley stuck between the Tigris and Euphrates in the Southeast, with not much more on hand than one of Carlos' weapons of choice, a Swiss Army Knife.

They sat winded on the roadside recovering from the morning run, and stared out on the unappealing view in front of them: the brown pallor of dull rolling hills in the Northern Iraqi countryside with only a closed down oil refinery and chemical weapons plant visible on the desolate horizon.

The quiet of the moment was broken when a small beat up pick up truck rumbled up the road from the other side of the hill. Much to their surprise when it reached them, the driver pulled over and turned off the ignition. An immense older Caucasian male with a full head of shocking white hair brushed straight back, with thick black framed sunglasses approached them. His khaki multi-pocketed safari outfit looked as though it had been slept in. Another person remained in the passenger's seat, but out of view due to dark tinted windows.

In broken but passable Arabic the man asked, "Excuse me. I'm trying to get to Kirkuk. Have I passed it?"

Both the man's question and the circumstances of his presence were inherently suspicious to all. At just past sun up, why was a foreigner driving a truck with a payload of cargo headed for Kirkuk, a prominent base of the Kurdish rebel alliance against Saddam Hussein?

Without waiting for the more senior drill sergeant to assert his proper command, Omar stood up and took charge, holding his rifle in ready position. "What business do you have in Kirkuk?"

"Nothing that concerns you young man. I thought there was a highway around here. Do I just turn around and go back up the same road to get there?"

"I asked you a question. I want an answer. Let me see your papers and I want to inspect your truck," Omar demanded.

"Blow it out your ass," the man calmly replied.

Although Omar was visibly displeased with the man's rude comments and the others were likewise taken aback, nobody budged.

"Look old man, don't give me a hard time. Just show me your papers."

"Are you stupid or deaf? I'm not showin' you nothin'!" The old man turned on his heels and started walking back towards the truck. Omar followed and just as the man reached the door, Omar tapped him hard on the shoulder.

"Hey. I'm talking to you. I want some answers." The physically imposing Omar firmly grabbed the man's arm, clenching it tightly.

"Let go of me you big dumb fuck. I don't want to hurt you," the man said, pushing Omar with his free arm. Omar released the man's arm but pointed his rifle so that its barrel touched the foreigner's chest.

"What are you gonna do punk, shoot me because I asked for directions?"

"Give me your papers now," Omar screamed. No one noticed that the passenger had slipped out of the truck and was crouched down by its tail.

In one swift, fluid motion the old man pushed the rifle straight upwards with the palm of his left hand, sidestepped to his right and kicked Omar on the side of the knee. As Omar lost his balance and was falling to the ground, the man followed with a solid knuckle clenched blow straight to the face, grabbing Omar's rifle midair. Omar, flat on his back, looked up to see the rifle pointed at his head. Before anyone else could react, the old man's passenger fired a gunshot in the air, freezing all in their tracks.

"Rule Number Two — *Know Your Enemy* and never underestimate him," Carlos announced matter of factly. He looked down in disdain at Omar. "My friend, you have a long way to go."

The old man bent over and extended his arm to his young victim. "Let me help you up."

Carlos nodded at each of the men, starting with the drill sergeant as he called each of them by name. "Romel. Ahmed. Khalil. Omar. This is Seve Dolchino. You may recall I mentioned him the day we first met in Baghdad. He was my mentor and he's here to help me train you." All eyes shifted to Seve, who leaned against the truck door, smiling.

Carlos looked specifically at Omar and said, "Now you know

why his nickname is the "Bull." Everyone but Omar laughed.

"I trust you've all had an enjoyable seven weeks," Carlos said. When no one answered, he added, "How should I interpret your silence?" Again there was no reply. After the experience of witnessing Siddig Saleh almost lose a finger in his fervor to defend the honor of Saddam Hussein and Iraq, everyone was guarded about what they said in order to avoid an unnecessary unwinnable confrontation with Carlos.

"Alright. Have it your way. Put your gear back on boys. It's time for another run."

"No, wait," Khalil blurted out. "We've just gone through almost two months of physical hell, and I'm not sure why. This isn't what we signed up for. We were all in good physical shape the day we met. Better than most."

"So what have you learned from this?"

"That we have to be Olympians to become terrorists?" Khalil snapped.

"I didn't ask for a smart answer, Khalil." Carlos poked him in the chest. "There was a lesson in your training. What is it?" When no one replied, Carlos exhaled deeply and shook his head showing them he expected much more.

"How about self reliance?" Carlos asked. "Didn't you learn to trust your instincts to get you through the wilderness with basically no resources available? What do you think it's like out on the streets in the middle of some city when you're being hunted and you've got no money or weapons or anyone you can trust? If you can survive the desert, mountains, forests and rivers, I guarantee you'll be able to manipulate your way around a city when you've got absolutely nothing."

Carlos noticed Ahmed grinning. "Ahmed. What's so funny?"

"I was going to say something like that, but I was afraid that if I said the wrong thing, you'd take my head off."

"The only way you'll learn is to talk with me. You'll know when to speak and when not to. When I ask questions, that means I want to hear what you have to say." Carlos then softened his tone. "I also want you to feel that you can talk to me about anything else that's on your mind. From now on I'm also your father. Understood?"

Everyone voiced acknowledgment of Carlos' ground rules.

Carlos had long been a student of both war and philosophy and how the two more often than not mixed. In Carlos' learned view, terrorism was merely a form of war and in reading the teachings of great warriors ranging from Sun Tzu to George Patton, Carlos accepted a common precept of leadership that ran like a thread through the centuries. A general as the leader of men must not be only tough and demanding, but has to show compassion and warmth as well, so that his troops will follow him until the ends of the earth if necessary.

Carlos walked over to Omar, leaned over and softly asked, "You're okay?"

"Yeah, I'm fine," Omar said, even though his nose and head ached.

"Good. Next time put the old man on his ass." Carlos offered Omar his canteen, who gladly downed its contents.

"Now, are there any other thoughts about the past few weeks?"

Leaning back on both elbows, Khalil asked, "Maybe I'm wrong, but is it possible you think pushing us to our physical limits will make us tough enough to accomplish our goals?"

"Good, Khalil! You're right on track. Rule Number One is *Discipline.*" Carlos paused and looked intently at each man so as to emphasize his point. "Discipline. There's a definite correlation between physical strength and willpower. Your ability to succeed will often be a direct result of your own self-discipline. There will be times when you're under extreme pressure and dead tired, but you'll have to keep going because your mission or your life or both will depend on it. That's when you'll find out what you're really made of."

Seve motioned to Carlos that he had something to add. "Look boys, war is fought with large armies of men working together. In terrorism it's a one man battle. Self reliance, personal discipline and strength will *never* be more important," he stressed. After a long pause he added, "But don't look at me as the example."

"Yeah, you fooled me," laughed Omar, now recovered from the quick beating he'd received.

"No son, Carlos was right. You've got to *know your enemy*. You antagonized me without having the slightest idea about who you were dealing with. You just can't do that. You have to always maintain the ability to either control or walk away from a situation. And if you don't know, don't act."

Carlos interrupted Seve and announced, "There's a cooler with drinks in the back of the truck. Throw your gear in there, cool down and in a few minutes we'll talk some more about our goals.

Ten minutes later Khalil, Ahmed and Omar sat in a semi-circle in front of Carlos and Seve. Romel stood guard, leaning against the truck and facing away from the group, staring off into the Iraqi countryside.

Carlos commanded their attention. "First, never forget this. Terrorism is war. Guerilla war. And to become a warrior you'll now master crafts like electronics, disguise, bombs and martial arts. You're also going to learn English. It's the universal language and you've got to know it. Most important, I will teach you four fundamental rules that will become your personal philosophy. Anyone know what I'm talking about?"

Omar cautiously raised his hand.

"Just speak up when you want to talk. I want an open dialogue," Carlos ordered.

"You seemed pretty serious when you told me to know who and what I'm dealing with before jumping into an unknown situation."

"Good. My precise words were *"Know your enemy and never underestimate him."* That's Rule Number Two."

Seve lectured, "This requires thinking...intellect...work. To really *know* your enemy you have to *study* him. You have to understand how he thinks and then place yourself in his shoes. Only when you fully understand his strengths, weaknesses and viewpoints, can you attack his strategies and set your plan."

"Never start out planning an offensive attack in any mission,"

Carlos explained. "All you have is a goal. Like hijacking a plane. Knowing the enemy allows you to structure your offensive tactics to achieve that goal."

"Carlos, I understand what you mean by knowing the enemy, but I don't really get what you mean by this offense and defense thing. It sounds like a soccer game," Ahmed said.

"Let me give you an example. By December 1975 I had spent over three months in Vienna with five comrades from the Baader-Meinhof gang planning the invasion of the OPEC headquarters to make sure every contingency was covered. We obtained a complete set of floor plans to the Texaco Building where OPEC was located, and we each memorized the structure's layout completely, including hallways, staircases, alarms, phone systems and windows. Everything. We knew about every security guard in the building and even what weapons he carried. We obtained personality profiles on each of the OPEC ministers to anticipate how they might react to getting caught in the middle of a gunfight or being taken hostage. That's what I mean by defense. We then planned our offensive attack around all the information we'd learned about the building and OPEC, being able to anticipate items we knew we'd have to deal with. Nothing was left to chance."

"The first thing Carlos did when he entered the OPEC lobby was kill a security guard. This showed the world that Carlos was dangerous and had to be taken seriously," Seve added.

"Right. I also shot a member of the Libyan delegation and wounded someone else from Kuwait. That *really* scared the shit out of them." As Lenin once said, *"The product of terror is terror."*

"You know you have Carlos to credit for opening the door to the marketplace of terrorism for sale," Seve added. "After OPEC, all the governments began hiring Carlos -- or others like him -- to do their political dirty work. You three are the next generation of international terrorists and there's an almost unlimited market out there just waiting for you."

"Let's get back on track. They'll learn about that later." Carlos said. "The third rule is simple and it grows out of the first two. *Be organized. Anticipate. Be flexible.* If you have the discipline to do this job, and you take the time to know your enemy, you'll already be organized. Then all you have to do is be flexible enough to improvise without panicking when something doesn't go the way it's supposed to."

"That sounds logical," Omar commented.

"Remember, no matter how much planning you do, nothing will ever go exactly the way it's supposed to. If you're too rigid, too stuck on your plans, you'll end up dead. You have to anticipate problems and spontaneously generate alternatives to them. Most important, you have to survive."

"Listen to Carlos," Seve said. "Even if you don't finish a job, the fact that you even tried sends a strong message. Pulling it off is better of course, but what's it mean if you get killed? Nothing."

Carlos nodded in agreement. "Let me give you an example about being flexible from a job I did once. I was carrying four bombs, all on timers, set to explode simultaneously to level a building, and on a tight schedule, planned down to the final seconds. I planted the first bomb, no problem. I went to hide the second bomb and there's a group of people standing right where it was supposed to go. Now I've got a few choices. I could just take the package out of my briefcase and leave it there for everyone to see, or I can stand around waiting for the group to take off. Better yet, I could be flexible and modify my plan, which is what I did. There was a bathroom twenty feet away. I walked in, sat down in a stall and waited for about two minutes until I figured they left. When I came out they were gone, so I planted the bomb.

"Same job -- right after I planted the final bomb, some son of a bitch maintenance worker I didn't see picks the fuckin' thing up and brings it to me as I'm walking away. Now my schedule's totally screwed up. I'm holding about eight pounds of plastic explosives almost ready to detonate. What did I do? I didn't panic. I simply killed the man, replanted the bomb and took off. And to this day, I haven't been linked publicly to the job, which is just how I want it."

"Was that the attack on the U.N.?" Khalil asked.

Without changing facial expression or showing the slightest emotion, Carlos responded, "No, but whoever did that job knew what they were doing." Carlos thought that later, after he knew for sure that Omar, Khalil and Ahmed could be trusted, he might tell them the truth. For now, there was no point in it.

"My story illustrates something that every skilled warrior must learn. The character of war is of continuous change. You have to be ready to anticipate and alter your plans when faced with changing circumstances. You got it?"

Again everyone nodded.

"All right," Carlos continued, "Who can tell me the fourth rule?"

The terrorist trainees looked dumbfounded.

"*Success in warfare is based on deception.* Who knows what I mean?"

"I do," Khalil blurted out. "My father used a similar phrase in his police work. You mean that nothing should be as it appears, so that the other side never knows your real intentions."

"That's close. So how do you reconcile this rule with what we've talked about this morning?"

"Well, you tell us we need to know our enemy and to attack his strategy. If we do this, I would think deception means we should use diversions, aliases, disguises, lies. Anything to send the enemy off in the wrong direction."

"Excellent, Khalil. Nicely said." Although Carlos' sixth sense had told him early on that Khalil stood out above the others, it was still too soon for Carlos to announce his plans for Khalil; doing so would have a negative impact on motivating Omar and especially Ahmed, and they too had important future roles to play.

"Deception will be just as important in dealing with those around you," Seve added. "Sometimes you'll have to lie to those you trust, not only to protect them, but to protect yourself as well. Just remember that a good lie has to be based in truth, so that much of the lie is in fact the truth. A good liar also has to practice lying, so that the truth can never be read through his eyes. You'll learn to talk in ambiguities. It sounds crazy, but this is something we're going to work with you on."

Khalil rose from a cross legged position on the ground and walked up to Carlos. "How do we know that you're not lying to us now? That there isn't some hidden plan or agenda affecting us?"

Few things ever dramatically surprised Carlos, but Khalil's question did. "Because I'm not," answered one of the greatest liars alive. "But if you don't believe me and you want to leave and go back to your simple life, you may."

"I don't believe you but it's all right," Khalil said in a strong voice. He paused and added a bit softer, "If you've lied to us so far, I presume it's because you have a good reason for doing so. I'm not even sure I really care. I want to train with you anyway."

Seve rocked back and forth, stunned at Khalil's comments. Fortunately, Carlos seemed impressed by both Khalil's guts and perceptions. To show his command over the group and situation, however, Carlos gave a low almost sinister laugh and then shot Khalil a look that would freeze Medusa. Khalil inched backwards fifteen feet and sat down again, actually a little shaken but mostly fascinated by the strength of Carlos' silent power.

Carlos realized his impenetrable command over the men had taken hold. "Today was your first lesson in terrorist philosophy. You heard my four rules, my creed for survival. Now it is yours. One, *self-discipline..* two, *know your enemy..* three, *organization, anticipation and flexibility* and four, *deception.* Do not forget this acronym. Live by it. *DEAD... Discipline, Enemy, Anticipation, Deception. D.. E.. A.. D..* Now repeat it."

They did.

"The day you hit the streets and forget these four rules is the day you'll be dead. If you follow them, you stand a chance to live and spend the incredible money you're going to make, and to know what it's like to have true power." Carlos separately stared straight into the eyes of Khalil, Ahmed and Omar who each solemnly looked back with an expression of acceptance and determination to succeed. Their lives had all changed that morning and they just realized it.

"You've all had plenty of time to rest. We're going to run back to camp now, at least most of us." Carlos puffed out his cheeks and stuck out his stomach in a good natured mocking of Seve. Everyone including Seve laughed. The guard had already climbed into the truck to drive Seve back to camp.

"You're going to run, too?" Omar asked Carlos.

"What do you think? That I'm too old to go four kilometers? After all, that's what I ask from you."

In a classic demonstration of leadership by example, Carlos led Khalil, Omar and Ahmed on the difficult hilly run back to camp. On the last mile, none of them could beat Carlos in his challenge to race, finishing over 30 meters ahead of them all.

TWELVE

Gaza Beach, Israel

B AD MEMORIES made Norman Richards' skin itch. Years ago, on his first business trip into Gaza Beach, he made two incredibly stupid mistakes. The first was driving his Mercedes, and the second was wearing his finest alligator boots. He stood out in the sand ghetto, and the Palestinian youths who presumed Richards to be some Israeli slumlord trashed his car, beat him up and stole his boots. He learned a good lesson though, and today he wasn't taking any chances, riding in a borrowed old white pick up truck, wearing a beaten dirty pair of tennis shoes.

He pulled up to park in front of the White Mosque, spiritually situated for over 400 years in the center of town. The Islamic house of prayer, with its traditional dome and appended 80 foot tower, badly needed a coat of white paint to do its name justice. Hundreds of people of all ages milled about the Gaza Beach flea market which started in front of the mosque, wrapped around the building, and stretched for three blocks down the road to the West, away from the Mediterranean Sea.

It was readily apparent that conditions had worsened since his last visit. Gaza Beach was home to over 50,000 Palestinian refugees, and the Mossad estimated that up to 45 percent of its residents were supporters of Hamas, the militant Islamic Resistance Movement, whose goal was the complete destruction of Israel. From what he could see, Richards believed it.

Only 300 yards up the dirt road that led into Gaza Beach, he witnessed what was the daily ruckus of a young and angry mob of Palestinians burning tires and throwing rocks at a platoon of helmet wearing, shield yielding, scared shitless 18 year old Israeli soldiers. Just across the street from the White Mosque, two men stood on the roof of a burned out, three story concrete building, brandishing machine guns and waving the outlawed red, white and green Palestinian flag. People below went about their business as if these events were nothing.

Richards picked his trusty, long barrel .44 magnum off the seat next to him and checked the safety and chamber. The CIA and Mossad may have totally screwed him over three months earlier in the raid near Baqaa that killed Abu Nasir, but at least they did one thing right — they salvaged his Smith & Wesson. He slipped the gun into the shoulder holster parked inside his bluejean jacket, exhaled deeply and stepped out into the crowded marketplace.

The salty smell of the Mediterranean Sea, combined with the garbage that hadn't been picked up for weeks, struck Richards immediately. So did the sight of a hundred Arab merchants conducting business out of portable tents, tables and from the back of their trucks, haggling feverously with old men and women over everything from food to gold.

Driving a junker and wearing Nikes made Richards feel no less conspicuous than any of his previous visits to Gaza. He was sure he was the only non-army Anglo anywhere in a five mile radius and that he'd either be taken as he looked, like an American, or alternatively, as an Israeli, neither choice being particularly attractive considering the locale. There was one thing for sure: Richards wasn't in the mood for a confrontation. With his survival instincts on full alert, he weaved his way in and out, through the hoards of people arguing over a shekel as if it were a life and death matter.

Richards saw no need to cruise the area any longer than necessary. He walked up to two teenage Palestinian boys leaning against bent up bicycles ten feet from the entrance to the Mosque. They looked like serious troublemakers -- unfortunately, just what he needed right now.

"Can you take me to Ghassan Kassem?" Richards asked in Arabic.

The boys looked straight ahead as if Richards didn't exist.

"Ex-*cuse* me. I need to see Ghassan Kassem. He's a friend. Can you take me to him?"

The taller of the two boys responded, "Who's he? Why would we know him?"

"Everybody does and you know it."

"Never heard of him. Besides, you piece of filth, even if I did, I wouldn't help you." The boy spit on the ground just missing Norman's shoe.

"Alright, let's try this," Richards said. Reaching into his right pocket he pulled out a small wad of Israeli shekel bills and waved twenty shekels in front of the boy's nose.

"Okay," the boy said, "I might know where he is. But my time is worth more than that. For 200 I'll take you to him."

"Forget it, gutter rat," Richards said, stuffing the money back into his pocket. "Someone else will help me for 50." He turned and slowly started to walk away.

"150," the boy called out.

Richards spun around. "70."

"120."

"Last offer. 50 now and 50 when I see his face."

"How do we know you're not here to kill him?"

"If I was, how would I escape Gaza without being killed myself? I know that Mr. Ghassan keeps at least one bodyguard with him at all times, and has eyes on every corner of the city. I'm his friend. Maybe when someone else takes me to Mr. Ghassan, I'll tell him about how you wouldn't help me. You can explain yourself to him later."

The tall boy looked at his younger friend who smiled broadly and nodded. One hundred shekels represented material wealth. He held out his hand signaling for payment of the retainer and announced, "Let's go."

As they wound their way through the middle of the packed marketplace, Richards felt his back pocket every few seconds to make sure his wallet hadn't been swiped by one of the expert pickpockets who roamed the area. At the end of the market, they slipped through an opening in a long row of rusted 55 gallon drums filled with concrete and stacked 12 feet high, strategically placed by the Army as a barricade to deter demonstrations. After walking up the dirt street for another block they stopped at an unassuming, two story square concrete building containing one small window per floor, and badly in need of paint, just like every other building in Gaza Beach.

"He lives here. Pay up."

"Not yet. Not 'til I see him," Norman said.

"No. If Kassem sees we brought you here, we have a problem. We don't want problems with Kassem. We just want money."

"Too bad. Stand right here," Richards ordered, positioning the boys on his left, out of the front door's line of sight. He pulled out another 50 shekel bill, clenched it in his left hand and knocked hard on the door. Only a few seconds passed before a strapping Arab in his early twenties answered the door. He said nothing, letting the rifle strapped across his back and the automatic pistol in his hand speak for him.

"I need to see Ghassan Kassem. Is he in?"

"Who are you?" The guard demanded as he threateningly raised the pistol to chest level.

"Richards. Norman Richards...I know, tell him it's Boomer."

"You're Norman Richards?" the bodyguard asked, a look of amazement on his face.

"Yeah. That's me."

"Come in. Mr. Kassem has mentioned you before. I'm sure he'll be happy to see you."

Immediately before entering the house, Richards opened his left palm and one of the youths snapped up the bill. Once the door closed, they galloped down the street.

"Mr. Ghassan is resting right now, but I'll get him. Before I do, you need to hand over any weapons you're carrying. I'll give them back when you leave."

Richards tendered his .44 magnum, and lifted his pant leg to retrieve the nine inch Legionnaire's double edged stainless steel blade that accompanied him everywhere. The guard was particularly intrigued by Richards' 8 3/8" long gun, which he inspected closely, an uncommon weapon in the Middle East.

"I'll get Mr. Ghassan now. Please make yourself comfortable." The bodyguard motioned to the couch.

Richards was impressed by the furnishings in the tiny front room. Rich multi-colored Persian tapestries adorned one large wall and almost every square inch of the floor. European Lladro statues and Baccarat crystal filled a curio cabinet. An overstuffed paisley print couch took up almost an entire wall with a large color television sitting opposite. As Richards scanned the room, it dawned on him that between a career in law and the positions of influence Ghassan Kassem had held for over 50 years in Palestine, it was natural that he would acquire wealth, even residing in Gaza.

A photo gallery on another wall formed an historical collage of Ghassan Kassem's life, showing him with every prominent Arab of the last forty years: Gamel Abdel Nasser, Anwar Sadat, King Faisal, King Hussein, The Emir of Kuwait, Muammar Qaddafi, Saddam Hussein and Yasser Arafat. Staring at the pictures, Richards contemplated Kassem's amazing life. Rising from the depths of Gaza's abject poverty, Kassem fought and beat every social obstacle possible to become educated, ultimately graduating from law school in Cairo. He started his law practice fighting for the rights of the poor and dispossessed Arabs of Palestine, founding the first Palestinian legal aid clinic, and his stature as a lawyer grew immediately. In 1948, with the formation of Israel, Kassem assumed the unofficial

role of spokesman for the civil rights of the Palestinians now left
without a homeland.

Over the years, Kassem's public role evolved into initiating peace-
ful anti-Israeli protests to obtain both basic liberties and a Palestinian homeland, activities often publicized in the international press.
Ultimately Kassem came to be regarded as the non-terrorist, non-
violent patriarch of all Palestinians throughout the Middle East.
Though never elected to political office, he had the incredible ability to sway the masses just by his pronouncements. Kassem could
start or stop a labor strike in Israel just with his proclamation that it
be so. When Yasser Arafat formed the Palestine Liberation Organization, even though Kassem had never preached violence as a means
to the end, Arafat sought Kassem's counsel and support. Arafat
was not alone. At one time or another, every face pictured in
Kassem's gallery looked to Kassem for friendship, guidance or approval.

By 1983, Kassem became such a powerful voice and alleged
threat to U.S. Mid East interests that the U.S. government approved
a plan for his assassination, to be carried out by Richards with the
willing cooperation of the Mossad. After the event, the world press
was to receive false reports about Kassem being murdered by his
own people for engaging in unaccounted for treasonous acts with
Israel. Kassem would also be blamed for directing violent terrorist
attacks, which would assure that even in death he would be discred-
ited as a hypocrite.

Because it was contrary to Richards' beliefs to kill a respected
man of peace, he questioned his orders, specifically to Sam Phillips
and then to higher CIA sources in Langley. The official response
was that the hit was necessary as a matter of "National Security."
Richards believed otherwise.

At that time, nobody had the contacts or grasped the intricacies
of the politics and people of the Mid East like Richards. He told
Phillips and the CIA "Suits" that taking out Kassem ultimately would
only bring destructive results. Then, rather than carry out the order,
he set up an underground meeting with Kassem warning him of the

plot. The assassination attempt failed miserably, and Kassem pledged to Richards that he owed him a life for saving his life. Norman Richards, CIA agent, who had blown his intelligence cover, immediately gained acceptance into much of the Arab community.

Richards then quit the Agency and Kassem sent word to Richards that he wanted a meeting. They spent a full day together discussing regional politics and the prospect and need for a region wide Arab-Israeli peace. A true friendship evolved between the two men. Kassem then served as a personal reference for Richards to various Arab organizations and revolutionaries, helping him get started as an arms trader, since he was done as a spy. After a ten year association, however, this was the first time Richards stepped foot in Kassem's house.

"So, you live." Richards' daydream was interrupted by the familiar low throaty voice of Ghassan Kassem standing next to him. The short and stooped severely grey and balding man touched Richards' arm, confirming his presence.

"I'm here," Richards replied with a shrug, then checking his own pulse.

"That's good." Kassem smiled in surprise of seeing his presumably dead friend alive and well. "I heard the Israelis shot you in Jordan. I wasn't surprised. I thought for a long time you'd end up someone's victim. I think you still will."

Giving a traditional Arab welcome, Kassem then reached up and gave Richards a soft hug and a kiss on both cheeks. Richards reciprocated out of obligation but cringed never having felt comfortable abiding by that Arab custom.

"So, I know you wouldn't come to see me here unless it was very important. Let's go sit down. I'm old. I get tired standing."

The hulking guard followed them into the front room. Kassem instructed him, "Get us some cold drinks. Then walk around the block for an hour."

Richards waited for the guard to leave. "He seemed to know who I was. Particularly when I told him that "Boomer" was here for you."

"The day I heard you were killed I told him about you. After all, you saved my life. How could I not feel something over your loss? Now tell me, what's on your mind? Why are you here?"

Richards spread his right hand across the lower half of his face and rubbed downwards a few times. "Ghassan, I've got a major problem. I have to help the U.S. find out who blew up the U.N. in Geneva. If I don't do it, either I get extradited back to the U.S. where I go to jail or they'll take me out," Richards said as he slid his index finger across his throat. "If I do it, I lose all my credibility and business in the Mid East and almost certainly get shot by some pissed off Arab. Either way, I probably fucking end up dead over this goddamn mess."

"I'd say there's a good chance half of the Arab world will want you dead once they see you're alive anyway. Just on the presumption that you set up Nasir."

"I know. But I *didn't* do that. I was set up."

Kassem nodded. "Well Norman, where exactly have you been the past few months?"

"Convalescing," he lied. Richards lifted his shirt to expose his artificial scars.

Kassem looked at Richards' chest for a split second before turning his head away. "And you want me to arrange your safe passage through the region?" Kassem wisely anticipated.

"What I really need is for you to get me back into Baqaa so I can talk to Nasir's people. If I can get just a few minutes to prove myself to them, I think I've got a chance to survive this whole thing. But if I don't get up to Baqaa right away, I'm history."

"And what makes you think they'd even see you?"

"I have something they want and if I can get it to them, I can reestablish myself."

"Okay. No promises, but I think I can get it done. Now what's this about the U.N.?"

"I got this from the top. The U.S. is upset it hasn't solved the bombing yet. They don't have a clue who did the job, but all of the CIA's top analysts come up with a Mid East profile."

"Of course. Who else to blame besides the Arabs?" Kassem frowned.

Richards put his palm up in an authoritative gesture and spoke firmly. "No. Listen Ghassan. I've had three months to think about this. Nobody has told me so, but I know I'm right."

"Fine, lets hear it."

"I know that another serious round of peace talks have been ongoing between the PLO and Israel. The PLO is to guarantee Israel's security by handcuffing Hamas, and Israel is supposed to give back land and allow more self rule. That's the long and short of it, and somehow I have to believe you've gotta be right in the thick of it."

What Richards said was true and Kassem was stunned because the new talks were absolutely top secret. Still, the Palestinian statesman controlled himself. Years of diplomacy taught Kassem how to mask his emotion to avoid inadvertently disclosing information. On the other hand, Richards years of experience as the premier U.S. Middle East operative taught him a thing or two on how to gauge the truth of a statement by looking directly into one's eyes. Kassem's total lack of expression confirmed that what he said was right on point.

"I was told to consider any Islamic fanatics that would disrupt peace with Israel as suspects for the Geneva bombing," Richards said. "As I thought about it later though, that didn't make sense. Even if some crazy militant somehow learned about the talks, why would the Palais des Nations be a target? The Knesset, yeah. The U.N. — I don't think so, especially since no one we take serious has even claimed the crime. And you know the intellect here. You do the job, you take the credit. Sometimes you take the credit when you don't do the job. I think the CIA was giving me a message to pass along to you and your friends."

Kassem leaned forward, now intrigued by the scenario that Richards had started to paint. "Go on."

"First, watch for the arrest or maybe assassination of select leftist leaders if the bomber's identity isn't revealed soon. That'll put pressure on everyone to find out who did it, because the leftists will go crazy on PLO leadership, and Arafat can't afford that. Second, and more important, whoever does cooperate will be rewarded after whatever peace deal is reached. Those who don't help will get nothing. There will be clear winners and losers. You see?"

Kassem nodded pensively. The implications of solving this crime, or perhaps not solving it, were far reaching. There was an incredible amount at stake in the future months for every Arab power broker that struck a good deal with Israel, and whoever won this game was guaranteed to hit the jackpot.

"Ghassan, I didn't ask for things to be this way, but right now I have the Israelis' ear. If you can get me back into Baqaa, think of what I can do for you in return. We could arrange for the world to learn it was *you* that brought self-rule to the Palestinians throughout Israel. You've been working for this your entire lifetime."

"I understand. And I know what to do. Where are you living?"

"I just got back into my old place in Jerusalem."

"Good. In a few days I'll send you a message. You must go now. I'm tired."

As Richards walked to the front door, Kassem said, "You know Norman, you have such insight. You never cease to amaze me."

"I know." Richards grabbed his weapons from a coffee table, tucked them away and slipped out the front door.

THREE DAYS LATER AT 10:45 A.M., Norman Richards was crashed out on his couch sleeping off the after effects of yet another serious night of drinking. One leg lie flat on the black leather and the other dangled aimlessly off the side. He was still dressed in the same clothes that he put on the previous morning. It took almost two minutes before the pounding on the door startled him out of his slumber. Bleary eyed, he stumbled to the door, sniffing and grunting on his way. He opened it, turned his face and jerked half his body away from the light. Once his pupils finally adjusted to the brightness, he looked down to see the same two young Palestinian boys who had led him to Ghassan Kassem.

"Mister. I'm supposed to tell you: Tomorrow. 10:00 a.m. Baqaa. Same place. Be on time."

"Uh huh."

"I'm also supposed to give this back to you." The boy's outstretched hand gingerly held two 50 shekel bills.

"Nah," Richards coughed. "Keep it."

"No. We'll get in big trouble."

"Alright then, we don't want that. I'll take it."

The boys looked sad as they gave the money back and turned to walk away. Before they could get ten feet, Richards called out, "Hey, would you guys do me a favor?"

The younger boy turned and gave Richards a quizzical look.

Richards waved the money and said, "Go buy me a newspaper at the corner and keep the change."

"Really?"

"Yeah." The boys grabbed the cash and disappeared down the street. Richards yelled after them, "And keep the damn paper too."

THIRTEEN

Baqaa, Jordan

NORMAN RICHARDS SLAMMED HIS HAND on the steering wheel of his jeep and shook his head in disgust while staring blankly out the window at Abu Nasir's ex-safehouse. He instantly regretted his action, knowing that as always, the welcoming committee of Nasir's friends waiting inside were no doubt watching his every move. They would sense his anger and frustration and use it against him.

The deteriorated condition of the all too familiar looking structure was no surprise. The fact that the front of the house looked like a parking lot with an assortment of cars and pickups did. Nasir's people never publicized their clandestine activities. Today they were sending a message that any unwanted intrusions would be met with force.

He walked toward the building remembering his last visit three months ago. It seemed there were more bullet hole pock marks in the front wall than before, but then again, maybe not. The same tacky yellow and brown print curtains still flapped around the broken windows and caught his eye.

He didn't have to knock. The door opened as if operated by an electric eye, confirming that whoever was inside was watching him. He instinctively put his arms up in the air and walked in. Twelve gun toting Arabs encircled him. Richards was so overwhelmed by the Arab manpower that the situation appeared comical, and he made a brief nervous laugh as he faced his accusers.

"Could we put down the guns?" Richards blurted out. "Those things make me nervous."

A strikingly handsome Arab stepped forward and replied, "Oh yes, Mr. Norman. Then of course you won't mind handing over the big one that you're so famous for."

"You mean my 44. I don't have it. It's on my front seat along with my knife. I'm clean. Go check." Richards spread open and lifted his bluejean jacket and turned around to prove that he wasn't carrying any weapons. "Do you want me to strip?" Richards asked, anticipating the Nasir group's security procedures.

"In a moment. You're sure you didn't forget anything?"

Richards shook his head no.

"If you're lying, I'll kill you." The man smiled, his teeth shining like fluorescent lights.

"You know, you're a good looking guy," Richards replied. "I bet you don't have any trouble getting dates, huh?"

The Arabs all gave Richards the same, *"What are you talking about?"* look.

"Apparently everything I heard about your big mouth is true," the leader said sharply. "Ismael, check him."

"You mean, *you're* not going to do it?"

The leader glared irritatingly at Richards and his chest heaved.

Ismael approached Richards and in a remarkably swift motion, he cocked his elbow and scored a direct powerful blow to Richards' face, breaking his nose and spraying blood everywhere. Richards' knees buckled beneath him and he crumbled to the floor semi-conscious.

He lay on his back holding the side of his face, instinctively fighting the natural urge to moan. Instead, he muttered, *"You motherfucker"* under his breath. Speaking louder he added, "Well now we've confirmed I wasn't carrying any weapons in my nose." Richards steadied himself on one knee. Blood continued to flow freely from his nostrils onto the ground. "Sorry about messing up your floor. Send me the cleaning bill."

"Your mouth never stops, does it Mr. Norman?" the leader asked.

"My name is Mr. Richards, not Mr. Norman."

The room turned silent. Nobody thought the slur to the Arab custom of addressing even someone as low as Norman Richards with respect was funny.

"Search him Ismael," the Arab loudly commanded.

Ismael leaned over and picked up Richards like a bag of garbage and placed him squarely on his feet. He brusquely groped Richards' body, confirming the absence of weapons or a recording device.

"Why are you here? Why have you asked our friend Ghassan Kassem to intervene on your behalf? If you don't have good answers, you die today," the Arab said, with a hostile bite in his voice.

Richards stood up straight, wiped his face on the sleeve of his bluejean jacket and calmly answered, "I figured that when you found out I was alive your people would come looking for me. I wanted to present myself to you first. By the way, what's your name?"

The man's eyes narrowed as he whispered, "Salim."

"Salim, I understand why you would think I was involved in the attack here when Nasir was killed. But I had nothing to do with it. I was a victim too. Look." Richards lifted his shirt revealing his "scars." He turned in a full circle, displaying his hairless chest like a trophy for all to see.

"Is that supposed to impress me?" Salim asked.

"Yes. Look," Richards continued, "if this scar was my only proof of innocence I wouldn't have bothered coming. But you know what I was supposed to deliver to Nasir back in February."

"Of course."

"If I could finish my delivery, would you still want it?"

"What kind of stupid question is that?"

"Presuming I deliver, would that convince you enough to take me off your hit list, and also, to pay me in full? Nasir still owes me money from last time."

"You dare to ask for money? Many good men died that day, including my oldest brother. The answer is no," he yelled. "I don't trust you. I condemn you." Salim's voice rose in crescendo and his face reddened with emotion. The silence in the room was deafening.

Richards nervously wiped more blood off his face. He'd come back to Baqaa hoping to reestablish his credibility, and instead, he was now facing execution.

Just as Richards began to hyperventilate, a familiar voice came from the back of the room. "Fortunately for you Mr. Norman, it's not his decision to make. Your fate rests with me."

Stunned, Norman Richards watched the guards part for Abu Nasir, who walked toward him. Though his hair and trademark mustache and goatee had gone pure white, there was no mistake -- it was Nasir.

"You're surprised I see."

"You could say that. Kassem didn't mention that you were alive."

"As I understand it, you didn't ask. Then again, we were relatively surprised to see you survived as well. Nobody else did. Just you and me. Our lookouts in the hills said you appeared to be seriously wounded in the raid. When you disappeared afterwards, we presumed you didn't make it."

"Well it sure looked to me like you died. I was only a few feet from you. You got hit right before I got shot."

"I took two bullets. But we're not here to talk about our health. We can discuss that later, if there is a later. What is it you can deliver, and as Salim says, why should we trust you?"

"The Stingers. You want 'em, I got 'em."

"That is a good answer. When I heard from Kassem that you were alive and wanted to meet with us, I presumed it was to speak for the Israelis. But I can hardly believe they'd let you continue to sell us arms, and particularly deliver these missiles."

Richards experience as a spy had taught him to be a good liar, but he also knew there were times that only the truth would work. He was smart enough to recognize that the Palestinians would ask him and others a lot of questions, and not just today, but perhaps forever. His story had better always remain consistent and it was easier to remember the truth than it was a lie.

"I won't lie to you. It's a long story, but the Mossad and CIA have agreed to let me stay in business as long as I help them with something. I swear to you -- I had nothing to do with the attack here. In fact, they used it to set me up, and now they're extorting me."

Richards spent the next half hour disclosing to Nasir the details of the attack on Baqaa and his relevant part in it.

After Richards finished the soliloquy of his ordeal, Nasir rubbed his goatee repeatedly in contemplation.

"Abu. The man is Iblis; the devil himself," Salim said, his voice rising. "He *must* die." The others unanimously murmured their assent to Salim's dicta.

The simple raise of Abu Nasir's hand silenced the entire group including Salim. "So Mr. Norman. How long will it actually take for you to get me the Stingers?"

"If I deliver, you're gonna pay me, right?" As a psychological ploy, Richards intentionally overstated the importance of the money issue to provide an air of confidence in his ability.

"My word is always good. I told you before that you would get paid, but only when there is full delivery."

"Fair enough. I can get you the goods in thirty seconds. They're in my jeep. Your Stingers, the guns, ammo, all of it. Go look."

Nasir smiled faintly. Salim's upper body jerked straight up in disbelief. With the flick of his wrist, Nasir dispatched two men to the jeep to confirm Richards' boast.

"And by the way, bring in the bag that's on the front seat," Richards yelled after them.

The group stood in awkward silence until the guards returned, each struggling with a small crate. One of the men commented that Richards' jeep was packed full. Nasir barked an order at one of the men to take an inventory and transfer the weapons into the Arabs' vehicles.

Richards smiled in self assurance. "I was always good in math. Let's see. You only paid $5000 last time, remember? Now you owe me $37,000 more." Richards put out his hand, palm up.

Nasir was taken aback. "I don't have your money with me today. How could I know you'd come with this delivery?"

In a gesture atypical of business arrangements in the Mid East, Richards nodded in understanding and then advised Nasir, "That's okay. I trust you."

Nasir nodded back and Richards then looked over to the other of the missile toting guards and asked, "Would you please get that package from my jeep?" Nasir waved the man away again. The guard quickly returned with a small sealed cardboard box which he placed on the cracked cement floor in front of Norman Richards. The American leaned over and ripped the sealing tape with the course edge of his key. He pulled out and displayed two bottles of a yellowish liquid, proudly announcing, "Siddiki, special blend. Gila." He put the bottles on the ground and removed a stack of plastic cups from the box, which he handed to the guard standing to his right. The Arab took one and passed the rest down.

Richards walked in a semi-circle, pouring healthy shots of the 120 proof booze to all. Half of the Arabs smiled at the opportunity of sipping this distinctive Arab moonshine, even with an untrustworthy potential adversary. The other half looked perturbed, maybe even insulted by the obvious bribe. Richards considered it progress that even half the men were willing takers. Given a choice ten minutes ago they would have all lynched him.

"Mr. Abu. Last time we were together you said we would share Siddiki. I can think of no better time to do so than now, if you will be kind enough to allow me to toast to your good health." Richards raised his own glass and said, "With Allah's blessing, may you live to be 100," before bowing deeply as a sign of respect to Nasir.

Everyone raised their cup and sipped their drink -- everyone except Salim, who let his cup drop onto the floor, splattering the alcohol all over. "I will never drink with you, American pig."

"Salim, you will treat our guest with respect," Nasir said, enunciating each word for emphasis.

Although Nasir's reference to Richards as a "guest" was a positive sign, Richards knew not to make too much of it because of Nasir's general sense of manners and formality.

"Mr. Abu. It's okay. I understand," Richards injected to open his first round of personal peace talks with Salim. "When we consider everything that's happened, if I was him I might not trust me either. Especially if I lost a brother. I know I'll have to prove myself again to all of you, and today is only the beginning."

Nobody disputed Richards comment. Stinger missiles and a round of drinks only opened the door. He had yet to walk through it. Salim, however, continued to glare at Richards.

"Look. I'm not stupid," Richards continued. "You're going to check out everything I've told you today. If you catch me in a lie, I'm a dead man." Richards didn't wait for confirmation. "Here's something you're not supposed to know. I had a big fight with the Mossad on this before they finally gave permission for me to deliver the Stingers. I had to convince them I'd never regain my credibility with you or anyone else to get information on the U.N. bombing, unless I was able to deliver the missiles."

"You might have been right about that," Nasir agreed.

"Well, get an expert to check them out. The Mossad disconnected the modulators. All you have to do is reattach the lead wire." Richards shook his head and snorted in a bit of acting to show disgust, "This is how they deal with me. You know, sell the weapon, but don't tell them it's broken."

"I'm not impressed," Salim cut in. "You know we'd come after you if they didn't work. You had no choice but to tell us."

Richards jumped up and poked Salim hard in the chest. "Look, you rat's ass. Do you think I had a choice about any of this? Do you think I wanted to get in the middle of that goddamn commando raid and get shot? Do you think I wanted to get put out of business? I might be crazy but I'm not stupid."

The group was shocked at Norman Richards' outburst, and a couple of the guards raised their weapons in alarm. All the progress Richards made with Nasir's group in the last hour seemed lost in a flash. Nasir motioned the weapons down and stepped between the men.

"Enough! Both of you!" Nasir looked at his top aide and said, "Salim, Mr. Norman is known as a fighter, and a good one. He would hurt you." He turned his head and lectured Richards, "And you. Whether I believe you or not doesn't matter. If you touch him, I will shoot you myself. And this time, you will not survive."

Richards exhaled deeply and bit his upper lip, angry at himself for his loss of control.

"Mr. Abu, Mr. Salim, I'm sorry." Richards bowed his head to his younger adversary and then extended his hand, which was refused. He paused for another moment and spoke slowly and passionately. "Mr. Abu. I don't care who blew up the U.N. Its got nothing to do with me. The CIA and Mossad know that by compromising me and screwing around with my Arabic friends and business associates, that I become highly motivated to convince you and people like Kassem to give up the bomber. No one's going to be safe until it's done. I didn't ask for any of this. All I want to do is survive." Richards ran his fingers through his hair and exhaled deeply, showing his frustration.

Nasir didn't seem particularly moved. "I'll be candid with you Mr. Norman. I still don't understand one thing about your story," Nasir said.

"What's that?"

"Why did the CIA have to discredit you? Why couldn't they have just hired you back on assignment to resolve this U.N. matter? We all know you were supposed to be their top field man in the Middle East for many years. Although with your irrational behavior and that mouth, I don't know how."

Richards smiled, pleased that Nasir had asked such an easy question. "Because they knew I'd never voluntarily help them out. I left on bad terms. We still don't get along." Richards shook his head. "You can confirm that. Ask Kassem. Ask Bassiouni in Egypt. Ask anyone."

"A good response," Nasir replied blandly.

"Also a true one. And I'll tell you this. The CIA and Mossad will make life miserable for everyone until they find out who blew up the U.N. Whoever cooperates now stands a better chance of getting a bigger piece of the settlement pie with Israel, and you know that's coming. Those who don't help will get hurt."

"If we find out who did the bombing, we want something big for it," Nasir said. "A concession. A prize. Motivate us. Things can't get any worse here. Israel has already tried to kill me, and my people have nothing that can be taken away."

"Tell me what you want."

"Not yet."

"Do you know who did it?"

Nasir responded with a noncommittal smirk and raise of the eyebrows, the kind of look that made it impossible to either confirm or deny whether Nasir knew the identity of the culprits.

Richards shrugged his shoulders back in response. "Well, whatever. I came here today primarily to reestablish myself with you. I presume you got the rest of the guns out of my Jeep?" Richards looked at the guard who'd been delegated that task, and who nodded affirmatively in response. "Good. Mr. Abu, I'll trust you on payment for this stuff, but I think that it's only fair if you get it to me within a week or so."

This was yet another goodwill gesture by Richards. He could have insisted on returning for his cash the next day. Not that he would have necessarily received it, or that there was much he could do about it if Nasir wanted to stiff him. Still, the Middle East wasn't a territory generally known for extending generous credit terms on anything, whether it was buying shoes in the marketplace or Stinger missiles from an arms dealer.

Richards shook hands with Nasir, but didn't attempt to do so with Salim. He made a half-bow to the rest as he left the house. As soon as he hit the dirt path, he breathed a sigh of relief. He had survived. He would survive.

Not even ten seconds after Norman Richards pulled away, Nasir cornered Salim in front of the group. "What kind of performance was that?"

"He deserves to die for what he did and we should have killed him. He's the enemy."

"Maybe, maybe not. Regardless, never let the enemy know how you feel or what you're thinking. You know better!"

"Fine. Sorry. But you don't believe him, do you? You can't!"

"Yes I can. He delivered the missiles to us, and that was without knowing I was alive. And he also comes with a high recommendation from Ghassan Kassem. I must take that seriously."

"It's all a scheme."

"We'll see. But that's not the point today. If I kill him now and he is the enemy then I don't find out what he's really after. If he's clean, and it's possible, then we can use him for our own purposes in the future. Either way, what does it matter? We got weapons we didn't expect to see. We can always kill him later."

Salim shook his head and said, "Yes. Yes we can."

FOURTEEN

Baghdad

"I REVIEWED YOUR ENGLISH TEST scores today with Mr. Jabara," Carlos said, "and it seems none of you are taking your studies serious enough. I'm inclined to impose an earlier curfew starting tonight. Omar, your score was particularly pathetic. What do you have to say for yourself?"

"I did the best I could. I got an 88. That would be a high grade at the university."

"You're not at the university. I expect perfection from you and you better expect it from yourself. Remember rule number one -- discipline."

With his peripheral vision, Carlos spotted Ahmed al-Sharif rolling his eyes. "What's your problem?" Carlos barked, as he snapped his head all the way around. "Were you satisfied with how you did?"

"I got a 93."

"I expect 100 and I'm not joking. That goes for you too," Carlos said to Khalil al-Sharif, who'd scored a 96.

"Carlos," Khalil said half raising his hand. "We're learning the language on an accelerated basis. What does it matter if..."

"I don't want to hear it," Carlos interrupted, "from any of you. English is the universal language. No matter what country you're in, it could help you establish a cover or save your life in an emergency. None of you will go into the field until you speak it fluently. Perfectly. How can you expect to travel through Europe or the U.S. if your only language is Arabic? Rule number four -- deception. Do you understand?"

The young terrorist prodigies collectively nodded their heads, grasping the significance of Carlos' point.

"And remember, if all things are equal among you when we're done with your training, whoever speaks the best English goes to America with me."

Again everyone nodded.

"Good. We'll be starting French next. Probably in a month or so. Now, can any of you guess why I brought you to this hellhole?"

Nobody answered. They were sitting in the open lobby of a filthy, barely lit, four story tenement on Haifa Street in the south end of Baghdad. Until allied bombs had smashed into the building during the Gulf War, making it structurally uninhabitable, it held 24 modern apartments. At Carlos' insistence the building was donated to his mission and minimally rewired with electricity and a few other special fittings. It now served as his personal urban terrorist training center.

"We're going to spend a fair amount of time in this pit, and these are some of the more practical lessons we'll go through," Carlos said. "You're going to learn offensive and defensive measures on how to shoot your way out of a building to avoid arrest or murder. We're also going to have drills in a high rise building, a bank or something like that, and a house out in the country. I need to expose you to as many different scenarios as possible."

"Ahmed, remember a couple of days ago we were talking about the correct procedure for quick firing your pistol while maintaining sight alignment? What do you do?"

"When I raise the gun to fire it, I center the front sight in the notch of the back sight, with the top half of the target visible through the sights."

"Good. Khalil, how do you aim?"

"At the center of the object, with the sights in focus so the target itself is sort of a blur."

"Excellent. For the next few weeks I want you to keep these rules in mind and work hard on improving the fundamentals of moving and shooting. Don't be so concerned right now about your target scoring. With time, accuracy will come. Seve has a shooting drill that will help you."

Seve lumbered over from the opposite end of the room. "You don't have to fire your gun for this exercise, and you can pretty much do it whenever you have spare time, like in your barracks at the end of the day. Carlos, demonstrate for me."

Carlos stood alongside Seve and pulled his Beretta from his shoulder holster.

"First drill," Seve started. "With your arms relaxed at your side, quickly bring the gun up to eye level and squeeze off two shots into the target."

Carlos snapped his arms from a limp position to being fully outstretched, and he ripped off two live rounds into a door forty feet away on the opposite side of the lobby, shooting right between Omar and Khalil. The two holes in the door were only an inch apart.

Omar and Khalil looked at each other with their eyes popped wide open.

"The next drill is basically the same, except you add a target," Seve continued. "Start with one target and then move to the other." Before anyone could protest, Carlos whipped off two shots between Omar and Khalil, then two more between Khalil and Ahmed. His shooting was near perfect. The first new set of bullet holes were right next to the previous set he had just made in the door. Khalil sighed heavily and ran his fingers through his thick black curly hair. Omar and Ahmed appeared equally startled.

"Carlos, you just missed me," Khalil said in a high pitched squeal. "You could have shot me."

Carlos looked back at Khalil and nonchalantly responded, "Anything's possible." Looking at everyone else he added, "I want you to practice those drills every day. Work on improving your reaction time and the mechanics of sight alignment. I guarantee that even if you practice with empty chambers, your shooting will improve when you move to real targets."

Trying to act professorial, Seve lectured, "I presume you'll always be carrying a handgun, but if you think you'll be in a situation where a gunfight's likely, there's no finer weapon to carry than a 12-gauge repeating combat shotgun. Its got excellent hit probability, high firepower and terminal ballistics. A handgun will only get you so far in a firefight."

Carlos walked over to the front door and pulled five weapons from a wooden crate next to it. "Here guys, take these."

Carlos' students eagerly lined up for their handout.

"This is the Benelli M3. It's got a self-loading mechanism with a combination automatic and pump action," Seve explained. "Everybody take six shells and watch how I load it."

Carlos leaned against the front door watching Omar, Ahmed and Khalil curiously inspect every inch of their weapons after they filled their barrels.

Seve held the shotgun out in front of his body. "When handling this weapon, it's critical you position it properly by fitting the buttstock square against your shoulder, with the muzzle pointing downward." As Seve illustrated the technique, the others mirrored his actions.

"Right," Carlos said stepping forward. "These things have a major recoil, so if you get the chance to set up on a shot, try to lean forward a bit like this," he demonstrated. "See how my knee is bent. This helps the body recover from the recoil for subsequent shots."

Khalil, Omar and Ahmed stood a few feet away opposite Carlos, imitating his every move.

Seve continued, "Now if you're in a combat situation, the gun should be kept in this down position at all times, except when going upstairs. The half second you'll save by being prepared to fire could be the difference between taking out the enemy or being his victim."

Seve walked over and inspected the trainees' form. "No Khalil, you've got the buttstock too far in on the collarbone. Move it out an inch so that it fits squarely in the soft spot of your muscle," Seve said, as he repositioned the shotgun.

"Seve, do you mean we actually keep the shotgun locked on our shoulder as we walk?" Ahmed asked.

"Anytime you face a potential confrontation with the enemy you've got to be ready to fire first," Carlos answered. "Remember rule three -- anticipation. You have to be prepared for anything to happen every minute of the day. You can never let down your guard. Never."

Seve waited a moment before speaking, recognizing that Carlos' last message was the most important point the trainees would hear all day long. Then he reperched the shotgun onto his shoulder, muzzle down. "Let's say you hear something behind you. Don't just turn your head. Pivot your whole body so that the gun moves with you in case you need to fire it right then." Seve showed the maneuver with surprisingly smooth coordination considering his age, weight and slow reflexes.

"Now go take ten minutes and walk around the building with your shotguns in ready position," Seve instructed. "Get used to the feel of the weapon. Go up and down the stairs. Run. Walk. When you get up to the third floor, empty your chambers into the walls. Pretend you have an enemy stalking you. Then take him out. And remember, these are live rounds. Try not to kill each other."

Khalil, Ahmed and Omar vanished down the hall like kids off to play with new toys. Seve lit up a cigarette and sucked down the smoke in long hard drags. They sat in silence listening to the pounding feet of Omar, Khalil and Ahmed running wild through the building.

"Captain Sabar sure has been cooperative," Seve said.

"Yeah, almost too cooperative though. We have to be careful

around him. He's smart, curious, violent, dangerous."

"Sounds like you," Seve said, wholly serious.

Carlos smiled and replied, "Supposedly all he knows is that we're training the men to be terrorists. But just yesterday he asked me what they're going to do when we're all done."

"So Ilich, maybe it won't hurt to tell him the truth."

"Fuck no. I know Sabar respects me, especially since I saved Saddam's life in the restaurant a few months ago, but you know the Mukhabarat always has its own agenda."

"Like all secret police. The KGB wasn't any different," Seve added. "Are you concerned about him being jealous of your influence over Hussein?"

Carlos nodded affirmatively and for a moment seemed lost in thought. "I have to get close to Sabar. You know -- maintain close relations with the adversary. I can control Saddam, but I'm not so sure about Sabar. He's got his own incredible resources and powerful allies. I'm going to need his cooperation for a while still, and he can hurt me bad."

A second later Seve and Carlos were interrupted by the distinct powerful sound of a shotgun blast reverberating through the building. Other explosions followed, and the noise continued for five more minutes until all three of the six-shot magazines were depleted. Carlos felt slight relief when Omar, Khalil and Ahmed all returned, smiling and unharmed.

"So what do you men think?" Carlos asked.

"This thing is unbelievable. I bet it would take down an elephant," Omar responded.

"Not quite, but close," Carlos smiled.

"I still like the Uzi more though," Khalil said.

"I do too. It's partly a matter of taste. You can see the tactical advantages as to why you might want to use the shotgun, though. You can blast through anyone."

"There's no reason we can't carry them both," Omar added.

"That's true, especially since the Uzi's so light," Carlos replied. "Most of the time, you'll probably carry more than one weapon.

Now, grab your Berettas and the Benellis and follow me upstairs."

As the group stood on the edge of the stairway landing between the second and third floors, Carlos lectured, "Knowing how to properly use your weapon is critical, but if you don't know how to use the physical surroundings as well, you'll get killed for sure."

"Watch this," Seve said.

All eyes turned to the large man as he raised his own Beretta and shot two rounds through the lower midsection of a door at the end of the hallway. He walked the 20 yards to the door, opened it and put two fingers through one of the holes in its backside. He yelled down the hall, "So what do you think would happen if you use a door like this for cover?"

Nobody needed to answer.

"Seve. Get out of the way," Carlos yelled back.

Knowing what was coming, Seve scampered for cover. Carlos pumped his 12 gauge shotgun into the door; his aim was perfect and the barrage of lead blew the door right off its hinges.

"You guys get the message?"

Khalil, Omar and Ahmed all nodded.

"Most doors manufactured today have hollow cores. Standing behind paper will give you about the same amount of protection. Even a solid wood door might not shelter you from a bullet."

"So we use walls for cover?" Omar asked.

Carlos didn't answer. Instead, he fired two shots with his Beretta through a wall twenty feet away. The 9mm bullet punched a golfball sized hole through the front of the wall. "Go into that room. You'll see the bullet went right through the wall," Carlos said confidently.

"Plasterboard," Seve remarked. "It's got less stopping power than the damn doors."

"Knock on the wall here," Carlos said, and each of the men did. "You hear that. It sounds hollow. A real plaster wall won't have any reverberation. You'll even feel a difference on your knuckles. Rule three, anticipation. When you enter a building, stake it out. Learn its layout, its construction. Search for concrete or steel cover. You never know when you'll need it."

Seve walked over to the edge of the stairwell. "Here's something else for you to think about." He unloaded three bullets into the center of the stairs going up to the third floor, splintering part of the boards as the bullets exploded through the wood and into the ceiling. The group understood the lesson without the need to say more.

"I hope you understand the importance of true cover," Carlos said. "Don't confuse it with concealment though, which is where you hide until the opportunity to act against the enemy arises."

"Don't be afraid to hide, either," Seve chimed in, "especially if you have poor cover. Remember, the object is to stay alive, not to prove you're some macho man."

"Now everybody watch the correct technique for maneuvering around corners and doorways. Seve," Carlos motioned to his mentor with a broad sweeping motion and an open palm, as if he were introducing an act on stage. The scene drew a chuckle from the younger men, and a tiny bit of the mounting tension was released.

Seve tucked the Beretta into the front waistband of his pants and held his Benelli 12 gauge shotgun in the ready position against his shoulder. "Before you turn any corner, always take a quick peek to make sure the coast is clear." Seve disappeared behind the corner and then reappeared for a flash by barely sticking out one eye. His hidden voice remarked, "If you spot an enemy during your peek, take a half step back from the corner, lean out a bit with the weapon and then fire. This minimizes your body's exposure to potential return gun fire. Taking the half step back is important because otherwise you can't fire in a stable position and retain the wall as cover. Hopefully most of your enemies won't know to shoot through the wall. But you will."

A moment later, Seve's head, right shoulder and the shotgun aimed straight ahead were visible. "If it's clear, turn the corner and maneuver cautiously down the hall, staying to the side instead of walking down the middle. Keep your weapon in a fire ready position," Seve said as he proceeded forward in slow measured steps.

After about fifteen feet, Seve stopped and walked back to the group. "It's the same basic rule with doorways. Try not to stand in front of the door, and use the quick peek method. If you need to enter a closed door, always stay to the side opposite of where the hinge is. When you open it, jump back against the wall and count to three, because usually if the enemy's inside, their gunfire will start right away. Also, turn to the side at doorways because it limits the target exposure of your body. Any questions?" No one responded.

"Forget what you've seen in the movies," Seve continued. "Don't ever jump out into a hall or room with your gun ready. Use the quick peek. Also, don't walk with your gun pointed up. Keep it straight ahead, ready to fire. It's kill or be killed."

The men had focused so intently on Seve's lesson, they didn't notice that Carlos had slipped away to the steps behind them, but their attention turned quickly upon hearing his voice. "Also remember that probably the most dangerous spot to be caught in a building is a stairway because you're in a confined area with little choice for retreat. Always stay to the side of the steps, especially if they're wooden, because they creak and make more noise in the middle of the step."

Carlos squatted down. "Stay as low as you can, and keep your gun in fire ready position." Carlos suddenly fell to his stomach and yelled, "If you're going upstairs and you're fired on, fall to your stomach and return fire while sliding down to escape." Carlos fired his Beretta twice for impact as he wiggled down a flight of steps in only seconds.

"If you're going down stairs, retreating back upwards is difficult and gives little chance for escape. Stay low and hopefully you'll have greater firepower, which is usually one of the best ways to advance towards an enemy ambush if you've got no other choice."

"But Carlos," Khalil interrupted, "What do you do in a situation where you're basically surrounded, so you can't go upstairs or downstairs?"

"It's very simple," Carlos said matter of factly. "You die."

FIFTEEN

"**Y**OU GUYS AREN'T TIRED, are you?"

Exhausted, Khalil, Ahmed and Omar collapsed on the ground from their daily 90 minute aerobic and martial arts workout. Drenched in sweat, they collectively panted "yes." Carlos couldn't blame them, because his chest was also ready to explode. And because Rashid Sabar was present today, Carlos had pushed the men even harder than usual. As he gulped air, Carlos doubted that anyone in the Mukhabarat had ever worked this hard.

"Good. Get a drink, take a short rest and then go sit on the wall for fifteen minutes."

"Sit on the wall?" Sabar inquired. His back to Carlos, he was examining a machine gun riddled wall on the ground floor of the beat up apartment house that had become Carlos' terrorist training headquarters in Baghdad.

"Yeah, you'll see," Carlos nonchalantly replied.

"They're really coming along," Seve observed.

"There's progress," Carlos intentionally understated. "I will give them credit for this -- they're great athletes. I can teach them all the aikido and karate in the world, but I can't teach quickness or coordination."

163

"Aren't you concerned they'll hurt each other?" Sabar asked.

Carlos downed a large cup of water in three gulps. "They're already vicious with each other, but so far, we've just had typical stuff like broken noses and some bruises and sprains."

"Maybe they need some fresh bodies to practice on," Seve said.

"No doubt about it," Carlos agreed. "What do you think, Captain? The Mukhabarat must have a few martial artists who might enjoy some extra sparring." Carlos wiped his wet and red face with a towel.

"It can be arranged, but I'm not going to be responsible when your boys get injured."

Carlos smiled back in response, but thought, *"Asshole."*

"Alright guys, break time's up. To the wall," Carlos ordered.

Everyone remained still until Khalil finally stood up. He took a large swig of water, leaned over and extended his arms to pull both Omar and then Ahmed up off the ground and onto their feet. The men silently walked over to the wall, placed their backs against it, and then squatted down slowly until their thighs were perfectly parallel to the floor, as if they were sitting on chairs. Within thirty seconds, all three men were grimacing.

As head of Saddam Hussein's secret police, Rashid Sabar had inflicted more than his share of torture and pain over the years. Sabar thought he had seen it all, but he was clearly bewildered now, and he glanced over at Carlos.

"Go try it Captain. Give it one minute. I'll time you."

"I will. Maybe I'll learn something here today."

Sabar, powerfully built and in excellent physical condition, especially for a man of 52, took his place on the wall next to Omar. The moment he squatted into position his lower back and quadricep muscles tensed stiff, and he grunted in discomfort. By the time Carlos announced that only 15 seconds had passed, Sabar had enough, but his pride would not allow him to quit. At the thirty second mark acute pain shot through his lower body, which felt like it was on fire when Carlos finally announced 45 seconds down. Sabar found himself counting off the final arduous 15 seconds to himself. When the minute was finished, Sabar was sweating, breathing hard and sore.

"Quite effective, Ilich," Sabar panted.

Carlos smiled and replied, "So you learned something! As you can see, this exercise develops lower body strength for both building endurance and their martial arts training."

"Martial arts?" Sabar said.

"Yes. For strength, balance and discipline," Carlos replied authoritatively.

Sabar considered that every time he was around Carlos, he became increasingly impressed by the legendary terrorist's almost endless black knowledge of attack and survival weapons, techniques and strategies. It was true. Carlos was the master of these dark arts.

"Do you want a drink Captain?"

"Some of that water would be good. It's hot as hell in here. I think if you asked the president to reinstall the air conditioning in the building he'd do it."

"I'm sure. But I want it to be hot as hell," Carlos said. "I want them to be uncomfortable. The worse the better. My training conditions have to be harder than the real world, which is nearly impossible to duplicate because everything out there is so damn unpredictable. Making it tough is the only way they can be prepared for real life combat conditions."

Carlos walked over to a foot locker in the corner of the room, conspicuous because of its spanking new appearance in contrast to the rest of the half demolished apartment building. He dialed open a padlock, lifted the top and pulled out a sealed quart of Stolichnaya.

"I can't offer you any ice," Carlos smiled, "but will you join me anyway?" Carlos' own confidential sources in Baghdad had confirmed Sabar's taste for Russian vodka, strangely enough, hard to obtain in Iraq, even for the Mukhabarat.

"Well, I've never had it warm and straight up like that before, but I guess there's a first time for everything," Sabar replied with a grin, displaying his seldom seen smile.

"Even the label says, 'Cool Before Drinking,' Carlos said. "But here's a better idea. Take this bottle home, throw it in your freezer and enjoy it later."

"I can't," Sabar said, putting his hand up like a stop sign.

"No, I insist. You've really been helpful the past few months and this is just a small token of my appreciation," Carlos said, feigning sincerity.

"The president told me to provide you my fullest cooperation. I'm only doing my job."

"And you have." Carlos walked over to the head of the secret police and handed him the bottle. "Please. Take this. Don't insult me."

"If you insist," Sabar said, genuinely surprised by Carlos' modest but politically significant gesture.

Carlos knew he had just scored important points with the one Iraqi official who could jeopardize his relationship with Saddam Hussein. Carlos would do what was necessary to keep relations with Sabar positive, even if he totally distrusted him. No sooner had Carlos tallied the imaginary score in his mind, than Sabar interrupted his train of thought.

"So Ilich. We're on the same team. Tell me. What do you really have planned for these boys?" Sabar looked Carlos square in the eyes in his search for the truth.

Carlos knew the query would come sooner or later, but he wrongly calculated that his little bribe would put the issue off for a while. Instead he just opened the door to the question.

Stonefaced, Carlos answered, "My only job is to train them to be terrorists. All modesty aside, I'm supposed to make them clones of myself so they can perform selected services for President Hussein when they're all done with my program."

"There's no particular mission they're being trained for?" Sabar asked suspiciously.

"Nope."

"Then why does it take so long to train them? You've trained other soldiers in the desert in eight to twelve weeks."

"That's right. And like you said, those men are soldiers. Infantry. When Seve and I are done with Khalil, Ahmed and Omar, they'll be generals, leaders. President Hussein doesn't have any home grown talent like that available to him, and I won't be here forever."

It was a convincing lie, Carlos thought, and a perfect example of Rule Four. *Deception.* Mixing the lie with the truth.

"What's wrong with the Cave? Why not train there?"

"I thought about it, but it was too comfortable. I like this dump. Besides, this is top secret. Only you and a couple of others know what I'm doing. Nothing remains a secret in the Cave."

"Are you going back to the desert?"

"I doubt it. The American satellites are tuned in to every square inch of sand out here. They've monitored virtually every training mission anybody's ever gone through in the desert. It's too high risk. This place is perfect."

Sabar didn't completely accept Carlos' answers although the Jackal's eyes told the truth and the responses seemed logical. And as Sabar had observed, nobody could train a terrorist better than Carlos. Yes, he would give him the benefit of the doubt, at least for now.

Intentionally changing the topic, Carlos asked, "You can stay a while longer can't you? I was just about to start a little course in knife training."

"Sure. Why not."

"Good," Carlos said looking down at his watch. "They've got about another minute on the wall."

Sabar had forgotten about the wall, and when he looked over and saw Omar, Ahmed and Khalil all perfectly composed and staring straight ahead in a trancelike state, he was completely amazed. "I'm impressed."

Carlos felt great satisfaction by the acknowledgment from his colleague. "Now you can see the true importance of the exercise is honing their ability to focus. Not just building leg strength."

Sabar nodded and made a mental note to start using the wall as a Mukhabarat training technique.

"Alright men, that's it," Carlos ordered across the lobby. "Stretch your legs for a minute and come over here."

Only seconds had passed before Ahmed, Omar and Khalil sat cross-legged on the dirty concrete floor in front of Carlos, hungrily waiting for his next instruction. He opened his Swiss Army Knife to its large blade, and flung the red and silver instrument fifteen feet across the room into a plasterboard wall, where it stuck right in.

"Remember that?" Carlos asked, reminding them of how he had thrown the same knife into a wall the day they'd first met at the Cave. "Any of you think you can do that?"

Ahmed walked over to extract the knife, and confidently replied, "I can." Plucking the weapon from the wall, he cocked his arm and whipped the blade into the opposite wall where it bounced off the hard surface and fell harmlessly to the ground.

"One more try. I can do this," Ahmed said, wearing a look of disgust at his first failure.

"Don't bother," Carlos said.

"Omar. Since we started working together you've been bugging me about learning how to throw a knife. But a knife is a limited use weapon. I use one only in three circumstances. First, when I don't have a gun, and you know how often that is. Second, when I need silence to dispense death and a gun would be too loud. And third, when I want to leave a lot of blood for effect. It sends a message to whoever finds the body, like by slicing a throat or cutting out a heart."

Carlos was totally serious as Omar, Ahmed and Khalil all grimaced at the gory thought. Sabar, however, agreed with the message and smiled. Of course, Sabar, "the Executioner," had used a knife much like an oversized scalpel many times over the years for torturing and permanently silencing enemies of the State. Sabar had never thrown a knife, and had no need to. To him it was just a butcher's tool.

"Throwing a knife with any degree of effectiveness is extremely difficult, and even with practice, you'll only be able to throw from one or two specific distances," Carlos said.

"What do you mean?" Khalil asked.

"A knife will rotate only a few times in its trajectory where the point is facing the target. Unless you're capable of adjusting the speed and estimating distances, you should expect the knife to rotate once every six feet," Seve answered.

"I can stick a knife anywhere up to 15 feet. I'm only fair up to twenty feet. I've never seen anyone hit a target over thirty feet, so you should understand, this is purely a close range weapon," Carlos said.

"You remember how you taught us why we might want to use one gun over another?" Ahmed asked.

"Yeah," Carlos replied.

"Well is there any type of knife we should try to carry?"

"Nah. I've never seen a knife that can't be thrown," Carlos answered.

"Right," Seve added. "You've seen Carlos can even throw that shitty little Swiss Army Knife pretty well. But it couldn't stop someone unless it was a lucky hit. You really need to have a heavier blade. It's difficult to master, but the technique of throwing is actually very simple," Seve said as he removed a long shiny silver black handled dagger out of the same yellow foot locker that held Sabar's bottle of Stoli.

Carlos took the knife by the handle, cocked his arm all the way back behind his shoulder, and in a hard karate chop motion, released the weapon at the precise moment his arm was fully extended, snapping his wrist and sending the knife spinning across the room. Surprising no one, the eight inch blade was buried two inches deep into the wall.

"See?" Carlos questioned. "There's no magic to it. Just aim and let it fly. But make sure that when you release the knife, your hand is open, almost like a handshake. With practice you'll learn to control the knife by how hard you snap your wrist." Empty handed, Carlos repeated the throwing motion over and over, while his men observed and simulated the procedure with him each time.

Seve yanked the knife out of the wall. "You can each try it a couple of times right now, and we'll work on it some more at the end of the day. Keep in mind that the wall is a much harder surface than a human chest."

Khalil, Omar and Ahmed all threw the knife three times, each getting it to pierce the surface once. Sabar had never thrown a knife before and was eager to try, but didn't dare for fear of failure and embarrassment. He made a mental note to give it a shot in private later at the Mukhabarat's headquarters.

"In fact, I want you to add into your daily routine a few minutes of throwing practice. We'll get a target put upstairs in the pistol range hallway in the next day or so," Carlos advised.

Knife throwing was just another in a long list of items Carlos required his students practice or study every day and night. Their current curriculum included martial arts, target practice with everything capable of firing a bullet, electronics and mechanical engineering including wiring and machinery repair, political and social sciences, reading a variety of articles Carlos clipped from news services worldwide, and the study of English and French languages. They had already been schooled in basic table manners and etiquette, typing, photography and first aid.

Failure to study or otherwise follow Carlos' instructions was a violation of Rule One, *Discipline*, and was dealt with severely. Rather than just punish the wrongdoer, everyone was punished equally. No sleep for a full day with a doubling of activity for that 24 hour period. This made the trainees responsible for each other, which was crucial to building the team concept often necessary in carrying off terrorist missions. Carlos also knew it was inevitable in the real world that there would be days that they'd have to pull an all-nighter, and the only thing that could prepare them for that most physically and mentally demanding task, would be to actually experience sleep deprivation under pressure circumstances.

"Go upstairs to the dojo," Carlos told the men. "We're going to work on defensive measures to knife attacks."

On the second floor of the apartment building, Carlos had converted one of the apartments into a mini-gym filled with mats, a heavy bag and free weights. Once upstairs, Carlos put his arm around

Seve's much larger shoulders and guided him over to the center of one of the mats.

"If you're being held at knifepoint, whether you're ordered to do it or not, put your hands in the air." Carlos announced and demonstrated, as Seve actually poked Carlos in the ribs with the same stiletto that had just been thrown into the wall downstairs. "You're going to want to distract the assailant. Rule Four. Deception. Start talking to him and watch his eyes. Maybe beg for mercy. Flick your hand. Twitch your head. Do something subtle. Then, the second you've caused the slightest diversion, slash down on his arm with one hand and use the two-finger eyestab with the other. This should immobilize the assailant. Then side step, grip the arm holding the knife with both hands, and forcefully sidekick into his knee a few times. Do *not* try and wrestle the knife away," Carlos emphasized. "That'll get you stabbed in the gut. If he hasn't dropped the blade yet, slide your hands up and either jerk his wrist or a finger backwards until it breaks. I guarantee he'll drop it then."

Carlos had performed the drill in deliberate slow motion, barely touching Seve as he described each step, so that the men could more quickly pick up the choreography.

"Who knows what's next?" Carlos inquired.

"Kill him," Omar shouted out.

"Right." Seve spit back. "But not until you've gotten whatever information you need from him first."

"Now, who wants to practice on me?" Carlos asked.

When there was no response, Seve called out, "Fucking girls," disgusted that no one would volunteer.

"Khalil. Come here," Carlos said.

Khalil reluctantly stood up and said, "I don't want to do this. I know there's something you haven't shown us."

Carlos stared like a hawk at Khalil, not responding to his charges.

"Do you have to use the knife? What about a pen or something else?" Khalil said.

Again Carlos remained silent forcing Khalil into a standing position opposite of him.

Just as Carlos touched the knife blade to Khalil's chest, the young Arab started coughing and his face almost instantly turned red. Khalil put his hand around his throat and gasped, "I'm choking. Help me. Air."

Ahmed jumped up from the floor, startled by his brother's unexpected physical condition.

Carlos remained stationery but moved his head closer to Khalil to look into his suddenly bulging eyes. The instant that Carlos altered his position, Khalil spun around counterclockwise and released a perfectly placed circular back kick into Carlos' hand, dislodging the knife. His momentum carried his right arm through into a vicious chop to Carlos' side, followed by another series of body and face blows. Carlos fell to the ground dazed. Khalil picked up the knife, held it to Carlos' throat for a moment, then tossed it away and calmly asked, "Is that what you meant by diversion?"

The room was dead silent. The shock of Khalil besting Carlos was obvious on everyone's face, especially Seve.

Still lying on his back, Carlos burst out laughing and then sprung to his feet like a cat. "Awesome. Excellent." Carlos hugged Khalil, an amazing show of affection for the older terrorist, and exclaimed, "My boy, you're going to make something of your life." And Carlos just kept laughing.

SIXTEEN

Amman, Jordan

"HIS MAJESTY WILL SEE YOU NOW," announced a leathery faced middle aged manservant. Cloaked in a floor length black silk thobe and matching black and gold beaded gutra, he gracefully bowed, welcoming the guests of Jordan's King Hussein. "Please follow me," the servant said, unfolding an arm outwards in a grand gesture.

In unison, Yasser Arafat, Ghassan Kassem, Abu Nidal and Abu Nasir stopped chattering and rose from their high-backed red velvet chairs. Two rows of forty such matching chairs sat opposite each other in King Hussein's walnut panelled formal reception room. Their heels clicked down a thirty foot gallery of chandelier lit polished wood until they passed through double bronze doors, where they sank into two inch deep royal blue carpeting. The Royal Consultation Center was used only for the most important diplomatic meetings. Arafat, Kassem and Nidal had previously visited it and rooms just like it all around the world, so they were no longer impressed by its splendor. Abu Nasir, however, having lived his entire life in the Baqaa refugee ghetto, was awestruck by the incredible resplendence of the centuries old Ma'wa Palace.

173

His eyes gravitated upwards to the eight foot in diameter, 10,000 piece, sparkling crystal chandelier which hung from the thirty foot high ceiling. The walls were covered with colorful priceless paintings and Persian tapestries. Statues and busts occupied selected positions throughout the room, whose centerpiece was a twenty foot long dark mahogany table with an intricate gold design etched into its border.

King Hussein rose from a chair at the head of the table and with a broad smile, warmly received each of the guests. Nasir was surprised to find that Saddam Hussein and another man, who also stood to exchange greetings with the others, were already seated in the Consultation Chamber. King Hussein introduced Saddam Hussein and Rashid Sabar, a "security officer" to Nasir, the only one not to have previously met the Iraqis.

"Chairman Arafat has requested that we get started right away because he has a very hectic schedule today," King Hussein announced, motioning for everyone to take a seat. "I understand he's already been in Syria this morning, and that he's flying directly from here to Egypt."

Yasser Arafat revealed his famous toothy cherubic grin. "I thank you all for coming on such short notice, and I especially thank King Hussein for his gracious hospitality in offering the use of his magnificent palace for our meeting," Arafat said, bowing his head in respectful recognition to the King of Jordan. The impeccably dressed monarch nodded back with a pleasant smile to the leader of the Palestine Liberation Organization.

"You have all heard the news. History has been rewritten," Arafat confidently announced. "I am here to invite you to participate in the process of finalizing the peace with Israel, and to share in the spoils that will result from this accomplishment."

Before he could continue on, the infamous terrorist Abu Nidal, interrupted Arafat, the ex-terrorist turned peacemaker. "Yasser. I will never forgive you for acknowledging the Zionist government's right to exist, but now I hear you renounce all violence against it as well?"

In a strong and still confident voice, Arafat responded, "Yes." Arafat knew his longtime friend and ally would not be receptive to peace. After a moment's pause Arafat added, "Abu. Your presence here today is important. I know your voice reaches those in the Popular Front's General Command and other PLO factions who oppose this peace. But as my friend and long time compatriot, I ask you to take back to them my views on the benefits of peace. Especially to Ahmed Jibril, who I hear has already placed a price on my head."

"Yasser, there is nothing you can say to me that will ever change my view on driving the Jews into the sea. That is the only solution I will ever support. I would die for it and so may you," Nidal calmly replied. "And I have no control over Jibril. No one does. You know that."

Nidal was right about Jibril, but Arafat also believed in his own ability to persuade Nidal and perhaps even Ahmed Jibril that they were wrong about ruling out peace. Thus, Ghassan Kassem was invited from Gaza to Amman, to provide credible firsthand testimony that Hamas, the militant Islamic movement primarily located in Gaza, which had crippled Israel with street guerilla warfare since its founding in 1987, was lining up behind the peace process. Perhaps Yasser Arafat couldn't change minds, but maybe Kassem, the respected Palestinian ambassador of goodwill, could.

"We in Gaza are excited by the prospect for real peace. We received partial autonomy a few years ago with the Oslo Accords and the Hebron Agreement, but now we have a future," Ghassan Kassem said. "It will be difficult. Israel has occupied Gaza and the West Bank for too many years. Our youth know nothing but hatred for the Jews, who hate us as well. But there is no future in hate. Abu, perhaps later you will give me a few moments to talk in private, eh?"

Abu Nidal shrugged. It was hard to say no to Ghassan Kassem. "I will. But Yasser, it's hard to take you seriously. For twenty years you fought the Jews, then a few years ago you made peace, then you renounce the peace and tell the Palestinians to fight Israel, then you make the peace again. I think you're crazy."

The room was silent, mostly because nobody could disagree with Nidal's assessment. Arafat raised his arms in the air, looked to the skies and responded with a smile, "I am crazy. Like a fox." He paused and said in a solemn but hard tone, "I know what I'm doing."

"I doubt that," said Saddam Hussein under his breath.

"Only two hours ago I finished a positive meeting with President Assad in Damascus," Arafat said. He picked a small piece of paper from his green PLO army suitcoat and read, "Syria supports the rights of the brotherly Palestinian people to decide what they see is suitable for their future." Assad told me this statement would be released to the press today."

"Hardly a resounding endorsement," Saddam Hussein said sarcastically. He twirled a long Cuban cigar between his thumb and index finger and blew a jet stream of smoke straight up in the air. "Captain Sabar, please advise the Chairman of our position."

Rashid Sabar rose from his deep cushioned blue leather chair. He spoke slowly and deliberately to Yasser Arafat. "President Hussein has not forgotten your loyalty to the country of Iraq during the war with America. There are many ways that we will show our friendship to you, to the Palestine Liberation Organization, and to all Palestinians. But one thing we will not do is support peace between Arabs and the Jews. We are sorry."

Arafat had fully expected the anti-Zionist proclamation from Iraq, just as he had with Abu Nidal. Regional politics, though, were such that it would have been considered a terrible insult not to have invited Iraq to accept peace, since he was seeking approval from virtually every other Middle East country. And he knew better than to ever insult Saddam Hussein.

"Mr. President," Arafat said to the Iraqi leader, "I remind you that the United States refused to participate in the last coup attempt against you to help advance peace in the region. I urge you to not rule this out so fast."

"I'm sure the U.S. was only concerned with advancing its own interests here," Hussein responded. "Don't tell me the Americans care whether I live or die. They've tried to kill me at least three times. History shows exactly how they feel about Iraq." The volume and sarcasm in Saddam's voice had increased dramatically so that the tension in the room was now palpable.

"What makes this new peace settlement so great?" King Hussein asked skeptically, trying to subtlely intervene by slightly changing the topic. "It doesn't establish a Palestinian state. It doesn't allow Palestinian refugees to return to Israel. So how will it benefit Jordan?"

"I voice the same concern for all displaced Palestinians throughout Baqaa and Jordan. Yasser, you do not speak for these people," Abu Nasir authoritatively declared, putting his hands behind his head and reclining back in the executive leather chair. "We want to know how this will better our lives."

"I've been troubled about these matters for over thirty years," Arafat said, stroking his salt and pepper scraggly beard. "Complicated problems never have simple overnight solutions. I am sorry we can't accomplish everything at once. I wish it was possible. But a united parliament of Palestinians from Gaza, the West Bank and Hebron is a starting point. Your concerns can only be resolved in the future by your ratification of the concept of peace now. Ultimately the whole Arab kingdom will be involved in this process and then these other issues *will* be solved," Arafat said.

The meeting's participants remained silent, contemplating the truth of Arafat's comments, although Saddam Hussein caught Abu Nidal's attention and rolled his eyes at Arafat's absurdity.

"Let me tell you what's been resolved so far that will impact on all of you," Arafat continued. "There is a massive region wide economic development program which will be sponsored by the United States. They're talking about 11.6 *billion* dollars for construction and high technology engineering. That's just government money, not private investment."

"Listen to yourself, Yasser. Who wants the infidel's dirty money?" Abu Nidal shouted scornfully.

"Dirty money? Don't be stupid. Any of you. There is *no more money* coming from Russia. The United States is the only super-power left, so either play the game, or get left behind," Arafat snapped back, his large dark eyes gleaming. "Do you want to get left behind?" Arafat asked King Hussein.

"My greatest economic concern involves water," the King replied. "Jordan has only 15 to 20 years of water resources left before our agricultural and food security is threatened. The groundwater supply in the West Bank continues to fall, and we're losing water to Syria out of the Yarmuk River. We must have an agreement to share water technology and resources, perhaps through building desalinization plants or pipelines from the Mediterranean. Or maybe by sharing the supply of water from the Galilee through Israel's National Water Carrier Project."

"It is possible. Desalinization for all of Israel and Jordan would cost less than $10 billion," Arafat said, surprising all by his command of the facts. "The issue has already been anticipated and discussed."

King Hussein replied with a positive "Hmmm" and nod of approval.

"I would expect such foresight," Abu Nasir said. "We all know the next war with Israel will be over water if this problem is not resolved."

It was impossible to disagree with Nasir's comment. The shortage of water was a severe problem throughout the Middle East, and in a very real sense, water was the region's most precious commodity, not oil. The Arab countries frequently bickered among themselves that one nation improperly diverted the flow of water from the limited available fresh water supplies, to the detriment of another.

Ghassan Kassem stood up and pensively placed his index and forefinger vertically over his mouth as he thought through the situation. Everyone waited patiently for Kassem to expound his wisdom as if it were the gospel.

"I've known you all for many years," Kassem started, speaking in a low voice and typically expressing himself with dramatic hand gestures. "I know right now your hearts say no peace with the Jews, and perhaps with good reason. But your brains say otherwise, and if they don't, then you are all fools. Peace is the future. This is the first time that we as Arabs are presented the opportunity to become partners with the Americans. And the fact is, we've long been jealous that Israel has had that exclusive pipeline to their money and technology. In only a few years we will no longer have to be regarded by the Europeans and Americans as The Third World."

Kassem's assessment was right and Yasser Arafat had come to that same conclusion and didn't seem embarrassed about admitting it. For many years, King Hussein had sought U.S. aid and longed for more, because Jordan lacked the natural oil reserves that blessed many of the other Arab states. Abu Nasir's Palestinian refugees in Baqaa were subsidized 90% by United Nations charities; 90% of which was provided by the United States. Even Iraq had long been funded by the United States, and that enduring partnership was the predominate reason Saddam Hussein had failed to take seriously George Bush's warnings about leaving Kuwait, thus in part leading to the Gulf War. Only the pure ideologue, Abu Nidal, whose funding concerns were different than those of the other leaders in the room, didn't care about obtaining financial aid from the U.S.

"Of course, every nation has its own agenda," Kassem continued, "because each of our needs is different. For instance, it seems obvious that Jordan's primary concern is water management. Your Majesty?" Kassem rhetorically nodded to King Hussein, who responded with a flick of the wrist, his trademark gesture signifying agreement. "And we in Gaza remain in dire need of jobs, food, clothing and medicine," Kassem added.

"Who would ever have thought I would serve as the lead Arab voice for peace with the Jews?" Yasser Arafat said, shaking his head in amazement, then glancing at Abu Nidal and Saddam Hussein. "The fact is, if we want better lives for ourselves and our children, then we have to tap into the resources available through the Zionists. And we can do that only by making peace. Besides, what do we have to lose?"

"You are correct, Yasser," King Hussein said. "Now is the time for peace. So long as the terms of the peace pact open the door for economic prosperity and fair treatment for the refugees, Jordan will endorse your plan."

"Abu?" Arafat questioned.

Nasir maintained relationships with many of the militant circles in the Middle East, including Abu Nidal, which opposed and would seek to disrupt peace. But he understood that he too had no choice but to support it now. How could the Palestinians of central Jordan not line up as well with their brethren?

"Baqaa affirms your peace," Abu Nasir said, with no emotion in his voice.

Arafat knew it was useless to debate the issue further with Abu Nidal or Saddam Hussein, so he didn't waste his breath on them. "I appreciate your support. You won't be sorry," Arafat said, nodding to King Hussein and Abu Nasir. "Unfortunately, there's another issue in this peace settlement that I need to address today, and it is something we all have to deal with, whether you support this union or not. It affects everyone," Arafat said, directing his comments specifically at Abu Nidal, Saddam Hussein and Rashid Sabar.

"What?" Sabar sharply asked.

"Finding out who was responsible for blowing up the U.N. in Geneva," Arafat said.

Saddam Hussein took a deep breath and his heart skipped a beat, but showed no visible emotion at hearing about Carlos' exploits, knowing that if the truth was told and the attack was tied to him, it could topple his government and maybe cost him his life.

"How could this possibly affect me?" Saddam asked.

"Because I've been told that even if you fully comply with the U.N. Gulf War directives, the U.S. will keep the embargo in place until the bomber is turned over. Regardless of who he is or where he comes from," Arafat replied.

Saddam Hussein was shocked, yet he remained stonefaced.

"And you," Arafat said to Nidal. "Even though I don't believe it, the rumor is that it was your handiwork in Geneva. If you think the Americans wanted you dead before, you should hear how they talk about you now."

"I've heard this garbage before," Abu Nasir said.

"What do you mean?" Arafat asked.

"He knows Norman Richards, Yasser," Ghassan Kassem advised.

"Who's that?" Sabar asked.

Immediately suspicious upon hearing an Anglo name, Saddam Hussein's bushy eyebrows also narrowed in curiosity.

For a moment the room remained quiet as nobody, even Kassem, wanted to claim knowledge of Richards. Finally though, Kassem spoke up. "Richards is an American weapons dealer who lives in Israel. He also happens to be an ex-CIA agent and supposedly one of their best. He's trustworthy and I consider him a friend, but there is certainly a wild, unpredictable streak to him."

"So what does an arms dealing spy have to do with the peace process?" King Hussein asked.

"The Americans believe that Richards' contacts and credibility in the region are better than any of their current local operatives, and that he stands the best chance of finding out who did the bombing. All of us except for our brothers from Iraq know Richards, and I imagine they'll learn about him before the day is out," Yasser Arafat smiled.

There was no point in Saddam or Sabar responding. Sabar had already made a mental note to pull up the Iraqi secret police files on Norman Richards. If he was as noteworthy as it appeared, there would be an extensive dossier on him.

Arafat continued, "As Darwin Weisser, President Tate's National Security Advisor explained to me last week, Richards cut some deal where the U.S. made him the point man in the Mid East on investigating the bombing while agreeing to let him continue with his arms business," Arafat said.

"Sounds a little too convenient," Sabar said skeptically.

Ghassan Kassem somewhat reluctantly felt compelled to come to his American friend's aid, "The way I heard it, and I have no reason to believe it's anything but the truth, is that the United States extorted Richards. In fact, this Weisser and his henchman -- someone named Yarmuth -- are right in the middle of it. They told him if he didn't go out and find who did the bombing, they'd extradite him back to the States and prosecute him for treason."

"Will someone please tell me what this has to do with peace?" King Hussein demanded impatiently.

"Oh yes," said Arafat, "Of course. The bottom line is that while the U.S. will publicly support the peace, their money will not flow here until the U.N. bomber has been turned over. And since the object of this exercise is money, it is in all of our best interest to cooperate on this. It's been made clear that whoever turns the person or group over to Richards will receive special dispensation."

"Are you saying that the U.N. bombing is going to hold up the peace process?" King Hussein said incredulously.

"Yes, that's my basic assessment. And of all people, Norman Richards is the man in the middle," Arafat replied.

"You'll get no cooperation from me," Abu Nidal said, folding his hands and resting them on the table. "The U.N. is scum. A joke. I don't know who did that job in Geneva, but if I find out, I'll kiss his feet for the service he performed for all of Islam. I've dealt with Norman Richards before, and I too believe he's simply caught in the middle of this mess. But let me say today, that if I learn anyone does cooperate with him to facilitate this peace, they will die. I will pull the trigger myself if I have to."

"My friend Abu is right," Saddam Hussein announced glancing down at Sabar. "Iraq has publicly condemned the U.N. bombing, but we will not lift a finger to help solve this crime. Yasser. Your peace is illegal and unholy, and we will take no action to support it."

"Besides, what makes the United States so certain that Arabs were behind this plot?" Sabar injected. "Nothing stays a secret in this region, and it appears that none of us here knows who was involved. The Americans should look elsewhere, instead of making us their scapegoat, as usual."

"Captain Sabar raises a good point," King Hussein said. "It sounds to me like this is just another example of prejudice against Arabs. We are being blamed for something we didn't do."

Yasser Arafat nodded his head in agreement and stroked his beard thoughtfully for a moment before responding. "I raised this issue with the Americans. Even they admit it is possible. Apparently though, they have checked out all non Mid East terrorist groups from around the world, and they are convinced it wasn't someone like the IRA or the Red Army. By process of elimination and in consideration of geopolitical factors, they keep coming back to a Mid East profile."

"You should hear yourself Yasser," Abu Nidal said. "You are already speaking for the imperialists."

"Not at all. I'm speaking for all Arabs."

"Wrong," Saddam angrily blurted out. "You are a *traitor*. And you do not speak for Iraq! You do not speak for Iran. Nor for the Egyptian fundamentalists. And we will see how long Syria and Hamas support this travesty you call peace!"

Arafat ignored Saddam. "If our economic goals can be achieved by something as simple as turning in a criminal to the Americans, and we improve our face with the rest of the world for doing so, then there is no question. It must be done. You especially have to gain by cooperating," Arafat said, pointing his finger at Saddam. "Unless it was one of your people who did the bombing."

Abu Nidal shook his head in disgust at Arafat, hardly believing he was in the company of the same militant terrorist who had been his close comrade in arms against Israel for twenty years.

Saddam Hussein feigned irritation, knowing he would never turn Carlos in, especially in light of his present mission concerning the Americans.

Rashid Sabar shook his head too, focusing on remembering and finding out about Norman Richards.

SEVENTEEN

Jerusalem

NORMAN RICHARDS' OUT OF TUNE VOICE screeched a Rolling Stones song into a brown beer bottle which made a perfect improv microphone. His tight bluejeaned hips gyrated in measured rhythm as he danced and jumped about the room to the thunderous beat from the jukebox blasting at Ema's Club. As Richards finished his best song and dance imitation of Mick Jagger, he stumbled into the arms of the laughing, dizzy looking, chesty blonde he met only an hour earlier. She giggled and quivered as Richards drunkenly slurped his tongue down her neck and into her ear promising he could provide her with satisfaction. She believed him. But two beers and three shots in sixty minutes would make a lot of people believe almost anything.

Richards turned the girl sideways, put his arm around her shoulder and leaned against the bar. Slamming his beer bottle down on the bar loud enough to be heard over the music he yelled, "Bartender. Zvi. Gimme some whiskey."

A stocky, half-bald, bartender strolled over to Richards. "Normie, what do you need buddy?"

"A short one, Zvi. Just another short one. And get it quick before I pass out," Richards instructed.

"No problem. She need one too?" the bartender asked.

"I dunno." Richards turned his head so that his face was about two inches away from hers. "You want another one Penina?"

"My name's Ilana. And yes."

"Penina wants another one," Richards said.

"It's Ilana," she said impatiently, rolling her eyes.

"Yeah. Right. Sorry," Richards said, confusing last night's date with this evening's new found friend. "Ilana wants another one Zvi. Make it Vitamin Jack."

The bartender reached down into the bar's speedrack and whipped out a bottle of Jack Daniels. He filled two shotglasses with the Tennessee whiskey, but before Richards could grab the shooter and polish it off, a hand reached in from his side and snatched his drink away.

"Hey Boomer. How you doin'?" Sam Phillips asked, slapping Richards on the back. "I've been sitting back there watching you for about fifteen minutes. I promise you, you don't need this," Phillips said as he turned the shot upside down onto the floor.

A slack jawed Richards sobered up in a jolt at both the unexpected sight of his old CIA nemesis and the tragic loss of his cocktail. "What the fuck are you doing here?" he asked in a soft voice but acerbic tone.

"We have to talk," Phillips replied. "But first, don't you have manners? Introduce me to your pretty young friend here."

Richards glared at Phillips but then said, "Yeah, sure. Leora this is Sam. We used to work together."

"I said it's Ilana," she barked, now glaring at Richards.

Phillips shook his head at Richards' bad program with women and snorted, "You're such a jerk."

Richards raised his eyebrows in guilt, having now confused the girl with his date for tomorrow. He cursed his blunder, knowing that now he wouldn't get lucky with Ilana tonight. Unless, of course, he could get a few more drinks into her.

Phillips pulled a thick rubber band bound wad of Israeli bills out
of his pants pocket, and peeled off a 100 shekel note. He gently
took Ilana's hand and pressed the bill into her palm. "Take this.
Sometimes when my friend drinks he doesn't behave so well. Don't
hold it against him. Do me a favor. Give us ten minutes to talk and
then come back. Okay?"

The girl smiled and stuffed the bill into the pocket of her very
short shorts. "I think I'll just walk around for a few minutes." She
leaned over and pecked Richards on the cheek and flitted away into
the crowd, apparently already forgiving the minor matter of Richards
forgetting her name.

The moment she was gone an incensed Richards poked Phillips
in the chest and said, "Who the fuck do you think you are pulling a
bullshit stunt like that?"

"Hey. Calm down Boomer. I was trying to make sure you still
got your rocks off. It looks like it may work."

"First, I've told you before and I'll tell you again. Don't call me
Boomer. Second, stay the hell away from me. I got nothin' to say
to you."

"Sure you do. You owe me a status report on your U.N. investigation, and I want it now."

Richards grabbed Ilana's half-filled beer bottle from the bar and
poured the frothy alcohol onto Sam Phillips feet. "Jesus, that was
really rude," he said, opening his palms in the air and then placing
them across his chest feigning sincerity. "I can't believe I did that.
I'm *really* sorry," he said sarcastically.

Even in the dim light of the smoky bar it was easy to discern that
Phillips face turned flush with anger, and he raised his arm and fist
to throw a punch.

Richards quickly raised his index finger and with a stare, warned,
"Don't do it, Sam. I'll hurt you. And it'll be fun. — No, wait. I'm
wrong." He raised both hands and motioned for Phillips to come
get him. "*Do it*. C'mon."

Phillips slowly lowered his arm to his side. It took all of his willpower not to punch Richards, and only his knowledge that Richards

could and would beat him senseless prevented him from throwing the first punch.

"Now buddy boy," said Richards, "speak your peace and then leave me the fuck alone."

Phillips glared at Richards, then began. "It's been eight months since you've supposedly been on board with us. You haven't told us shit about the U.N. bombing and we don't like it. We want some answers. *Now*."

"You're a stupid fuckin' monkey, you know that? You got a thousand people all over the world looking for the assholes who hit the U.N. Obviously nobody's found anything, cause here you are shakin' me down." With a wave of his arm Richards caught Zvi's attention and signaled for another drink.

"Don't give me any shit, Norman. I want to know what you've been doing. Who've you talked to? What have you heard?"

"I ain't heard shit. Don't you fuckin' think that if I knew who it was, or if I had anything important to say, I'd tell you, just so you'd leave me alone?" Richards said as he started scratching his head intensely.

"One never knows," Phillips said, thinking *"What an asshole."*

"Right. Whatever you say," Richards said, thinking *"What an asshole."*

Phillips watched Richards continue to claw away at his scalp. "You got a fungus growing up there? Try soap and water occasionally. It'll clear that shit right up."

Richards frowned and stopped scratching.

"Norman, please. Just tell me. What's going on?"

"Nothing's happening. Zip. Squat. I've talked to every high powered source of information I know in the Middle East, and there isn't a soul who has a clue about the bombing."

"What about Abu Nidal? We have reports it may have been him."

"It wasn't Nidal. I just saw him about a week ago and believe it or not, the son of a bitch brought the bombing up to me. I couldn't fucking believe it. I guess he was at some meeting with a bunch of Arab leaders about this peace thing with Israel, and Arafat told him the U.S. thought he did it. He also said the State Department has made it public knowledge that it's my job to find the bad guy. He thought that was pretty funny."

"So how do you know it wasn't him?"

"Because he said so. The fuckin guy would love to take the credit for it. It'd make him a hero with most of the Arabs. But most of these terrorists have this strange sense of honor about their work. He'll only claim what he's responsible for. And I can tell you this. He's not afraid of the U.S., so that wouldn't stop him from telling me the truth. It wasn't him. I'm sure of it."

Phillips rubbed his chin in thought, accepting Richards' analysis as accurate. Despite Richards personality shortcomings, he had miraculously remained the best source and judge of information in the Middle East available to the Central Intelligence Agency.

"Okay. How about the Iranians? Or Saddam?"

"I don't have any direct reliable contacts in Iran right now. Most of my old sources either moved out or got killed. The fundamentalists don't trust me simply because I'm American. I think they'd shoot me if I showed up in Teheran."

"Then you should go."

Richards ignored Phillips' crack and continued, "I spoke to Ghassan Kassem about Iran because he has ties there with the fundamentalists through people he knows in Hamas."

"Wait a second," Phillips said. "I thought Kassem was independent. He's not supposed to be part of Hamas."

"He's not. But he's still the big cheese in Gaza and that's where Hamas operates from. Ghassan tells me that Hamas is getting some serious funding from the Iranian fundamentalists, and that no one has ever mentioned the U.N. job. And these people have notoriously big mouths. The job must not have been sanctioned out of Iran or we'd have heard about it by now. For what it's worth though, go tell your friends Weisser and Yarmuth that Hamas' public support for the Mid East peace is hanging by a thread. Hamas' leaders are for it, but there's too much pressure from the people and from the Iranians and other hardliners."

"Thanks for the tip."

Richards shrugged his shoulder in response.

"Norman, do you have anything on Iraq?"

"I asked Nidal about Iraq, and he told me that if it was Saddam's job, he'd have heard about it from his friend Rashid Sabar, who runs the Mukhabarat."

"What do you think?"

"I don't know. I used to have a pretty good file on Sabar. He's a vicious crazy animal and totally loyal to Saddam. I don't think he'd tell Nidal if he knew. I have a hard time pinning this on Saddam, though. He had too much too lose and nothing to gain by ordering that job. Besides, he's got so many enemies inside Iraq that even if Sabar kept his mouth shut, a hundred others wouldn't. Look how easy it was to uncover the Iraqi assassination attempt on President Bush a few years back. Nothing stays secret in that country."

"Yeah. We basically had the same assessment."

"You got anything else?"

"Nope. Nothing."

Richards tossed down a new shooter of Jack Daniels in one gulp and grimaced for a second as the alcohol burned through his insides. The men stood in silence for about thirty seconds, looking straight ahead.

Phillips finally broke the silence. "Norman. I really didn't come in here tonight looking to have a problem with you. Remember, we had some good times once. And I'll even admit I made some mistakes throwing my weight around with you at times I didn't need to. I'd like to straighten things out. What do you think?"

Richards turned and faced Phillips, and put his hand on his shoulder.

"Are you serious?"

"Yeah. Before I came here tonight I gave this a lot of thought."

"Good. Then leave me alone." Norman Richards turned on his heels and started walking away. "I've got to find whatever her name is."

EIGHTEEN

Baghdad

OMAR RAFSANI CAREFULLY MEASURED out a quarter cup of magnesium powder, and poured the sandy textured substance in a thin stream onto the silver nitrate already packed into the clear glass jar resting on the table in front of him. He sealed the container and turned it over repeatedly until the white and silver powders meshed together to become one new shade of gray. Reaching over Omar's shoulder, Carlos removed the lid and mixed the newly blended ignitor onto the top of the gelled gasoline incendiary pellet bomb Khalil al-Sharif had concocted in a coffee can under Carlos' instruction only minutes earlier.

"Remember that the explosive is extremely delicate in this state," Carlos reminded Khalil, Ahmed and Omar, speaking English. "Now that the powder is mixed with the gel, the slightest bit of moisture will act as a fuse, causing the detonating agents to react."

"And if it that happens and you're not prepared for it, your ass will be disintegrated in no time flat," Seve added, taking a symbolic precautionary step backwards.

Carlos spit into the mixture. "Now Omar, the bomb is alive," he announced calmly. "You've got about thirty seconds to disengage this thing before the magnesium burns through to the gas gel and we all die. *Do it.*" The powder already started smoking giving off a powerfully acidic smell.

"Huh?" Omar looked bewildered.

Carlos pulled the Beretta from his shoulder holster, clicked off the safety and stuck it to the back of Omar Rafsani's head. "Do something, or I'll kill you right now. 25 seconds left."

Seve gave Carlos an *Are you out of your mind look?*, but it was too late to argue. Khalil and Ahmed froze in their seats next to Omar, astonished by Carlos' actions.

For five seconds Omar intently studied the explosive, analyzing where to start. Knowing the delicacy of the material and that the wrong movement could expedite sending them all to kingdom come, he considered his possible courses of action. He exhaled deeply and bit his lower lip, realizing that no product or device could terminate the ongoing chemical chain reaction. And, there was nothing within arm's reach to even experiment with in this desperate situation. The wisp of smoke turned into a bright white flash of fire as the magnesium mixture fully ignited.

"Goddammit, do it, you fuck!" Carlos screamed, slapping Omar's head. As the seconds continued to tick off, the tension in everyone but Carlos' face became heightened.

Seve screamed, "Carlos you're insane," and barreled out of the room and down the hall.

Ahmed and Khalil rose from their chairs to follow Seve. Carlos pointed his pistol at Ahmed's skull and ordered, "Sit." They did.

Taking a deep breath, Omar picked up the coffee can, and with his arms outstretched he walked in a quick but even pace to the window. As fireballs began to randomly shoot up from the can, a putrid choking smoke filled the room, gagging its prisoners. He expertly kicked a hole through the glass and tossed the bomb out of the window, heaving it as far out and away as possible. Two seconds later a deafening explosion echoed through the building. Omar looked down to see a swath of fire burning on the pavement below.

"Good thinking. Good instincts," a facially expressionless but satisfied Carlos said.

Seve walked back into the room sucking hard on a cigarette. Shaking his head he said, "Sometimes I really think you're either downright fucking crazy or just plain suicidal."

Carlos shrugged his shoulders and softly responded, "Well, I'm *definitely* not suicidal."

"Carlos, what would you have done if I hadn't figured out what to do?" Omar asked.

"You had about three more seconds before I'd have told you, and then I probably would have shot you later," Carlos answered, sounding sincere. Omar believed him but Seve knew better. Carlos had too much time, sweat and emotion invested to just summarily execute him.

"Ilich. What happened out there? A chemistry experiment go bad? You almost killed me." Saddam Hussein laughed standing in the doorway, surprising Carlos' trainees by his sudden unexpected presence, and speaking the first words of Arabic that they had heard in almost two weeks.

"You're late. You could have seen for yourself," Carlos said to the Iraqi dictator. "But don't worry. I've still got a good show planned for today. You remember Omar, Ahmed and Khalil?" Carlos motioned to each man with an open palm in sequence.

"Of course. How are you men?" Saddam asked, stepping forward and greeting each of the young terrorists with vigorous handshakes. An entourage of men, including Rashid Sabar and ten Republican Guardsmen trailed Saddam into the room.

"Your professor has told me great things about you," Saddam said, gesturing grandly towards Carlos. "I understand your instruction is almost complete."

"Correction. Their instruction will never be complete," Carlos quickly replied with a smile.

"Naturally," Saddam agreed.

"Put this stuff away," Carlos instructed with a sweep of his arm.

In a fluent display of teamwork, the men packed up the various chemicals and equipment from the table and quickly stored them away in a closet.

They sat back down at their work table and Saddam asked, "Ahmed, tell me the most interesting thing you learned this week."

Ahmed didn't even have to pause for thought. "Yesterday Carlos taught us how to blow out a phone system in a city grid."

"What?" Saddam asked, clearly not comprehending.

"Yes sir. It's pretty easy. You shear off and expose the wire on an extension cord, and then thread it back into the receiver and the phone line and plug the cord in. It sends 120 volts back through equipment designed to handle only six volts. It can take care of a whole phone system in a large building, or a full city grid in a residential neighborhood like this."

Carlos beamed with pride as Ahmed succinctly recited his lessons. Saddam's eyes opened wide. "I didn't even know that could be done. Did you?" Saddam asked Rashid Sabar.

"Of course," the head of the Mukhabarat lied.

"How about you, Omar?" Saddam asked.

"As you saw, we've been learning how to construct bombs. I can make a bomb out of almost anything now. Even soap or wax."

"Khalil?"

"For me, it's that I'm now fluent in English and French. I know I can travel anywhere and pretty much do anything and not get caught, so long as I keep myself focused," Khalil said confidently.

That moment confirmed again what Carlos had known almost from the beginning. Khalil was the one. His chosen. Starting the first day they met in the Cave and throughout their terrorist training, Khalil had excelled. Ahmed and Omar were superb students, but Khalil was the star.

"Let's go down the hall," Carlos said to Saddam and Sabar. "We'll have our exhibition in the dojo. Are your men ready?"

"I think the better question is, are yours?" Rashid Sabar replied.

Carlos' pupils gave each other a mystified look, contemplating what new and unknown challenge Carlos had set up for them. Seconds later the entire group moved down the hall.

"So how do you want to do this?" Saddam asked Carlos.

"I don't care. You make the rules."

"Good. No rules. I'll pick the matchups. Who's your best fighter?" Saddam whispered.

Carlos rubbed his chin in thought for a moment. "Omar is the strongest, Ahmed is the toughest, and Khalil is the quickest and has the most heart," Carlos said to Saddam. He turned and looked at Seve. "You agree?"

"Absolutely," Seve answered.

Saddam conferred in private with Sabar for a moment before the secret police chief announced loudly, "Let's just first try a simple matchup between Ismael and Omar."

"Just give me a moment to talk with my men," Carlos said.

Carlos and Seve huddled with Khalil, Ahmed and Omar. "I don't want to put any pressure on you, but you're each gonna have a fight to death with one of these goons," Carlos said.

Each man gave Carlos the same blank look. Seve exhaled a lung full of smoke into the center of the group.

Carlos nodded rapidly to reemphasize the point. "Wake up you assholes. Saddam's men have instructions to kill you or at the least, to maim you. It'd be a good idea for you to try and do the same to them. Understand?"

This time they all nodded affirmatively.

"Good. Remember: Discipline. Enemy. Anticipation. Deception. Now go sit down and prepare yourselves. Focus."

"I didn't know you set up a death match," Seve whispered to Carlos as the men walked away in contemplative silence.

"I lied, but they don't need to know that. And guess what Saddam meant when he said 'no rules'."

"Isn't this a bit risky? We don't know who they brought in."

"So now we'll really see what they can do."

"You and your tests," Seve smirked.

"They'll thank me one day," Carlos said. "Besides, you always tested me."

"Let's get started," Saddam Hussein announced impatiently.

"So, when you say no rules, you mean it?" Carlos asked Saddam, more as a reminder to Omar than because he needed to have the question answered again. Omar and Ismael already started circling each other, staring into the others eyes searching for signs of weakness.

"Are there rules out in the streets?" Saddam asked.

"Of course not," Carlos replied.

"Then there are no rules today," Saddam announced.

"Good. Just the way I like it."

A second later Ismael lunged at Omar, leaping high and twisting in the air attempting to plant his foot in Omar's throat. Omar sidestepped the move, grasping Ismael's leg as it was coming down, and tried to snap it in half. Ismael fell with a scream and a thud but bounded back up quickly, brandishing brass knuckles on both hands. He repeatedly punched at Omar's head with wild full arm swipes but barely kept missing, his undisciplined frustration growing with each errant swat.

As one futile blow swept past Omar's head, he grabbed Ismael's stray arm with his left hand and exerted his full body weight on the man's wrist, bending it backwards with all of his strength until it broke and fell limp. Ismael screamed in agony and Omar seized the opportunity to step behind Ismael and put him in a chokehold. Grabbing and twisting the man's now useless wrist, Omar palmed it with the brass knuckles side up and forcefully punched Ismael in the face and skull with his own broken hand and weapon continuously, until Ismael's features were fully bloodied. Omar didn't stop until Ismael fell to the ground unconscious, and for good measure, he kicked his adversary in the throat. The whole match was over in less than 30 seconds and Omar hadn't broken a sweat. He looked over at Carlos and smiled broadly. Carlos nodded his approval.

Omar looked down sullenly at his gasping but otherwise totally still victim. Surprising everyone, Omar leaned over Ismael, petted him on the hand and spoke softly in his ear for a few seconds before walking away and sitting down between Ahmed and Khalil.

"Get this man out of here!" a red-faced Saddam Hussein commanded. Sabar motioned to two of the guardsmen. They picked Ismael up by his arms and legs and started carrying him to the corner of the room. "No," Saddam yelled again, pointing to the window. "Out there. Like the garbage that he is." The guards stopped in their tracks, shocked by their president's order. "Do it now or you will join him," Saddam ordered. The men did as they were told, dropping a seriously injured, but certainly mendable Ismael out of the second floor window onto the street below.

Seve turned to Carlos and said in a low voice, "I guess this is a fight to death."

"Well, we know he hates to lose. This should be interesting, because I'm sure Saddam sent his weakest man up first," Carlos answered, as he brushed his hand through his hair.

"Ahmed. You'll fight Latif now. And think about Ismael," Saddam said gruffly.

One of the guards who was leaning casually against the wall holding a rifle stepped forward and stripped off his military fatigue shirt. At 6'5" and 250 pounds, Latif's physical presence was most notable among all others in the room.

As Ahmed stood up, Khalil announced, "Waste him. Don't let him touch you."

Omar added, "Fight hard," and he shook Ahmed's hand.

Ahmed had barely moved onto the mat when Latif charged him, maneuvering Ahmed into a crushing bearlock grip from behind. Ahmed kicked his right heel back with full force onto Latif's shin, and then crushed down on the man's instep. He slipped his hands up just enough to grasp Latif's left little finger which he bent sideways, causing Latif to loosen his grip.

Latif shook the ache out of his left hand and snorted through his nose. The adversaries squared off again and circled around each other, their shoulders hunched in anticipation and their eyes glaring at the enemy, searching for an opening in the other's defense. Ahmed shifted to a traditional attack stance with his feet positioned perpendicularly. He inched towards Latif who sneered and spit at him.

Latif lunged at Ahmed again, this time throwing a sequence of high kicks aimed for Ahmed's chest and head, each of which Ahmed narrowly dodged. Latif kicked past Ahmed and spun around to try again. As he moved past Ahmed this time, however, Ahmed swung his right arm out with cat like quickness, snapping his wrist hard so that his clenched fist struck the back of Latif's head in the soft spot just below the skull at the top of his neck.

Latif crumbled to the floor unconscious, shocking the room's spectators who remained silent for a few seconds, but for gasps of surprise from Seve and Saddam.

"Yesss!" Ahmed exclaimed, thrusting his fist up in the air. He then removed a set of the brass knuckles off his right hand that belonged to Ismael until five minutes earlier, and he laughingly taunted Saddam, wagging them in demonstration.

"What? Explain yourself!" Saddam Hussein demanded, his face bright red.

"Rule Number Four," Omar yelled back. "Deception."

"Huh?" Saddam said.

"Remember, you said anything goes," Ahmed reminded Saddam.

Two guards dragged Latif off the mat. Sabar escorted them out of the room, giving orders to shoot Latif.

Carlos walked over and patted Ahmed and Omar on the back. "Nicely done." He turned to Khalil and warned, "Prepare yourself. I don't know what's next, but it won't be easy. They'll want your head." Carlos glanced over his shoulder to see Rashid Sabar and Saddam Hussein speaking with another soldier who was loosening up with a fluid sequence of technically perfect punches, kicks and grabs. Khalil quickly realized that his opponent's moves proved a level of martial arts skills far exceeding his own training. Khalil walked around the dojo to loosen up, merely stretching his limbs and neck and doing light calisthenics.

Saddam walked up to Carlos and announced loudly, "Ilich. I know the work you've gone to with your men and you've done well, but I don't care. I've told Mohammed to kill Khalil. And he can do it."

Carlos frowned in acknowledgment of his favorite soldier's apparent death sentence, recognizing Saddam would not accept a 3 - 0 shut out very well. Seve looked down at the floor in contemplation that Khalil's minutes on earth might be numbered.

Khalil looked over at his group and confidently announced, "Don't worry."

He stepped to the edge of the mat and bowed slightly to his adversary who nodded back. As opposed to the high intensity approach Latif demonstrated right before his match, Mohammed's dispassionate stare displayed a totally calm and collected presence which Carlos and Seve both read as pure danger. Even though they lost, Ismael and Latif were fighters. It was clear that Mohammed was a killer.

"Start," Saddam Hussein instructed.

Mohammed stepped forward and produced a pearl handled switchblade from the back of his pants. He pressed a button and a six inch gleaming silver blade instantly protruded from his clenched fist. Mohammed pointed the knife at Khalil and stopped. "You will suffer for the pain inflicted on my friends," he announced. He moved towards Khalil brandishing the weapon as if it were a natural extension of his arm. Khalil stood motionless.

"Move," Ahmed yelled at his brother. "Don't let him touch you."

"Focus! Discipline!" Omar added.

Just as Mohammed was within striking distance of Khalil, the young terrorist dove forward in a perfect tumble, ending up ten feet away and acrobatically jumping back to his feet. Mohammed's eyes narrowed and he immediately continued with his offensive, again stepping towards Khalil, this time aggressively slicing the air with the blade in a symmetrical movement. He threateningly narrowed his distance to Khalil with slash after slash, which Khalil continued to just barely avert.

In seconds Khalil found himself cornered on the end of the mat, and Mohammed sliced upwards from his left. The weapon gashed Khalil across the chest shredding his shirt and slitting open eight inches of his skin on a diagonal.

Carlos bit his lower lip and Seve lit a new cigarette off one he was still smoking. Ahmed rocked back and forth in anxiety and yelled, "Khalil! Stay back! Remember defense!"

"No. Rule Two," Khalil calmly responded with his back to his friends.

"What?" Ahmed yelled again. "Defend yourself!"

Blood dripping from his flesh, Khalil maneuvered around the mat while Mohammed continued to stalk him, still relentlessly swiping at his body with the knife. After two minutes of the cat and mouse game, Mohammed chased Khalil back into a corner again, and attacked with the same previously successful cross body slash. This time, Khalil landed a series of three strong direct shots to his enemy's kidney and throat, followed up by a leg sweep that took Mohammed down to the floor where Khalil jumped on him.

The room changed from silent intensity to near pandemonium as everyone started yelling support for their man. Khalil and Mohammed rolled over and over as Mohammed continued to grip the knife. Suddenly the larger and stronger Mohammed finally overpowered Khalil. Practically sitting on Khalil's chest and further pinning him down with his left arm while holding the knife in his right hand, Mohammed started to push the knife down towards Khalil's face. When the point of the blade was only three inches from his eye, Khalil manipulated his free right hand to the top of Mohammed's head. Seconds later Mohammed's entire head of curly hair was engulfed in fire and smoke.

Mohammed dropped the knife and jumped up screaming and slapping himself in the head, trying to douse the flames that Khalil had created with a disposable lighter now visible to the others. When he managed to do so, Mohammed howled, "You die now," and he charged Khalil. Khalil whipped his arm back and then forward releasing Mohammed's knife which whizzed through the air like an arrow and caught Mohammed square in the throat, stopping him in motion as if he had hit a wall. Mohammed gurgled in his blood and dropped to both knees, his hands clutching his throat.

Khalil walked over to Mohammed and yanked the knife out,

wrenching the weapon upwards as he did so. With his left hand, Khalil grabbed Mohammed by what was left of his hair and jerked the dying man's head up, causing blood to shoot out of his wounded throat like a fountain. With his right hand and the knife pointed at his own bleeding chest Khalil said in a soft but cold voice, "You see this. Now *you* die." Clutching the knife he slammed it into the man's heart, then looked over at Saddam Hussein and Rashid Sabar before he twisted the totally buried instrument upwards. He kicked Mohammed over onto his back, and stood over him, panting and dripping sweat mixed with the blood running from the gash across his chest.

Carlos looked deep into Khalil's eyes and saw the steel icy glare of a man who had no fear of death and no compunction about killing. Seve, breathtaken by Khalil's incredible performance, read Carlos' eyes the same way and a chill rose up his back in respectful recognition of Carlos' heir apparent. Everyone else was astonishingly silent, oblivious to Khalil's mental state, rather, completely taken by his shocking deadly victory over the supposedly invincible Mohammed.

Ahmed walked over to Khalil and gave him a brotherly hug. "Are you all right?"

Khalil looked down at his bloody chest and calmly replied, "I'm fine."

"You were unbelievable. You're also crazy."

Although it was out of place, Carlos laughed at Ahmed's suggestion of lunacy. Whenever Carlos pulled off the unexpected scheme, or survived when the odds were especially stacked against him, by almost always utilizing the most unorthodox of methods, his compatriots had countless times accused Carlos of being crazy. And he'd always responded, "No, just sly." Khalil had proven he too could be a jackal.

Saddam Hussein and Rashid Sabar strolled across the room to Carlos. Much to everyone's surprise, Saddam wrapped his arm around Carlos' shoulders. Smiling broadly he said, "I guess you just proved to me that all that money I paid you was well spent."

"More than you know," Carlos responded.

"Where did you get the lighter from? How did you know you'd need it?" Sabar cross-examined Khalil, amazed that he was alive and Mohammed, his top young Mukhabarat agent, was dead.

"It's Seve's. He leaves his cigarettes and these disposable lighters all over the place," Khalil said, handing the lighter back to its rightful owner. "When we walked into the room I had a feeling I'd need something extra for defense. Carlos taught us that if you think about it, you can turn almost anything into a weapon."

"That was pretty gutty drawing him to the ground, Khalil," Carlos commented.

"I saw right away that he was a more experienced fighter so that my fists alone wouldn't keep me alive," Khalil responded to the group, all circled around him listening intently. "I had to let him think he could take me out when I was cornered the first time, but it was really the only way to plan my attack. Rules Two and Three."

"What are these numbered rules you people keep mentioning?" Saddam Hussein asked Carlos. Rashid Sabar nodded his head showing he wanted to know as well.

Carlos looked to his star pupil to provide the explanation.

"Rule Two is *"Know your enemy"* and Rule Three is *"Anticipation,"* Khalil replied. "We have a set of rules, sort of a creed that guides us in how we train, plan and survive." He smiled politely and turned back to Carlos and Seve, adding, "The rules are now an instinctive part of my natural thought process. You said this would happen."

"Yes, and now that it has, and after what you've done today, I can see there's not much more I really can teach you," Carlos said.

"Ilich. My first reaction was anger when I watched your men take out mine," Saddam Hussein said. "But I have to congratulate you. You have trained the ultimate soldiers for me." Saddam shook hands with Carlos and Seve, and with his hand still outstretched he continued, "Khalil, Ahmed, Omar, I welcome you to my service. You've earned a handsome bonus for your hard work the past eight months."

Rashid Sabar moved from Saddam's side over next to Carlos, and he draped his arm around the terrorist's shoulders just as Saddam had done minutes earlier. "I've been telling him for three months how good these guys are, and not just in fighting. Wait til he sees their other talents. My friend, you are a genius. I should send my son to you."

"No, not really. Seve's the genius. He taught me most of what I know. I'm just passing it on." Carlos looked at his men and said, "Go have some lunch and relax. You've earned it." They left and Saddam excused his remaining Republican Guardsmen as well.

Once the door was closed, Carlos told Saddam, "I appreciate your comments on the progress of my men, and it's true, their potential is incredible. But the fact is, they're still basically untested in real battle. All they really went through this morning was a tough fight. Big deal. It doesn't prove anything. What they need is a real test. Combat."

"What are you getting at?" Saddam asked.

"Rashid, remember last month I talked to you about putting them through a raid, where they have to really fight to survive?"

"Of course. You wanted me to stage an attack, right?" Rashid answered.

"Exactly. Would you set that up for us?" Carlos asked.

"Where and when?"

"Here. Today. Now. If we want to see what they're really capable of doing, let's give them a test that'll be equal to what they'll see on the streets. And then if they pass that, maybe we'll try a black box drill next."

"A what?" Saddam asked.

"It's a training drill where the men sneak into a high security public building and plant a fake bomb and get out safely, or something elaborate like that," Seve answered. "The KGB originated the concept."

Saddam nodded approvingly, then turned back to Carlos. "Ilich, are you suggesting that Sabar send in men with *live* ammunition to raid this building?" Saddam asked.

"Absolutely. What good will blanks do?"

"This may seem inconsistent, even odd, but now that I see what assets your men will be, I don't want them hurt. We have too much invested in them. I already lost three good men today."

Carlos exhaled deeply and clicked his tongue on the roof of his mouth. "They're nothing more than a theory right now. They're knowledgeable and talented, but extremely raw. I don't know what they can really do under true life and death pressure. And most important, I don't know if they can kill." In fact, Carlos now knew better about Khalil.

"What are you talking about, Ilich. You saw how they didn't hesitate to kill only fifteen minutes ago."

"False. I saw Khalil act in an emotional self defense type situation."

"They really could get killed now, though. It would be a waste. I veto it," Saddam announced sticking out his chest in a show of his power.

"Tough. It's my call to make. That was part of our deal and I'm holding you to it," Carlos replied, shocking everyone with his bold assertion of authority over Saddam. "You can't send these kids out on an any kind of real mission until we know what they can do. Look, they're almost like sons to me and I've got a lot invested in them too. But I have to make sure they can kill. You of all people should understand this. They have to learn to like the taste of blood."

Saddam, perplexed, rubbed his head. On one hand, he hated the thought of anyone, including Carlos, telling him what to do, especially in front of Sabar. On the other hand, Carlos was the most ruthless terrorist in history, and it would be foolhardy not to let him finish the program he had embarked on so successfully.

"Mr. President," Carlos said. "Please let me finish what I've started. I'm confident in their soldiering skills, but I must watch them kill."

"Fine. Captain, set it up however Ilich requires," Saddam instructed Sabar. "I want to monitor the event with him though."

"YOU GUYS DID GOOD TODAY. I'm proud of you," Carlos said to Khalil, Ahmed and Omar in a rare display of positive reinforcement. "But don't get too comfortable. If you think this morning was a challenge, you haven't seen anything yet."

The men all stopped eating their sandwiches simultaneously, and looked up at Carlos attentively.

"Seve and I have arranged another test for you, and it begins in about -- eighteen minutes," Carlos announced, looking at his Rolex.

"You mean we actually get a little advance notice this time?" Khalil asked.

"Yeah, I thought that since this place is soon going to be swarming with about a dozen well-armed Mukhabarat agents who think you're involved in a plot to kill the president, that I'd give you at least a little notice," Carlos dryly responded. He was tempted to give them no notice, but then he knew they'd stand no chance, having no clue what the secret police were there for.

"You're serious, aren't you?" Omar asked.

"Totally. But aside from fighting for your lives there's a little bonus in this for you if you can pull it off," Carlos replied.

"Like what?" Omar asked.

"For each live Mukhabarat agent that you take prisoner, Saddam will give you 5000 dinar."

"You might also want to know," Seve cut in, "that Carlos insisted the Mukhabarat be given shoot to kill orders."

The men didn't even blink.

"So let me make sure I understand this," Khalil said. "They're supposed to kill us, but we're supposed to take them alive?"

"Not all of them," Carlos answered. "Kill whoever you have to in order to stay alive. If you have to kill them all, then do it. But take the rest captive. With the stockpile of weapons we've got here plus your knowledge of the building, you have the upper hand even though you'll be outnumbered. And since you're down to about 16 1/2 minutes now, I'm getting the hell out of here and I suggest you do some emergency planning. Let's go, Seve."

As soon as Carlos was gone Khalil took over. "Let's go upstairs.

I've got an idea. We should use the triangular patterned defense."
"Excellent," Ahmed concurred as Omar nodded his agreement.
Fifteen minutes later, despite their attempt at a surprise entry, eight heavily armed Mukhabarat agents announced their arrival as the heavy wooden chair Omar had wedged against the front door crashed to the ground. The four agents who tried to slip in from the back fared no better as one man opened fire in surprise at his armed reflection in a large mirror Ahmed had strategically placed only four feet opposite the door.

Seconds later Khalil screamed out in fury, "You pathetic traitor pigs will never take me alive. I die for Allah." Khalil raised his gun, fired one shot and fell hard to the floor.

Within seconds all twelve of the Mukhabarat agents scampered and stomped up the creaky wooden steps to the source of the gunfire. At the top of the steps they turned the corner and found Khalil lying 25 feet down the hallway on his back, blood covering his face and the wall, his hand still clutching his automatic weapon.

"The scum. He killed himself. Too bad. I wanted to do it to him," the leader of the commando group said.

"We should take his body with us and hang it in the square, just to send a message to his friends," another agent replied as the platoon walked at ease down the hall towards Khalil's body.

"Wait. That's right. There's supposed to be two more," the leader said.

"They're cowards. They probably split once they heard us come in," someone else answered.

"To where? And how would they have known about the raid? Think! The chair? The mirror?" the leader questioned.

Almost simultaneous with the leader's last word, Khalil opened fire on the group, keeping his finger tightly pressed to the trigger of his AK-47, while he remained flat on the ground barely even picking up his head. A millisecond later, Ahmed and Omar appeared from the darkness of opposite doors behind the Mukhabarat agents unloading their machine guns into the crowd, who had no escape from the surprise hurricane barrage of crossfire. Within seconds the shooting had stopped without the Mukhabarat even having raised a gun to fire, much less getting a shot off. Eight Iraqi government agents lay dead on the ground, two were down and wounded and the other two remained standing miraculously uninjured but in shock from the stunning attack.

"Throw your weapons down," Omar yelled firing a shot into the ceiling to emphasize the point. The survivors listened and put their hands up without being asked to do so.

"We did it! We pulled it off!" Khalil yelped as he burst out laughing from his group's accomplishment. He jumped to his feet and keeping his weapon trained on his four prisoners, he stepped over corpses to congratulate his comrades.

Ahmed looked down at the pile of twisted bodies before him and the numerous puddles of blood that had already started covering the floor. He tapped one of the corpses with his foot and said, "It's one thing for Carlos to test us in a shoot out like this, but he damn well better not ask us to clean this mess up."

"Don't worry, I won't," Carlos said, his voice surprising the men as it resonated from a speaker down in a corner near the staircase. "Very impressive work. You've proven yourselves to be quite capable," he added.

Through the wonders of technology, Carlos, Seve, Saddam and Sabar were burrowed together in the building's basement in a specially built high-tech security room, watching the proceedings as they unfolded on remote video by live feed two floors above.

Khalil, Ahmed and Omar looked at the videocamera screwed into the top corner next to the speaker as they stripped off the American made Kevlor bullet proof vests, kept on site and frequently used during training, but fortunately not needed today.

"You've been downstairs this whole time?" Ahmed asked.

"Where else? You didn't really think I'd miss the show did you?" Carlos replied.

"Now what?" Omar asked.

"Kill the survivors."

"I thought you wanted them alive?" Khalil inquired.

"There's no need for witnesses," Carlos instructed. "And don't worry, you've earned your bonuses. But I want you to each take one."

"Okay," Khalil replied, understanding the gravity of the new orders.

One of the survivors boldly announced, "You wouldn't be dumb enough to shoot me. I'm Mukhabarat." He defiantly crossed his arms across his chest.

Khalil raised his eyebrows and replied, "You'd be surprised how dumb I am." He changed clips in his gun, raised it and emptied four shots into the man's chest. The force of the bullets smashed the agent into the wall where his feet slid out from underneath him until his dead body sat like a rag doll on the floor. Gobs of blood painted vertical streaks on the wall from the bullets that exited out of his back.

Omar walked up to the other unwounded man and placed the barrel of his Beretta at the man's skull. Before the agent could protest, Omar announced, "Say goodnight," and he pulled the trigger.

Ahmed reached one of the wounded men, barely conscious from the shock of being shot and the quick loss of blood, doubled over in pain. The man looked up, their eyes met, and Ahmed's prey hoarsely whispered, "Ahmed? Help me. I'm cold. Get a doctor."

"Oh my God! Jamil!" Ahmed shouted, astonished at the sight of one of his closest friends. "Khalil. It's Jamil!"

Jamil moaned in agony and Ahmed watched his complexion turn increasingly pale and waxy. "Please help," he coughed. "I need water."

"Shoot him," Khalil instructed coldly.

"How can you shoot me? We're friends," Jamil struggled to say.

Ahmed shook his head and replied, "No. Not anymore. Sorry." Realizing his new duty exceeded the bonds of friendship, Ahmed fired one shot into the middle of Jamil's forehead, then unloaded three shots into the other wounded man's chest.

After Ahmed finished the last execution, in the darkness of their cell, Saddam Hussein quietly opined to Carlos, "Ilich. They were perfect, and as you had hoped, it certainly appears they like the taste of blood."

Carlos placed his hands on Seve's shoulders, who was sitting at the monitor in front of him. He smiled and truthfully responded, "Yes. It does."

NINETEEN

Baghdad

"I COULD GET USED TO THIS," Omar said as he played with the buttons and knobs on the control panel in the back seat of Saddam Hussein's iron plated Mercedes limousine. Windows rose and fell and lights clicked on and off. "I've never been in one of these things before."

"Enjoy it while you can," Ahmed replied. "This is probably the last time you'll ever ride in one."

"Not if you're any kind of terrorist," Carlos thought. Aloud he said, "Alright. Listen up. Let's try and focus for just a few more minutes. We're all done today. You're pretty much on your own from now on." Carlos spoke slowly, looked directly into the eyes of Khalil, Ahmed and Omar, and chopped his hand into the air with every well founded point. "Never forget the rules, no matter where you are or who's around. *Discipline...Enemy. Know your enemy... Anticipation...Deception.*"

"You make it sound like we're driving right into enemy territory," Ahmed injected. "We're going to work for the president."

"Make no mistake. I'm loyal to President Hussein," Carlos said emphatically. "But you still better watch your back. There's going to be people surrounding him that will be suspicious and jealous of you just because you're moving right to the top. Everyone can be dangerous in their own way. *Everyone.*"

"Let others do the talking and boasting. Be strong by silence," Seve added. "Unless there's a damn good reason for it, *never* tell people what you're thinking. Your words could be twisted. Misinterpreted. Used against you."

"Seve's right," Carlos said. "Presume that everyone will lie to you about anything."

"Yeah, and don't forget, the best way to find leaks and liars is to feed misinformation to those whom you suspect betray you," Seve added. "When the lie comes back to you, then you'll know who can't be trusted. Deal with those persons accordingly. In private. Do you understand?" Seve asked, requiring an affirmation from each man.

After a few moments of reflection Khalil asked, "So what's planned for us today?"

"The president will personally give you your new orders," Carlos answered.

Five minutes later, the limo pulled up to the main gate of Saddam Hussein's palace. The moment the car came to rest inside the grounds, a brigade of sixty Republican Guardsmen, from scattered positions around the external perimeter, cohesively molded into two long lines forming at the car's door and ending at the front entrance to the palace. Saddam Hussein and Rashid Sabar stood waiting at the palace's open, 15 foot tall double brass doors.

"Wow, what's this!" Ahmed exclaimed as he stepped outside, straightening the buttoned jacket of his olive green Republican Guard's dress uniform.

"An official hero's welcome," Carlos said.

"We didn't do anything. We're not heroes," Khalil said.

"Don't tell them that," Seve whispered, motioning to the two lines of soldiers.

As the group strolled down the man made color guard aisle, the soldiers twirled and spun their rifles around in unison. A ten man drum corp beat out a rhythmic compelling allegro in synchronization with the honor guards' movements. Just as they reached the end of the aisle and stood before Saddam Hussein, the president sharply clicked his black boot heels together and saluted the group, a greeting naturally returned by the young soldiers.

With a broad grin and sweep of his arm, Saddam escorted his guests inside the palace. Once the door was closed he extended personal greetings to each man. Noticing the awed expressions on their young faces at the foyer's lavish decorations, he graciously offered and gave an impromptu full tour of the palace. An hour later the entourage finally entered Saddam's private office and was seated around Hussein's desk. Saddam stood behind his chair with his back to the group. He turned to Khalil, Omar and Ahmed and dramatically announced, "This is your palace. The people's palace. You are always welcome here."

Sabar then walked over to Carlos and placed one hand on his shoulder saying, "Let me thank you again for dinner last night. My wife said it was one of the most engaging evenings she's had in ages. She's so happy that she and Magdelena have become close, as have you and I," Sabar said warmly, displaying a personal side nobody thought existed.

"It was our pleasure, and you know our feelings about you and Leila are reciprocal," Carlos said, giving a gentle pat on Sabar's back.

"What's this about?" Saddam Hussein asked, obviously bewildered.

Carlos and Sabar glanced at each other for a moment before Sabar answered. "We have worked together much in the past year. At first I didn't trust Ilich, and I'm sure it was reciprocal. But soon we realized that we were on the same team and had a great deal in common."

"Wonderful. I never thought I'd see the day," Saddam smiled. "My two best maniacs together." Everyone laughed at Saddam's characterization, which pleased him immensely.

Though Saddam and Sabar assumed the friendship was sincere,

Carlos, a master manipulator of people, knew Sabar held true power in Iraq. He knew he could not afford to have him as an enemy, so it was better to make him a friend. Befriending Sabar was a job though, not a pleasure.

"Speaking of teams, I have something here to welcome you to mine," Saddam announced to Khalil, Ahmed and Omar. He reached into the inside pocket of his jacket and withdrew a batch of sealed envelopes, handing one to each man. They looked at each other and then at Carlos, unsure if etiquette allowed for their opening to inspect the contents.

Saddam answered the unspoken question. "Go ahead. Take a look. There's 100,000 dinar in each. You've earned it and you'll continue to earn it. And Mr. Dolchino, we never had an arrangement, but here's something for you too," Saddam said giving Seve an envelope. "Captain Sabar has told me your involvement in this project was almost as significant as Ilich's."

"That's very kind of you," Seve responded, genuinely surprised. In truth, Seve expected nothing. He was just happy to help and be part of the action.

"So what will you do next?" Sabar asked Seve. "You are welcome to stay here." Saddam Hussein nodded his head in agreement.

"No offense," Seve replied wheezing through a cigarette, "but I kind of miss European food and I still have my antique business in Geneva. I'm going back there in a couple of days."

"Just remember you're welcome here anytime," Saddam Hussein said.

"So what do we do with this?" Ahmed asked, grinning and thumbing through the wad of cash.

"Whatever you want," Saddam replied. "It is yours. A bonus. Captain, tell them the rest."

"We have set up new furnished two bedroom apartments for each of you a few blocks from here. You'll find them quite comfortable. You'll also get a State automobile, fully equipped and later in the day you'll be meeting President Hussein's tailor. We cannot send you out in public in your present wardrobes."

"What do you mean *send out in public?*" Carlos asked.

"We've decided to take them on a diplomatic mission to some of our European embassies to meet foreign Mukhabarat staff," Sabar replied authoritatively.

"Don't you think you'd be better served if less people, not more, know who they are?" Seve said, aghast that Sabar would publicize the arrival of the secret police's new star terrorists. "Look at Carlos. Everybody knows his name, but hardly anyone knows what he looks like."

Carlos agreed, "It's one of the things that's kept me alive."

"No. We want them to know our station chiefs," Sabar curtly answered. "And here are your diplomatic passports," he added, passing out the thin books, as if the act of doing so was now the end of the debate.

"You've got thousands of agents all over the world," Carlos blurted out. "It's reckless to tell the world that these guys exist. You don't do that with anyone else. Goddammit, you won't be able to keep this secret and they'll be marked by every foreign service. They *need* their anonymity." Carlos was always capable of controlling his emotion around Saddam Hussein, and this outburst was calculated to drive home the seriousness of the error he perceived his Iraqi colleagues had apparently committed to make.

"Too bad. It's done," Sabar answered.

"Is it?" Carlos asked Saddam.

Saddam didn't answer.

"It is *not* done," Carlos quietly said. "Khalil especially is not going anywhere unless I say so."

Sabar strolled across the room and leaned over, placing his face three inches away from Carlos'. "My friend. We have come a long way together. This is not your call. Do not challenge me. Khalil no longer belongs to you."

"If you say so," Carlos said angrily.

Omar said, "I don't see what the problem is with..."

"Shut up," Carlos interrupted. "Didn't you fucking learn anything from me? Like when not to talk?"

Omar took two steps back, wholly intimidated. The room was dead silent. Carlos folded his hands, placed them on his lap and stared at Saddam. "Whose call is this?" he finally said.

Saddam wrung his hands together before stammering, "Well... uh... you're both wrong." After a pause he said, "Ilich, We need to talk." Saddam pointed towards the door and Carlos followed him out.

Standing just outside his office, Saddam said, "Do you really need Khalil for your mission in America? There are things Sabar and I have planned for him with the others."

Carlos looked at Saddam with a stunned expression. He shook his head and said, "What are you talking about? Just yesterday you said you clearly understood Khalil *is* the mission."

"I thought about it some more. I gave *you* $50 million to do this. Even the day you saved me in the restaurant you swore to me you'd honor your contract, even if I was dead."

"Listen, you know to pull this off, I'd have to stay in America for six months straight and then have access to the buildings where we need it. I could never do that. I'm good for three to four days in the States at one time and that's it. The mission would never succeed with me running it. But it will with Khalil."

"He's too young. He has no experience. It's ridiculous."

"Saddam, I'll telling you the truth. He's better than I was at his age. I promise you. I'll go to Washington and set it all up. You know the plan. Yesterday you said it was perfect. Unstoppable. And Khalil will be able to finish it off. The fact that he's young and nobody will know him will work to his advantage."

With a heavy sigh Saddam nodded, and said, "Sabar's not going to be happy. Let's go back in."

The moment Carlos and Saddam stepped back in the office, Sabar snapped, "What's going on here?"

Saddam authoritatively marched back behind his desk, and standing over it, said, "These men are now under the jurisdiction of Captain Sabar, who has my full support and confidence. But Rashid,

Ilich has to continue his work with Khalil."

"Why?" Sabar suspiciously asked, giving Carlos a dirty look.

Ignoring the question, Saddam said, "To settle this thing, Ahmed and Omar will go, and Khalil will stay."

Rage surged through Sabar's body at the thought that Saddam didn't fully support him. While Carlos may have become his new trusted friend, relationships were expendable when it came to the invasion of his power and influence over Saddam Hussein. However, Sabar wisely remained silent rather than take a chance on jeopardizing his own standing with Saddam.

Knowing that he still needed Sabar as an ally, Carlos spoke up. "Rashid. Don't be so upset. I'm not trying to invade your turf. Part of my compensation for training these three was that I get to borrow Khalil a little bit for my own personal use," Carlos said, mixing a lie with the truth. "I've got to hold President Hussein to our deal."

Sabar smiled faintly, trying to rein in his temper, wanting to give Carlos the benefit of the doubt. He wasn't sure if he would, but said, "Okay, I don't blame you. I'd do the same thing if I was you."

"Good. Thanks." Carlos rose from his chair and shook hands with Sabar, calculating that the demonstration of unity was important not just for Saddam Hussein, but for Khalil, Ahmed and Omar as well.

"I'm glad that's settled," Saddam Hussein remarked, visibly relieved. "I guess we can get back to business. After Omar and Ahmed return from their travels to Europe they'll start their permanent assignments."

"Omar, you'll be joining my staff, and will serve as the Mukhabarat's special envoy for Palestinian affairs," Sabar said.

"What does that mean?"

"You'll facilitate the flow of information and anything else we send to our friends in the PLO, Hamas and whoever else requests assistance. In fact, later this week we're going to Syria so you can meet Abu Nidal."

"It's my honor to serve and do whatever you need," Omar replied.

"Ahmed. You're coming to work for me here in the palace," Saddam Hussein said.

"What am I going to do?"

"Everything. One day you may be a bodyguard, the next you could be off on a mission."

"Mission?"

"What kind of work do you think you're capable of doing for me?"

"I've been trained to handle pretty much anything," Ahmed answered.

"That's what we think too. Especially after seeing your performance during the black box drill at the bank last week. You took out eight policemen. Incredible! So use your imagination."

Ahmed smiled excitedly.

"What about me?" Khalil spoke up, concerned by the unusual references about his future.

"I was just getting to you," Carlos quickly replied. Measuring his words carefully, he added, "You probably remember that when we first recruited you and started your training, Seve and I said that one of you was going to stay on and work with me for awhile. Well, you're it."

"Good," Khalil said, instantly realizing that he had gotten the best position. The money had to be more plentiful and the adventure more extreme with Carlos. Besides, who knew what to really expect from the volatile Saddam and Sabar. While Carlos was not necessarily predictable, Khalil had learned exactly what his mentor would demand from him. "I remember you had some special project you were working on."

"I've always got a special project going. You were my project for the past year. Now we'll figure out a new one," Carlos said, trying to diffuse Khalil's reference to a project and keep secret his plans to annihilate the U.S. government. "But the first thing you're going to do is go back to school."

"I thought we completed our training."

"You did. I said *school*."

"You mean school school?" Khalil asked incredulously.

"Yes. School school. It's critical for our future together for you to continue your education. It's not for very long. I want you to experience life in the West for a little bit. You're going to America. You'll see the clash of civilizations out there where it's the world versus Islam."

"I don't care. This is not fair. They get to start work now. This is what I've trained for."

"What they're doing is irrelevant to what you're doing. While they'll be off possibly getting themselves killed, you'll be living in pleasant surroundings with a lot of money, playing around, meeting girls and studying. You've got the better deal. Trust me."

"Khalil, read between the lines," Saddam Hussein extraneously added. "You'll be off setting your cover as a student, and once that's accomplished, you'll get to kill President Tate." Saddam walked over to Khalil, gave him a big smile and put his arm around his shoulder. "You'll personally be responsible for rendering the United States helpless to assist Israel for my attack on it the next day. Your work will help start and finish the Holy War we attempted before and couldn't achieve. Your role is crucial. The Arab world will rally around all of us and embrace us. Together we will *all* be heros!"

Carlos was stunned as Saddam disclosed their most inviolate of secrets, yet he remained silent. Out of the corner of his eye Carlos saw Rashid Sabar shifting a dark stare back and forth between him and Saddam Hussein.

The words had barely left Saddam's mouth and Sabar felt the insult. Recognizing he had been duped at least in part by Carlos, another cold rage rushed through his body. The deception played upon him would not be tolerated, and he would learn the truth. One way or the other. No matter what.

TWENTY

Miami, Florida

THE DOOR TO THE CAPTAIN'S CABIN flew open and an immensely fat man in a filthy work shirt and blue jeans, with a four day old beard waddled in. A freshly lit cigar dangled from his mouth, partly covering a week's worth of body odor.

"Hey Chico," the man bellowed. "Customs and INS just left. Everything's fine. Totally routine. The same two guys that always do the check. They could have cared less about the Crew Manifest. They only give a shit about the cargo and getting their import taxes paid."

"No walk through?" Carlos asked, rising from a cross-legged position on the floor.

The captain shook his head no. "Now's a good time to go. Another ship just came in. They're busy with that."

"Good. Then I'm out of here," Carlos announced, reaching into his pocket and handing Alberto Clemente a thin stack of fresh American greenbacks folded in half and held together with a paper clip. The captain of the *El Blanco Sol* started to count the cash on top of his four drawer bureau in a deliberate fashion, slowly placing one bill on top of the next, mumbling the tally out loud.

"Alberto, what's wrong with you? It's all there," Carlos said, seemingly insulted that his longtime boyhood friend from the streets of Caracas, Venezuela apparently didn't trust him.

"The last few guys I did this for tried to fuck me over," the captain responded. "Don't take it personally."

"How long have we known each other?"

"Long time. Since we were kids."

"I ever rip you off before?"

"No," Alberto said, while thinking, *"I never gave you the chance."*

"Then why do you treat me this way?"

"I'm sorry Chico," Clemente said, hanging his head while stuffing the thirty $100 bills into his pants pocket. Carlos had already paid him $3000 when he first boarded ship.

"Fine. I forgive you," Carlos said, lightly slapping the humongous man on the arm. "But only if you stop calling me Chico."

"Can't help it Chico. Been doin' it all my life."

Carlos let it drop. "You'll be here next Friday? No one else? Right?"

"Yeah, yeah, yeah. Every nine days I hit Miami. I haven't been off this schedule in four years."

"Good. Tell me the plan again," Carlos ordered.

"At 9:00 p.m. we meet at the bench outside of the Sharper Image store at Bayside. I'll get you back on the boat, don't worry. There'll be a name for you on the manifest with matching papers. I've got the system down. Trust me."

"I trust no one," Carlos thought to himself. "Of course," he replied.

In terms of risk, flying in and out of the U.S. was probably the most unsafe location in the world for Carlos due to the sophistication of the law enforcement agencies' computers, capable of confirming his true identity in seconds. Thus, although Carlos remained skeptical about his friend's capabilities, he nevertheless believed that smuggling himself in and out of the U.S. with Clemente's help on the *El Blanco Sol* was the safest means to avoid detection.

"Walk me out of here. I don't know my way around the ship," Carlos said in a ploy to obtain the security of being escorted by the ship's captain.

In fact, from virtually the moment Carlos slipped aboard the *El Blanco Sol* two days earlier in Caracas, he hadn't left the captain's quarters, solely to avoid detection by other potentially untrustworthy crewmen. All of his meals were delivered by the first mate, a powerfully built dangerous drunk who earned $1000 both for the service and to keep his mouth shut.

The accommodations were cramped and dirty and had to be shared with Clemente. But at least they were air-conditioned with a window providing a full view of the ocean. Carlos spent most of his time propped up against a wall where he either slept or read with amusement a Spanish translation of a popular American author's best seller supposedly about him and some American agent suffering from an identity crisis. But that was fiction, of course. He picked up the paperback in Caracas after an arduous flight schedule that took him from Baghdad to Riyahd to Mexico City to Caracas, his hometown for the first ten years of his life and then intermittently thereafter.

Dressed conservatively in pleated navy slacks, a white dress shirt and a red patterned tie, Carlos disembarked from the ship unnoticed. One could easily have assumed Carlos to be a port authority official, even with the overnight suitbag in his left hand and the briefcase in his right. As it turned out, nobody even looked twice at him as he nodded and smiled his way past numerous truckdrivers and longshoremen occupied with their own affairs. Still, he walked at a brisk pace among the white and sea blue painted warehouse docks and gravely blacktopped truckyards to avoid being seen on the main roadways of the Port of Miami.

Just as Alberto promised, there were plenty of cabs waiting for fares at Terminal 9, the luxury cruise line passenger terminal. Carlos was relieved to get an air conditioned taxi, since his shirt was already soaked in sweat due to the oppressive heat and humidity of Miami. Five minutes later he was checking in at the front desk of the Miami Hyatt Regency as Carlos Martinez, providing his corporate American Express Platinum card in the name of Seltaeb, S.A. to guarantee payment.

Anyone checking out Seltaeb S.A. would find that it was a corporation organized in Grand Cayman Island with one shareholder and one director, the Royal Toronto Trust 775408. The most experienced investigator could search forever and never locate a Seltaeb office, employee, ongoing business or hard asset. Nor would any sum of money influence the Royal Toronto Trust Co. to disclose who owned the beneficial interest in Trust 775408. At least for so long as its $15,000 annual management fees were paid and seven figure low interest paying deposits were kept on site. And since the trust company was authorized to automatically withdraw its fee every January 1, Carlos' secret account would remain intact forever.

Eager to get on with the business that brought him from Iraq to America, and for which Saddam Hussein had paid him 50 million Swiss francs, Carlos quickly showered and changed into a single breasted navy blue Armani suit, the only other dress clothes he carried. He folded a wash cloth in half and placed the sharp edge of a six inch hunting knife into its crease and carefully tucked the makeshift sheath into the backside of his belt. It wasn't that Carlos expected trouble today -- he just liked to be prepared for it.

Unable to fly with weapons, Carlos needed something besides his hands for protection. It was a $300 amenity, but Alberto Clemente obtained the knife for Carlos on short notice. Clemente could have easily procured a gun for Carlos as he requested, but there was no way he would put a semi-automatic weapon into the hands of one of the world's most deadly terrorists while he was a stowaway on *his* ship.

Carlos strolled out of the hotel and over the Brickell Bridge only yards away, stopping half way across to watch a racing boat thunder down the Miami River, before he continued on into the heart of the Miami banking district. Well dressed, the Chameleon blended in perfectly with the lunch crowd of bankers and lawyers walking along the palm tree lined, glitzy high-rise bordered Brickell Avenue.

Carlos entered the airy green marble lobby of the Barnett Tower and elevated to the 25th floor, where the Banco de Caracas rented half of the floor. The bank's primary purpose in Florida was to serve as a financial intermediary to funnel personal fortunes in and out of the U.S. for a wealthy South American population based in Miami. It also happened to be Carlos' bank because it was willing to turn a blind eye to facilitate certain transactions that ethical American bankers would shy away from. Often, the bank earned hefty fees for nothing more than opening and closing accounts, cashing checks and wiring funds around the world.

A young Latin receptionist with wavy long black hair greeted Carlos with a pleasant, if not suggestive red lipsticked smile. "May I help you, please?"

"Good afternoon. I have an appointment with Luis Ramirez," Carlos said, returning the most charming of smiles.

The woman provocatively leaned over her desk. "Your name sir?"

"Carlos Martinez. Seltaeb Computers."

"Yes Mr. Martinez. And would you care for a drink sir?"

"If you wouldn't mind, I'd like some Cafe Cubano."

"Certainly," the receptionist said, tossing her hair over her shoulder. She picked up a phone and made two short calls, before advising Carlos that Mr. Ramirez would be out shortly.

Five minutes later a portly, bald, late middle aged man, in a shiny light gray suit with a bold striped tie, appeared from a door behind the receptionist. He peered at Carlos over the top of his gold framed bifocals and walked up to him with an outstretched hand. "Mr. Martinez?"

"Yes sir," Carlos said, and they exchanged a firm grip.

"Sorry to keep you waiting. I'm Luis Ramirez. Please come with me."

Carlos dutifully walked in silence a half a step behind the banker down a long emerald green carpeted hall adorned with tastefully expensive modern art. They walked into a large corner office and yet another beautiful young woman followed them in, carrying a tray holding a white china coffee pot and the tiny matching cups appropriate only for the jolt packed Cafe Cubano. The instant she left and the door closed behind her, the banker turned around with a big toothy grin and enveloped Carlos in a suffocating hug, planting a kiss on each of his cheeks. Carlos returned the affection plus a rub on the shorter man's glossy head.

"Ilich. My God boy. What's it been? Four years?"

"A little longer than that, Uncle Luis."

Luis Javier Ramirez was a first cousin to Carlos' father, Jose. While the genealogy charts would never technically list Luis as an uncle, he'd held that title in Carlos' household for as long as they both could remember, and Ilich Ramirez Sanchez was Luis' favorite "nephew." They had limited contact since Carlos became famous in the early '70s, but there remained an unbreakable bond between the two men when they were together. Luis had become a U.S. citizen in 1977 and served as President of the Miami branch of Banco de Caracas since 1982. No one else was more trustworthy or better qualified to serve as Carlos' banker for the Americas and the Caribbean. Jacques Ruf had held that job for Europe until he'd gotten greedy. Luis Javier Ramirez would never get greedy, at least insofar as handling Carlos' account was concerned.

"Jesus Christ. I couldn't believe it when I heard from you a few days ago. You said you were calling from Caracas?"

"Yep."

"You're getting brave, maybe stupid. Coming in through the Miami Airport can't be very safe."

"I didn't fly in. Do you remember Alberto Clemente? The fat kid that lived down the block? He used to hang with Jaime, my brothers and me."

Luis scratched his cheek for a second. "You mean -- uh -- what was his name, Dogface?"

"That's him," Carlos laughed. "Well he's the captain of a freighter now. He slipped me in through the Port of Miami this morning. It was a breeze."

"Does he still look like a dog?" Uncle Luis asked, totally serious.

"Yeah, like a big fat fuckin' bulldog," Carlos said with a laugh. "He hasn't changed a bit."

"Good," Luis howled. "Speaking of your brothers, I talked to both Vladimir and Lenin recently. They tell me your parents are really fighting a lot now. If you call them it might help."

"Who fucking cares? They've been divorced for almost twenty years. They like to fight. Let them fight."

Luis slapped Carlos hard across the face. "You show some respect *por tu familia*. I don't care who you are, Mr. Bigshot. You don't talk that way about your parents around me. You understand?" Luis poked Carlos in the chest with his index finger.

Carlos hung his head in feigned embarrassment. "Yes. You're right. I'm sorry. I know Elba's in London. Where's Jose this month? I'll call them before I leave," Carlos lied.

"Caracas."

"Give me their numbers."

Luis moved around the side of his desk, sat down, thumbed through his rolodex and scratched out some numbers. "Here."

Carlos stuffed the slip of paper into his pants pocket and walked over to the floor to ceiling window. "You know, I always loved this view." He gazed out over the downtown Miami skyline to the Northeast, the broad expanse of the teal blue Biscayne Bay straight ahead to the East and Key Biscayne to the Southeast.

"I know. I've been in this office for years and the view's never gotten old." Luis moved next to Carlos and together they stared out over Miami.

A few seconds of silence was broken by Luis. "Hey, I'm hungry. Let me treat you to lunch. Wherever you want."

"Sounds good. How about that stone crab place on Miami Beach you took me to last time?"

"Well, almost wherever you want. That's Joes. They just closed for the summer. Where else?"

"Nowhere," Carlos said looking down in disappointment. "Never mind. I'm kind of in a hurry anyway. I'll just get something on the road."

"Whatever you want," Luis shrugged. "So you want to see what I've got for you?"

Carlos nodded, gulped down his Cafe Cubano in two swigs, and poured himself another.

Luis walked over to a grey metal file cabinet in the corner, unlocked it and withdrew a briefcase from the second drawer. He moved back to the desk, sat down, manipulated the combination on the attaché, opened it and spun it around for Carlos to inspect the contents.

Carlos nodded again, this time with a huge smile. "Excellent!" He opened his own briefcase and not bothering to count, started transferring mixed stacks of U.S. bills from one case to the other. There was no need to verify the amount.

"A hundred grand from the Seltaeb account," Luis said. "And here's the checkbook. Just got it an hour ago," he said, handing him a blue vinyl rectangular item that he pulled from his suitcoat. "You sure you won't need more than 25 checks?"

"Probably won't need more than five. But don't be surprised if some very large checks come through. What's my balance anyway?"

"A little more than $16 million. That $10 million score that came in from Ruf's bank in Geneva was impressive. What'd you do to earn that?"

Even though Luis was one of the few people in the world who could safely ask Carlos *anything* about his business, this time Carlos just gave him a blank stare as his answer.

"Sorry," Luis said, raising his eyebrows in guilt.

"You heard Ruf killed himself, didn't you?" Carlos announced.

"No!" Luis replied, his head jerking back and his eyes opening wide.

"Yeah, he shot himself in the head sitting on the crapper in some disco in Geneva."

"Strange way to go."

"That's life," Carlos shrugged. "Strange guy," he added, sipping his second cup of Cafe Cubano.

Luis thought he understood the message of what really transpired with Jacques Ruf, but decided against trying to confirm it.

Carlos then removed a Beretta from his uncle's briefcase. He pointed it out the window looking down the sights. "Nicely done," Carlos said, closely inspecting the gun. "I didn't think you'd be able to score this for me."

"It wasn't easy. Getting this kind of cash together was a pain. Getting the gun was nearly impossible," Luis said.

"Impossible? You're president of a bank," Carlos said. "You can do anything."

"Florida has a three-day waiting period for buying handguns. That one's hot, and finding you a Beretta was really tough. I could only get one extra clip," Luis said.

"How resourceful," Carlos deadpanned as he put the clip into the side pocket of his suit jacket. "But this is what's really excellent," Carlos said, holding up a shoulder holster.

"Good," Luis beamed, pleased by his success. "So can you come for dinner tonight? It'd be a great surprise for Aunt Maria. She'd love to see you."

"No thanks. Actually, I'm leaving town early this evening," Carlos lied.

"Where to?"

"New Orleans," Carlos lied again.

"Will you stop by again on your way out of the country?"

"I would if I was leaving out of Miami. I'm meeting another ship that's gonna take me through the Gulf and back to Caracas."

"Well, at least I got to see you for fifteen minutes. That's better than nothing," Luis frowned.

"There's one more thing I want you to do Uncle Luis."

"Anything."

"Take a million out of the Seltaeb account for you and Aunt Maria. I've never given you a cent for anything over the years. You deserve it. And I can't spend it all anyway."

"You're familia. I couldn't," Luis exclaimed. "No way!"

"Do it," Carlos instructed, nodding his head with a grin.

"Thank you. I accept," Luis said, stunned. Luis had almost $2 million stashed away, but this was a windfall he never expected.

"Is there anything else I can do for you then Ilich?" Luis offered.

"Yeah. Lose twenty pounds. You got fat," Carlos said, teasingly sticking out his stomach.

Both men laughed and hugged. Carlos turned away from Luis and locked his briefcase. "I'm sorry but I've got to go. I've got a couple of other stops before I leave town."

"I'm not surprised. I'll see you out."

Minutes later, Carlos had hailed a cab and gave the driver instructions to Sixth and Alton Road on Miami Beach. The cabby chatted away, but Carlos ignored him and stared out the window at the Biscayne Bay, bounded by the Port of Miami on one side of the MacArthur Causeway and mansions lining Star Island on the other.

The cab pulled up to Sunburst Motors, a neon lit turquoise and pink stucco converted gas station with circular columns out front that fit the motif of the local art deco architecture perfectly. Carlos dropped a $20 bill on the front seat and told the driver to keep the change.

He hadn't been looking at the inventory of used cars any more than fifteen seconds before a skinny little slightly balding man with a wispy mustache stepped out of the front door.

"Iggy Rodriquez here," the man said in a high pitched, heavily accented squeal with an outstretched hand. "Whatever you want, we got. If we don't got it, we'll get it. If we can't get it, nobody can. What's your name?"

Carlos looked down at the man's hand for about five seconds before begrudgingly putting out his to match the greeting. He answered, "Eduardo Lopez."

"Eduardo Lopez! I got a cousin named Eduardo Lopez."

"Yeah right," Carlos thought. "Really. That's great. So does that mean I get a deal?"

"Nobody beats my deals. Especially cousins, cousin. By the way, nice suit. You're a lawyer right? You gotta be a lawyer dressed like this."

"No, I'm a general contractor," he answered.

"Oh, that's big money too. So tell me, what are you looking for?"

"Something pretty new. It doesn't have to be fancy. Just make sure its got a good engine."

"I got a '92 Regal in great shape. Beautiful car. Best one on the lot. See it over there Eddie? The white one."

"It's Eduardo," Carlos said sharply.

"Eduardo. Right. Sorry."

"How much?"

"For a cousin. Twelve five. A special deal for today only."

"I'm not gonna try and bargain you down on the price. Just be sure it's in great shape."

"Absofuckinlutely. Scuse my language."

"Iggy, here's a hypothetical situation for you. I drive the car a few thousand miles in the next week and it breaks down. I get unnecessary aggravation. This makes me unhappy. I come back here and cut out your heart. And have fun doing it. Do you understand what I'm getting at?"

"I see your point. And I don't know a good cardiologist. I tell you what. Forget that car. Let's take a look at the blue Cutlass over there. It's not quite as nice as the Regal, but it'll run like a virgin pony. It's in perfect shape."

"You're sure?" Carlos said, pointing his index finger almost into Iggy's nose.

"Positive. Let's go for a test drive."

"Don't need to. Do I?"

"No, no, no. The car works," Iggy excitedly said.

"Okay. How much?"

"Eleven three."

"Too much. I'll give you ten."

"What do you mean, ten?" Iggy whined. "You just said you wouldn't try and bargain me down."

"That was for the Regal. I'll give you ten grand for the Cutlass. Cash. Right now."

"Eduardo, don't fuck with me. Nobody pays cash. Nobody has cash."

"I got cash. My car was stolen. This is the insurance proceeds. I got judgments against me all over the place. Every time I put money in the bank I get garnished. I lose the money. Now I keep cash. Ten thousand. Take it or leave it."

"You want mats. Mats are a hundred bucks extra."

Carlos' death stare into Iggy's eyes was his response.

"Okay, okay. Ten grand. Can't use the mats without the car anyway. Consider them a gift for a cousin. Let's go cool down inside and do the paperwork." Iggy tried to put his arm around Carlos' shoulder, but Carlos knocked it away.

An hour later Carlos pulled up to the Hyatt, and parked the Cutlass across the street from the hotel to avoid registering a car to his room. Ilich Ramirez Sanchez would leave little evidence that could trace the itinerary and whereabouts of Carlos Martinez, Eduardo Lopez, or any other alias used by Carlos during this most sensitive of business trips.

He spent a couple of hours strolling down Flagler Street, the retail district of downtown Miami, and that evening confined himself to his hotel room. He dragged himself out of bed early the next morning and pushed himself through a vigorous workout in the hotel's gym. Upon returning to his room, and with *The Today Show* blasting on the television in the background, he pushed himself even harder through his high intensity martial arts drills. After a cold shower and full room service breakfast, Carlos checked out. He paid the bill in cash, personally ripping up into tiny pieces the Seltaeb charge card slip the desk clerk returned to him.

Minutes later, Carlos was behind the wheel of his Cutlass, heading up the ramp of Interstate 95. An open map of Florida lay on the seat next to him, and a few others for the South Atlantic states highlighted with yellow fluorescent marker were folded neatly on the floor for review when needed.

Carlos calculated that the 1100 mile drive to Washington D.C. would take about 19 hours. The flat tropical Florida scenery changed to rolling hills and greenery the further north he drove. Carlos thought out his itinerary over and over as the minutes turned into hours. Staying out of trouble was important, so his cruise control was set at 59 miles per hour.

Staying fresh was important too, for Carlos knew that although he had a limited amount of time in the American Capitol to accomplish his agenda, doing it right was critical. He could push himself and drive the distance in one sitting, but he wouldn't. The maps showed Walterboro, South Carolina to be the halfway point up I-95, and ten hours on the road seemed like enough for one day. While the accommodations at the Days Inn a 100 yards off the expressway were sparse, they were adequate enough for one night's discreet lodging.

A second solid day's drive completed through the scenic countryside of South Carolina, North Carolina and Virginia put Carlos into the heart of metropolitan Washington D.C. right at the end of the evening rush hour traffic. He navigated through the web of the Capitol Beltway of 95 to 495 to 295 to 395, through the D.C. streets to the J.W. Marriott, the hotel chain's flagship stop where Carlos Martinez had a suite waiting for him.

When Carlos finally reached his room, he kicked off his shoes and fell onto a couch. He lay back contemplating the hard part of his mission that waited ahead and the potential impact its success would have on world history.

TWENTY-ONE

Washington, D.C.

"HOW YA' DOIN'? I'm Jay Friedman," the fortyish tall and balding man said through beaver like cheeks while shaking Carlos' hand vigorously. He glanced at his Cartier watch noting that it was 9:15, an important point for billing purposes.

In that instant, just by noticing his gold watch, gold cuff links and Gucci shoes, Carlos sized up the man as all flash, which was just what he needed. He handed the lawyer a Seltaeb business card listing both a false Mexico City and Miami address and phone number. Carlos always carried business cards with him in various languages with numerous addresses and types of businesses. Something for every occasion and people always bought it. "Nice to meet you Mr. Friedman. I'm Carlos Martinez. Seltaeb Exports. Thank you for seeing me on such short notice."

"No problem. Please, have a seat." Friedman gestured to a chair opposite his desk. "Would you like some coffee?"

"No thanks."

"Okay. Before we get started, how'd you get my name?"

"Another lawyer I've used in the past, Dobson Hill recommended you," Carlos said. He had expected the question and was prepared to lay out a whole fabricated story if he had to.

"Never heard of him."

"Really? Dobbie's supposed to be one of the top lawyers in New York. He's heard of you. He said you're known for your expertise in international trade and corporate law. I hear you get things done that nobody else can do. That's what I need, and I want the best." Although Carlos spoke impeccable English, now he employed a thick Spanish accent to enhance his Latin cover.

"I don't know if I'm the best," the lawyer said, believing that he was, "but I imagine I can help you. Let me tell you about my firm."

"Okay," Carlos said, pushing his nonprescription wire framed glasses up the bridge of his nose. "Although I'm sure you're good. And what a location," he added enthusiastically, looking out of the lawyer's Union Station office window at the Capitol dome only a couple of blocks away.

"I need to be close to Capitol Hill as well as city government. Anyway, Friedman & Nadler was formed 15 years ago. You're right about our corporate and international specialty, but I also do some zoning and real estate work. Maybe that's how Mr. Hill knew of me. Doesn't matter, though. Whatever your business problem is, we can take care of it. Frankly, I'm best on the kind of matters where things have to get done behind the scenes, especially with the government. I've been around a long time and I know a lot of people. I especially know how the wheel is greased, if you know what I mean. And to be sure, I'm not cheap."

"I didn't expect you would be. I've never seen a cheap lawyer yet," Carlos said, telling the truth for the first and last time in the day.

"You get what you pay for," the lawyer confidently smiled.

"What is your fee structure?" Carlos asked, not really caring, but deciding to play the game.

"I charge $350 an hour plus an extra provision for results at the end of the matter. Since we haven't done business together before it's a firm policy to have you sign a fee agreement. You'll also have to pay a retainer to be applied against future fees."

"How much?" Carlos asked, fingering his fake thick salt and

pepper mustache that nicely matched his freshly greased back black hair, and painted grey temples.

"That depends on the job. Tell me about your business and why you've come to see me." Friedman grabbed a legal pad and his Mont Blanc pen to start taking notes.

"My company exports fruits, flowers and other commodities and perishables from Mexico, South America and the Caribbean. So far, our business has focused on the Florida and Texas markets."

"Other commodities?" Friedman questioned, raising his eyebrows.

"It's not what you think," Carlos emphatically answered as if he were insulted. "No drugs. Occasionally we dabble in oil. Usually from Mexico or Venezuela."

"Yeah, sure," Friedman thought. "In this country, everybody's entitled to a lawyer and I believe in the sanctity of the attorney-client privilege. You can speak freely with me."

"Yeah, sure," Carlos thought. "Good. But my business is clean. Because we're principally located out of Mexico, we see many new trade opportunities developing in America due to the NAFTA treaty. We'd like you to form an offshore corporation as a subsidiary to Scltacb's existing business, solely to handle transactions and goods along the East Coast. It's a natural expansion route from Florida. We also need a bank account opened up in Washington right away so I can make an initial deposit to purchase a letter of credit and to get some offices opened up here.

"Fine. But why an offshore corporation? If you already have a Florida or Texas corporation for your existing business in the U.S., you may not need to incur the cost that follows with a separate new corporation," Friedman said.

"It's a good thought, but my business partners and I don't want our names in the public records, and frankly, we don't want to pay any more U.S. taxes. We made that mistake once. We won't do it again. Attorney-client privilege, right?"

Friedman smiled. "You still may not be able to completely avoid that."

"We have excellent creative accountants," Carlos said. "How long will it take for you to set this up?"

"Consider it done."

"How's that?"

Friedman clasped his hands behind his head and replied, "You're not the first client to come in needing something like this. I have what I call shelf companies. They're already formed and registered in the Netherland Antilles with me listed as the sole director. All I have to do is change the director to yourself, or for a small fee, I can remain the director." Friedman placed his index finger to his temple to further the suggestion. "If anonymity is important to you, it may be worthwhile for me to stay on as the director."

Carlos pretended to contemplate his options for about ten seconds. "Yes. I think that's what we'd prefer. Can we also keep the official corporate address at your firm?"

"That's what most of my clients do. I have a standard set of agreements that I'll need you to sign, and then you're pretty much in business. Let's see what companies I've got on the shelf," Friedman said. He pivoted his leather chair to his computer and typed about fifteen keystrokes, while data almost simultaneously blipped onto his screen. "Hmmm. Things have been busy. I've only got one company left right now. *Pluto Associates, N.A.* If you don't like the name, we can do a name change by fax."

"No, Pluto's fine as long as we can do business in some derivative of Seltaeb."

"Sure. Of course. Are your offices going to be in D.C., Maryland or Virginia?"

"Washington. Definitely."

"Because technically we need to register the dba, the tradename of the company, with the Business Services Division of the Department of Consumer and Regulatory Affairs. I know the Chief Clerk there pretty well. Laura Michaels. A real party girl. I can push this right through. What's the tradename going to be?" Friedman asked, pen to paper.

"I'll let you know. There's a few possibilities. Right now, let's just keep everything in Pluto."

"No problem."

"Maybe I should keep the Pluto name permanently? Make it harder for the IRS to trace," Carlos asked pensively.

"Keep Pluto," Friedman advised.

"Did you say you can also open a bank account for us?"

"Yes. You may have noticed that Washington Federal has a branch in the lobby of our building."

"I saw."

"I open accounts for clients with them all the time. I even keep a stock of their signature cards and corporate resolution forms here. They do whatever I ask."

"We'll need a checking account."

Friedman pushed a button on his telephone and after a high pitched beep, a woman's voice promptly responded, "Yes, Mr. Friedman."

"Anne. Please bring me in a blank checking account signature card for Washington Federal. Then type up one of their corporate resolutions with today's date for Pluto Associates, N.A. listing me as the sole director. Also xerox a copy of the corporate charter."

"Yes sir," the voice politely responded.

"I take it you're a fisherman," Carlos said, having observed a six foot blue sailfish plastered as a trophy on the wall behind the lawyer's chair.

"Yeah. I've got a condo in Palm Beach. I try to get down there as much as I can during the winter, although I caught that thing in the Keys."

A moment later, a frumpy woman with dyed red hair, wearing reading glasses and a flower print dress, knocked once and entered the office. "Excuse me," she smiled at both men. "Here's the signature cards, sir." A second later she was gone.

Friedman scribbled some information on the index sized cards and then asked, "Who's going to be authorized to sign on the account?"

"Just me and one of my partners," Carlos replied.

"Is he here in town to sign the card?"

"No. But I can sign his name. I've been doing it for years. That's not a problem is it?" Carlos said in a serious tone.

"Nah, I don't care," Friedman smiled. "Just don't tell the bank. They'll never know because they clear 100,000 checks a day. Print and sign both names on the two lines at the bottom," he added handing the card to Carlos. "In fact, here's a blue and black pen. Do one in each."

Carlos took his time writing out the information, and when he had finished, the two signatures were dramatically different.

Friedman examined the card for a moment and announced, "Barak Hamas. I hope to meet Mr. Hamas soon."

"He'll be coming here sometime in the next few months. I presume we'll have a continuing need for counsel?" Carlos said, knowing he was pushing the perfect button with Friedman.

"I'm sure," the lawyer smiled, pleased with the prospect of picking up yet another long term client. "The bank will require an initial deposit to get the account opened. How do you want to handle that, Mr. Martinez?"

"Can I give you a check from the company's Florida operating account?"

"Of course."

"Good. Who do I make it payable to?" Carlos asked, retrieving from inside his briefcase the Seltaeb checkbook that Uncle Luis gave him at Banco de Caracas.

"Pluto. Sign it on the back and write, "For deposit only."

Carlos paused in thought for a moment before writing the check and giving it to Friedman.

Friedman leaned back in his chair and delicately held the ends of the check between his thumbs and forefingers at eye level. "$1.25 million," he whistled. "This'll get your account open. Jesus!"

"We're a high volume business. We know in the beginning we have to spend money to make money. You can also see now why we like to keep the taxing authorities out of our affairs and our names sheltered."

"I understand."

"Let me pay you for this while my checkbook's out. How much?" Friedman rubbed his chin for a few seconds trying to think up the maximum he could get away with charging. "$4000. That'll include everything related to forming Pluto, serving as director for a year, and opening the bank account. I also need another $6000 as a retainer."

The average corporate lawyer might charge less than half of that, but also wouldn't be as pliable. Carlos' friends had found him the right counsel, and the fact was, the price was irrelevant.

"I'll make you a deal. Here's $5000 for your services which includes a bonus. In a couple of days I'll give you a local address where you can send future bills, and we'll pay you within ten days of receipt. Is that fair?"

"That's fine."

"Your partner isn't handling any of my work on this is he?"

"She. No. In fact, she doesn't even know you're here."

Carlos was exceptionally pleased with the answer. "Then what do you think -- should I just make the check payable to you?" he winked, already starting to write it to Jay Friedman.

"That'll work," Friedman said, unable to hide his glee.

"I'm staying at the Marriott. Send my copy of the papers and the bank account information over there. Also tell the bank we may keep the account in a Seltaeb name. I'll let you know for sure."

"It'll all be there before five, Mr. Martinez."

"You know. I'm sorry. I should have said this before. Call me Carlos."

"Great. And call me Jay."

"Good. I'm looking forward to working with you Jay," Carlos said, standing up and extending his hand. "I'll call you in a day or so."

CARLOS CHECKED THE ADDRESS on the ripped out newspaper advertisement in his hand with the number etched into the double glass door ten feet away. He looked up and shielded his eyes from the sun, surveying every angle of the mansard roof on the ten story red brick apartment building. Carlos estimated that the structure was about 50 years old. It looked to be well kept although with an outdated electrical and ventilation system, evidenced by the boxy air conditioners that dangled from almost every window.

He walked back twenty yards to the corner of 23rd and H Street and cased every building in sight in all directions. Two young women strolled past him, and he interrupted their animated conversation.

"Excuse me, ladies. I'm sort of turned around. Could you please help me for a moment?" he asked in a proper English accent. Notwithstanding Carlos' extensive world travels, this was his first trip to Washington, and he really had lost his sense of direction.

"Sure, what are you looking for, mister?" a long-legged ponytailed blonde asked through a thick Boston accent.

"George Washington University's that way. Right?" Carlos asked, pointing to his right.

"Yeah," responded the girl. "In fact, even some of those buildings across the street belong to the school."

"Okay, good. So that means the Kennedy Center is that way?" Carlos asked, pointing in the other direction.

"Right. You see those tall buildings three blocks up?"

"Uh huh."

"That's part of the Watergate complex. The Kennedy Center is next door," she said, pointing slightly over to the southwest.

"Great. That's what I thought. Thanks a lot."

"Anytime," the blonde answered. Both girls smiled pleasantly, and walked away.

Carlos spent the next half hour walking around the block and the alley behind the apartment building, inspecting every square foot of its surroundings to assure that the external perimeter of the structure posed no security threat, and provided emergency ingress and egress. Arriving back at the front, he read the small notice posted on the double glass doors advising of apartments for rent and entered the building. He picked out "Building Manager" from the typeset directory and dialed *100 on the security phone. After providing a few second explanation that he was seeking to rent a unit, a harsh buzzer sounded, inviting him in. Carlos pushed the heavy door open and noticed the manager's office only a few feet up past the entry on the black and white spotted granite floor.

Almost simultaneous with his knock on the door a low raspy voice bellowed, "C'mon in."

Carlos pushed the door open to find an immensely fat man sitting behind a cheap veneer desk, a double cheeseburger in one hand, a pickle in the other, with bulging cheeks stuffed full. His jaws worked furiously to process the food, as he announced with a full mouth, "Stan Lefkowicz. What da ya need? An apartment?"

"Two."

"You mind if I eat while we talk?"

"No. Please, go right ahead."

"Good, cause I wasn't gonna stop anyway," he belched. "Nobody ever rents two apartments at once. What's your story?"

"My name's Carlos Martinez. My company is expanding into the D.C. area," Carlos said, handing the man a business card. "We'll have people coming and going here all the time. We've found it's chcaper to have a couple of nice apartments available than it is to pay for hotel rooms."

Lefkowicz stared at the card for a few seconds. "Yeah, I guess that makes sense. So Mr. Martinez, what kind of business is Seltaeb in?"

"Exports. Everything from computers to food. I'm sure you heard of us. Last week we brokered that jet engine deal between the Pentagon and Peru?" Carlos said, enjoying his own ability to convincingly lie.

"Oh yeahhh," Lefkowicz said, nodding his head as if he really knew what Carlos was talking about. "That was you guys, huh?" He dipped the cheeseburger in a gob of ketchup and stuffed another quarter of it into his mouth. "Have a seat," he mumbled. "I've got one, two and three bedrooms available."

"One bedrooms. Both of them."

"Okay. Let's see what I got," he said, digging a black binder out from a mess of junk scattered on a credenza behind him. "There's one on the fourth floor, two on the seventh, and one on the ninth."

"I like the idea of both units being on the same floor. Can I see the two that are together?"

"Right now?" Lefkowicz asked packing his mouth full again.

"If possible. I'm sorry to inconvenience you, but I really have a busy schedule, and I'm only in town for a couple of days. If I like them, I can sign the lease today," Carlos said politely but firmly. The fact was, Carlos had studied the street map of Washington and had scoured the rental ads to find the perfect location for his apartments. This was it.

"Okay," Lefkowicz moaned, resigned that he was going to have to finish his other double cheeseburger later. He grabbed his bag of french fries off the desk before he hoisted himself up. "Lets go," he said, lighting up a cigarette.

They quickly arrived at the identical seventh floor apartments which were three doors down from each other, both looking out over the heavy traffic tree lined H Street. They were clean and relatively modern, but unfurnished.

"I'll take these, but I need you to help me get furniture."

"What do I look like, the Yellow Pages?"

Carlos sighed and gave him a look of frustration. "Will you please take care of it for me?"

"Are you nuts? You think I'm your personal shopper? I manage this building. That's it."

"I'll pay you."

"If you paid me a thousand dollars I wouldn't do it."

Carlos pulled a wad of cash out of his pocket, counted out ten $100 bills, held them out, and said, "I told you I'm very busy. Here's a thousand dollars. Please take care of it."

The obese landlord ran his hand through his thinning curly hair and crinkled his large proboscis. "Well I do have some time after work today, but how am I gonna pay for the furniture, and who's gonna sign the contract?"

"We'll work that out downstairs. Now listen, I want both of

these units. Furnish them nicely. T.V., V.C.R. The works."

"It'll take three days for me to do a credit check."

Carlos peeled off another $100 and handed it to Lefkowicz. "I guarantee my credit is better than anyone in this building. You can call my bank in Miami from downstairs."

"We'll call from my office," Lefkowicz said, stuffing the bills into his pants pocket. "And I bet the furniture company can get the place filled in a day or so."

"Perfect."

Carlos and Lefkowicz spent the next 15 minutes calling Uncle Luis Ramirez at the Banco de Caracas to confirm Seltaeb's impeccable credit, and then Jane's Joint about renting furniture. Carlos watched in disgust as Lefkowicz wolfed down the second burger while talking on the phone.

"Mr. Martinez, the rent is $1600 a month plus electricity. I'll need payment of the first and last month, plus an extra month as a security deposit."

"No problem. That's $9600," Carlos said, calculating the amount due as quickly as he was speaking. "Obviously you'll take my check."

"Sure. The lease is our standard form and it's not negotiable. No changes," he said sternly.

"Give them to me. I'll sign them right now. They have to be in Seltaeb's name though. Not mine."

"How do you stay in business? Are you always this easy?" Lefkowicz blurted out, half-joking and half-serious.

"I know what I want. I get things done," Carlos replied, sharply enunciating his words and providing an icy glare to match, having grown tired of this big bore.

Lefkowicz shuddered and quickly responded, "I didn't mean nothin' by that. Sorry." He put his hand up in an acknowledgment of guilt.

"No offense taken," Carlos said softly, though not changing his glare. "By the way, you'll help get phones set up in each apartment, won't you?"

"Well I've never done that for any other tenant, but I guess under the circumstances it won't be a problem."

"Thank you. Then this is for your trouble," Carlos said, tossing him another hundred.

"You don't have to dó that," Lefkowicz said insincerely.

"No. I insist. I know this is an inconvenience for you."

"Well if you insist," Lefkowicz smiled, quickly snatching the bill off the desk.

"Now I'm sorry but you must excuse me," Carlos said. "I'm late for another appointment. I'll call you later and come back for the keys. Make sure you take care of the furniture and phone today or I'll be very unhappy."

As soon as Carlos closed the door behind him, Lefkowicz pulled out and recounted the most amazing tip he was ever paid, laughing out loud about what a sucker that Mr. Martinez was.

"MR. JOBLOVE. I have not traveled thousands of miles to hear you tell me that your university will not accept my son as a student," Carlos said through a thick but impeccable Middle Eastern English accent. "I simply cannot accept this," he added, pounding his fist into his hand to drive home the point.

"I'm sorry Mr. Hamas, but the application deadline for the fall semester closed over two months ago. There's nothing I can do. Classes start in only seven weeks."

"I don't care. Look at his training," Carlos said, pointing at the perfectly forged college transcript sitting on the man's desk. "Straight A's in every math and science course at Oxford. The International Summer Science Institute at the University of Paris. Barak could attend any engineering school in the world but he wants to come here. I know his qualifications are better than 98 percent of your existing students," Carlos said, his voice pitched with intensity.

"Yes, Mr. Hamas. You're right. But that's not the point. George Washington University has strict admissions rules that we must apply uniformly so as to be fair to everyone. I'd like to help but my hands are tied."

"Aren't you the director of admissions?" Carlos asked in exasperation.

Joblove ran his hands through his thick curly brown hair and took a deep breath, letting it out slowly. "O.K. I'll do this. I'll accept his application right now for the spring semester. Barak can start classes in January. Perhaps he could travel around the U.S. for a few months until then."

"I am not sending him to the United States to go on a holiday. I presume you saw on Barak's application that King Fahd is our cousin. The royal family of Saudi Arabia has important plans for Barak, and we do not wish them delayed. I would really hope we do not have to turn this into a diplomatic affair." Carlos straightened the white silk gutra around his face that he unfolded from his briefcase and slipped on in the bathroom of the university building just moments before his meeting.

"Sir, I'm very sorry. If some superior authority tells me to change the rules, I will. Until that happens there's nothing I can do." The university bureaucrat took off his thick gold wire framed glasses and polished the lenses on his shirt sleeve.

"Okay. How much do you want?"

"What do you mean how much do I want?" Joblove asked indignantly, knowing exactly what Carlos meant.

Joblove's response told Carlos the man wasn't bribable. Since he had occasionally run into scrupulous men before, he knew how to weasel out of the situation. "I'll pay you. In Saudi Arabia when conventional methods of negotiation fail, sometimes money takes care of the problem. Is that not acceptable?" Carlos said in a convincingly innocent tone.

"Sir. This is not Saudi Arabia. This is the United States. We do not do business here that way. I do not do business that way."

"Stupid naive asshole," Carlos thought. "I certainly did not mean to offend you, Mr. Joblove. Please accept my humble apology. This is how we always do things back home." Carlos bowed his head for a few seconds as a gesture of respect, and looked back up. "There has to be some acceptable way we can solve this though."

"I don't think so."

In feigned thought, Carlos stroked his fake goatee.

"What about a properly documented gift to the University? Would that do it? Perhaps $50,000." Carlos believed that in almost all circumstances the influence of money would ultimately prevail to persuade action in what might otherwise be an unsuccessful proposition.

Joblove rubbed his chin contemplating the revised offer, and it was certainly an intriguing one. "I've never heard of anyone being admitted to GW under circumstances like this before, but I suppose either the dean of students or the president of the university could authorize a special admission."

"Especially considering Barak's qualifications," Carlos chimed in.

"Yes, that would help justify a positive decision."

"Can we call someone right now? I think we should make it sound like it was your idea, so you get the credit," Carlos said politely. He extracted his checkbook from the inside pocket of his suit jacket and waved it at Joblove for emphasis.

Joblove smiled and answered, "Yes, let's see here..." He reached into his top desk drawer and thumbed through a small address book. He tapped out a phone number and stared down at the phone console while it rang.

"Ms. Cherry. This is Andy Joblove. How are you?"..... "Good thank you. Is President Matthews available? I have to talk to him right now. Can you interrupt him? It'll only take 30 seconds, but it's really important..... Great. Thanks." Joblove looked up and said to Carlos, "The president of the university is in a meeting, but I think he'll take my call."

A second later his eyes shifted back to the phone. "Michael. Sorry to interrupt you. I've got a Mr. Ismael Hamas, a cousin to the King of Saudi Arabia sitting in front of me right now. He has an extremely talented son, really an incredible record, who wants to start in the engineering school in August. I understand he's also been admitted to MIT." Joblove winked at Carlos. "I explained to him the admissions deadline policy, but apparently his son really has his heart set on coming here. ...Yes, over MIT. ... I had an idea. Mr. Hamas would fund a $50,000 endowment *today* if we could make an exception on the admissions policy. Is that possible?"

Joblove grinned and he gave a thumbs up gesture to Carlos. "Yes. Of course," he said into the receiver. "No, I don't know if housing is an issue, but if it is, we'll do what we can.... Very good.... Yes... Right. Talk to you later."

As Joblove was hanging up the receiver, Carlos handed him a signed $50,000 check on the Seltaeb account with the payee's name left blank. "Make it payable to whomever you think appropriate."

"Thank you very much, Mr. Hamas. President Matthews was very pleased," Joblove smiled. "Barak needs to be here for registration and orientation by August 14th. Does he need student housing? I was told to assist you with that if he does."

"No. We're devout Moslems. Barak has special dietary needs so I'll have to find him an apartment off campus where he can cook for himself."

"Yes. That makes sense," Joblove said. "But I should warn you. It's possible that not all of his credits from Oxford will transfer over. The Dean of the School of Engineering will have to determine that. He may lose a few courses, but he should still be pretty close to junior eligibility."

"Excellent," Carlos said. "We're presuming that he'll be here for at least two years anyway. I'm sure he'll be pleased that he just gets to come here."

"Good. And we're pleased to have him. We'll have a packet of information for Barak to help get him started, plus a supplemental information sheet he'll have to complete for university records. Shall I mail it to you?"

"No. Can I pick it up in the next day or so?" Carlos asked.

"How about tomorrow?" Joblove responded. "We'll have his admission letter typed up by then also." Joblove rose from his chair and escorted Carlos out of his office.

"That'll be fine," Carlos said.

"And if you need anything else, just let me know. And again, thank you for your generous donation."

The men shook hands.

"Yes. Of course," Carlos said, pleased with yet another success.

"IMPRESSIVE BUILDING," Carlos thought, admiring the front facade of the massive bronze columned, white Italian marbled Kennedy Center. He checked his Rolex: 3:40 p.m. He still had about twenty more minutes to kill before his final meeting of the day, so he decided to take another walk along the north side of the immaculately landscaped building to the willow lined backside of the music hall that bordered the Potomac River. After a couple of minutes of mindlessly gazing out over the water at Georgetown Park a fair distance away, and the Watergate Plaza just next door, he decided to get on with the business at hand.

He entered the Hall of States with its bold red carpeted lobby and large flags of each of the fifty United States hanging from the ceiling almost 100 feet up. He followed the sign leading him to a glass double door with *The John F. Kennedy Center for the Performing Arts Executive Offices* emblazoned in gold paint. He had barely pulled the door open into the reception room, before a middle aged woman greeted him from behind a desk.

"May I help you sir?"

"I'm here to see Dorothy Khouri," Carlos said in his Mideastern English accent. For this visit Carlos left the headdress in his briefcase, but still wore the fake goatee.

"You must be Mr. Hamas. Dottie's been expecting you. Please have a seat and I'll ring her," the receptionist said, motioning to two chairs.

A minute later a sixtyish silver haired woman with regal posture stepped out of an elevator directly next to Carlos' chair. "Mr. Hamas. I'm so pleased to meet you," the woman said, sizing up Carlos from head to toe with one quick glance through her bifocals. "I'm Dottie Khouri, Director of Administration."

"Ismael Hamas," Carlos said in a low soft voice. He gently took the woman's hand and gracefully bowed at the waist. "I am very pleased to meet you also."

The woman blushed. "You're the only one of our Benefactors I've never met. You must really be a friend of the arts to donate $500,000. I can't tell you how much our Board of Trustees appreciates your contribution and how important it is to our long term financial security. Thank you."

Carlos politely took her hand again and smiled, but instantly had second thoughts that maybe he dramatically overpaid to close this transaction. But then again, this was a deal he had to close and the check was already written. "I've talked to King Fahd about building a palace like this in Saudi Arabia, but it will never happen. Did you know we still don't even have movie theaters in Saudi Arabia?"

The woman shook her head no and asked, "Mr. Hamas, if you don't mind me asking, why did you select the Kennedy Center for your generosity?"

Carlos laughed. "Good question. My son Barak will be starting engineering school at George Washington University in just a few weeks. I want him to experience culture. To see there is another world out there. He will learn the importance of the arts through my contribution to your center."

"How lovely," Mrs. Khouri said. "Would you like a tour of the building?"

"I was hoping you would ask."

Carlos followed Dottie Khouri out of the administrative offices, and down the long corridor of the Hall of States, which led into the two football field long Grand Foyer in the back of the building. "The Eisenhower Theater is here on the end, and the Opera House is the theater right over there in the middle."

"This is quite a room," Carlos said marvelling at the sheer size of the Grand Foyer, accented by 18 spectacular Orrefors crystal chandeliers donated to the Kennedy Center by Sweden. Over 40 countries gifted some elaborate item from their culture or natural resources to commemorate the building and its namesake. "I imagine you could throw quite an impressive party in here," he added.

"We can, but we don't do it often. Most of our parties are upstairs in the Roof Terrace Restaurant, although every year we host a reception in the Grand Foyer for the Kennedy Center Honors Gala which tributes very special American performers for lifetime achievement. And then of course, we also hold the National Ball here every four years."

"The what?" Carlos said.

"The National Ball. Every four years on the evening of a new Presidential Inauguration, we hold the National Ball here."

"I don't understand."

"All of the heads of the federal and state government join the president here for a very large and prestigious party. We have one band set up down here at this end, and another one all the way down at the other end near the Hall of Nations."

"Ohhh, I see. The president comes here to celebrate his new term." Carlos said.

"Of course, but actually he and vice president only show up for about an hour because they have so many other inaugural balls to attend. You see the middle doors over there leading into the Opera House?"

"Yes."

"Well the president actually comes through the theater to make his entrance into the Grand Foyer, and usually stays on a special platform up there, which we bring out just for this one party."

"That must really be a security nightmare."

"Like you can't imagine. And it's not just because of the president and the vice president. Every one of the senators, governors, Supreme Court Justices, cabinet members and so on who attend the party all need protection. You can't get into the building, no matter who you are without going through a metal detector and showing a special pass. It's complicated."

"I'm sure it is. But it sounds like you've done it so much, you know how to plan for it."

"Of course, and the plans don't need to change that much from inauguration to inauguration, which makes it easier."

Having heard all he needed about the inaugural festivities, Carlos changed the topic. "So what kind of work will you have for Barak when he gets here?" he asked.

"Excuse me?" Dottie Khouri asked, totally caught by surprise.

"Work. What will Barak's job be?"

"Uh...well...uh..."

"You do have a job for Barak don't you Mrs. Khouri?"

"Of course. But we haven't placed him into a position yet," she said, wondering who was supposed to have taken care of this. After all, she couldn't afford to have a public relations problem with the Kennedy Center's single largest individual donor this year -- especially one related to the King of Saudi Arabia. "Tell me what are Barak's talents?"

"He's very mechanically inclined. He can fix anything. That's why he's studying engineering."

"Then I'm sure we can find a spot for him in the maintenance department. There's always something that needs repair in this building," Khouri offered.

"That would be terrific. But you know what I would really appreciate?"

"*I can't wait,*" she thought. "No. Please tell me," she responded, trying to placate Mr. Hamas.

"I want Barak to see firsthand how the upper class of Western society conducts itself. It's much different here than in Saudi Arabia you know. Can you also arrange for Barak to work as a waiter at some of your special functions?"

Dottie placed both palms across her cheeks in surprise and thought. "Mr. Hamas. A totally independent company apart from the Kennedy Center operates the restaurants and catering here. But...uh...I'll do the best I can."

"The best you can? I would be very disappointed if you can't assist me with this minor accommodation. Very disappointed. On the other hand, I would be very pleased if you were able to take care of this for me. And I know how to express gratitude. You understand what I'm saying, don't you Mrs. Khouri?"

The Kennedy Center's major domo gritted her teeth and smiled as sincerely as she could. "Yes, Mr. Hamas, I think one way or another we can take care of this for you."

"Perfect," Carlos smiled back.

"When Barak arrives in Washington, have him come see me. I will personally take him under my wing, Mr. Hamas."

"Excellent." Carlos replied. He looked at his watch. "Mrs. Khouri, I'm sorry but I just realized how late it is. I'm supposed to meet our consulate general for an early dinner. Would you be kind enough to excuse me?"

"Of course. And anytime you're free, please come back and we'll finish your tour."

"Thank you so much," Carlos said, firmly shaking Dottie Khouri's hand. "I think you'll enjoy working with Barak. He's a hard worker and he won't give you any trouble."

"I'm sure he won't," she replied, relatively pleased Mr. Hamas had left without asking for anything more.

TWENTY-TWO

"WHO WAS NEXT?" the skinny bespectacled desk clerk asked in a high pitched squeal to the four men all dressed in suits crowding around the counter underneath the "BLUEPRINTS" sign at the City of Washington, D.C. Building and Zoning Department. The heart of operations for all real estate development in D.C. was divided by an eighty foot long counter that ran the length of the room, segregating workers, file cabinets and desks on one side, and a slew of impatient noisy people waiting in various lines on the other. The phone rang nonstop and the swinging double glass entry doors opened and closed almost continuously with people from all walks of life coming and going.

"I was next," a tall man with greasy black hair and wire framed glasses responded, sticking up an index finger for emphasis.

"Excuse me, sir. You're wrong," Carlos curtly insisted, glaring deep into the eyes of the man who claimed his rightful position. "I was next." Actually Carlos wasn't next. He was last.

"I'm sorry," the larger man said, backing off. "My mistake."

"No problem," Carlos responded with a polite smile.

Another man muttered "asshole" under his breath and he too suffered the chill of Carlos' death stare. The other men stepped out of the way as Carlos moved up to the counter.

"How can I help you sir?" the clerk asked.

Carlos looked down at the man's name badge and read it to himself, *"Alex Brookes."* "Mr. Brookes. You're the fourth person I'll have talked to in the department. I'm very frustrated." Carlos noticed that the other men were eavesdropping. "Can I step behind the counter?" Carlos asked, lifting his head in the direction of the other men. "This is sort of a private matter."

"Yes sir. Come right here through the gate," Brookes answered.

After the others were out of clear earshot, Carlos continued, speaking softly nevertheless. "I've been trying for over an hour to get copies of the full building plans to The Kennedy Center."

"Who are you?"

"Jordan. Nicholas Jordan. I'm an architect from Chicago. I'm designing a music hall similar to The Kennedy Center. Here's my card."

"You came all the way from Chicago to copy the plans to The Kennedy Center?"

"Yes. Of course."

"Well that sure was a waste of time and money." The clerk laughed and shook his head.

"What? What do you mean?" Carlos asked, shocked.

"That's a *federal* building. The Army Corps of Engineers maintains the plans for all federal buildings. The Department of Building and Zoning keeps full plans only for non-federal buildings in the District of Columbia."

"Well then, where is the Army Corps of Engineers located?"

"Beats me. Maybe at the Department of Interior. Or the Pentagon. Nobody's ever asked me for federal plans before. But I bet you'll need an FOI request also."

"A what?"

"A Freedom of Information Act Request. It's a formal request you make to the government to get copies of public documents and information."

"Oh." A pit in Carlos' stomach started to grow.

"Yeah. You better get a lawyer too," Alex Brookes said, crinkling his nose with a sniffle.

"I have one," Carlos said, already trying to think of a great lie to tell Jay Friedman about why he needed The Kennedy Center plans. This assignment would put to test the attorney's boasts about his ability to get things done in Washington.

"Hope he's connected, Mr. Jordan," Brookes added.

Carlos wanted to punch the twerp, but he restrained himself. "I don't understand. I called the department before I came here and was told that you had the plans to every building in Washington. I know you need them for building code purposes."

"Of course."

What do you mean, *"of course"*? You just said you don't have the plans here for federal buildings."

"Plans. Full plans. Blueprints. Nah. I don't have those."

"What *do* you have?" Carlos asked.

"Microfiche. But microfiche isn't the full plans. And you can't copy microfiche here."

"Are you saying you have the microfiche of the full building plans for The Kennedy Center?"

"Of course."

"Why didn't you say so?" Carlos said sharply.

"You didn't ask for microfiche. You asked for plans. You specifically said, *"full building plans."*

Carlos looked at Brookes harshly. In barely a whisper he said, "May I please see the microfiche for The Kennedy Center?"

"Certainly Mr. Jordan," Brookes said looking back down at the business card to refresh his memory as to his customer's name. "The microfiche machines are over there," Brookes pointed to the other side of the room. "You know how to work microfiche?"

Carlos didn't, but he'd figure it out. "Of course."

"Give me five minutes. I'll have to find it and bring it to you."

"Take your time," Carlos sarcastically replied.

Brookes' absence gave Carlos sufficient time to read the xeroxed instructions taped next to the machine to learn how the contraption worked. A few minutes later the clerk delivered a white 5" x 7" envelope to Carlos, who sat cross-legged tapping his fingernails on the table.

"You know you have to sign these out, don't you?"

"No, I didn't. But what do you want me to sign?"

"Nothing. I already signed for you."

"Then why did you tell me?" Carlos asked, exasperated by the moronic city worker.

"I wanted you to know. That's all."

"Let me make sure I understand," Carlos said fingering the envelope. "These are the microfiche to the full building plans for The Kennedy Center?"

"Yes sir. I thought I explained that. Is there anything else you need right now?" Brookes said, rolling his eyes at yet another one of the stupid people he had to deal with every day.

"No. I'm all set," Carlos responded, grateful that he was.

"Good. When you're all done, put the microfiche into the tray on the counter over by where that big fat man is standing," Brookes said loudly, pointing. Then he turned on his heels and walked away to help his next victim.

Carlos flicked on the machine and after manipulating the 3" x 5" mylar sheets under the focus glass a couple of times, he was able to confirm the name "Kennedy Center" on the miniaturized blueprints displayed on the screen in front of him. He looked around the room to make sure nobody was paying attention to him before placing the plastic sheets back into the envelope, and then into his briefcase. Feeling incredibly lucky he nonchalantly but briskly walked out the front door.

AN HOUR LATER CARLOS leaned against the ornate green Victorian style light pole across the street from the George Washington University administration building where Andy Joblove conducted business. He checked his watch: 11:48. His eyes were glued to the front door and would remain there until Joblove appeared, whenever that might be.

A few minutes after noon people started streaming out of the building. Increased lunch time automobile traffic and the volume of bodies exiting the doors required Carlos to quickly zero in on each face.

Finally, at 12:40, Joblove spun out of the revolving doors with a magazine tucked under his arm, and started heading east up Eye Street in the direction of the White House, only a few blocks away. There was no question that Joblove, obviously preoccupied, didn't spot Carlos. The assassin's eyes locked onto the back of his prey and he darted through moving traffic to catch up to him, though Carlos stayed 12 feet behind Joblove.

Conditions for attack on this very busy public street were excellent, as more people filled the sidewalk around them from neighboring buildings, providing the natural cover that would shield Carlos. He moved to the left of Joblove and inched up behind him by taking larger half steps one at a time. Placing his right hand inside his side suitcoat pocket, Carlos slipped a plastic cap off the hypodermic needle he had carefully set in his jacket early that morning. He manipulated the syringe to the middle of his hand, resting the short cold needle against his middle finger. When the weapon was properly positioned and shielded in his palm, Carlos lifted his cupped hand out of the pocket and dangled it at his side.

At the corner of Pennsylvania and 20th, Carlos saw his spot when the throng of about 15 people surrounding him and Joblove came to a forced halt at a red light. Carlos politely squeezed his way through the crowd until he was right up behind Joblove.

The moment the light turned to a green *"Walk,"* both men stepped off the curb. With a straight right arm that barely moved, Carlos jabbed the clenched needle into Joblove's left hamstring through his pant leg, instantly propelling 5 cc.'s of the deadly potassium chloride into Joblove's bloodstream. Simultaneous with the impact of the needle, Joblove yelped in surprised pain. It only took an instant for Carlos to give the injection, and his hand had already moved away by the time Joblove's arrived to rub out the sting from this mysterious sudden attack.

Joblove stood still in the middle of the street massaging his leg, without even attracting a single concerned glance from the stream of preoccupied people passing by. He also failed to notice the face of the well dressed man, Mr. Ismael Hamas, who was behind him and who also scooted right past. Not that he would have recognized him anyway since the bearded Arab that he met only days before bore little resemblance to the clean shaven, glass wearing Latin who just stabbed him.

Carlos kept walking at the same pace as before, leaving the rest of the crowd by turning off Pennsylvania, a block up at 18th Street. He strolled up the street and stopped at the next corner where he nonchalantly dropped the used syringe onto the street, sliding it down into the sewer grate with his foot.

Twenty-five minutes later, in the middle of a bite of his chicken salad sandwich, Andy Joblove clutched his chest and throat. Seconds later he was dead.

The killer drug had already dissipated into such minute traces that only the most sophisticated of medical tests would pick it up, and it was determined by the coroner that Andy Joblove died from a heart attack. And one potential witness who could identify Mr. Ismael Hamas, a Saudi Arabian millionaire who didn't exist, or Ilich Ramirez Sanchez, who did, was now permanently incapable of doing so.

FIVE MINUTES AFTER WALKING OUT of Canter's Deli carrying a hot corned beef sandwich on rye, Carlos walked into Stan Lefkowicz's office.

"Mr. Lefkowicz, how are you today?" Carlos said warmly, leaning over to shake the fat man's hand.

"You're late," he replied. "You said you'd be here at 12:30. It's 1:45. I told you I wanted to go out for lunch today."

"I know. You're right. I'm sorry. But here, I picked this up for you." Carlos handed Lefkowicz a brown bag with the sandwich.

"What's this?" the man asked, ripping the top of the bag open before peering inside, even though anyone with half a sense of smell could tell what Carlos was carrying.

"It's from Canter's Deli. I saw their menu on your desk the other day. I figured you liked the place."

"Yes master! I forgive you. Thanks," he said, grinning broadly while unwrapping the sandwich. After removing a side of cole slaw and a dill pickle from the bag he finally looked up at Carlos incredulously and asked, "No potato pancakes or fries?"

Carlos replied with a sullen grin and soft, "Sorry."

"Ahhh, no big deal I guess," Lefkowicz shrugged as he squeezed some mustard out of a packet on to the corned beef.

Just as the ravenous building manager was ready to attack the sandwich, Carlos interrupted him by tossing a $50 bill onto his desk. "Mr. Lefkowicz, I know it's not fair of me to ask you to do this, but I'm really in a hurry. Could you please show me the apartments right now and give me the keys so I can get out of here?"

"What the hell. What's another five minutes," Lefkowicz said. "Let's go. Oh yeah, I got something for you." Lefkowicz dug through a drawer in his desk and handed Carlos a sealed envelope, adding, "There's copies of both leases for you, and two sets of keys for each unit. The gold keys are for the front door to the building, and the silver keys are marked for each apartment."

"You got the furniture delivered, right?"

"It came this morning. Looks great, too, if I say so myself."

"Both apartments?"

"Of course."

"Did you get the phones set up?"

"Yeah, yeah, yeah," Lefkowicz said.

"Great," Carlos said, enthusiastically patting Lefkowicz on the back.

Lefkowicz escorted Carlos upstairs to inspect how the furniture in apartments 704 and 710 turned out, and Carlos continued to praise the landlord's work. They exchanged small talk until they returned to the office, where Carlos took off his suit jacket, lay it across the guest chair and rolled up his dress shirt sleeves. Lefkowicz plopped himself down and promptly started chewing his sandwich again.

"Mr. Lefkowicz, do you have a pencil?"

"Sure," he replied through a full mouth. He reached into his desk drawer and handed one to Carlos.

"Thanks." Carlos then pulled the Beretta provided by Uncle Luis from his briefcase and pointed it at Lefkowicz.

Lefkowicz chuckled and chewed. "What is this, a fuckin' robbery? You gonna take back all the money you gave me?"

"Not quite."

"Then what's the gun for? You gonna shoot me?"

"No. Too messy. Besides, if I put a bullet in your head, the police will know you were murdered. When they find you dead I want them to think it was an accident."

At that moment Lefkowicz comprehended the seriousness of the situation. He turned white and slumped in his chair. Carlos walked around the desk and placed the cold metal gun barrel square onto Lefkowicz's temple.

"Eat."

"What?"

"I said eat. Put as much of that sandwich in your mouth as you can."

Terrified, Lefkowicz looked up at Carlos.

"Do it," Carlos commanded, clicking back the hammer on his Berretta.

Lefkowicz instantly began shoving the sandwich into his mouth. After Lefkowicz's jaws were stuffed full, Carlos demanded that he open his mouth. The moment he did, Carlos slipped his left arm in a vice lock around the man's forehead, and with his right hand, forcefully pushed the corned beef and bread deep down into Lefkowicz's throat with the pencil. Lefkowicz violently started kicking and bucking while choking, but Carlos' hold was far too powerful for Lefkowicz to escape. Devilish sounds escaped from his throat as the pencil vanished almost all the way down his rapidly closing windpipe.

Carlos extracted the makeshift plunger and relaxed his grip while Lefkowicz thrashed, frantically gasping for even the tiniest wisps of air. With a quick snap of the side of his hand, Carlos punched Lefkowicz hard in the soft spot at the back base of the skull, rendering him instantly unconscious. He grabbed Lefkowicz by his thinning curly hair and yanked his head back, pinching the man's nostrils shut, and lodging his palm under his mouth, closing it. Despite his comatose state, Lefkowicz gurgled and shook. As vomit slowly started seeping out of Lefkowicz's mouth, Carlos leaned the man back in his chair so that gravity forced the vile substance back down his throat. Lefkowicz's involuntarily movements became slower and slower until finally his body fell completely limp. Carlos grabbed Lefkowicz's wrist and confirmed the lack of a pulse.

Carlos pushed the corpse forward and the man's head smacked onto the desk. Vomit and food spilled out of his mouth all over the spread out mess of papers. Satisfied that Stan Lefkowicz was positioned perfectly for someone to conclude the poor man choked to death on a corned beef sandwich, Carlos quickly straightened himself up. Without looking back at his second victim of the day, he left the office.

ONCE CARLOS SPOTTED Jay Friedman's secretary in the lobby of the Union Station office, he immediately headed for the pay phones in an alcove near the bank entrance. He walked close to the wall with his face down to avoid having his likeness recorded on the security cameras overhead. It took five rings before someone picked up the line that Carlos dialed.

"Friedman & Nadler," a man answered.

"Mr. Friedman, please," Carlos said through a thick Spanish accent, already recognizing his lawyer's voice.

"Speaking."

"Mr. Friedman. This is Carlos Martinez."

"Mr. Martinez. How ya' doin'?" Friedman asked jovially.

"I'm O.K. Listen, I know it's late, but I wanted to come see you in a few minutes. Are you going to be there for a while?"

"I can wait. Where are you?"

"The Marriott. Just finishing a meeting. I have a bunch of xeroxing to do. Can I bring it by for your secretary to copy for me?"

"My staff has left for the day, but you can bring it here and we'll do it for you first thing in the morning and then have it delivered to you."

"That's fine," Carlos said, smiling into the receiver as one possible obstacle...potential witnesses...was now not a concern. "You know, I'm leaving again in a couple days. I was hoping to meet your partner before then."

"I'm sorry Mr. Martinez, but Mrs. Nadler is out of town on business today. She'll be back Wednesday. You can meet her then if you're still here."

"Okay. How about if I get there within a half an hour?"

"I'll be waiting."

Three minutes later Carlos slipped into the Friedman & Nadler reception room, opening and closing the front door silently, before turning the lock behind him. He kept a handkerchief webbed in his hand preventing fingerprints from being left behind. Having learned the layout of the office from his previous visit, Carlos glided from office to office confirming the absence of others.

"Good evening," Carlos announced, standing in Friedman's doorway.

Visibly startled, the lawyer suspiciously declared, "I thought you were at the Marriott?"

"I lied," Carlos shrugged. "Listen, I only have a couple of minutes. Tell me -- those papers you sent me confirmed everything's all set up for Pluto Associates, right?"

"Yes. That's what my cover letter said," Friedman replied frowning. "Mr. Martinez, what's going on here?"

"Nothing. I thought I'd take you to dinner. Did you call your wife to tell her I was coming up?"

"No."

"Anybody else?"

"No, goddammit. What's this all about?"

"I have to show you these papers," Carlos said, advancing towards Friedman, withdrawing the envelope from his inside jacket pocket given to him hours earlier by Stan Lefkowicz.

The lawyer apprehensively leaned back in his chair as Carlos approached him. Within a split second of coming into striking distance, Carlos violently chopped into Friedman's throat breaking his esophagus. He followed up with another powerful and perfectly placed blow square into the man's nose, driving fragments of bone into his brain. The unconscious man slumped to his side, blood flowing from his mouth and disfigured nose.

Carlos removed lightweight white cotton gloves from his briefcase, carried all the way from Iraq in anticipation that they might be needed somewhere where his fingerprints could not be found. He slipped them on and quickly leafed through the mass of papers on and around Friedman's desk and through his drawers to assure no Seltaeb or Pluto documents were lying around. He then walked quickly over to Anne's desk to make the same check, careful not to disrupt the order of a single scrap of paper.

Carlos then pulled Friedman's diamond ring off his little finger, unfastened his gold watch, took his wallet from his back pocket and stuck them all into his own pants pocket. As quickly and quietly as possible, Carlos ransacked Friedman's office, pushing files, papers and the telephone off the desk onto the floor, turning over the guest chairs, knocking over a six foot tall plant, and spilling a cup of coffee onto the carpet. Looking at Friedman, Carlos realized he appeared too neat to have just been involved in a death rumble. He full fist punched Friedman under the right eye, untucked his shirt, ripped his shirt pocket and yanked his necktie to the side.

Next he picked up a Mont Blanc pen and in kindergarten quality printing, he scratched in big letters onto a legal pad, *"BLACK TALL GOLD TOOTH."* He then dragged Friedman to the side of his desk, turned over his desk chair, and loosely wrapped the pen into the man's right hand, placing the legal pad next to the still body. Finally, Carlos withdrew his Beretta from his shoulder holster, stuck it in Friedman's belly and pulled the trigger.

The gun echoed louder than Carlos liked, which was why he had saved the shooting for last. Within twenty seconds, though, he was calmly standing at the elevator holding his briefcase with his suitcoat buttoned, looking like a typical businessman. Only nine minutes after entering Friedman's office, Carlos disappeared out of the building without drawing the slightest suspicious look from anyone.

Once he hit the street and started walking in the direction of the Capitol, Carlos removed the stolen jewelry from his pocket. Keeping his arm straight he imperceptibly dropped the ring on to the sidewalk, and about 50 paces up, he did the same with the watch. Eventually people would chance upon and keep the items, being totally without the means to find their true owner. A block up on Massachusetts Avenue, Carlos stopped at a newsstand and bought a magazine, dumping it in the public trash only a few doors up. But the real utility was in the small brown bag obtained in the purchase, now used to wrap Friedman's wallet which ended up in the garbage at a McDonalds in the next block.

At about 9:30 p.m. the Union Station building cleaning service discovered the beaten and bullet ridden corpse of Jay Friedman. The police investigators on the scene concluded that the prominent attorney was the victim of an armed robbery and had died in a violent struggle with his assailant.

Friedman's dying declaration, an unfinished scribbled note on a legal pad prompted a D.C. police computer search of all African American men over six feet tall with a gold tooth. The press would sensationalize this brutal murder, even though the police search was for the wrong man.

Just as he planned, no Washington cop would hunt down Ilich Ramirez Sanchez. To celebrate a successful day of murder, Carlos went back to his hotel to order a steak dinner from room service. Naturally, he asked that the meat be served rare. Bloody.

TWENTY-THREE

W ALKING BRISKLY, Carlos turned the corner at the bottom of the hill where Wisconsin Street ended at K Street, at the south end of the commercial district in Georgetown. The traffic on the Whitehurst Freeway roared directly overhead, and the rushing water of the Georgetown Channel flowed by thirty yards across the street.

The setting was perfect, just as Carlos thought it would be. A sequence of shadowy buildings and highway girders hid a dark and empty K Street. When he'd scouted out the location during the weekend there had still been sizable crowds partying and meandering about the streets of Georgetown at 11:30 p.m. But this was a weeknight. People had work the next day and it was already late.

He pushed open the windowed and wooden door of Chadwicks Bar & Restaurant and was hit by a jet stream of cold air, a welcome relief from the disgustingly humid Washington summer night. He was pleased to find the place empty, for the most part. Halfway down the 20 foot oak bar, a bartender was hunched over, engrossed in serious pick up conversation with a coed easily 15 years his junior. On the other side of the establishment, two longhaired throwbacks to the 60's sat at a table laughing away over nonsense that

263

could only be funny after the fifth beer. Nobody bothered to look up at Carlos as he cased the joint. The second level appeared empty, but to be sure, Carlos walked upstairs to confirm the absence of others.

Back downstairs, the dim lights reflected practically no glare off the brown brick interior walls and low ceiling. Three divided booths hid in the shadows underneath the steps in the back, perfect for private conversations. Carlos sat down in the last booth facing out towards the front door, providing a full view of the room.

A stringy haired waitress appeared at Carlos' table from a back room adjacent to the bar to take his drink order. Even though he really didn't feel like having a cocktail, he ordered a beer to avoid looking conspicuous just sitting in an empty saloon late at night without something in front of him. The waitress was back with a bottle in 30 seconds and, after collecting her three bucks, she disappeared again.

Finally left along, Carlos checked his Rolex. It was 11:36 -- nine minutes before his guest was due to arrive. When Carlos called the meeting only 40 minutes earlier, his instructions were unequivocal -- if the man wasn't there by 11:50, Carlos would leave. The schedule had to be precise to assure security. Carlos calculated the man had just enough time to get dressed and drive to Chadwicks, hopefully hitting the green lights. There was not enough time to place a full security team at the checkpoint as might be desired, although Carlos recognized the call for a Code I National Security Alert could be made from a car phone during the drive. But under the circumstances, he doubted it would be.

Precisely at 11:47 p.m., a tall thin man with graying temples and thick glasses stepped through the front door. Without moving his head, his eyes fully scanned the bar. Carlos leaned out of the booth and signaled with an extended index finger, quickly catching the man's attention.

No sooner had the man sat down giving Carlos an uncertain stare, showing lack of recognition, and no handshake or other physical or verbal greeting, than the cocktail waitress reappeared.

"Just water please."

"I heard you didn't drink," Carlos said.

"You heard right." The man then leaned over about a foot from Carlos' face. Sharply enunciating his words he said, "Who the fuck do you think you are calling me at home and insisting on this meeting? This better be damn good or I'll have your balls cut off. Operation Quinn has been closed for years."

"You don't know who I am?" Carlos asked in perfect English. The man shook his head no.

"You don't know who I am?" Carlos repeated, this time in Russian.

Again the man shook his head, but this time his attention was seized having heard the distinct communist language.

Carlos repeated the identical question over twice more, first in Spanish, then in Arabic. Then he sat back and took a swig of beer, his expression smug.

For almost 30 seconds Brendan Richter, the longtime director of the CIA, sat staring deep into his inquisitor's eyes before he put his right hand across his mouth in shock. "Oh my God," he mumbled slowly. "It's you -- Sanchez -- Carlos."

"Yes. I believe we've never formally met, Mr. Richter. It's about time after all these years," Carlos said, extending his hand. Richter reluctantly took it and Carlos squeezed hard, finally letting go when the cocktail waitress dropped off Richter's water.

"How did you get my private number?" Richter asked.

Carlos just rolled his eyes, snorted a laugh, and shook his head in response. Richter realized he wasn't going to get an answer, nor was he really surprised that Carlos obtained it.

"I gave you instructions. How do I know you don't have an entourage waiting outside?" Carlos asked.

"I don't. That's not how I work."

"Sure," Carlos replied, knowing better, but believing tonight Richter was probably telling the truth because of the sensitivity of potential issues raised by Carlos simply uttering the phrase *Operation Quinn* on the phone. "You wearing a bug?"

"No. Search me if you want," Richter said, not meaning it.
"I will."

"You're crazy for being seen with me."

"The same could be said of you. But frankly Richter, I don't believe no one's outside covering you and that you're not wearing a bug. I'd just as soon not be your sitting duck in this death trap."

"Like I said, I'm here alone. But you can bet I'd prefer to not be seen with you either," Richter agreed.

"Don't worry, nobody knows what the *infamous Carlos* looks like," Carlos said truthfully. And besides, tonight The Chameleon was wearing both phony sideburns and a mustache, thick black horn rimmed glasses, a rubber mole on his left cheek and his hair parted far over to the side, all amounting to a never before used disguise. For all Richter knew, this was how Carlos now looked everyday, since it was well known throughout intelligence circles that he regularly underwent plastic surgery to change his appearance.

Carlos abruptly rose from the bench and announced, "Follow me. I know where we can go." He headed straight out the front door, leaving the CIA Director with no choice but to follow if he wished to continue the dialogue.

Carlos walked directly across the street towards the Potomac, and Richter quickly caught up to him. Prior to entering Chadwicks, Carlos had observed that there were four cars parked in the lot adjacent to the water. Now there were five.

"Where'd you park?" Carlos asked.

"Over there. As you instructed," Richter gestured to his right. "If you want, we can take a drive in my car. It's secure."

"For who?" Carlos shot back. "We'll have all the privacy we need over there." Carlos pointed to an open spot behind some bushes a few yards up, right on the bank of the river. The light from the full moon was all the light there was, and the reflection of the black and white ripples on the water formed a hypnotic, almost hallucinogenic pattern.

When they reached a secluded gravel jogging path Carlos surprised Richter by quickly frisking him. With the sophistication of listening devices, Carlos couldn't be sure Richter wasn't wearing a body bug, but if so, it wasn't anything noticeable. He did find a semi-automatic pistol lodged in a shoulder holster.

"Take the gun out slowly, remove the clip and put it in your pants pocket," Carlos instructed, not wanting to touch the weapon himself and leave fingerprints for Richter's records.

"Fuck you. If you're going to kill me, then just get it over with. But I don't think you're stupid enough to do that, and I don't think that's why you wanted to meet with me."

"It's true that if I wanted you dead, you would be already. But you should know my profile. I wouldn't hesitate to kill you if the reason or just the mood suited me. So do it!"

Deciding it wasn't worth the risk, especially since he knew Carlos could disarm him anyway, Richter followed instructions and put the clip in his pocket. For above all things, Carlos was the most cold blooded of assassins.

"Interesting view here, isn't it?" Carlos said.

"Yeah, that's the Kennedy Center across the water," Richter solicitously answered, pointing to his left. "And that's Virginia over there," he added, now pointing to his right at the lighted high rise office and residential towers that dotted the landscape of Rosslyn. "But you didn't call me here for a geography lesson."

Carlos smiled. "Your reports a couple of weeks ago on the Israel-Jordan peace talks were very instructive. Absolutely first rate," Carlos said.

"That's what you pay me for," Richter replied. "I'll also tell you we've just heard Saddam is thinking about making another move on Kuwait. Pass this on to him. If he does try it, this time we'll finish the job. And frankly, we'd rather not. We're better off with him in power than one of those lunatic fundamentalists."

"Can you get me a memo on that? Like the one you faxed a couple of years ago when Tate ordered the hit on Hussein after you bungled that Marine raid on his compound? That got me a lot of mileage."

"Sure. But there's always a price."

"No professional discount?" Carlos asked with a half grin, not really expecting an answer. "And how come that order was never carried out?"

"Tate put it on hold when our State Department analysts said Hussein's possible successors were less predictable than that madman."

"Good move," Carlos replied.

"So Carlos, you're right. It is kind of amazing we've never actually met before. It's okay if I call you Carlos isn't it?" Richter asked sarcastically.

"Since we've done so much business together over the years, I'll honor you and say yes," Carlos retorted, equally sarcastic.

"Well *Carlos*, it's clear you don't have anything on Operation Quinn. I figure that means since you're here, you got my message. But somehow I didn't get the $5 million from you yet, and that really aggravates me. I'm at the stage of my life where I just don't want aggravation. You know what I mean?"

It was seldom necessary to have to repeat things twice for Carlos. "Richter, the problem I have is that it really wasn't made clear why I should pay you a cent more than I already have over all these years," Carlos replied, his lips drawing tight and his eyes narrowing as his blood pressure started to surge. "Explain it to me. I want to hear it in your words." The terrorist stood toe to toe with and glared at the CIA director.

Richter lit a cigarette and blew the smoke in Carlos' face. "I'll put it to you straight you slimy shit. We've been searching for way too long to catch the jerk off who blew up the U.N. in Geneva. It's pretty amazing that we haven't gotten anywhere on the case, and nobody seems to have a clue about who did it. You know what that tells me?"

"That the CIA is as incompetent as ever."

Richter scowled in hatred at his enemy, yet sometime business associate. "It means it was you."

"You think so, huh?" Although Carlos appeared nonplussed by the accusation, his heart raced.

"Only a handful of terrorists could have pulled off that job. Only one person could have kept it quiet. Only one person would have *wanted* to keep it quiet. Somebody with a lot to lose if he got caught. See, the short list of suspects we looked at would all have motives for publicizing their work. But not you, because it would mess up your own safe haven deal with Iraq." For emphasis, Richter jabbed his index finger into the chest of his smaller adversary.

"Of course you have no proof." Carlos smacked Richter's hand away.

"Who the fuck needs proof! I can manufacture proof. You should know that. I just want confirmation and $5 million to keep it quiet."

Carlos' eyes narrowed, he took a deep angry breath and simply said, "Fuck -- you."

"Doesn't matter," Richter shrugged. "Either give me $5 million and I nail somebody else for it, or don't, and I fabricate all sorts of evidence against you. It's your choice. Of course, if I announce it was you, then Saddam won't be able to shelter you any longer. There'll be too much pressure on him and he wants those U.N. sanctions lifted. You tell me. Who's he gonna take care of? Himself or you? I'd say within a week you'll have no place to go. Five million's a bargain," Richter laughed, clearly pleased with himself.

"What you're really suggesting is that either I should expect to be arrested somewhere or more likely killed," Carlos concluded, the heat in his voice rising.

"Not at all," Richter drawled out with a sarcastic smile.

"I'm not stupid. This isn't even a real shakedown. It has nothing to do with Geneva. It concerns the PLO and Israel peace process. Saddam and I have been major obstacles. You take me out and discredit him a little more, but not enough to lose him, because now you can control Saddam, but you can't control me. So whether I give you $5 million or not, I have to die. And the peace stays on track."

"Carlos, I don't want to kill you," Richter lied, unconvincingly. "I've used you on jobs before and I'd use you again. We've both made a lot of money off each other," he said, finally telling the truth.

"I've never worked for you. You've worked for me."

"Believe what you want," Richter replied.

"Your story is bullshit. If there was even a touch of legitimacy to it you wouldn't still be busting Norman Richards' balls about finding out who trashed the U.N."

"So you found out about him." Richter shrugged, clearly unconcerned.

"You *are* stupid. How could you possibly think I wouldn't?"

"And you my friend are a relic. A fool. Your time has passed," Richter scoffed.

"On the contrary. The older I get, the better I get."

"Yeah, right. That's why you're stuck working for Saddam Hussein."

"It's great money. I'll work for whoever pays me."

"That's why you can afford to give me the $5 million. Think of it as if you're buying a license." Richter paused for a long moment, shook his head and opened his eyes wide. "What are you really doing here? You didn't come to Washington just to talk about this. You could have obtained all the information you wanted from me through our normal channels."

Carlos remained silent, and even through the dim light Richter could see the dark expression of hate and anger peaking on Carlos' face. "You're here on a job, aren't you?" Richter realized.

Carlos' continued silence was a full affirmation.

"We had a deal that you were supposed to stay out of the U.S., and in return I'd leave you alone and sell you information. I can't overlook this."

"If you were going to leave me alone, then why the extortion and what's all this shit with Norman Richards?"

"Your concern over Mr. Richards only confirms your involvement in the U.N. job," Richter said. "You overstepped the boundaries of decency on that one, Carlos."

"Who the fuck are you to talk about decency? But you've got to admit, it was a great piece of work. A masterpiece."

"You killed hundreds. That was inexcusable. You'll have to pay."

"False. When are assholes like you gonna wake up and realize that only men like me can bring about change? That's why you're so scared of me and why every government in existence has paid me to do its bidding."

"Not anymore. Your days are over and you know it."

"You're so stupid," Carlos said spitefully. "My masterpiece has been painted. You just haven't seen it yet. But you will." He made a low wicked laugh.

Richter gave Carlos a quick look of curiosity and said, "The only thing in your future is your immediate death."

"I should just kill you," Carlos said in a matter of fact tone.

"An unarmed man? You're so brave," Richter said, extending his arms open wide and smiling. "But as pissed off as you are right now, buddy boy, even you know better than to fuck with the director of the CIA."

Carlos stood perfectly still except for his heaving chest, his black eyes staring right into Richters.

"Now listen up. I'm going to do you one last favor," Richter said. "This will be our last communication. Ever. After today we have no more business. Frankly, if I brought you in or killed you right now I would be a hero. A world hero. But you know what? I don't want the aggravation of having to explain what the hell I was doing with you in the first place. Even if I win, I lose. I'm giving you 24 hours to leave the country. If you're still here in a day, anything can happen. And if I don't get my money in three days, you're dead. I'll find you myself if I have to. Now go. Get out of my sight."

Carlos brushed his hands through his hair, his mind flying in a thousand directions. His outrage was so deep he was shaking, almost hyperventilating. The night was pitch black and muddled, yet everything seemed so clear. There was only one answer. One solution to a problem he knew he could never escape from; the infinite power of the U.S. government that could be used against him.

Carlos exhaled deeply, turned around and with his back to Richter said, "You made a big mistake fucking with me Richter."

At the same time, he slipped his right hand inside his jacket, and in a flash turned around and pumped two shots from his Beretta directly into Richter's head from close range, blowing off a good portion of his skull. Carlos stood above the dead man watching a large pool of blood immediately flood the area around his feet. He then kicked him in what was left of his face, spit on the corpse and said, "You piece of shit. Never fuck with me! Never!"

Carlos grabbed Richter by the feet and dragged him five feet to the retaining wall. Trying to be careful so as not to get blood on himself, Carlos pulled and pushed the corpse over the ledge and into the water where the current slowly swirled around and enveloped the face down body, carrying it upstream until it washed aground an hour later at Potomac Park near the Tidal Basin.

Carlos returned to the Marriott where he checked out past midnight, claiming some sort of family emergency. He drove south to Florida, stopping only in out of the way spots and politely minding his own business. Two days later and right on schedule he met Albert Clemente in Miami and smuggled himself out of the country, before the nationwide hunt for the killer of the director of the CIA could get its man.

TWENTY-FOUR

HEADLINES WORLDWIDE CELEBRATED the surprising arrest of the notorious terrorist "Carlos the Jackal" in the Sudan, and his immediate extradition to Paris where he would be jailed for the 1975 murder of two French Secret Service agents. No government, including the French, stepped forward to offer any details about what had led to the unexpected capture of Ilich Ramirez Sanchez. Not a single newspaper, magazine or television station worldwide displayed a current picture of the face of the Chameleon. Then somehow within days, the story mysteriously disappeared off of the wires.

The truth could not be told. The United States called in favors as it had never done before, not only to assure Carlos was found and brought to swift justice, but to make sure America's motivation for instigating the arrest remained permanently publicly silent. If the truth was told, the unexplainable would have to be explained. And the repercussions could be so severe that the power structure of Washington could topple under the weight of the monstrous failings of its security apparatus.

Carlos never realized that when he brutally murdered CIA Director Brendan Richter, that he left behind the damning evidence that would be sufficient enough in any court to obtain a conviction.

Unfortunately for the United States, that evidence could never be publicly released, and the country was led to believe Richter was just another victim of random violent crime. So while Carlos would get away with that murder, he would now be called to pay for the others he had committed over the years.

Carlos' first mistake was violating his cardinal precept: Rule Number One. Discipline. He lost it. Completely. For his intent behind seeking the clandestine meeting with Richter was not to kill him, but merely to confront the American spy chief over his $5 million extortion demand. To be sure, Carlos had his own proof of the director's multi-million dollar profit from the Columbian cocaine trade, which he knew would stop Richter from proceeding with his bold threats. Carlos just never got around to sharing his knowledge with Richter. He lost control instead; he was undisciplined.

Carlos' second mistake was a violation of Rule Number Two - Know Your Enemy. Prior to the meeting, Carlos anticipated that one way or the other, as director of the CIA, Richter would have some means in place to cover his tracks for the night, especially considering the unusually suspicious manner in which the meeting was called. Carlos guessed correctly that Richter had come alone to Chadwicks. But despite his cursory pat down of Richter across the street in the park, he guessed wrong about and didn't find Richter wearing a wire.

Carlos should not have been expected to find the stickpin sized microphone hidden in Richter's suitcoat lapel. But once he shot Richter, he should have been smart enough to grab the victim's car keys and search his BMW. Basic cleanup. If he had, he would have found the sound activated tape recorder in the glove compartment that chronicled the entire sordid conversation between Carlos and Richter. Matters such as Richter's admission of selling state secrets to Carlos, Richter's extortion over Carlos' destruction of the U.N. and the terrorist's admission of the crime, and the actual gunshots extinguishing Richter's life could have remained permanently silent, and Richter's death would have been shrouded in mystery. Carlos could have gotten away with yet another murder.

Instead, the FBI located Richter's car the next day and the National Security Council heard the telltale tape, Carlos' fate was sealed. And seven weeks later in the Sudan it was delivered. His arrest was supposed to be the end of the line for Carlos. But what the French and U.S. authorities did not know and would not learn is that it wasn't. Ilich Ramirez Sanchez' most spectacular act of terrorism; his plan for the destruction of the U.S. government was already in place and could not be stopped. Even with him behind bars.

TWENTY-FIVE

"I'M SORRY SIR. I don't have an opinion on the issue."

"Wrong answer, Mr. Hamas. This may be an elective course but if you want to stay in it, I expect you to participate in our discussions." The professor scowled and pointed a sharp index finger at his student.

"I've answered questions all semester, sir. I just haven't been in this country long enough to figure out which of the Bill of Rights is most important." Barak Hamas, known to his Iraqi family, friends and fellow terrorists as Khalil al-Sharif, tried to sound respectful and sincere, hoping he could manipulate his way out of the discussion.

"You've done all the assigned reading?" the professor asked, stroking his beard.

"Yes sir." The continuous reply of "sir" was something drummed into Khalil's head by both Carlos and the Republican Guardsmen training.

"Where are you from again, Mr. Hamas? Iran?"

"Saudi Arabia."

"They don't have a Bill of Rights there, do they Mr. Hamas?"

"No." Khalil didn't really know the answer, but he figured that the professor did, and that the answer was inherent in the question. "So if King Fahd told you to select one of the first ten U.S. amendments and it would become the law of the land in Saudi Arabia, what would you pick?"

Khalil rubbed his chin in thought for a few seconds before responding, "Well I guess if there's one thing that's always bothered me, it's that sometimes our people get accused of crimes and sent to jail without ever having a trial, much less a jury trial. Sixth Amendment, right?"

Simultaneous with the professor replying "yes," a female voice blurted out from the back of the room, "What kind of shallow thinking is that?"

"Miss Klein. Could you be any more rude about allowing Mr. Hamas the right to state his opinion?" the professor declared sarcastically.

"I absolutely could. And that's my point," the woman spit back. "How can anyone from a repressed society not think the most important right is the freedom of speech? It's the foundational right upon which all other freedoms are based. If the people in Saudi Arabia had the true right to stand up and express their beliefs, they'd be able to fight back against an injustice like not having the right to a jury trial."

Before Professor Wilhoit could interject, Khalil responded, "And what if I don't think it's healthy for the people to speak up and interfere with the way the government's run? You think it's good that every day you open the newspapers and see nothing but criticism of President Tate? Do you ever see a newspaper article or TV report that says, "The president did a good job today?" No. And I don't want it that way in my country."

"The president is accountable to the people who elect him. We're free to say what we feel," Debra countered.

"Let them say it in the next election. Isn't that what your so-called democracy is about," Khalil shot back.

"Oh yeah. It's real fair that you go to jail in your dictatorship simply for expressing a viewpoint," Debra sniped.

"Wait a second!" Professor Wilhoit yelled, raising his arms in the air. "Debra, Barak is entitled to his opinion. Don't you realize your attack on him is a form of repressing free speech?"

"I prefer to think of it as an exercise of my free speech."

"Touche," the professor smiled. "Okay, here's what we're going to do, because we only have about two minutes left today. Next Tuesday we're going to have a classroom team debate. Mr. Speyer, you and Mr. Kwart both spoke in favor of due process. Be prepared to argue the Fourth Amendment. Ms. Klein and Mr. Hamas have demonstrated a level of mutual respect that should make them fine teammates. You two get together outside of class and fight it out over the First or Sixth Amendment. I don't care which one you pick, just try not to kill each other. After your presentations the class will vote on who wins. The winners get their grade raised a half a point at the end of the semester. That should motivate you. Understand?"

Debra Klein grunted, fell back in the chair, tossed her long brown wavy hair around her shoulder and crossed her arms.

"Ms. Klein's enthusiasm is noted," Wilhoit dryly added. "People, don't forget to check the syllabus. That's it for today."

Twenty some college students filtered out the door, the professor in their midst. Khalil closed his spiral notebook and slowly loaded it and a textbook into a briefcase. Almost all the other students carried backpacks.

"Can I buy you a cup of coffee?"

Khalil looked up to see a pair of sparkling blue eyes and perfectly straight bright white teeth smiling down at him. Khalil gave the woman a blank look.

"Look, since we're going to have to learn to like each other, we might as well go get some coffee."

"Nobody said we were going to have to like each other. We only have to work together."

"Good thing, because I don't like you already," she said.

"Then we're even. I don't have time for loud mouth opinionated snobs," Khalil replied, giving her a cold, Carlos-like stare.

The look disarmed her. "Wait, wait. Hold on. I don't even know you enough to dislike you. At least yet. Can I try again?"

Khalil's expression didn't change but Debra, apparently undaunted, stuck out her hand. "Call me Debra. I'll even buy you a donut with your coffee."

"You're not going to leave me alone until I say yes, are you?"

Her hand was still extended, but his three second glance at it caused her to drop it to her side.

"My dad always says I don't know what the word 'no' means."

"I'm not surprised. And please, call me *Mr. Hamas.*"

Debra's eyes widened but before she could say anything, Khalil continued, "That was a joke. You don't get it?"

Through a burst of laughter she said, "Maybe you're not the stiff I thought you were after all."

"No, I probably am. Barak Hamas. Nice to meet you." He finally put out his hand as a show of good manners. She grabbed it quickly and shook it vigorously.

"What's your major, Debra?" Khalil asked, not really knowing what next to say.

"Journalism. You know, communications."

"I understand why," he said blandly.

She didn't know if it was a compliment or an insult, so she simply asked, "What's yours?"

"Engineering."

"Ooooh. So what are you doing in an American Civics class?"

"My father thought it would be good for me to learn about your country." Khalil mixed the truth with a lie. Carlos had helped him pick his electives.

"What does Barak mean?"

"What do you care?" he rudely responded, trying to limit the intrusion into his privacy, his alias.

"You're right. I don't." She muttered *"jerk"* under her breath, now concluding his "communication" comment was meant derogatorily.

He shook his head. "If you must know, Barak was the name of the prophet Mohammed's horse that he rode when he ascended to heaven in the 7th Century from the al-Aqsa Mosque."

"Oh yeah. That's the mosque that's at the Dome of the Rock near the Western Wall in Jerusalem. It's one of Islam's holiest shrines."

"How did you know that?" Khalil asked, impressed.

"I read a lot. And I've been there. Different cultures interest me. You know Hamas is the militant wing of the PLO?"

"No? Really?" Khalil convincingly deadpanned. Actually, the young terrorist had put a lot of thought into selecting his permanent American alias. And Carlos and Saddam Hussein thought *Barak Hamas* was a brilliant choice.

They left Rome Hall and were greeted by a strong cool breeze. Debra stopped walking and pulled Khalil back by the arm. "Don't get mad, but where'd you learn to dress? You look like you just came off the ship." Khalil was wearing a white short sleeve dress shirt, straight black pants and tie shoes. He started to put on a navy blue polyester jacket, his thin blood chilled by the wind.

Khalil was flabbergasted. Women simply did not speak that way where he came from. "Don't you have any manners?"

"Not really." She smiled with a half tilt of her head that shifted her long hair off her shoulder.

"You think you look so great?" he chided.

"As a matter of fact, yes. This -- is the style." Debra emphatically waved her hands from head to toe. She was tall and thin, her athletic frame slightly hidden by an extra bulky black sweatshirt, loose fitting faded bluejeans and black hiking boots. Her father called them Nazi boots.

"Maybe I'm inexperienced," Khalil said, "but are you...what they say...hitting on me?"

"Are you kidding? My grandma would roll over in her grave."

"What?"

"You know. A nice Jewish girl like me with an Arab like you."

"You're Jewish?" Khalil said.

"With a name like Debra Klein? What did you think I was, Irish?"

"Actually I didn't think about it," Khalil replied. "How many Kleins do you think there are where I come from?"

"Good point," she conceded. "Does it bother you?"

"No, of course not," Khalil lied. He had been indoctrinated to believe Jews were evil. In fact, Israel's extinction was no doubt part of the operation for which Ahmed, Omar and he had trained so hard, and one of the underlying reasons for his existence in Washington. Still, there seemed to be something redeeming about this particular Jew -- not by any stretch of the imagination in a romantic sense, but certainly in the intellectual.

"Good. Then what are you doing on Friday afternoon? I'll take you shopping. You don't need to look like such a schlemiel."

"A *what?*" Khalil said, looking befuddled.

"A schlemiel...Never mind." She decided trying to explain it would only instigate yet another negative verbal exchange, and she probably shouldn't have even used the word.

"Why are you interested in what I wear, anyway?"

"Look at you," she said, scanning him from top to bottom. "Someone's got to be. I bet you don't have any friends here yet, do you."

She was right. And that's the way it was supposed to be according to the plan. But even if the conversation had adversarial undertones, Khalil enjoyed it, not having had anyone much to talk to the past two months since his arrival in D.C.

"I probably have more friends than you," he said.

Debra saw right through him. "Yeah right. You're such a liar. What are you afraid of?"

"Nothing. What are you talking about?"

"It's because I'm Jewish."

"You're crazy." He waved his hand as if dismissing the point.

"You're full of shit, Barak," Debra said, poking Khalil in the chest with a sharp red fingernail. She walked away from him, then turned and snapped, "You're no better than me and I'm no better than you. Don't you get it? Isn't that what they're trying to fix in the Mid East right now after 3000 years of fighting? No wonder your name is Hamas."

"You don't know what's going on over there," Khalil yelled.

"Oh, and you do?" Debra stopped and said.

"Yes. I do," Khalil responded, certain that he did.

"Then what are you afraid of? That whatever you think of Jews might be wrong? Just tell me the problem and I'll leave you alone." Debra stared Khalil down, her hands firmly planted on her hips.

"I don't have a problem," he replied meekly. What else could he say? Certainly not the truth.

"Really? Well then, now that that's settled are you one of those rich Arabs or one of those poor Arabs?"

Startled, Khalil responded truthfully, since he had basically an unlimited expense account, set up by the now dead lawyer Jay Friedman, and Carlos, before his untimely arrest. "I'm a rich Arab."

"Good, then you've got no excuse for looking like that. Maybe we'll even get you a real haircut," Debra said, alluding to Khalil's unshaped mop of curly hair. "Meet me in front of Mike Kelly's Friday at 3:00, and bring lots of money. You can buy me coffee and a donut then. And be prepared to discuss our assignment." Debra turned back around and quickly sped off, not giving Khalil a chance to say no.

Khalil stood there shaking his head, amazed and slightly amused by how cleverly Debra manipulated him. He thought Carlos would approve and tell him to try and fit into his surroundings.

KHALIL CHECKED the white-faced, gold and stainless steel Rolex gifted to him by Carlos only days after he returned from Washington in June. It was time. 11:48 p.m.

He opened his apartment door and barely sticking his head out, peeked down the hallway in both directions. It was empty, as expected. He stepped out into the open and slowly closed the door of #704 behind him, assuring that it would shut silently. He glided three doors down the hall to #710, slid a key in the lock and quietly closed that door behind him as well.

He flicked on a dim yellowish vestibule light to find the fully furnished apartment immaculately spotless, as if no one lived there, and in fact, no one did. Since Carlos and Stan Lefkowicz had inspected the rental furniture in the apartment months earlier, no one but Khalil had stepped foot in the premises, and this was only Khalil's third visit.

Wasting no time, Khalil moved straight back to the bedroom, closing its door behind him to prevent sound from traveling to the hallway. He pulled a ham radio off the top shelf of the walk-in closet, placed it on a small desk resting flush to the windowed wall and plugged it in. The unobtrusive radio measured only 3" high by 6" wide by 8" deep, packed with switches, knobs, red and green diodes and band meters.

He deftly attached two exposed wires comprising a makeshift antenna to the back of the device, and unwound ten feet of cable straight across the floor. He then opened the window and felt along the outside wall, quickly locating another thin piece of wire clipped taut onto the window frame from the roof two stories above, and connected it to the radio.

It had taken two hours of discreet very late night work, but when Khalil first arrived in Washington, he ran a hidden wire along the apartment rooftop's perimeter copper gutter and down into unit 710, serving as a fixed vertical antenna. One of the reasons Carlos selected this building as the D.C. home for Khalil was because he knew its copper trim could be rigged as a booster conduit for assisting in surreptitious ham radio communications.

It had all been prearranged before Khalil left Baghdad. Carlos mandated that communicating through ham radio was necessary to guarantee Khalil's security. Long distance phone calls in and out of Baghdad to Washington created the prospect for U.S. government surveillance, not to mention traceable evidentiary phone company records. Mail to Iraq, besides being slow, was also too susceptible to interception. Periodic short ham radio discussions, while conceivably subject to recording by the CIA, FBI or NSA, could not be traced by the Feds, absent a miracle. And if the conversations were limited in choice of words and spoken in English, they wouldn't even be suspect or scrutinized by some security analyst for content. Thus, on the second Tuesday of every month at 12:00 e.s.t., which was 8:00 a.m. Wednesday in Baghdad, Khalil checked in with Ahmed to discuss appropriate business.

If circumstances were such that an emergency telephone communication to Ahmed was necessary during his stay in Washington, Khalil had instructions on how to present himself to the Iraqi embassy in the Capital. This would be a neat trick since no one in the embassy even knew Khalil al-Sharif existed as a living person, much less was stationed in the U.S. as an agent of the Iraqi government. And his mission remained so secret in Iraq that even Rashid Sabar didn't know of the pseudonym Barak Hamas or the actual purpose of Khalil's extended stay in Washington, not that he didn't try to find out. Still, the right sequence of words uttered by Khalil to the embassy's resident diplomat would unequivocally establish Khalil's credentials not only as an agent of the Mukhabarat, but as a right-hand to Saddam Hussein, someone not to be ignored

And if he was in deep trouble -- operation or life threatening trouble -- once Khalil stepped foot in the Iraqi embassy, the Americans couldn't touch him. For such a worst case scenario, he held an authentic diplomatic passport in his own name, that as a matter of international law assured his diplomatic immunity for anything and everything. After all, Khalil al-Sharif was still a valuable asset to the nation of Iraq, even if his present mission somehow turned out to be a disaster. He had to be protected. He had a future.

Today's job involved utilizing sophisticated equipment and antennas, a bit of training and some luck in getting a sun spot cycle that favored establishing radio communication with an isolated receiver a remote half a world away. Khalil's tuner was set at the 80 meter band CW, frequency 3.004 MHz, perfect for nighttime transmissions, assuming the weather and the sun cooperated. If communications couldn't be established on that band, Khalil had a sequence of other frequencies to tune down to.

At precisely midnight, Khalil turned on the machine and was

greeted by instant static and a white light that flashed across the tuning band. He fiddled with the filter knob which significantly reduced the clicky, dusty noise, but didn't touch the preset frequency off the 80 meter band where communications were established the only other time the equipment was used, exactly one month ago. He repeated "hello" into his hand held microphone over and over for a minute, until he was convinced reception would not be achieved on that band. He then clicked to the 40 meter 7.003 MHz band and started over. Finally he heard a response.

"Anybody out there? It's Boston calling," a familiar voice declared.

"Chicago here. Who's that?" Khalil asked into the mike, knowing full well it as Ahmed.

The i.d. code provided for Ahmed to first identify himself as a Boston resident. Khalil was to be from Chicago. The object was two-fold. It established a password for the brothers to positively identify each other, and if anyone unwanted was listening in on the conversation, they would be misled about the actual whereabouts of the speakers.

"It's Al," Ahmed said.

"Your big brother Kevin here," Khalil responded, using his code name.

"Any news on Uncle Carl?" Khalil asked. Everyday Khalil checked the newspapers and the Internet for reports out of France on Carlos. Somehow, even though it had been only two months since Carlos was arrested, the story about the capture of the most notorious terrorist ever, disappeared out of the press.

"Not much. All we've heard is that he hasn't said much to his hosts, and that he'll be gone for a long time," Ahmed answered. Khalil understood the message: Carlos wasn't cooperating with the French authorities. Who knew if he'd see the light of day again as a free man.

"Anything new with Omar?"

"Yeah. He's been spending a fair amount of time in the West, training kids and slipping supplies to those who share your last name."

This was big news. The West meant Gaza. Iraq had never directly assisted Hamas before. The support had to be provided secretly, however, because although Saddam Hussein continued to rail against a PLO-Israel peace, he maintained a relationship with and continued to feel a sense of obligatory support for Yasser Arafat, one of the few Arabs who didn't abandon Saddam during the Gulf War. Still, if the peace process could be undermined, it would be. In the interest of all Arabs, it must be.

"Is he with the captain?" Khalil asked, meaning Sabar.

"I think he reports in to him and gets some general direction, but for the most part he's on his own, although he's got about a dozen men with him."

"What kind of supplies?"

"Use your imagination."

"That's what I thought."

"So how's school? You learning anything?" Ahmed asked.

"Yeah, a lot," Khalil answered. "But I'm kind of bored. Not too many people to talk to."

"I can see how that would be tough," Ahmed said, genuinely sympathetic. "It's not for too long though. Maybe you'll find someone at work or in class to do something with occasionally."

"I guess so."

"Just remember to keep a low profile."

"Right." Khalil almost told Ahmed about his encounter earlier in the day with the Jewish girl, Debra Klein, but decided it was too complicated to get into in a short conversation. Besides, in a couple of days he'd blow her off anyway.

"How's work?" Ahmed asked.

"Good. They've got me doing a little bit of everything. One day I'm a waiter, the next day a guide, but mostly I'm in maintenance, cleaning the grounds and fixing things in the center."

"That sounds good."

"Yeah, I really like it. I've even seen some decent shows. I work as much as they let me since I've got nothing else to do but go to class and study."

"That's good. Let them learn to trust you."

"That's what I figure also. I volunteer for everything, especially the dirty jobs."

"Did you take care of that lady that runs the place yet?"

"Not yet."

"What are you waiting for? Uncle Carl told you to solve that problem as soon as you got there. His picture's been all over the place. It increases the risk of her figuring things out."

"No way. If she was going to, she would have already."

"The risk remains. Eliminate it," Ahmed curtly ordered.

"I'm aware of the situation."

"Then deal with it."

"I've got to be extra careful, because it can't come back to me, and I can't leave town afterwards. I've been planning, and I think I have her routine down. It'll be done in the next few days. Besides, she's been instrumental in getting me set there."

"Fine. Then just do it."

Khalil was ready to tell Ahmed to shut up when Ahmed changed the topic.

"I meant to ask you last time. How's your apartment?"

"Comfortable. Nicer than what you're used to. I just met the new landlord. Some guy named Clifford Savitar. Seems pretty sharp. He asked about Seltaeb and why we've got two apartments."

"That shouldn't be a surprise."

"It wasn't. I told him that I get a lot of company and that Seltaeb was my father's business and he put the apartments in the company's name for tax purposes. He bought it. As long as the rent is paid and I don't cause trouble, he'll leave me alone." In fact, the question was contemplated by Carlos, and an answer was prepared and rehearsed. Rule Number Four. Deception.

"Have you found the material yet?" Ahmed asked.

"Gimme a break. I just got here. There's plenty of time."

"Kevin. Have you found the material?"

"Yes. I'll be going after it soon. Very soon."

"Good. It's been three minutes. Time to go."

"Talk to you next time, Al," Khalil acknowledged, checking his watch. Ahmed had already disconnected on his side, half a globe way. Khalil knew his brother was right. It was time to start putting the plan in motion.

KHALIL WAITED PATIENTLY for the precise conditions that finally ripened on this night. There was no moon and the wind blew scattered strips of cold drizzle. A perfectly bleak evening to ensure a negligible amount of people walking around the high rent residential district of Georgetown. Especially at 9:45 on a weeknight. Meaning a minimal amount of potential witnesses or interference.

Khalil was sequestered in the black shadows of willow trees on a red brick paved sidewalk, across the street from a two story white colonial townhome. The right side of the house was still fully lit. Not what he wanted, but not unexpected. The whole left side of the house was dark except for a faint light peeking through the back of the second floor. Just what he wanted. And expected.

The street was empty, almost surrealistically out of focus from the combination of the light mist of water sprinkling from the sky, glowingly illuminated by sporadically placed street and house lights. Cloaked fully in black, Khalil blended into the pavement as he bounded like a panther across the street and up the townhouse's eight metal steps, two at a time. He had already positioned into his fingers a set of chrome picks. At virtually the same moment he hit the top step and stood before ten foot high dark double wood doors, he extended his hand into the front lock to manipulate its tumblers. His peripheral vision picked up the name *Khoury* over the buzzer and mailbox A. It took nine seconds of touch, feel and twist, but the front door swung open, and Khalil stepped in and silently shut it behind him.

A television blared through the door of the apartment to the right. Silence to his left. Although the main entrance to apartment A was on the ground floor just three feet away, Khalil crept up the stairs directly in front of him, taking care to stay on the far inside of the steps, their quietest point, wiping his wet rubber soled shoes on the carpet with each movement to avoid leaving footprint evidence once he got inside the apartment.

He moved to Dottie Khoury's unit and eavesdropped. Silence. Or maybe a faint radio. Decision time. Go in with the picks or not. No. When discovered it might bring a scream. The plan was set. Don't stray from the plan -- there was no need to.

He held his breath and knocked firmly at the door three times. This was the only weakness in the plan. Khalil had to hope that the neighbor wouldn't appear. Fifteen seconds passed with no response. He knocked again and moments later heard the distinct sound of feet shuffling towards the door.

"Who's there?" a voice barked.

"Shit!" he thought. It was bad enough he had to knock at the door, but he forgot that such an obvious question might be asked once he did. There was no other choice. He could only hope the neighbors wouldn't have heard the knock or his name.

"It's Barak. Barak Hamas."

"Barak?" the voice questioned from behind the door.

"Yes."

The door opened a crack confirming for Khalil that it held a safety chain as he estimated. Dottie closed the door, rattled the chain and five seconds later reopened it. She stood barefoot, dressed in a shiny pastel flowered housecoat with her hair wrapped in a towel. Her face looked a lot older without makeup.

"Barak, what exactly are you doing here at 10:00 at night? Is there something wrong? How come you didn't use the buzzer? Why are you up here, not downstairs?" The words flew out of her mouth rapid fire.

He wanted to tell her to shut up, but said instead, "I'm sorry. Your buzzer must be out. I knocked downstairs but you didn't hear me." He reached inside his new black parka, purchased days earlier with Debra Klein, and pulled out a fresh red rose. He shyly offered it to Dottie. "I had to see you," he smiled.

"Oh Christ," Dottie replied, reluctantly taking the flower from him through the door's opening. "Come in."

He did, closing the door behind him, making a mental note to wipe the doorknob before he left.

"Barak. This is very sweet of you. I'm flattered. I really am. But this is impossible. I --"

"I know," he interrupted, reaching into his jacket and retrieving a hunter's knife with a five inch serrated blade.

"Oh my God," Dottie said. "Why do you have that? What's wrong with you?"

"Don't talk," Khalil ordered, putting his index finger up to his lips. "I'm not here to hurt you. Just do what I say."

"What do you mean do what you say? You stupid punk. Do you have any idea the people I know? You're not going to get away with this. You're --"

"Shut up," he said, threatening her chest with the knife. "You will do what I say or you will have trouble."

Dottie froze. Khalil's calm voice but black steely eyes actually scared her more than the knife.

"I said I wouldn't hurt you. Now let's go to the back."

"Oh my God. You're going to rape me!" she screeched.

"No...I'm not...Look." He put the knife back.

"Then what are you going to do?"

Khalil gently grasped her arm and led her to the rear of the apartment. They stood in front of Dottie's bathroom door. "Start the bath. I'm going to watch you bathe. That's all."

"You are sick. You are fucking sick," Dottie sneered, now surprising Khalil by her coarse language.

Khalil took two steps toward her before she declared, "Alright. Alright." She started the water, not taking her eyes off Khalil, and not even testing it for temperature. They stared icily at each other in silence for almost a minute. When the tub was half way filled, Khalil instructed her to turn the water off.

"Take off everything," he unemotionally directed.

As Dottie Khoury begrudgingly stripped, Khalil removed his jacket and rolled up his sleeves past his elbows. She gave him a suspicious and scared look, turned a bit to the side and crossed her arms over her breasts.

"Get into the tub and lie down."

"I don't want to. I won't." Tears streamed down her face.

"Dottie, don't make me hurt you. Do you want me hurt you? I don't have to. I don't want to. But I will." Khalil's voice resonated with truth and death.

Realizing she had no choice, she stepped into the tub, crossed her legs under the water and covered her chest again. Khalil approached the tub and sat on the rim inches away from her, and softly placed his hand on her cheek. She started to shake. "Barak, why are you doing this?"

He smiled at her, and responded, "Sorry. You're a nice lady. But this is business." Before she could respond, he slid his hand from her cheek to the front of her face, palming it like a basketball. In one forceful motion he slammed the back of her head against the porcelain rim of the bathtub, rendering her unconscious. He let go of her face and she slowly slid below the surface of the water. Khalil placed his hand down into the water over her forehead, and kept her submerged. He watched 90 seconds tick off his Rolex while bubbles popped to the surface. When he was sure it was over, he wiped two fingers over Dottie's eyelids and closed them.

Khalil picked up the towel Dottie previously turbaned on her head, folded it neatly and hung it on the towel rack next to the tub. He flicked the heat lamp on, and knocked a bar of soap into the water. He pulled a handkerchief from his pocket, wrapped it in his hand and closed the bathroom door behind him, being careful not to let his fingertips touch the metal. He briefly looked around the apartment before quietly exiting back out the second floor, first retrieving the rose he brought Dottie, then wiping the doorknob clean of the fingerprints left from when he entered. Less than half an hour later he was back at home, and asleep without remorse.

Khalil al-Sharif proved that he learned his lessons well from Ilich Ramirez Sanchez. He proved that he too knew how to get away with murder.

TWENTY-SIX

"WHY WOULD YOU DO THIS?" Khalil asked, looking down at a gift wrapped box sitting on the edge of Debra Klein's kitchen table.

"Because, Barak, despite the fact that most of the time you're an obnoxious creep, somehow you've become one of my best friends, and friends are supposed to do nice things for each other." Debra softly touched Khalil's shoulder. "Besides, it's Chanukah. Jews exchange gifts on Chanukah," she said with a wink.

She waved at the box as a signal for Khalil to open his present. He stood there more than a little bit dumbfounded.

"I'm sure not Jewish. As you might say, don't you think your grandmother will..uh..turn over in her grave over this?"

Debra burst out laughing. "Just open the gift."

"But I don't have one for you."

"That's okay. You don't need to."

Following their forced classroom partnership by Professor Wilhoit, Debra Klein and Barak Hamas developed a most unique, strictly platonic chemistry of mutual affection. Perhaps it was just that as much as they were different, they were also very much alike. Giftedly bright, independent and stubborn, self-disciplined yet vocally acerbic, and competitive to a fault.

Debra felt one difference between them. She had a cold exterior that masked a warm heart. Barak just seemed cold throughout. She attributed it to his upbringing and culture. Somehow though, she knew that behind his hard shell, there was a different person than Khalil's chosen facade.

Hardly tearing the paper at all, Khalil methodically unwrapped the package, revealing an oversized bright multi-colored wool ski sweater, carefully folded in a Nordstrom box. With a genuine delighted grin he held it up to his chest for size and at Debra's urging, he pulled it over his head. It fit perfectly and matched his bluejeans and Timberland boots. Khalil's dress had become Americanized.

"Debra, this is very nice," he said. "With this weather it'll come in pretty handy." It was an atypical tough Washington winter, with temperatures in the 20's and snow falling every week since Thanksgiving.

She figured that was his way of saying thank you. "I'm glad you like it."

"When are you leaving for Pittsburgh?" Khalil asked.

"Tomorrow. Right after my Communications Law final. You're still welcome to come with me. My parents house is huge and they never mind when I bring a friend. And they know all about you."

"No. Thanks, though. The Kennedy Center has all these holiday special performances and they need me to work as much as possible because everybody wants time off. They gave me three days between Christmas and New Years and I really want to go see my cousins in Detroit."

"I guess I don't blame you. I know you don't have any other family here. It'll be good for you."

During one of their first conversations, when Khalil thought Debra was just some woman in his class he'd have to tolerate for a few weeks, he told her the only family he had was his father in Saudi Arabia, and a few cousins. Fortunately he never forgot the lie, because once he made the statement, it could never be retracted without raising unnecessary suspicion. Lying had become natural to Khalil as Carlos said it would. He had been trained to lie. His life was a lie. Even now, long after arriving in Washington he lied to Ahmed in their monthly Ham radio talks by not telling his brother about his friendship with the Jewish girl. A lie of nondisclosure.

Debra changed the subject. "When's your last final?"

"At the end of the week. Satellite Engineering," he said as he leaned forward and took a sip from his oversized mug of hot chocolate.

"You know, if engineering wasn't so math and science oriented I think I'd be tempted to switch majors," Debra said. "You study some really cool things."

"You should see the internship I've got next semester with the U.S. Navy in their ship and submarine research facility."

"I can't believe the sensitive areas the government gives students access to."

"Yeah, I can't either. But I heard we all passed some sort of security clearance."

"Geez. I would hope so. You know Barak, when you graduate here you're going to be really marketable. You'll have skills and experience nobody else in Saudi Arabia will have."

"Yeah, that's true. I think I already do," Khalil said as he thought to himself, *"And if you only knew."*

EVERY MINUTE OR SO the door to Saladin's Cafe opened and slammed as patrons came and went, each time propelling a blast of unseasonably cold air through the crowded smoke filled noisy Arab diner. Omar Rafsani and Ahmed al-Sharif couldn't believe it. A Who's Who of terrorists convening for a strategy session sat right at a front window table in a renown cafe on Said al-Jabri Avenue, perhaps the main boulevard in the Martyrs' Square district of Damascus.

Carlos would never approve. Then again, the infamous terrorists Fathi Shkaki and Yehia Ayyash could get away with just about anything in Syria. And since their personal security wasn't threatened, and Saladin's was where Shkaki required the meeting, there wasn't much of a choice in the matter if they wanted to talk with him.

While most of the world considered Fathi Shkaki and Yehia Ayyash gutless murderers, they were welcomed by the patrons of Saladin's and treated throughout the Middle East as respected leaders. And the more they killed, the greater their following.

Ahmed was amazed Shkaki and Ayyash were so bold as to casually sit in a public place, drinking coffee and conspiring another round of attacks on the Jews, while cordially accepting congratulations and signing autographs for anonymous well wishers. Since Ahmed had been occupied with other sensitive missions for Saddam Hussein and Rashid Sabar, he had not yet observed firsthand the typical Arab terrorist lifestyle. Omar, on the other hand, having spent his time travelling through the region paying any zealot he could to perform terrorist acts, knew well that these men and others like them had attained almost a mythic fame among the Palestinian people.

In contradiction to his Egyptian medical schooling, the founder of the Islamic Jihad, Fathi Shkaki, sucked hard on another nonfiltered cigarette. He'd indulge in at least 60 of them today. Cloaked in a heavy black woolen sweater with a red and white scarf draped around his neck and down his chest, Yehia Ayyash, "The Engineer," sat back absorbing the conversation and activity. This star soldier of the militant al-Qassam brigades of Hamas was recording into his photographic memory every relevant syllable of conversation within earshot.

A short old man with thin grey hair and a mouth of crooked and missing teeth, proudly displayed through an ever present smile, delivered a tray with bowls of falafel, hummus and fasooliya, being a bean stew, and a basket of the Arabic flat bread, khobz. The arrival of food signaled the visitors who converged around the table to disappear. Ahmed picked up a brass pot and poured himself and the others their third two ounce cup of Bedouin coffee, heavily laced with cardamom. The old man used a large silver spoon to dig out and slop large portions of what looked like dog food onto everyone's plates.

"So Omar, this is your friend Ahmed we've heard so much about,"

Shkaki said, stroking his short greying beard and peering at Ahmed through dirty gold wire framed glasses.

Both Omar and Ahmed nodded.

"And I understand you come directly from President Hussein?" Shkaki said.

"I do," Ahmed replied through a mouth full of hummus.

"With cash?"

"I don't carry it," Ahmed said. "But we can get you pounds, dollars, marks, yen, whatever you want. And it can be wired anywhere."

"Good. Then we can talk. Have you met Ayyash before?"

"Not 'til today," Ahmed answered. Then looking over at Ayyash he said, "But I know you got your start on the Tel Aviv bus job a few years ago. They call you the Engineer because you can make a bomb out of anything. You're 30 and come from Rafat, over on the West Bank. Shall I continue?" Ahmed asked.

"No need." Yehia Ayyash replied, impressed.

Ayyash wasn't a spy. He was just a fanatic. In October 1994, the Engineer designed the bomb which another Hamas zealot carried aboard and blew up the Number 5 bus along with 21 passengers in Dizengoff Square, in the cosmopolitan heart of Tel Aviv. That job, the first big terrorist act contracted for by Omar, brought Ayyash international notoriety. The thirteen others that followed catapulted Ayyash to the top of the Mossad's most wanted list, and guaranteed if he stepped foot in Israel again, he would be shot on sight.

"What's your body count so far?" Omar asked the Engineer.

"I don't know. I lost track. About 200 dead, 600 injured. Something like that," Ayyash replied nonchalantly.

"Very impressive," Ahmed said.

"Shkaki's got me beat. Big numbers."

"That's not true. I've never killed anyone. People I know have killed Jews. Never me."

Ahmed and Omar knew that technically, Shkaki was being truthful. But when he said people *he knew* had taken care of such deadly matters, it was also common knowledge that every Islamic Jihad terrorist act was approved by Shkaki before it was carried out, although it was impossible to trace an attack directly to him.

"So...So far we've done little deals," Shkaki said, exhaling cigarette smoke through his nose while taking a bite of food. "Small business. Now I understand from Rafsani that Hussein wants to do a big deal. Big business."

"That's why we're here," Ahmed agreed.

"Hussein is our friend. Hussein is Arafat's friend," Shkaki scowled. "What's going on here?"

"It's simple. We are committed to destroying the peace with the Zionists," Omar responded. "We want to kill Jews. I think we can agree that's what we all do best."

Shkaki puckered his lips reflecting on Omar's comment. Ayyash burst out in a loud resonant laugh for about five seconds and then abruptly stopped, instantly reassuming his normal serious demeanor. In that moment Ahmed realized that the Engineer, brilliant as he may be, was a relatively unstable character.

"The Jews want a real peace, not a bloody peace," Omar continued. "They will not continue to tolerate acts of terrorism or breaches of their security. They will have to retaliate. Each attack discredits Arafat and puts more pressure on him to put Hamas and Jihad in line. The more Arafat comes down on Arab brothers, the greater the revolt against him. Ultimately he will fall and so will the peace."

"So what do you propose?" Ayash asked.

"Stepping up the attacks," Ahmed answered.

"Yes. But what do you want with us?" Shkaki said.

"A contract as big as you want. We'll pay you by the job. As many as you want. And we'll give you a per head bonus."

"Per head?" Ayyash asked, intrigued.

"For every Jew you kill, you get so much."

"How much?"

"How much do you want? Don't be a pig, though. Remember you've done a lot of this for free for years now. For the cause."

"500 pounds per mission, 100 a head," Ayyash responded.

"No. 1000 pounds per mission, 250 a head," Shkaki said. "Maybe

Hamas works cheap. The Jihad will not."

Ahmed shook his head acting dismayed by their responses. "You people are ridiculous. We came to make a deal that works for everyone. You're both way too high. Let me speak privately with Omar for a moment."

Omar and Ahmed rose from their chairs and took a few steps away. Shkaki and Ayyash watched them closely. Ahmed whispered to Omar, "Morons. I would have paid three times as much as Shkaki asked." He started flailing his arms and whispered again, "Act like you're upset with me." Omar responded by also animatedly waving his arms in feigned anger while whispering meaningless words into Ahmed's ear. They continued the charade for a few moments, then Ahmed grabbed Omar by the arm and led him back to the table.

"If I come back to Iraq without an arrangement I might as well not come back at all," Ahmed said, wearing an irritated expression. "Shkaki, you've got to help me. You have nothing to lose in this transaction. Every attack makes you a hero. I'll go as high as what Ayyash wants, but I can't pay Hamas one fee and Jihad another. Please. Take the deal."

There was no reason not to. The fact was, Shkaki was thrilled with the idea of bringing in more money to the Jihad organization, particularly since competition for cash among the Arabs was fierce. It could be used for an infinite number of projects from buying weapons for his soldiers to supplying medicine and food to the refugees in his village. "I accept."

"There's one other condition," Omar announced. "We want it known that Hafez Assad is funding you."

"Syria?" Ayyash asked. Even Shkaki looked puzzled.

Ahmed put up his hand to silence Omar so that he could explain it himself. "Yes. Prime Minister Ben-David used to be Chief of Staff of Israel's armed forces. His distrust of Syria runs deep. If Ben-David thinks that Assad continues to sponsor terrorism, it becomes impossible for Israel and Syria to make peace."

Shkaki leaned back in his chair reflecting on Ahmed's analysis.

He smiled and announced, "Today is Chanukah. I want you to meet who's going to deliver a Semtex gift to Jerusalem tomorrow." Shkaki raised his hand straight up in the air, snapped his fingertips a few times and dropped it back to his side.

A moment later the waiter escorted a skinny young man to the table and motioned him to sit at the empty chair he pulled up next to Shkaki. His eyes were intensely wide open but there was a strange sense of calm about him.

"Do you know who I am?" Shkaki asked.

"Yes sir. You are Fathi Shkaki. Leader of the Jihad. You are a hero to me and all in my village. It is an honor to meet you. It is an honor to work for you," the man said humbly, lowering his eyes as he spoke.

"What is your name?"

"Jamil Houwri," he said looking back up.

"Jamil, do you know these other men?"

"No sir."

"Well you should. They too are heros. This is Omar Rafsani, Ahmed al-Sharif and Yehia Ayyash," Shkaki said, motioning to each man as his name was mentioned.

"Oh Allah! You are Ayyash! You're the Engineer!" Jamil excitedly declared. "You're a legend!"

Ayyash remained stonefaced.

"Excuse me. I'm sorry." Jamil said, realizing his emotion was out of place.

"Hmmm," Shkaki murmured, the corners of his mouth turning down. "How old are you, Jamil?"

"22."

Shkaki shook his head no back and forth repeatedly. "You are too young to die."

"No I'm not. I am ready. You must let me."

Shkaki stared deep into Jamil's eyes for a few seconds. He dropped his voice an octave and said softly and passionately, "Giving your life for Allah...for your people...this is a serious matter."

"I'm telling you I'm prepared," Jamil replied.

"Why? Why are you prepared to die?" Shkaki sharply asked, sticking his index finger in the young Arab's chest.

"Because I am from Kalkiya. I lived near Abdel Rakim Souwi. When he blew up the bus in Tel Aviv he died a martyr. A hero. He brought honor to himself and his family. You know what I have seen and lived with in Kalkiya. My family and I have nothing. The enemy deserves to die. Let me die a martyr killing them for Allah so I may enter heaven. I cannot get there any other way."

Shkaki rubbed his chin, contemplating the man's desperate plea. He looked over to Ayyash who raised his eyebrows and shrugged his shoulders. Shkaki then smiled broadly, placed his hand on Jamil's shoulder and announced, "You're a fine man. We shall let you enter heaven."

Jamil sighed heavily, put his hand over his heart and declared, "Oh thank you, Mr. Fathi."

Shkaki smiled. "Tell me the plan." Of course, Shkaki knew it.

"Actually it is modeled after one of the attacks Ayyash planned a couple of years ago. There's a Bank Leumi branch on Jaffa Road at Zion Square in Jerusalem. At 11:30, when the bank is very busy, I'll walk inside and once I'm near a crowd of people, I'll blow myself up."

"Who made the bomb? What is the material?" Ayyash asked.

"One of Abu Nidal's people. It's made out of five pounds of something called Semtex."

"Five pounds?" Ayyash chuckled. "It'll bring down the whole building."

"It will?" Jamil grinned.

Ayyash smiled in response.

"Ohhh, then I have been truly blessed."

"Yes. You have," Shkaki agreed.

Shkaki raised his hand straight again and the old waiter instantly reappeared. Jamil and Shkaki stood, and Shkaki embraced Jamil in a firm hug, kissing the young man on each cheek. The restaurant turned silent for a moment and then broke out into rousing cheers. As the waiter led Jamil away, a stream of outstretched arms tried to pat him on the back or shake his hand.

"Consider tomorrow's job free," Shkaki laughed.

Ahmed felt like replying that he had no intention of paying for it, but he decided to keep his mouth shut.

"Do your people have any idea that we've ever paid you before?" Omar asked Ayyash.

"Of course not," the Engineer replied, "but they wouldn't care about the money. We use it for good purposes. I do not profit. I own nothing. Look at Shkaki. He still lives in a camp. Our people die because they want to. It's an honor. A privilege."

"We understand," Ahmed replied. "But what if your people knew their families would be specially taken care of if they gave their lives for you. What do you think would happen then?"

"We'd have 50,000 volunteers."

"And what if on one particular day we wanted say...200, 300 suicide attacks all at the same time, and we'd pay triple for that. Could it be arranged? Would you be interested?" Omar asked.

"Very much," Shkaki quickly replied.

"I can make it as big as you want," Ayyash added. "With enough time, and an advance payment, I could personally arrange 300."

Ahmed reached inside his coat and pulled out two sealed white envelopes. "An advance is a reasonable request," he said, sliding the envelopes across the table, one for Ayyash, one for Shkaki. "Here's 20,000 each. For expenses. But there isn't much time. We'll be in touch with the details. But get to work."

Both Ayyash and Shkaki slipped the envelopes inside their garments.

"One last thing," Omar said. "If we hear as much as a rumor about this from anyone...*anyone*...the deal's off."

"And I promise you, I'll be back for a refund," Ahmed added. "And a pound of flesh."

TWENTY-SEVEN

SINGING OUT OF TUNE as she pounded the beat of the drum from *Jumping Jack Flash* on the steering wheel of his new customized GMC van, Norman Richards sped down the now familiar road from the West Bank of Israel into Jordan's Baqaa Valley. He accelerated into the blind turn of a tight bend in the brush laden broken road, and slammed on his brakes to avoid colliding into a man frantically waving his arms next to a jeep lying on its side. Richards yelled "goddamn" as he averted catastrophe with his van stopping only feet away from the accident. He surveyed the wreck before him, turned down the music and focused on the Arab signaling for his help.

"What the hell happened here?" Richards asked, stepping out of the van.

"We lost control coming out of the turn."

"Anybody hurt?" No bodies were visible.

"No."

"That was lucky."

"Yes."

"But now Mr. Richards, your luck has run out," a voice announced coming out of the brush from behind him. "I've waited a long time for this."

Norman spun around to find Abu Nasir's chief aide, Salim, standing next to his van with a pistol pointed straight at him. Six other men climbed out of the brush.

"You killed my older brother. Today I finally get to kill you."

"Fuck," Richards blurted out, his mind quickly dissipating into a fog. He fought hard to gain control of his senses. "In the raid by the Israelis?" Richards blurted out dumbfounded, but knowing the answer. "I didn't kill anyone. I was wounded myself. Nasir knows that's true." Richards had lived the lie for so long, that he now seemed to believe it himself.

"Nasir's a stupid old man. I will be in charge soon."

"The Israelis are to blame," Richards stammered.

"I didn't believe that story when you came back begging for mercy before, so don't waste your breath now," Salim said.

Salim motioned to the downed jeep and within a minute his men had turned it back upright, jumped in and drove away.

"Ismael, frisk him," Salim ordered to the remaining man, the one who flagged Richards down.

"Don't bother," Richards replied. "I know the drill."

"Good. Then give your gun to Ismael. Slowly."

Ismael kept his weapon trained on Richards, who following instructions, carefully opened his blue jean jacket, removed his .44 magnum from its holster, and handed it to the Arab by the barrel.

"The knife too."

"Oh, you want that?" he said bending over and pulling it from the sheath attached to his calf. Looking up at Ismael's eyes, he suddenly recalled his past experience with the man. "Wait a second. I remember you. You're the fuckin' guy who broke my nose." Richards paused for a moment and shook his head. "You broke my fucking nose," he said excitedly, slashing the air with the knife for emphasis.

"Correct," the Arab cackled. "That's me."

Richards took a threatening step towards Ismael, but before he could say or do anything more, Salim fired a shot into the air, stopping Richards in his tracks.

"Mr. Richards, I will not tolerate your antics today," Salim declared.

Richards had already concluded he would soon be dead and therefore had nothing to lose. "Fuck off you smelly asshole. I'm not gonna take your shit either."

Salim stared at him coldly. Even though Richards could have reached out and touched the hatred, he could have cared less. In fact, he felt like instigating trouble. "Can I ask one question?"

"What?" Salim said curtly.

"You've got a daughter, don't you?"

"Yes."

It was a lucky guess. "Well, a couple of months ago, Nasir told me he was fucking her camel style. I was just wondering, is he still doing her or has he moved on to some other peasant whore?"

Salim's face reddened and his chest heaved. The gun in his hand shook.

Waving the knife, Richards continued, "Let's go. One on one."

Salim's nostrils flared and he pointed the gun straight at Richards' chest. "Drop the knife on the ground and step back," Salim said.

Richards shrugged and did as he was told, while adding, "O.K. Maybe you've got a point."

Ismael picked up the weapon.

"So why don't you just kill me right here and get it over with?"

"I can't torture you here. I want you to feel real pain before you die. Maybe I'll cut out your kidney and leave you on the side of the road."

Trying hard not to show his fear, Richards retorted, "As long as it's not my liver."

Ismael smacked him across the back of the head with the .44, almost knocking him senseless. Richards fell to his knees and rubbed his new bloody wound. Looking at the red liquid on his hand and then up at Ismael, Richards announced, "I'm going to kill you today."

Both Ismael and Salim laughed.

"Get into the van. You're driving," Salim ordered.

For the first time in a long time Richards fastened his seat belt. Ismael sat next to him in the front and Salim got into the back. Both kept their guns pointed at Richards.

Richards blew Ismael a kiss and said, "Try to keep your hands out of my lap."

"Drive," Salim demanded, intentionally placing the gun barrel on Richards' sensitive fresh head wound.

Richards gunned the accelerator and the van shot forward.

"Drive normal," Salim ordered.

"I am," Richards laughed as he flicked his Rolling Stones tape back on loud and sped up. The van was already at 60.

"Slow down!" Salim yelled, leaning over the front seat. The van bounced along the half paved road like a ping pong ball.

Ismael braced himself in the seat sideways with one arm extended straight onto the dashboard. "You're a crazy man. What are you doing?"

Richards stuck out his tongue, rattled his head like he was having a seizure, and panted in a deep voice, "Yeah, yeah, crazy."

"Slow down or I'll kill you!" Ismael screamed.

"You'll die too," Richards laughed.

"Cut it out!" Salim commanded.

"Hey, I'm only going 85. Chill out. We'll get where we're going faster."

"I said stop!" Salim yelled.

"You want me to stop?" Richards yelled back.

"Stop now!"

"You want me to stop?" Richards yelled again. The speedometer touched 93. The van was barely in control.

"I command you to stop!" Salim screamed again.

"Okay. If you say so," Richards replied.

As hard as he could, Richards slammed his foot on the brake pedal, instantly sending the van into an uncontrollable spin. The G forces from the sudden chaotic movement flung Ismael straight through the windshield and Salim over the seat headfirst into the dashboard. The van continued to spin wildly running over Ismael while Richards, who was restrained by his seatbelt, fought to bring the vehicle under control. A few seconds later he succeeded and although the van was off the broken road, it was miraculously upright and stopped. Richards looked down at Salim whose barely conscious body was strewn across the front seat, with a deep bloody cut across the middle of his forehead. Richards sat for a few seconds to catch his breath. When he recovered, he picked up Salim by the hair and as a testament to his nickname "Boomer," punched the Arab in the jaw, shattering it and knocking him out cold. He looked out of his rear view mirror and saw the bloody mangled corpse of Ismael lying face up on the ground. "You fucker. I told you I'd kill you today," he said while retrieving his gun and knife off the floor of the van.

Fifteen minutes later, Norman Richards pulled up to a small farmhouse just outside the Baqaa refugee camp. He jumped out of the van, slammed the door and pulled Salim out from the passenger side in a headlock. He dropped him hard to the ground, grabbed him by one ankle and dragged him moaning across the rocky path to the front door of the old rickety house.

For the first time in probably the twenty times that Richards had met with Abu Nasir, the door to the designated safehouse swung open before Richards even reached it. Nasir stood in the entrance looking typically regal in his white thobe and gutra.

"What happened here?" he asked, concern obvious on his face.

"You tell me!" Richards screamed.

Two bodyguards stepped past Nasir and approached Richards for the standard weapons search. "Get the fuck away from me," he barked, drawing his .44. In an instant the Arabs' guns were drawn and pointed at Richards.

Richards was unfazed. "Okay. You fuckin' guys want a shoot out? Let's do it and I'll waste a few of you. But you're not taking my gun. You already tried to kill me once today."

Nasir motioned to his men to lower their weapons. "What are you talking about?"

"You know fucking well what I'm talking about," Richards said, now aiming at Nasir. The Arabs raised their weapons again.

"No," Nasir said, shaking his head, "I really don't."

"Then ask this cocksucker," Richards said, kicking Salim in the stomach.

"We will. But I'm telling you I really do not know what is going on. If I wanted to kill you I could have done it long before today."

Norman thought about it and realized Nasir made sense. He frowned.

"Norman, why don't we go inside and get you a drink. You will tell me your story and we will see what Salim has to say."

Within minutes, Richards had polished off two glasses of siddiki and conveyed his saga to Nasir.

Practically the moment Salim appeared coherent, Richards began screaming at him, "Why were you going to kill me? What's going on here? It's not over your brother because you could have taken me out a long time ago if that was it."

Salim snorted contemptuously, but said nothing.

"Salim, I demand that you to tell me what happened today," Nasir sternly ordered.

"Shut up, Nasir. I have nothing to say to you. I'll die first."

"That can be arranged," Richards quickly replied.

Nasir was shocked at Salim's mutiny. "Tell me the truth. You have been my right hand for years. You are like a son to me."

"You're a traitor to me," Salim responded.

Nasir slapped him across the face.

"You're gonna talk right now, fuckhead, or I'll shoot off your toes, one by one." Richards cocked his gun and pointed it down. "You have 'til I count to three."

"One, two, three," Salim smugly replied.

"Have it your way," Richards said. "May I?" Richards asked Nasir.

"Why not?" Nasir begrudgingly okayed.

With that, Richards aimed down at Salim's left big toe, pulled the trigger and blew a hole through Salim's foot.

Salim screamed in agony as blood sprayed out of what was left of the shoe. "My toes. My toes. You shot off my fuckin' toes!"

"Not really, at least not all of them," Richards laughed, genuinely feeling satisfaction for crippling Salim. "It looks like I left three on that foot. Now I'll try the other foot."

"You're crazy! You're fucking crazy! You shot off my toes!" Salim kept screaming.

"Tell me right now or I'll do it again. Why did you attack me?" Richards asked, hoping for another chance to pull the trigger.

"I will die before I say anything."

"No you won't. I won't let you die. I'll only maim you." Richards pointed the gun at Salim's crotch. "You'll live through this, but you'll have to change your name to Sheba." All of the Arabs gasped, particularly Salim, whose face froze in shock. "Last chance. One... Two..."

"Okay, okay, okay. I'll talk."

"Smart move. Talk."

"Nasir is a traitor to Islam and his people. You are an agent of the imperialist Americans and the Zionists. Your conspiracy... your peace with the Jews must be stopped."

Richards exhaled a deep breath. "Wait a second. Let me make sure I understand this. You were going to kill me because Nasir and I are working to improve the life of your people through the peace pact with Israel?"

"You improve nothing," Salim said as he spit at Richards.

"You moron. Do you have any idea what I brought with me today?"

"I know exactly what you have. Forty cases of baby formula."

"Right. A donation from an Israeli assistance agency. *From Israel!* Don't you get it? Last week a truckload of vegetables. Next week computers. This wasn't possible even two years ago. This is good for your people. Look where 40 years of war with Israel got you," Richards said, shaking his head in disgust.

"We don't need Jewish help. We need them in the sea."

"Life in the refugee camp has already improved with peace,"

Nasir said. "Let your hatred go, Salim. It is blind. It is wrong. The only future for our people, for our children, is peace. Much can be gained from working with Israel."

"You deserve to die, Nasir. You have betrayed us all," Salim sneered.

Nasir stared at Salim for almost thirty seconds. He walked over to the window and stared out over the Jordan plains for another minute before he turned around and stood before Salim. He reached over and snatched Richards' gun out of his hand. He looked at Norman Richards and said, "At one time this man was my friend. He has shamed me and all Palestinians today. Please accept my apology. You and I will continue to work together."

Nasir then turned to Salim and announced, "Martyrs go to heaven. You are not a martyr. You will not see heaven." Salim's face turned to a mask of horror. It was the last look he would ever make. Nasir pulled the trigger sending Salim to hell.

TWENTY-EIGHT

Gary, Indiana

LOOKING IN THE REAR VIEW MIRROR of his parked rental car, Khalil combed his hair and straightened his tie. Opening the car door to a blast of barely breathable arctic air, he clutched his just-for-show briefcase, and rushed forty yards through the parking lot of Hoosier Chemicals into the soot covered, red brick, two story building. He grunted and tried to shake off the cold. Fortunately, once he was inside a wave of dry hot air enveloped him from a blowing vent directly above in the entranceway.

"Pretty damn cold out there today, isn't it mister," said a middle aged woman with red purplish hair stacked a foot high on her head, standing behind a counter that ran the width of the room.

Khalil was speechless for an instant having never seen a coif quite like that before. "Yes ma'am. Colder than I'm used to," he said in a Spanish accent he picked up from Carlos.

"You're not from around here?"

"Nope. Atlanta."

"Well be glad it didn't snow, too. You sure have come a long way. And during Christmas week, too. Ain't you got no holiday spirit?"

311

"It's my boss's fault. I guess business stops for nothing."

"Guess not. What can I do for you?"

"I'm looking for Dave Roberts."

"Good ol' Dave. Is he expecting you?"

"Yes ma'am."

"What's your name?" she asked, cracking a piece of gum.

"Roberto Aparacio," Khalil said. "Here's my card," he added, handing the woman a business card, while focusing on her huge mascara drowned blue eyes and fire engine red painted lips.

The Roberto Aparacio standing in the front office of Hoosier Chemicals bore no resemblance to the real Khalil. Today he hid behind a fake mustache and goatee, a greased down strong side part in his normally curly fluffed hair, and slightly tinted horn rimmed glasses. He worked hard at keeping his eyes permanently squinted. Even brother Ahmed might not recognize him right now.

"Antonov Plastics," she said reading the card aloud. "Why don't you fix yourself some coffee over there, have a seat and I'll track down Dave for you."

Five minutes later a tall middle aged black man with a shaved head walked into the room. "Mr. Aparicio?" he bellowed.

"Right," Khalil said, walking towards the man. "Nice to meet you, Mr. Roberts. Here's my card."

"Call me Dave."

"And I'm Roberto."

"I was able to locate two five gallon bottles and remeasure the carbonyl chloride into them. You're sure you don't want a whole barrel? Ten gallons isn't very much."

"No. My product development department says that even five gallons is more than enough. They don't need 50 gallons right now."

"You know we have to charge a premium for this because we don't normally stock five gallon containers and we had to break down a drum. It's gonna be $350.00 plus shipping, which'll probably cost at least the same."

"I don't care. It's not my money. I think it's ridiculous my boss sent me all the way here just to test the stuff."

"Yeah, I still don't understand why you've got to do that. Carbonyl chloride is carbonyl chloride."

"That's not what our chemists say. If the stuff isn't totally pure they can't use it, and the two other suppliers they've bought from in the past have contaminated products."

"What are you guys gonna use it for?"

"Styrofoam cups," Khalil replied. He had an answer prepared for everything. Rule Number Three - Anticipation.

"You can't do that. It's illegal. The government made one of them fast food chains discontinue using their Styrofoam cups made with carbonyl chloride because they turn to phosgene when burned. And man, that's one poisonous gas."

"Yeah, I think I heard something like that. But the R & D people say if it's pure and mixed with sodium, you don't have the phosgene problem, and then it's a lot cheaper to make than that other type of styrofoam."

"You don't say?"

"That's what I've been told."

"Well, follow me," Roberts said. The men walked down a hall that ran off the front office. Khalil memorized every step of the way as they made numerous turns passing a series of offices and other rooms.

"I've got the bottles all set up in shipping," Roberts said. They entered a large brightly lit room filled with metal drums, boxes, crates and various packing materials. "See, they're almost ready to go into their crates." They stood in front of a work table holding two small wooden crates stuffed with bubble wrap and two ice blue colored large thick bottles filled with liquid.

"Excellent. If the supply is good, I'll just take them with me today."

"What are you, crazy? That violates federal law. If one of these things break and any water touches the carbonyl chloride, it will hydrolyze and you'll have a phosgene problem that'll kill everyone anywhere close to the spill. You know what that means if it happens at an airport and someone tries to clean it up with a wet mop?

National headlines. Major catastrophe. This is serious stuff man, and we run a straight shop here. This has to be registered correctly. When all the paperwork is done, we'll ship it down to you, but not 'til then."

"Okay, I understand. But it was worth a try," Khalil said smiling. Roberts didn't smile back.

"Do you have just a couple ounce sample to do my test?"

"Right here," Roberts said, retrieving a plain glass sealed jar from behind one of the crates.

"We don't need gas masks to open this stuff in here, do we?" Khalil asked, pretty sure he knew the answer.

"Nope. Sitting by itself carbonyl chloride is just another solvent. It doesn't smell great, but it won't kill you."

"So what's your test buddy?" said Roberts.

"Simple. All we do is add a little salt," Khalil said, retrieving a tiny junk food salt packet from his pants pocket. "If the carbonyl chloride is pure it won't change color. If it does, it's no good."

"Bullshit. I'm a chemist by training. Sodium won't do nothin' to change the color of this stuff. Even if you put in a pound."

"We'll see. I'm just doing what I'm told." The fact was that Roberts was right. But the test was a necessary ruse for Khalil to make sure that he was led directly to where Hoosier Chemicals stored what he needed.

Both men peered inside the jar for about thirty seconds waiting for something to happen. Nothing did.

"This looks good to me. How long before you can ship it?"

"It'll go out tomorrow."

"Great. I'll call the company later today to issue a purchase order and arrange payment. Someone will call you tomorrow."

"Fine. Then it'll definitely go out tomorrow."

"Can you lead me out of this place?" Khalil asked. "I've got another appointment in Chicago I've got to get to."

AT 11:30 P.M., twelve hours after Khalil had left Hoosier Plastics, he passed the burning smokestacks of U.S. Steel in the heart of

Gary's industrial center, and pulled off Highway 20 back into the chemical plant's parking lot. He quickly cut his lights and pulled up parallel to the front door, facing back out to the street. Khalil had actually spent a few hours freezing in the parking lot the night before observing the activity at the plant as well as checking out the security system, an item he also closely inspected as he walked through the building earlier in the day with Dave Roberts. Right now there were only two cars in the lot, and Khalil concluded they were owned either by janitorial staff or night security guards. It didn't matter.

Still dressed and disguised as Roberto Aparacio, Khalil waited for someone to answer the front door after he repeatedly pushed the night bell. He prayed he had made the right call and wouldn't have to break in, because the alarm system was intricate, and once it was tripped, there was no saying how much time he'd have to finish his work and escape the building before the police would show up. And under no circumstances could he afford for that to happen. Tonight was critical. Without full success, the entire purpose for his being in Washington could fail; an unacceptable proposition.

Finally, after almost five minutes a young muscular black man dressed in a security uniform opened the front door.

"What do you want mister? It's near midnight. You don't have any business here right now."

"I'm very sorry," Khalil said. "Here's my card. My name's Roberto Aparacio. I'm from Atlanta. Earlier today I had a meeting with my good friend Dave Roberts. You know Dave, don't you? Anyway I left my briefcase here. I've got an 8:00 a.m. flight out of O'Hare tomorrow morning and I can't go without that case. Please, you gotta help me out. Here's fifty bucks. I know right where it is in the shipping room. You can even call Dave at home if you want to confirm this."

"I can't let nobody in," the security guard said fingering both the fake business card and the $50.00 bill. "Sorry. Somebody'll be here at seven in the morning."

"Look, my job is on the line. Here's another $50.00. It'll take two minutes, that's all. I promise. Have some holiday spirit," Khalil said, edging his body into the lobby.

"Well okay," the guard said, taking the second bill. "C'mon with me. You look pretty honest."

The moment the guard turned his back, Khalil grabbed his head from behind and powerfully twisted his neck while simultaneously breaking his spine with an uplifted knee. The guard fell to the ground, blood dripping from the corners of his mouth, gasping for air for a few seconds before his open eyes went blank. Khalil picked his money and business card out of the corpse's hand, shoved them back into his pocket, and put on a pair of thin black leather driving gloves.

Moving quickly and silently he retraced the path down the hallways back to the shipping room, his Beretta 9 mm. pointed in front of him leading the way. Silently he entered the room and switched on the light. He was relieved to find neither the bottles of carbonyl chloride nor their packing crates had been moved.

After trying to pick up one of the bottles, he decided he had to get the liquid containers out of the building another way besides carrying them. He set the open crates on the ground and carefully placed the bottles in each. After pausing in thought for a moment he set the lids to the crates on each box, although there weren't any nails or a hammer to seal them with.

"Hey man, who's you?" demanded another tall young black security guard, suddenly appearing at the door to the room and totally startling Khalil. The guard started walking slowly towards the intruder with his pistol pointed straight out at him. "Don't move. Put your hands up."

"Hey cut that out!" Khalil yelled as he raised them high, aware that his Beretta was hidden from view on the table right in front of him. "Do I look like a fuckin' burglar?" Khalil exclaimed. "I just started working here yesterday. Special shift. Call Dave Roberts. Ask him."

"Fuck you, man. That's bullshit. There ain't no special shift," he sneered. "Yo' Frankie!" the guard yelled. "Get over here Frankie!

We got a problem!"

"There he is," Khalil screamed back, throwing his head in the direction of the door.

The millisecond that the guard turned his head was all Khalil needed. He snatched his gun and dove to the ground while the guard shot at him twice, narrowly missing with each bullet. Khalil tumbled forward and finding a barely clear line of fire between shelves, he squeezed off three quick shots wounding the guard with two of them. The man slumped to the ground bleeding from the shoulder and stomach. Khalil approached him slowly with his Beretta aimed straight at the guard's body.

"Don't kill me man. Don't kill me," the guard strained to whisper.

"I won't. Just tell me how many others are in the building. Tell me that and you live."

"Okay. Please let me live. Only one. My partner Frankie."

"What about maintenance?"

"No man. They leave at 9:00," he coughed.

"Thanks." Khalil smiled cruelly and pulled the trigger one more time, ending the conversation.

It took Khalil five more minutes to find a cart, load the carbonyl chloride onto it and then into his car. Once his car hit the Indiana Turnpike only a mile up the road, he ripped off his beard, mustache and glasses and threw them out the window in five minute increments. He didn't stop driving until he needed gas four hours later outside Toledo, Ohio. After that he didn't stop to rest for another four hours, until he found a Red Roof Inn just outside Pittsburgh. The bodies of Frankie and his partner were just being found by the time Khalil was 500 miles away, having left no direct evidence of his identity behind.

Of course, once the two containers of carbonyl chloride were discovered missing, a stunned Dave Roberts told the Gary Police about a suspect named Roberto Aparicio of Antonov Plastics in Atlanta. Roberts felt pretty miserable the next day when the FBI and the police told him Antonov Plastics didn't exist and no one named Roberto Aparicio lived anywhere in the Atlanta area. Although a good composite sketch of the prime suspect was put together, it sure didn't look anything like Khalil who was now safely 1000 miles away. Carlos would be proud.

TWENTY-NINE

KHALIL TRUDGED UP THE HILL past the infamous Watergate complex on his way to work next door at The Kennedy Center. He shifted a backpack filled with a textbook, sack lunch and thermos off one shoulder and onto the other. When he reached the white and grey marbled entrance at the archway of the Hall of States, he kicked the remnants of muddy slush off his Timberland boots so as to not drag unnecessary grime onto the red carpet. After all, he'd probably be the one to have to clean it up anyway.

Once inside the seventy foot high, football field length hall he was greeted by a lanky National Park Service uniformed security guard. "Hey Prince, how you doin' today buddy?" All of the guys working at The Kennedy Center had nicknames. Khalil became Prince when his colleagues learned he was the son of a rich Saudi Arabian oil shiek.

Khalil walked over to the towering caucasian and gave him a soul shake. "Shrimp, don't you ever stop working man?"

"No reason to. No work, no money. No money, no party. No party, no life. Might as well work."

"Get a life, Shrimp," Khalil laughed, playfully poking the man in the chest, then walking away. "You wanna play some more hoops next Sunday?" the man named Shrimp said loudly.

"I don't know. I stunk yesterday."

"No way, Prince man. You can't shoot, but you play some mean defense and you rebound like an animal. I got a dent in my ribs to prove it. I know Cook and Crash will play."

"Where at? G-Town again?" Khalil asked while backpedaling down the hall.

"Yeah. Tell everybody you see. The more the better. I'll get the gym."

"Consider it done," Khalil waved as he turned around and disappeared off the great hall into an alcove hiding elevators.

He rode the elevator down one level, slid into the men's locker room, removed his lunch and thermos from his backpack, and placed them on the top shelf of his locker. Just as Khalil changed into his work uniform, a navy blue golf shirt with *Barak* emblazoned in gold over his heart above the Kennedy Center logo, a middle aged man with a cigarette dangling from his mouth pushed through the door to the room. He announced his presence with a simple gruff and throaty attention grabbing, "Barak."

"Hi, Mr. Brumbaugh. I'm not late yet," Khalil said lightheartedly.

"Did I say anything to you about that?" Brumbaugh snapped, scratching the back of his curly haired head.

"No sir." Khalil said apologetically.

"I didn't think so. Listen Barak, a few of the guys tell me they think you're the best mechanic on staff."

"I don't know about that. I'm okay with electronics."

"Aren't you an architecture student or something?"

"Engineering."

"Same difference. What's your experience with furnaces? We've tried to get the goddamn heat in this building fixed right all winter long."

"In the fall I fixed the compressor on the air conditioner when it went down. But we knew what the problem was then. You don't know what's wrong now, huh?"

"If I knew what the fuckin' problem was I wouldn't have to be talking to you, would I?"

Khalil sheepishly shrugged his shoulders.

"I don't think the damn Army Corps of Engineers or the Park Service cares one goddamn bit about whether we melt or freeze in this place."

"Oh," Khalil replied, not really sure how to respond.

"Do me a favor. I'm taking you off maintenance today. I want you to spend some time going through the HVAC system to see if you can figure out anything to make this place more comfortable."

"Whatever you want sir."

"I want the fuckin' thing fixed," Brumbaugh coughed through a mist of smoke. "And I want those jackoffs in administration upstairs off my ass."

"I'll try. But remember, I'm only here 'til one today because of school."

"Barak, you get it done and I'll take good care of you." Brumbaugh looked intently into Khalil's eyes and then smacked him in the arm with an open palm.

"Yes sir."

The moment Khalil was sure Brumbaugh was long gone, he was back in the service elevator grasping his thermos, and exiting next to the kitchen on the Roof Terrace floor. He darted into an adjacent stairwell and flew up a flight of metal steps to the top floor of the building which housed the Kennedy Center's boilers, electrical and ventilation systems.

His eyes shifted quickly about the vast dimly lit space before him, searching for other building employees. As expected, the floor was empty, so he moved cautiously but swiftly down a cement aisleway enveloped by multi-colored furnaces, machinery, pipes and ductwork. Fifty yards down at a ceiling high generator and electrical junction box, Khalil turned and climbed into a narrow black crawl space no more than three feet wide behind the massive machine. With his back flush against the wall he inched his way behind the generator for about eight feet, continually gently extending his foot in front of him in search of a specially hidden object, finally stopping upon making contact with a five gallon commercial water cooler bottle swiped two weeks earlier from the kitchen.

Khalil squatted and reached under the machine. He fumbled around for a few seconds before retrieving a gas mask with a small red plastic funnel wrapped inside its head strap. Although he didn't really believe it necessary, as a purely precautionary measure he pulled the mask taut over his face, unscrewed the top of the thermos and poured a quart of carbonyl chloride through the funnel into the bottle. Absent the protection of the gas mask, if even an incremental amount of condensation was in the container and mixed with the chemical, the clear poisonous gas Phosgene would hydrolyze into the surrounding atmosphere and kill him with only a couple of breaths.

After he finished pouring, he removed a thick rubber stopper from his pants pocket and lodged it tightly inside the bottle before pushing the glass back under the generator where he heard it tap into a second empty bottle waiting to be filled. Praying to Allah, he then took the deepest breath he could before taking off and replacing the gas mask, and speed walking back to the stairwell. When he finally reached the stairs he exhaled, fully satisfied that he had safely deposited the delivery of the deadly carbonyl chloride to its intended destination. By the time he replaced the thermos back in his locker downstairs, not even six minutes had passed and nobody had missed him or observed anything suspicious. His detailed planning was paying off. It was taking him a while to smuggle ten gallons of carbonyl chloride into the Kennedy Center, but it could be done. And it would be done.

Four hours later Khalil was casually strolling down the Hall of States about to leave for the day, when he was stopped by the bellowing command of the building superintendent John Brumbaugh from halfway down the hall. "Hamas! Get over here!"

Khalil stopped in his tracks and walked slowly towards his boss. "Yes sir." He could see a scowl on the man's face from 40 feet away.

"What the hell did you do to the furnace?" Brumbaugh yelled, turning heads of the sightseeing visitors lounging about the great hall. "The damn thing seems to be working all the sudden." Brumbaugh pulled a Marlboro out of a hard pack and offered one to Khalil.

"No thanks. I don't smoke."

"Smart kid," he choked out through a mouthful of smoke. "So Barak, how'd you fix that fuckin' thing? Nobody else could do it for weeks. You did it in a few hours."

"I'm not really sure. I took out a bunch of parts and cleaned them, tightened some screws, adjusted the compressor. That's about it. I guess I got lucky."

In fact, it wasn't luck at all. About six weeks earlier Khalil snuck a large paper towel filled cardboard box onto the top floor. It didn't take a rocket scientist to know that if he removed the vent screen and stuffed the empty box in front of the primary air intake vent, that the heat in the entire building would get screwed up. Only a terrific sleuth repairman would go so far as to search for a furnace problem in the obscure spot Khalil sabotaged. Ultimately Khalil knew he'd get a chance to try and fix the mess that no one else could, because he always did. And after he was successful, Khalil would curry great favor with not only Brumbaugh, but with every other bigwig in the Kennedy Center who suffered through the uncomfortable climate in the building.

"So Barak, don't you think there's better things we can do with your time than keep you in maintenance?" Brumbaugh wheezed.

"Well, I'm not particularly fond of cleaning bathrooms or changing lightbulbs."

"How about if I talk to Mrs. Mehringer about moving you into the engineering department?"

"That'd be great. I don't want to seem ungrateful, but can I tell you what I'd really like?"

"Maybe. What is it?"

"When I first started here I worked a few times as a waiter, but I haven't done it much lately. Can I get some extra work as either a waiter or an usher, especially for the formal events?"

"Why would you want that? Isn't your father a sheik or something?" Brumbaugh asked. "You can't need the money."

"My father thinks it's important that I'm exposed to the upper class culture for when I go back home to Saudi Arabia after I finish school."

"You gotta be kidding?"

"No, sir."

"Well, what the fuck do I care. You've done good work. I said I'd take care of you. I'll see what I can do."

"Thank you, sir."

"You know, I guess that's probably not a bad idea for you. You're doing something with your life. Did you know the president is going to be here next week for some party? Maybe you'll get to meet him. I bet your father would like that."

"So would I. Very much, sir."

"Yeah, who wouldn't. But Barak, you've got to do me a favor, son."

"Yes, sir."

"Stop with that "sir" shit. Just call me John like everyone else. Okay?"

"Whatever you say, Sir John." Khalil smiled.

Brumbaugh chuckled and walked away. The spoiled rich Arab kid wasn't so bad after all.

KHALIL HAD SPENT AN HOUR in unit #710, his second and secret apartment, poring over the building plans to the Kennedy Center and meticulously laying out the antennae in anticipation of his monthly ham radio transmission with Ahmed. The two bottles of carbonyl chloride stolen from Hoosier Chemicals sat in the same closet as the electronic gear. By 11:55 p.m. Khalil's set was turned on and ready to go.

"Hello? Hello? Chicago here. Hello? Damn it!" Khalil sharply exhaled after his fourth attempt to make a connection failed. He fell back in his chair and massaged his closed eyes with his thumb and index finger. He kept trying for ten minutes, but no matter where

Khalil tuned the band, no response came.

Finally a voice squeaked through the airwaves. "Anybody out there? It's Boston calling."

"Excellent! Kevin here," Khalil quickly responded.

"Hey bro. It's Al," Ahmed declared.

The two-step city and name security code was complete. Khalil was relieved at finally making the very long distance connection with his brother.

"Where the fuck were you last month?" Khalil yelled.

"Sorry. I couldn't get through. I was in the West again."

As always, Ahmed's reference to the West meant he was in Gaza.

"Again?"

"Yeah, I've been there a lot lately. With Omar."

"How's all that going?"

"We're ahead of schedule. Everything's set with Hamas and the Jihad for about 300 suicide attacks to coincide with your project."

"Hey asshole, how about some discretion?" Khalil sniped, admonishing Ahmed to not be so obvious about such a public disclosure.

"Relax Kevin. You know this is secure, 100%."

"Yeah right," Khalil replied, knowing that at least in theory, Ahmed was correct. And with the exception of not disclosing most names and locations, their monthly conversations were increasingly less subtle in describing their plans. But so what? Even if some federal agency was eavesdropping, the wire couldn't be traced.

"We also just got Abu Nidal lined up," Ahmed advised.

"Who took care of that? The captain?" Khalil asked, referring to Sabar.

"No, I did. He made the introduction a long time ago, but that was it. We're really keeping him out of the loop. He still doesn't even know what you're up to."

"Good. What's Nidal responsible for?"

"The Knesset and hopefully Rabin."

"And the other 300 from the Jihad and Hamas?"

"Just random public targets. You know, where there's lots of

Jewish blood to be spilled."

"Nidal must have been expensive."

"Nope. He just wanted costs. He sees the big picture. This is the job of a lifetime for him. He's happy for the chance."

"So who knows the plan now?" Khalil asked, feeling a bit out of touch and dependent on Ahmed for information.

"Nobody knows about anything or anyone except Nidal, and all he knows is that he's part of some grand scheme. The only thing I've told everyone is to be ready in a few weeks, and not to proceed until they get the all clear on a radio broadcast."

"I don't follow."

"We had to figure out a way to coordinate the attack. The object is to hit Israel all at once. A blitz."

"Yeah, but what's this radio thing you mentioned?"

"Omar's developed contacts who operate a radio station in the West. Once we confirm your success, we'll broadcast a special message inviting the destruction of the Zionists. That will be the signal to go. But the president and I know that if you don't waste the Americans, and we go ahead with the bombing anyway, then we might as well move into the Cave and stay there the rest of our lives. That means you better get it done."

"I will," Khalil replied. "You're really on track."

"Yeah, it's pretty incredible. Think about it. You take out the leadership of the U.S. and we take care of Israel. All in one day!"

"Well, the hard part is still yet to come," said Khalil.

"That's true. Just keep your focus. Keep thinking D E A D. Discipline --"

"I don't need a lecture Al," Khalil interrupted.

"It's not a lecture. I'm just trying to..."

"Drop it," Khalil barked.

"Okay. Okay. So how's your life? Are things all right?"

"Work's fine. I got a promotion into engineering and I'm waiting at special events. School's fine. I'm still getting A's. Everything's fine. Next question." Months after moving to the U.S., Khalil still hadn't told Ahmed that his closest friend in Washington happened to be a Jewish girl.

"Okay," Ahmed said, "so how's the planning on your end?"

"Most of the hard stuff has been taken care of."

"What about that lady that Uncle Carl met with where you work?"

"Her? I thought I told you. She's been gone a while. An accident. She fell in the bathtub, cracked her head and drowned. A real shame. Nice lady. Tough break."

"You find the material yet?"

"Yeah. In fact I've already brought a lot of it in."

"Already?"

"I'm working with small quantities. I've got to be careful."

"What are you using, Sarin?"

"No Phosgene. Sarin's too volatile to temperature and storage conditions. That's what the Japanese used in that subway incident."

"I don't remember Phosgene."

"Yes you do. If you take carbonyl chloride and mix it with water, it hydrolizes into gas. The Germans used it in World War I. Even dispersed outdoors it killed thousands."

"Hmmm," Ahmed replied, not really remembering the detail from the poison gas lessons given by Carlos. "How much do you need?"

Khalil laughed. "Not much. I've got ten gallons of the stuff. I've triple checked my chemical analysis. A lethal concentration would be about a half a milligram per 1000 cubic feet for ten minutes. I'm gonna pump it in at a rate of twenty grams for about two minutes. It should take out the whole building almost instantly because even two or three breaths will be fatal. And since the gas is clear and odorless it'll be over before anyone knows what happened. *Nobody* walks out of there," Khalil authoritatively pronounced.

"Awesome. Imagine what that'll look like on T.V. going out live around the world."

"Yeah, I know. About 2000 bodies with bug eyes. Uncle Carl would be really proud," Khalil said.

"He'll never get to tell you. He's not going anywhere."

"Yeah, I kind of figured that," Khalil said sadly. "He's completely disappeared from the papers."

"Right. You realize that could be us one day," Ahmed pointed out.

There was a brief uneasy silence between the brothers before Khalil changed the subject. "Hey, I get to serve President Tate on Friday at work at some major function. I've been thinking of taking him out right then."

"What?" Ahmed asked, shocked by Khalil's remark.

"You heard me. I'll be right next to him. I already figured out how to kill him."

"Are you fucking crazy? Don't even think about it. If you get caught, everything we've done goes right down the drain. The CIA will also pick apart your alias and trace you back home. Is that what you want?"

"No, no, no. You don't understand. I'm not gonna shoot him or break his neck or anything like that. If I slip even two drops of carbonyl chloride onto his food after it mixes in his stomach, it'll kill him. It should even look like a heart attack. There's no way it can get traced to me."

"Oh, Allah," Ahmed moaned. "You've been away too long. You've gone nuts. Don't do it. Wait. You'll have your chance."

"We'll see. No promises. I gotta go. I'm tired. Talk to you soon."

Before Ahmed could respond, Khalil flicked off the power switch on the ham radio. A world away a stunned Ahmed could only respond with, "Oh shit."

"HORS D'OEUVRE, SIR? Hors d'oeuvre, ma'am?" Khalil repeated over and over as he spun around to minor variations of the same face. In response, outstretched hands picked diminutive colorful geometrically unique creations of food off his silver serving platter. He barely needed to move through the black tie crowd filling out the Kennedy Center's South Roof Gallery, before his tray was swiped clean and he returned to the adjacent Roof Terrace Restaurant kitchen for a refill.

As he reentered the reception, an incredibly stunning, curly coiffed blonde, wearing an ankle length black dress with a front slit running up her legs to Mount Venus, pressed her water balloon breasts against Khalil's arm. "I'd love to have a cocktail weenie," she smiled with a whisper and hardly a hint of innocence behind her silver dollar sized eyes.

"I'm sorry maam, I only have quiches," he responded with raised eyebrows.

"Oh no. I bet you have a maaaa-jor cocktail weenie," she purred.

"I'm not sure that's being served tonight," he smiled back, trying to stay out of previously uncharted waters.

"Now you've told me that you're not just one of those regular dumbbell waiters. You're *much* too quick. You must be a student. Law, I bet."

"Close. Engineering at G.W."

"Ahhhh, how did I know? What is your name?" she said, looking down at his namepin and reading *"Barak"* aloud. "Barak, what an exotic name."

"It's the name of the horse the prophet Mohammed rode up to heaven."

"Yes, a stallion," she observed with a tilt of her head. "Call me Hot Babe."

Just as Khalil realized he was overmatched, an elderly couple approached him and attacked the tray.

"Excuse me," he said to them all when the old geezers finished their feeding frenzy. He ducked away and thought to himself, *"Saved."*

Suddenly, the attention of all 600 present shifted to the middle of the room where some of the guests broke into applause as a small group exited the elevator. Khalil couldn't see what was happening through the crowd, but his instincts told him the guest of honor had arrived. He was proven correct a moment later when the orchestra stopped midsong, and the band leader dramatically announced, "Ladies and gentlemen, the President and First Lady of the United States, Walter and Dolores Tate."

The band broke into "Hail to the Chief," which was partially drowned out by thunderous clapping. The mass of people parted as the Secret Service led the Tates through the room to a podium bearing the presidential seal.

Smiling warmly, the president gave a five minute talk about the importance of dance in American society, during which he was repeatedly interrupted with rousing applause and laughter at his attempted humor.

Khalil kept his eyes trained intently on the president and the four Secret Service agents who surrounded him. The protectors' eyes peered straight ahead inspecting everything in their vicinity. Interspersed throughout the hall were at least another eight agents, their earphones and ill fitting suits indiscriminately standing out in the otherwise formally attired crowd.

A tightly controlled reception and photograph line formed to the side of the Tates. Khalil circled around the room with a full platter, always watching the roving Secret Service agents. He could see that other waiters unhesitatingly approached the Tates to offer food and drink. He picked up a fresh platter to serve those guests patiently waiting their turn to exchange greetings with the First Family.

Earlier in the day when Khalil went to work, the Secret Service was already planted in The Kennedy Center, well into their security preparations for the evening's event. Every person entering the building passed through a metal detector which checked for weapons. When the Service inspected Barak Hamas' backpack, having just come from school, they found nothing extraordinary. Just a textbook, legal pad, paper clips, pencils and a fountain pen. A fountain pen which they failed to closely inspect. A fountain pen not filled with ink, but with carbonyl chloride.

Right now the writing instrument was secured into place on his inside left wrist by his Rolex watch band and two rubber bands. Earlier in the week when Khalil recognized the potential opportunity that lay before him, he reengineered the mechanism of the pen to suit his clandestine purposes. With hours of practice he mastered placing as many drops of liquid out of the pen as he wished onto a spot the size of a dime, with the mere flick of his left fourth finger onto a retrofitted lever on the flaired head of the pen.

Khalil was certain that during the course of the evening the chance to approach and serve the president would present itself. During that brief moment, Walter Tate could help himself to whatever appetizer he wanted off of Khalil's tray, and Khalil would deftly drop his poison squarely on the target while handing the president a paper napkin. And after that, either the president's stomach juices or the next sip of champagne would start the chemical combustion process culminating with severe chest pains, then internal suffocation. The whole thing would be over in about two minutes. Since his heart would blow up, the coroner would report a heart attack.

"Now seems as good a time as any," Khalil thought. Before picking up a fresh platter, Khalil pulled the pen out three inches from inside his sleeve so that the tip rested just outside the cuff, not even visible. His heart started to pound as it never had before. He took a deep breath to help keep his focus and discipline.

Zeroing in on Walter Tate, Khalil went into a zone, closing out everything around him. There was no music, no crowd. Just a tray of food and the president. He glided out of the kitchen through the guests towards the official entourage. The event seemed surrealistic. The people around him moved in slow motion.

Khalil al-Sharif, arguably now one of the most dangerous men in the world was standing six inches in front of arguably, the most powerful man in the world. The secret service was six feet away. For the first time, in that moment, Khalil understood his own inate power. If he wanted to, he could have snapped the president's neck. But that wasn't the plan.

"Mr. President, would you care for an hors d'oeuvre, sir?"

"Sure," Tate said in his folksy drawl, picking a spinach quiche off the tray and holding it between his thumb and index finger.

"Here's a napkin for you, sir." Khalil lifted his left hand over the president's, extending a blood red square napkin between his index finger and thumb, while pushing bombs away from the pen with his fourth finger.

The President of the United States looked down at Khalil with a warm smile and a nod, "Thank you son." In one bite the appetizer disappeared into his mouth.

Khalil turned on his heels and walked back into the crowd. The mission was a success.

The president could be dead. Today, however, was only a test run. Water, not carbonyl chloride, really filled the pen's cartridge. However, Khalil now knew the Secret Service set up and what he was capable of achieving. Carlos was right. Rule Number Two...Know Your Enemy. But there were bigger things in store, and only weeks away. A bigger picture to consider. The next inauguration. The last inauguration.

THIRTY

"**I** REALLY CAN'T BELIEVE you brought me here," Khalil sighed, shaking his head at Debra Klein.

"Barak, chill out. What's the big deal?" she replied, her hands firmly planted on her hips.

"Taking *me* to the Holocaust Museum? Come on. There's got to be a point behind this somewhere," Khalil said.

"The architecture is brilliant, isn't it?" Debra remarked, ignoring Khalil. She turned slowly in a full circle. "Look at everything. The brick walls, the vents, the iron work. I guess they want you to feel like you're in a death camp."

"I do," he muttered.

"Then you can leave right now," Debra snapped. She then glared at him, turned on her heels and stormed off.

Khalil stood still for about three seconds. "No wait. I'm coming," he said chasing after her.

"Don't do me any favors," she said, not even turning her head to him while continuing to walk away.

"No. I promised I'd do this," Khalil said, stopping her by a gentle tug of the arm. "C'mon Debra. Let's go on the tour."

"I don't want to force you." The irritated expression she wore hardly belied the fact that's exactly what she wanted to do.

"Like you said before. Maybe I'll learn something."

"You will."

Minutes later they stood shoulder to shoulder in front of encased Nazi storm trooper uniforms at the beginning of the exhibition on the fourth floor. The hall was dimly lit, consistent with the somber mood of the thick line of visitors. Debra stood before the case and stared at the swastika. Even through the shadows, Khalil could see she was misty eyed.

"I'm not going to deny I had an agenda in bringing you here," Debra finally said as they walked through the exhibit.

He considered sniping at her, starting yet another round of sarcastic barbs that seemed to continuously flow between them, but decided against it. "So what's on your mind?" he asked as they moved through the exhibit.

"You know, even though we've become so close, there's still this -- this distance between us and I --"

"No there's not," he interrupted.

Debra clicked her tongue against the roof of her mouth and exhaled in frustration, "Yes there is. As well as I know you Barak, there's this side of you I can't understand for the life of me."

"I don't know what you're talking about," he replied.

After a moment's pause she finally blurted out, "The only thing I can figure is that our religions come between us."

"You had to bring me here to tell me that?"

"Yes, I did. I know they teach anti-semetism in the Middle East, but that's okay. I remember my Uncle Phil saying the only good Arab was a dead Arab, and to this day he won't buy a Mercedes."

Khalil shook his head.

"Anyway, it's obvious you can't deal with my being Jewish."

"Oh," Khalil said, now rolling his eyes but making sure Debra couldn't see him.

"But here I can show you something to make you think twice about wanting to push my people into the sea."

"I don't think that way," he lied.

"Maybe you do. Maybe you don't. But, deep down, I believe to you I'm a Jew and you're an Arab. And that's a conflict. Am I right? If there's anything to our friendship, tell me the truth."

Khalil bit his lower lip, wondering how he'd gotten into this position. The truth was that since he first arrived in Washington, his one true friend, the one person he could depend on, was Debra. He owed her the truth. At least to this question. "Yeah. You're right. Until we met, I always thought Jews were evil."

"Why? What have we done that's so wrong?"

Khalil looked down for a moment, unwilling to answer.

"Well?"

"Fine. You want to know? Israel stole our land."

"What? We stole nothing! Jews have been on that land for 4000 years! Tell me why we don't have a right to be there. And give me an intelligent response. Not that propaganda shit."

Not having an answer, Khalil shrugged, feeling a bit stupid.

"So, I guess there are two sides to the story."

"I guess," he replied sheepishly.

"Did you know Islam and Judaism have many similar beliefs?"

"I doubt that."

"It's true. Mohammmmed drew on principles of Judaism in his teachings. Tell me, who's considered the father of Islam?"

"Abraham," Khalil impatiently replied.

"Right. Do you know who's the father of Judaism?"

"No."

"Abraham. The same Abraham. The same Abraham whose son Ishmael built the Great Mosque in Mecca. What's it called, Kaaba?"

"Yeah," Khalil said, surprised by Debra's knowledge.

"You don't eat pork. That's the same as us keeping kosher. And isn't zakat, giving to charity, one of the important tenets of Islam?" she continued.

"Yes. I'm impressed." And he was.

"Well Jews have the same thing. It's called *zedakah*. It almost sounds the same."

Khalil mulled over his theology lesson. "I didn't know any of this stuff before."

"That's my point. I bet most Jews and Arabs don't either."

"How did you learn all this?"

"I read, you big jerk. I wanted to learn about Islam because of you. And by the way, it was Abraham who settled in the land of Canaan, which is now the same land known as Israel. So the Jews didn't steal anything."

"Ohh. So if Abraham was the father of my people and he settled in Canaan, then we have the same right to the land of Israel as the Jews, right?" Khalil answered, pleased with himself.

For a moment Debra was stumped. "No. You have the entire Middle East. We should be able to have a homeland. You do. I just think that if we educated each other, a mutual respect could develop and then all this killing could stop."

"It'll never happen. You can't change something that's been going on for centuries. A lot of Islamics believe it's good to die for the cause of hurting Israel."

"Then those are the people we should start with."

"You're so naive."

She ignored him, not wanting to believe the truth. They had been walking through the museum and were now standing before a solitary wooden boxcar. Debra took a deep breath and exhaled at the sight of it. "During World War II Hitler killed over six million Jews. The Germans would go into towns throughout Europe, round up all the Jews, and send them on these boxcars to the death camps."

"I know. I've heard."

"My parents tell me they lost their grandparents and most of their families. Something like 100 people. Imagine if some madman killed your whole family and tried to wipe out your entire religion."

Khalil was silent. He never had to think about it before, but it didn't sound right.

"How many people do you think could fit in there?" Debra asked, pointing at the boxcar.

"To the extent people are supposed to fit in a boxcar, I guess 30 or so comfortably."

"How about 60?"

"That would be tight."

"How about 100? For three days, without food, water or a bathroom."

"No way."

"Yes. Men, women and children. And what if that was your family? Your people?"

"I...I didn't realize." Rubbing his chin in thought he softly added, "That's very cruel."

"This is nothing. Wait 'til you see what the death camps were like. That's where the real atrocities were."

Forty minutes later Khalil understood what Auschwitz was. He witnessed the authentic wooden barracks, the grotesque torture performed on Jews by the butcher Mengele, the bales of human hair, and the model of the poison gas showers and crematorium.

After viewing the display of the thousands of victims' shoes, Khalil was visibly moved. He turned to Debra and solemnly asked, "Debra, I get the point. Can we go?"

"Yes. I've seen enough too."

When they got outside, the sky was burnt orange, unusual for a January day. Debra raised her arm to hail a cab.

Khalil pulled her hand down. "C'mon, lets walk."

"It's chilly out and it's getting dark."

"It's not that cold. We'll walk fast. It's only a mile."

"All right," Debra said begrudgingly. They headed up 14th Street with The Capitol lit up to their right down the Mall, and the Washington Monument majestically illuminated in The Ellipse to the immediate left.

Debra weaved her arm inside Khalil's, surprising him. Not sure what to do, he did nothing. They walked for a block in total silence, staring straight ahead. Subtlely tugging her arm, Khalil navigated Debra off the Constitution Avenue sidewalk and up and through the immense lawn of the Ellipse, as a shortcut up to the George Washington University district where they both lived.

Just as they passed a small cluster of bushes, two young black men wearing knit caps jumped out brandishing knives. The larger man, easily six inches taller than Khalil, stuck his knife three inches from Khalil's nose and screamed, "Mothufukka, gimme your watch and wallet or I kill you now. Bitch gimme your purse." The smaller man's knife threateningly slashed at the air around Debra. She froze in shock and terror.

"You guys leave right now and I won't hurt you," Khalil said calmly. "I don't want trouble with you. And I promise you. You don't want it with me."

Khalil's assailant moved the blade directly onto his cheek. "I'll start with your eye. Don't fuck with me."

In a flash, the other man placed his knife directly under Debra's chin, and added, "And I'll cut her throat."

"Please Barak," Debra trembled. "Do what he wants. It's only money. Take my purse," she told her assailant.

"It's not the money, Debra. It's the threat. And I don't like threats, especially to you."

"I'm gonna count to three man, then that's it," the first man shouted.

"One," Khalil shouted back.

"What?" the man said in bewilderment.

"I said *one*!"

"Man, you're crazy!"

"You know it! *Two*," Khalil shouted again.

"Barak. *No! No!*" Debra cried out.

Not understanding what was happening, the attackers stood frozen in their places.

"Three," Khalil shouted. In one fluid move, he kicked upwards with his right foot catching the little man square in the chest and sending him flying, while sweeping his left arm up and underneath his attacker's arm. He followed with an immediate punch directly to the throat. The large man fell to the ground, stunned for a moment before jumping right back up and lunging at Khalil with the knife. Khalil sidestepped the move and caught the man's arm. He twisted it downwards, breaking it and forcing the man to stab himself in the side. The attacker, now victim, let out an inhumane shriek

and fell to his knees.

The small man, still sitting, inched backwards, his eyes wide open. He got up and started to run away. Khalil ripped the knife out of his assailant's body resulting in another scream and whipped the blade through the black night. Ten yards away the other man went down clutching his hamstring and yelping, "My leg. Jesus, my leg."

Khalil grabbed Debra by the hand. "Let's get out of here."

She looked over her would be attackers and then at Khalil, clearly stunned.

"Well this is a first. I've never seen *you* at a loss for words," Khalil said calmly, as if absolutely nothing had just happened.

"Uhh. Yeah. Right," she whispered, tears starting to stream down her face.

"C'mon Debra. We've got to go," he said, gently reaching out for her hand and leading her away. "I don't want to have to deal with the police."

"You saved my life," she said softly.

"Mistakes happen," he smiled.

"No seriously. Barak, you saved my life."

"Well of course I did. I had to. Debra, you're my friend. My *Jewish* friend," he said, genuinely meaning it.

"Your friends and family don't know I exist, do they?"

He paused for a moment. "No."

She grimaced at the response. "What would they say if they knew you saved the life of a Jew?"

"You wouldn't want to know," he replied, truthfully.

She stared at the ground.

Khalil realized he hurt Debra and he didn't really want to. "No actually, they'd say that Allah would be pleased."

Debra half-smiled, wanting to believe it was true. "Can I ask you a question?"

"I may not answer it, but yeah, what?"

"Where did you learn that karate stuff? You were incredible."

"When I was in the army in Iraq."

"What?"

"Yeah, special training."

"No wait. You said Iraq. You're from Saudi Arabia."

For the slightest instant, Khalil's face turned to stone. Recovering, he said smoothly, "It was a special training program. I spent a few months there."

"I thought the Saudis and Iraq didn't get along?"

"Western propaganda."

"Oh. I see."

A couple of blocks later, Debra suddenly stopped walking. She tilted her head to the side and gave Khalil her best puppy dog look. Nudging up against his chest, she threw her arms around his neck and pulled his face into hers. Before Khalil knew what was happening, Debra thrust her tongue deep inside his mouth and began to gyrate her hips against him. Caught up in the moment, Khalil pulled Debra even tighter and closed his eyes. Debra reached down, grabbed Khalil's hand and placed it squarely on her breast. He intuitively massaged her spongy flesh, causing Debra to purr. He felt a strange rush of something he couldn't identify surge through his stomach, taking his breath away.

She moved her lips to Khalil's neck and worked her way up to his ear lobe. He shuddered.

She whispered, "Barak, take me home. I want you."

Her words were like a slap across the face and he pulled back, holding her by the shoulders at arms length. "No Debra. No. We can't do this."

"Why not? We're both just regular people who care for each other. We have so much in common. You know I'm right."

"It could never work. There are things about me I can't explain and you could never understand."

She looked up at him, tears running out of her eyes again. "I'm sorry. I'm such a fool. I should have known better. And now I've blown a friendship."

With a gentle brush of the back of his hand against her face, Khalil wiped away her tears. "No, Debra. You're wrong. You are special to me. And you always will be."

THIRTY-ONE

Baqaa, Jordan

"EVERYBODY LOOK HERE. To extend the buttstock, pull it out fully past the locked position, rotate it halfway around clockwise and then release the stock. You see how it springs forward and locks. Everybody understand?" Norman Richards asked, holding a NATO M249 Squad Automatic Rifle firmly across his chest. Four Arabs ten feet away nodded their heads in understanding, but the blank expressions on their faces said otherwise.

"Who wants to try it?" Richards asked, extending the rifle out toward them.

Nobody budged. Richards gently placed the gun down on the rocky ground right outside the same safehouse where the Israelis attacked him and Abu Nasir years ago.

"Did I mention it comes with a 100 round assault pack?"

Again, everyone nodded.

"Okay. Any questions about the specs or how this thing works?"

The group shook their heads no.

"Good. I can get as many of these as you want. Right now I've got immediate access to something like thirty dozen."

"That's at $1200 each, right?" asked one of the men.

"Ahbala. I *never* told you that price. They're $1360."

"No, no, Mr. Norman." The man smiled, showing yellow crooked teeth. Wagging his finger he added, "You told me $1200. But I'll go $1220." Ali Ahbala, an Islamic fundamentalist leader from a small Iranian city turned to his two companions who nodded their heads in agreement.

"You can say all you want about going up to $1220, but I'm not coming off $1360," Richards said, crossing his arms on his chest. "If you don't want them, I don't care. There's practically no net margin on these for me so I'm not giving them away."

Norman and Ahbala stared at each other for a moment, before Ahbala looked over to his associates for guidance. One of them whispered something into Ahbala's ear.

"$1260," Ahbala countered.

Richards threw his arms out to the side. "What's the matter with you? Are you fucking deaf? I said $1360."

"Hey, do you want to do business or what? I don't need you to insult me," the Arab shouted back, without a hint of anger showing on his face. He wasn't really insulted, this was part of the bargaining process.

"What insult?" Richards asked. "And even if it was, the price is still $1360."

Ahbala thought about it and then announced, "Our last offer -- $1300."

"$1300? Come on!" Richards yelled, kicking the dirt. He leaned back on the broken wood fence and pulled a tiny pocket calculator out of his blue jean jacket pocket and tapped in some numbers. It was all an act. His cost was only $765 per rifle, but that was none of their business. Just the fact that Ahbala and his entourage had traveled all the way from Iran told him they were real buyers. "Okay, fine. $1300. How many do you want?"

"Six dozen."

"How about you?" Richards asked the fourth man. Unlike the others, this man was dressed in a white thobe and gutra, had come to the presentation alone and so far remained silent. Because of his attire and goatee, Richards guessed that he was a Saudi. "What's your name again?"

"Yasser Sarraj. I didn't come for guns. I want computers."

"That's right. I remember. Laptops. I've got 486's, 200 megahertz, 33 meg of RAM and a 2.2 gig hard drive. Loaded with software. All in English though."

"We want them, too," Ahbala interjected. "How much?"

"$1550 each. I can get you 60 of them."

"What about a warranty?"

"A warranty? Are you kidding?"

"Not at all."

"No fuckin' warranties. You got it? You want them, fine. You don't, I don't give a shit."

"We'll take them."

"I'll take three dozen but I also want mainframes and a network," said Yasser Sarraj.

"Can't get that. What do you want a mainframe for?"

The man paused before answering, "My business."

"Do you mean like none of my business or the business that you conduct?"

"Both," he replied with a frown.

"Oh." Norman knew Sarraj was lying and that he wasn't just the typical village leader arming his people. "I can make some calls. No promises, but it's harder for me to get high tech stuff than it is to get guns. I'm gonna have to know where to send it, because that'll affect cost."

"I don't talk business in front of strangers," Sarraj said, tilting his head in the direction of the others.

"Fine, but I don't do side deals. Everybody pays the same price."

Sarraj stepped up to Richards, stared straight into his eyes and whispered, "Is that why your cost on the M249's is $765 each and you sold them to Abu Nasir for $900 each?"

Richards bit his tongue, surprised by the man's knowledge. After a moment's contemplative pause he whispered back, "Well maybe

you have a good point after all. Can you excuse me for a second?"
Sarraj nodded.

Richards walked over to the other men scratching the back of his
head. "Mr. Yasser's got some real private business. We've got to
respect that. Give me five minutes, okay?"

He returned to Sarraj who instructed, "Into your van. Let's go."

Richards obeyed, although his instincts told him to prepare for
trouble. "What the hell's going on here?" Richards demanded, casually dropping his left hand to the door's map compartment where
he kept hidden a loaded palm sized Derringer two shot .38 special.

"You never found who destroyed the U.N. in Geneva did you?"

Richards couldn't stop his face from going flush. Nobody outside Nasir's group, and the U.S. and Israeli intelligence was supposed to know that was his charge. "Who are you?"

"You don't know, huh? Well I know you. Norman Richards.
CIA agent gone bad. Now an arms, high-tech and odds and ends
merchant. But still employed by the CIA. Let's see -- sometimes
goes by the nickname of Boomer, is hot-tempered and -- you're an
alcoholic."

Richards didn't know how to reply, so he responded to the only
non-truth. "I'm not with the Agency any more."

"Sure," the man said sarcastically. "You have some important
friends around that tell me that, but I don't believe it. Regardless,
you're with them after today."

"Who are you? CIA? Mossad?"

"Neither. I'm a little surprised you don't recognize me."

"Sarraj. Yasser Sarraj," Richards mumbled, searching his
memory and coming up empty, although something about the man's
face was vaguely familiar.

The Arab took off his sunglasses. "Rashid Sabar. I work for
Saddam Hussein. Sound familiar now?"

Richards nodded his head in acknowledgement, wondering what
new trouble he was in. "Captain Sabar, the chief of the Mukhabarat.
The beard and clothing threw me off."

"Good."

"We've never met."

"No. And you didn't answer my question. You never found out who attacked the U.N., did you?"

"Why would I find out? It's not my concern," Richards replied innocently.

"Look, you American rat. I didn't come all this way to play games," Sabar said acerbically. "Word gets around. I know all about you, Sam Phillips and Dudi Bareket. Not too many people do, but I do. So where were you standing when you got shot? Inside, right?"

Richards bit down hard on his tongue and his chest began to pound. It was pointless to ask how Sabar knew about those events, much less who else knew. He took a deep breath presuming Iraq had a mole planted inside the Mossad. "Understand this right now, Sabar. I'm not doing business with you. That's the end of it." Richards opened the door to get out.

"It was Carlos," Sabar softly said.

Halfway out of the vehicle Richards stopped and looked back at Sabar, who simply nodded in confirmation.

"But he's in jail," Richards said. "The French have him."

"I know. I told the French he was in the Sudan. Use your diplomatic influence. Call Charles Pasqua, the French Interior Minister. Ask him."

Richards got back in and closed the door. "I don't believe you."

"Can you afford not to?" Sabar solemnly replied.

"Why are you telling me this? What do you want?"

"What do you think? Your help."

"With what?"

"We'll get to that. But first, pay attention because I will not say this twice. I realize you need to accept my credibility or you won't do what I ask."

"I don't think anything you say will make you credible." Nevertheless, Richards pulled a pen and a piece of paper from his shirt pocket.

"Go to Geneva. Check out the Grand Passage department store.

A crate of goods from there was delivered to Carlos' Baghdad home with governmental priority approval the day after the bombing."

"What else?"

"That's all I've got to prove it was Carlos, but I know I'm right. I can't place him in Geneva but I confirmed he was out of Iraq when the explosion occurred, and that when he returned the next day, Saddam was very pleased with him. And look into Seve Dolchino, too."

"Dolchino? The KGB Dolchino?"

"Who else?"

"I remember hearing that Carlos and Dolchino were close. And everybody knew Saddam was sheltering Carlos. But Dolchino?"

"That's what I'm getting to."

"You mean there's something *besides* the U.N. job?"

"I think the U.N. blast was just the beginning of something Carlos planned that is much bigger."

"What is this *I think* shit? Do you know *anything* for sure? You tell me Carlos blew up the U.N. but your only proof is that he had some stuff delivered from a store in Geneva. I don't trust you. I think this is a set up."

"Damn it!" Sabar exploded. "Just listen to what I have to say! I'm risking my life just being here."

"You think it's different for me?" Richards snapped back.

"If I wanted you dead, Richards, you would have been already," Sabar fumed. "I need you to deliver a message."

"I can't think of one fucking reason why I should trust you."

"Maybe I don't blame you, but it's irrelevant right now because the fact is, you're here."

"Then tell me. What do you really want?"

"I've come to realize Iraq can't go on any longer with Saddam running the country. We need to redevelop ties with old friends. Allies like America. Iraq's strongest point in time was when we were a team."

"Ahh, my good friend Judas Iscariot. Nice to meet you," Richards said dryly, symbolically sticking out his hand. "So you want a coup?"

"Believe me, I don't feel good about it, but I love my country and it's being ruined. And I'm afraid that Saddam has cooked up some master scheme that will destroy Iraq forever."

"So what the fuck does this have to do with me?"

"Deliver the message. I help the U.S. I want it to help me. I would think your bosses would be happy if Saddam was dead and Baghdad was friendly."

"Why me? Why not Sam Phillips or someone else?"

"You know my position, my responsibilities. Every minute of my day is accounted for. If I was caught talking to Phillips I'd be taken out and shot. Besides, I don't trust him. At least with you I can say I was buying weapons that we can't purchase because the U.N. embargo is still in place. But most important, both Abu Nasir and Ghassan Kassem speak well of you. I understand you have some peculiarities. You drink, you fight, you're vulgar, but at least you're honest."

"Am I supposed to be flattered?"

The men sat in silence as Richards pondered the situation. "All right," he finally said. "I'll listen to you. Make it quick."

"Good. Carlos and Dolchino trained three young Iraqi soldiers to be terrorists. They're now very skilled, smart, and cold blooded killers. They single handedly took on a platoon of my best Mukhabarat on a surprise raid and wiped them out without suffering a scratch."

"And I assume they now do Saddam's bidding."

"Correct. But here's the problem. Saddam's kept me away from them so I don't know their agenda. I just know that it's big. It may involve killing President Tate. They were supposed to work for me, but they haven't. One of them, Omar Rafsani was originally assigned to me. I took him across the Mideast introducing him to government leaders, terrorists, money men and so on. Saddam pulled him off my detail and now he and another of Carlos's men, Ahmed al-Sharif, have been setting up a massive operation with Hamas and the Jihad."

Paying close attention, Richards wrote down every word Sabar spoke.

"Anyway, a couple of weeks ago Saddam made a very strong remark about how he would be the undisputed leader of the Mideast in less than a month, and that we would never have to worry about Israel or the U.S. again. He said it was a done deal."

"What did he mean by that?"

"I asked him and he changed the subject. I couldn't push it."

"He can't be crazy enough to attack the U.S. Could it be atomic weapons?"

"No. We have plenty of material, but our bomb isn't ready yet. Besides, I understand that if it was used on Israel, the nuclear fallout would cover Jordan, Syria, Lebanon and all the critical Arab water supplies. Not practical."

"Wait a second. Hold on. You told me Carlos's two guys were dealing with Hamas and the Jihad. Those organizations don't operate in the U.S. At least directly."

"Right. That's where you come in. The third soldier has been living in the United States. And he's the most dangerous of all. Brilliant. Cold blooded."

"My kind of guy."

"I know he's been planted there for a reason and it must tie in with what Omar Rafsani and Ahmed al-Sharif are doing here."

"What's his name?"

"Khalil al-Sharif."

"Any relation to the other guy?"

"Brothers. Twins."

"Hmm. Nice twist. So where's he at?"

Sabar looked down, not wanting to answer, even though it was a legitimate question. The critical one. "I don't know. Maybe New York. Maybe Washington or Boston."

"Great," Richards said looking up and shaking his head. "So what the fuck am I supposed to do?"

"Find him. Stop him."

Richards burst out laughing but Sabar sat stonefaced. Seeing Sabar was serious, Richards said, "You're not joking, are you?"

"Find him."

"You're unfuckingbelievable! Why would I possibly consider trying to locate this Khalil?"

"Because if you don't he'll blow up half your country. Or do something equally extreme."

"The FBI can find him."

"Really? They haven't yet and he's been there for a while."

"And now they'll know to look."

"Yes, but only you will know *who* to look for," Sabar said, handing Richards a photograph of Khalil.

"Well now they will."

"No they won't," Sabar said, grabbing back the print. "I keep this. You memorize his face."

"What do you mean memorize his face? Gimme the goddamn picture," Richards said, trying unsuccessfully to grab it back.

"I'll kill you before I let you leave with it," Sabar said matter of factly. Richards could see that Sabar meant what he said.

"Why? What's the big deal if I take the picture to the professionals who can locate him?"

The big deal is that there's not going to be any hard evidence to trace this investigation back to me. Study the picture. Then go find him."

"Why me? I still don't get it."

"Because I do not yet trust anyone else in your government."

"Then why are you doing this?"

"Hopefully to open the door to trust. And to create an opportunity for me. I help you out and possibly save Iraq."

"You really think turning in your own countrymen is for the good of Iraq?" Richards asked sarcastically.

"You have no idea how dangerous these three men are, especially Khalil. Whatever it is they're up to was planned meticulously by Carlos and sanctioned by Saddam. Do you understand?"

Sabar took a deep breath and continued. "Look, I'll admit it. On one hand, I don't care if you Americans live or die, but unfortunately, the United States is the only superpower left, and Saddam just doesn't get it. The repercussions from whatever he's got planned will be devastating. Iraq will never trump the U.S. I realize that. I also remember what a friendly U.S. can do for Iraq. Plus, I hate to admit it, but I see a benefit to peace with Israel."

"This is real goddamn logical," Richards said shaking his head. "I go tell my old spy buddies that we've got to -- no, *I've* got to stop this wild man Arab terrorist from pulling off some unknown cockamamie scheme, and that I learned about it from Saddam's right hand man who favors peace with Israel. This is crazy. They'll never believe me!"

"Yes, but I imagine they will take you more seriously if you tell them what you discover in Geneva about the U.N."

It took a moment to sink in, but Richards finally understood the whole scenario.

"And try this one out. I think Carlos was the one who killed your CIA Director Richter."

"No way. It was a common street murder."

"C'mon Richards, you know better. The Director of the CIA is under watch every second of the day. His security is almost as tight as the president's. That is, unless he was doing something he shouldn't be doing."

"So why do you think it was Carlos?"

"Because just like with the U.N., he was out of Iraq when it happened and returned right afterwards. And also, you know how it was always the French that wanted to capture Carlos?"

"Yeah."

"Well the day after Richter got killed, the U.S. told the French they'd do whatever it took to help catch Carlos, even though for 20 years before that, the CIA never spent a minute trying to get him. Then suddenly I start getting calls from France, because you know, Carlos was living in Iraq. And then, after he's captured in the Sudan based on my information, the U.S. takes the Sudan off its black list of terrorist countries."

Richards whistled.

"I bet if you go home and tell that story to the right people you'll get all the cooperation you need to find Khalil."

"Okay. I see how this is good for you. What do I get out of it?"

"I thought you were smart."

Richards stared at him blankly.

"You get whatever you want. Not only from the U.S. who will owe you big time, but also from Iraq and every other country that hates Saddam and learns you helped get rid of him. You'll be a very rich man. And a very powerful one."

Richards lay his head back on the car rest and put his foot up on the dashboard. For two solid minutes he stared at the same spot on the inside roof of the van. He slowly turned his head towards Sabar and said, "Let me see that picture again."

Sabar nodded and smiled, handing Richards the photograph of Khalil. "This is from Mukhabarat files. He may look different. Just remember the eyes."

"Don't worry, I never forget a face. It's names I can't remember." Richards tapped on the notepad with his pen and circled *Khalil al-Sharif.* "Let's go," he said. "I still gotta get rid of those bums."

Richards and Sabar stepped out of the van and walked back to Ali Ahbala and his companions.

"Ahbala. Sorry. It seems Mr. Sarraj here was able to convince me to go into a new line of business with him."

"Ahhh, free enterprise. Very good," Ahbala said begrudgingly. "But you did not sell him my computers, I trust?"

"Nope. You want the 486's right?"

"Yes. Two dozen. But we want all 72 of the M249's."

"Fine. Then I need my 50% deposit right now." Richards started clicking away again on his pocket calculator. "That's $60,400.

One of Ahbala's men pulled six stacks of American bills out of his briefcase. "Here it is. Sixty thousand dollars."

"Good enough."

"When do we close?"

"Tomorrow. As always, the balance is due then."

"So soon?" Ahbala remarked.

"Yeah, well, I'm going out of town right afterwards. I wanna wrap this deal up."

"That will be fine."

Richards walked back up to Rashid Sabar. As they shook hands he whispered, "What if I have to talk to you? How can I reach you?"

"You cannot. No more talk. No more meetings. Unless, of course, you succeed." Sabar then gave Richards a cold hard stare. "One last thing. You don't have much time. Saddam was very specific. Something's going to happen. And soon."

RICHARDS REPEATEDLY BASHED on the front door of a boxy little whitewashed row home on a tree lined street in the heart of suburban Jerusalem. Although the lights were out, he put his ear to the door and heard music. After another two minutes of pounding, a light in the front room finally turned on.

Sam Phillips opened the door, standing in a barely closed mid-thigh bathrobe. Red faced and breathing heavily, his jaw dropped when he saw it was Norman Richards. "What the hell are you doing here? It's 2:00 in the fucking morning."

"Damn, you're observant. And normally it's me that's drunk and not you. We've got to talk. Now."

They were interrupted by a young girl of maybe 18 with flowing wavy brown hair and a towel barely wrapped around her prancing out from the back of the house.

"Sammie. Who's here?" she cooed.

"Your daughter?" Richards said facetiously.

"Someone's," Phillips replied.

"Cute."

"She's an athlete, man," Phillips whispered.

"Sammie," she impatiently demanded tossing her hair back off her shoulder.

"Sammie?...Sammie?" Richards teased.

Phillips mouthed "fuck you" to Richards and turned around to face the girl. "Hey baby, go back and lie down. I'll be there in two minutes. This is one of my business associates."

"Okay," she whined. "But hurry."

"Right baby," Phillips said, waving her away.

"Baby. You're not kidding," Richards editorialized.

"With the lifestyle you lead, you're hardly one to criticize."

"Who's criticizing. She's a grown teenager," Richards cracked.

"Make it quick. What do you want?"

"Are you sober? This is important."

"Sober enough," Phillips replied.

Richards then relayed in full his conversation with Rashid Sabar. Phillips was stunned by both the source of information and the magnitude of it. If he wasn't sober when Richards started, he was by the time Richards finished.

Rubbing his chin in thought, Phillips paced around his living room for a minute. "Norman, do you believe him?"

"Well, it's like he said. Can we afford not to?"

"Yeah. Right. This actually makes some sense. We've gotten some reports about suicide bomb attacks that are supposed to hit Jerusalem and Tel Aviv in the next few weeks. It must all tie together."

"Hamas and the Jihad are both big on that," Richards added.

"So what do you think?" Phillips asked.

"I think we have to go to Geneva," Richards concluded.

"Yeah, me too."

"Tomorrow."

"Right."

"I'll be back at noon. You take care of travel."

"It's done."

"Now go back and fuck," Richards smiled, patting Phillips on the shoulder.

Phillips threw his chest out, rubbed back the thin hair on his bald head and replied, "I think I will."

THIRTY-TWO

Geneva

WEAVING THROUGH THE CONGESTED cosmetics sec-
tion in the front entrance of the Grand Passage department store,
Richards' and Phillips' eyes darted like pinballs scoping out the
high heeled, mannequin like Swiss women maneuvering for position against each other at various counters. Richards barreled through
the crowd of ladies at one counter, brusquely interrupting a seriously involved conversation about mascara shades. "Excuse me.
Where's the manager's office?" he demanded.

The quadrophonic chatter of female voices ceased, and two
women gave him the same *"How dare you"* look, as Richards returned an impatient *"I'm waiting"* glare.

"It is that way," replied the cosmetician with raccoon painted
eyes. She pointed with an inch long red fingernail to the left side of
the store.

Richards turned and knocked his way back to Phillips without so
much as an "excuse me." He drew nasty stares for about three seconds before the women got right back to business.

"I love Geneva," Phillips announced, genuinely meaning it, as he admired the female scenery within eyeshot.

"Really, I hate it," Richards responded.

"No way. The French here are the greatest," Phillips insisted. "They're warm. Beautiful. They even speak English."

"Bullshit. They're a bunch of pompous assholes. They think their shit doesn't stink." Richards glanced back over his shoulder at the cosmetics counter.

Richards waited for Phillips' retort, but it never came. Phillips already concluded he wasn't going to bicker with Richards over every little thing. Only the big things. They had to work together now, communicate, and tolerate each other. Somehow.

Two minutes later they were standing before a middle aged, red haired, oval bespectacled secretary in the general manager's office. After incessant demands to speak with her boss and determining that the boisterous Americans weren't leaving, the woman finally paged him storewide over the intercom system. Henri Dumas miraculously appeared almost instantly.

"How can I help you, gentlemen?" the statuesque man asked, buttoning his double breasted suitcoat.

"If you please, we'd like to speak with you in private," Phillips said politely.

"You may speak freely in front of Ms. Labeque. She's my right hand and handles many of my personal affairs as well."

"Congratulations," Phillips said sarcastically. "But I don't care if she's your mother. Our business is private."

The Frenchman raised his eyebrows announcing, "Very well." He swung his arm to the side as an indicator for Phillips and Norman to follow him to his office.

"Now, what may I do for you gentlemen?" Dumas impatiently inquired, once behind closed doors.

"How long have you been working here?" Richards asked.

"I have been the general manager of the Grand Passage for 13 years," the man proudly declared.

"Good. About a year and a half ago a customer made an extremely large purchase in your store. We need to get some information about that."

Dumas laughed while fingering his pencil thin mustache. "Do you know how many customers we have here? Our sales are a million francs a day. I have no way of helping you."

"No. This was different. This was a very large purchase. Probably paid in cash."

Dumas looked mystified and shrugged his shoulders.

"A full shipping crate of goods was sent out of the store," Richards clarified.

Dumas' face remained blank for a moment while he concentrated on the issue before wincing, albeit only for a millisecond. Richards caught it.

"I'm sorry, but that does not sound familiar. There's nothing I can do to help you," Dumas said softly. "Excuse me, but I must get back to work. It is crazy out there today."

Dumas started to leave his office, but Richards clotheslined him with an outstretched arm. "Uh, uh. We're not done with you," he said, poking the man in the chest.

"Who do you think you are?" Dumas indignantly shouted. "Let me pass! And leave my office at once!"

"Sorry, can't do that," Richards calmly replied as both he and Phillips stood blocking his exit.

"That's it, I'm calling security. I demand an explanation!" Dumas excitedly pushed his fingers through his slicked back hair.

"Do it." Phillips answered. Looking at Richards he asked, "Should I tell him?"

Richards nodded.

"We *are* security," Phillips said.

"What do you mean?"

Phillips flashed a badge. "CIA. You've probably heard of us. And by the way, here's my Interpol and Swiss search warrants to tear apart your store."

"I've done nothing wrong," Dumas said guiltily.

"We didn't say you did. But, we do want some answers," said

Phillips. "And you're gonna give them to us one way or the other."
"Perhaps I remember a little bit. But it has been a while."
"Why would you remember anything?" Richards said, now testing Dumas. The fact was the store had thousands of customers a day, and Dumas, as an administrator, rarely had contact with any of them.

"We might be talking about something different, but one customer came to find me a long time ago, and I walked through the whole store with him. It was remarkable how much he bought."

"Ahhh, so you do know what we're talking about?" Richards said, this time more threateningly poking Dumas in the chest.

"Perhaps."

Phillips pulled a series of pictures from a manilla envelope and handed them to Dumas. "Do you see him here?"

Dumas skimmed through the photos. "I cannot be certain it is any of these men."

"They're the same person," said Richards.

"Oh, I see." Dumas looked up, amazed one person could appear so many different ways. "I'm sorry, I simply do not remember."

The prints showed various faces of Carlos taken over time, as well as CIA generated computer enhancements of possible disguises based on his looks when arrested. A few other pictures of non-suspects were thrown in for good measure.

Richards removed his .44 magnum from his shoulder holster and placed the gun barrel to the manager's forehead. "Listen carefully. If your memory doesn't get better right now, I'm going to permanently erase it."

Dumas bravely replied, "You would not dare. This is Switzerland. We are civilized. We have laws here."

"Big fucking deal," Richards laughed. "I'm not Swiss. I'm American. I do what I want. You know how we behave. Besides, you've heard of diplomatic immunity?" Richards clicked the gun trigger back halfway.

A little tear formed in the corner of Dumas' eye, who was frozen still and silent.

Phillips spoke up. "Norman, look, don't shoot the fuckin' guy. I'm sure you could get away with it, but think of all the reports you'll have to file. Just beat his brains out. That won't cause any problems."

Richards sighed. "Goddamn it. You're right. I don't have time for the paperwork this week." He tucked his gun away but instantly picked up a Victorian side chair and smashed it into Dumas' hand carved antique desk, sending pieces of wood flying across the room.

"Maniac! Lunatic! What is wrong with you!" Dumas screamed. "That chair is two hundred years old. It is worth thousands."

"I don't think so," Richards smiled. He held a wooden plank in his hand and looked at Phillips. "How much do you think it's worth?"

"I don't know. Three, four francs," Phillips said.

Ms. Labeque barged into the room. "Monsieur! What's going on? Are you alright?"

"Shut up and get out of here!" Richards yelled at her.

Though taken aback by Richards' coarse behavior, she stood her ground. "Monsieur Dumas, shall I call the authorities?"

"Tell her," Phillips commanded.

He raised his eyebrows and shrugged in frustration, "They *are* the authorities."

"Nooo," she said in disbelief.

"Yes." He nodded his head and made a helpless face. "You're excused Ms. Labeque."

She backed out of the room and no sooner was the door closed than Richards swung the piece of the chair leg at Dumas, intentionally missing by a few inches.

"Enough! Let me see the pictures again."

"Look carefully. This is serious," Phillips said.

"So I see," Dumas replied, glancing at the remnants of his chair. "May I ask why you are looking for this man?"

"Do you remember the explosion at the Palais de Nations?"

"Of course. Who could forget that? Such a tragedy. It was horrible."

"The explosion occurred within a day or so of when this person visited your store."

Dumas' face went flush as he instantly comprehended the purpose of the American's mission. "Mother of God! You mean?..." He put his hand across his mouth in shock.

Both Phillips and Norman nodded the answer.

This time Dumas closely examined every print. When he reached the photograph of Carlos taken at his arrest, he paused and looked up at the ceiling as if divine intervention would confirm his conclusive realization. "This is him."

Phillips gasped. "Are you sure?"

"Yes."

"You weren't sure five minutes ago," Richards said.

"This is him. I am sure."

"Well then, how the hell is it you are so sure?"

"Because he did pay cash and he gave me a generous gratuity."

"Good," Richards replied, satisfied with the admission.

"May I ask his name?" said Dumas.

Richards looked to Phillips for approval who nodded and said, "Why not?"

"He goes by Carlos."

"Carlos! *The* Carlos?"

"Yep. *The* Carlos." Phillips replied casually.

"Oh my God! He could have killed me!"

"True," Richards agreed. "But only if you got him mad. Like if he didn't like your shirt or something serious like that."

Dumas quickly and defensively replied, "I didn't know who he was. We have many rich people visit this store. He appeared to me to be just another one of them."

"I believe you," Phillips acknowledged.

"When you first came in I did not want to help you because we protect our customer's privacy," Dumas continued.

"I understand," Phillips said. "What else can you tell us? Who was with him? Did he give you a name? What did he buy? Anything can help."

Dumas squinted while he concentrated and lit up a cigarette. "He was here alone. He was well dressed. Polite, but didn't say much. And...uh...yes, we delivered his purchases in a crate to a hotel. I think it was the DuRhone. The delivery receipt would say for sure."

"You still have that?" Richards asked.

"Of course. It's in storage upstairs. If you give me a week I am certain we can find it."

"We don't have a week. I'll give you an hour?"

"An hour? Please be reasonable. It is a madhouse out there. I must take care of my store."

"I said an hour," Richards repeated, wagging his index finger at Dumas. "We'll wait." He walked around Dumas' desk, sat down in his chair and threw his legs across the table.

"I can't do it right now," Dumas insisted. "But I'll have somebody look tonight after the store closes. I can have it by tomorrow. Next day at the latest."

"Really? Well maybe I should make a few calls to padlock the store until you find it," Phillips snickered. "Can I use your phone?" He grabbed it, not waiting for a response.

"Fine!" Dumas exclaimed, throwing his arms up in frustration. "I've heard enough. Let's go. Right now."

"That's better," Phillips smiled.

A mere 45 minutes later, having sifted through a morass of boxes in a cramped, barely lit, poorly ventilated storage room, they located a receipt showing a major purchase and delivery for Jean-Luc Finet. Confirming Dumas' recollection, the goods were delivered to a certain Pierre Erne, Assistant Manager at Geneva's Hotel DuRhone. Richards stuffed the receipt into his pocket.

"You cannot take that," Dumas insisted.

"Try and stop me," Richards smirked.

"It is store property."

"Don't be ridiculous. It's a piece of paper that sits in a box."

"I know. I will make you a copy."

"I'm taking the original. It's evidence."

Phillips interrupted the bickering with a high pitched fingers in the mouth whistle. "Why are you morons fighting? We have subpoenas, remember? The document is ours."

"Well then," Dumas sighed, "at least the good news is that I am done with you two."

"You think so?" Richards quickly responded. "I think our friendship's just beginning. You'll probably be the key witness at Carlos' murder trial here."

"We may have to put you in protective custody," Phillips added.

Dumas turned pale. Laughing, Phillips and Richards turned out the light and left him sitting on a box alone in the dark.

STANDING INSIDE THE GREEN MARBLE and teak wood lobby of the Hotel DuRhone, Phillips and Richards surveyed the heavy flow of businessmen of various nationalities milling about the room and adjoining piano bar. Noticing that the blue blazored employees all wore name tags, they slowly walked around in search of a Pierre Erne. They found him leaning against a wall at the end of the long counter underneath a series of international time clocks.

"Pierre Erne?" Phillips asked.

The man snapped to attention. "Yes sir. How may I help you?"

"I was wondering if you could spend just a couple of minutes talking to us about one of your guests?"

Erne smiled and politely responded, "Sir, I am sure you understand how important privacy is to the visitors of the Hotel DuRhone. I would like to help you, but simply cannot." He smiled again.

"I certainly understand the need for privacy, but this is a little different," Phillips replied, just as politely.

"Oh? Please tell me how," Erne said, a slight edge to his voice.

Richards removed the Grand Passage receipt from his pocket. Reading from it he said, "This involved a Mr. Jean Luc-Finet. Does that name sound familiar?"

While his head remained motionless, the blink of his eye and heave of his chest was enough for Richards and Phillips to know they were on to something.

"I have never heard that name," Erne said softly. "And may I ask who you are?"

Richards leaned over and whispered the answer in Erne's ear. Erne winced and his chest ballooned out again. "Well of course we are always willing to help the authorities," he said with an unconvincing smile.

"Are you sure you don't remember him?" Phillips prodded.

"Finet?....Finet?..." Erne nervously rubbed his chin, pretending he was lost in thought. "No. I just do not recall that name. I'm sorry."

"Look, you little fuck," Richards snapped. "I know a liar when I see one. Maybe I should take you out of here in handcuffs right now, in front of everybody. What will that do for your job security?"

"I do not know what you are talking about," Erne replied emphatically.

"Sammy, this is why I hate the French," Richards announced. He shoved the receipt in Erne's face. "You see this? It's your signature for an eight foot crate of goods from the Grand Passage for Jean-Luc Finet. If a crate like that came in, it means a crate like that went out, and you took care of it."

Erne fought to keep his composure, which became harder when he saw others in the lobby watching the confrontation. "This is from a long time ago. And the DuRhone has many guests. How can you expect me to remember such an obscure item?"

"Because I'm not stupid. Your eyes and voice tell me that you do," Richards said. "And it was for the famous terrorist Carlos, and I think you know that."

"Gentlemen, please excuse me for a moment. I'll get the keys to a conference room where we can speak in private. This is not the place. I'll answer all of your questions. Is that acceptable?" Erne asked with convincing sincerity.

"That would be fine," Phillips answered. "Go."

Erne quickly disappeared behind the counter. They waited five minutes, then ten. After 15 minutes they realized something was dramatically wrong. Unfortunately, it took another half hour of frantic demands upon DuRhone employees before they determined conclusively that Erne calmly walked out of the back service entrance of the hotel, slipped into its parking lot and drove away.

Richards and Phillips walked across the street from the hotel and leaned against a guardrail, staring aimlessly down at the rushing green water of the Rhone River, ten feet below them.

"I can't believe that fucking guy hosed us," Phillips lamented.

"It was our fault. We were stupid," Richards said, not looking distressed at all. "It's not as bad as you think, though."

"How's that?" Phillips asked.

"His taking off like that is proof enough for me that Carlos was here. It also shows he's got something more to hide. It would have been easy for him to cooperate with us and just claim a case of bad memory. But he panicked. He must have done something else. Maybe he was involved in the blast."

"That's possible," Phillips said, puckering his lips in thought.

"Can you call the bureau chief here to get an Interpol computer check on him?"

"Yeah. I'll also have the Geneva police track him down," Phillips said. "In fact, we better get to a phone."

"They'll never find him. He's long gone," Richards opined.

"Maybe. Depends on his money, family. Who knows?"

"Nope," Richards shook his head. "He's running. That's why he split."

Phillips thought about it some more, then nodded in agreement. "Yeah, we better put Passport Control at the airport and border on notice also."

"Good. Let's go, Sammie. We've still got a lot to do here." Richards spit into the water and the men turned back into the direction of the Old Town.

WALKING UP THE COBBLESTONED ROAD, both Richards and Phillips admired the classic mixture of Renaissance and Gothic architecture unique to the Old Town section of Geneva. They stopped in front of a four story, whitewashed stone building with a brown mansard roof. Standing adjacent to the door, they tried to sneak a subtle glance inside the picture window partially covered by the *Antiquities* sign painted upon it.

"You're sure this is it?" Richards asked, the skepticism in his voice obvious.

Phillips looked down at a slip of paper. "Yep, 42 Rue de Calvin. The intelligence reports are usually accurate," Phillips replied, although a bit skeptical himself.

"Go figure. Whoever heard of a murdering spy becoming an antiques dealer?"

"Norman, just remember. He's vicious. An animal. His nickname was the "Bull." We don't want trouble with this guy so just watch your mouth," Phillips warned. "O.K.?"

"Yeah, yeah, yeah," Richards replied, rolling his eyes. He muttered "asshole" under his breath.

Richards pushed open the intricately carved wooden door to the shop and Phillips followed him in. Out of tune bells sounding almost like fingernails on a chalkboard clanged over their heads.

A moment later a grey haired powerfully built truck of a man appeared from a room in the back of the store. "Bon jour," he smiled congenially in horrible French, a cigarette dangling from his lips. The man's face matched the picture in the dossier they'd reviewed only hours earlier.

"Nostrovia," Richards replied.

Seve Dolchino frowned. This was Geneva. *Nobody* spoke Russian and very few in town knew his background. "Who the fuck are you?" he asked in his adopted Russian tongue.

"Loshka gavna v bochki moda."

Dolchino half-smiled and replied, "Shto ty priyibalsa ka mn'e."

Phillips smacked Richards on the arm. "Since when do you speak Russian? What are you saying?"

"He asked who I was. I told him "a spoonful of shit in a barrel full of honey". He said, "Why the fuck are you bugging me?"

"Oh Christ," Richards said.

"Don't worry. I'm making friends. This is under control."

"Hold on here," Dolchino interrupted, now speaking English.

"What are you, Russian or American?"

"Capitalist," Richards grinned.

Dolchino was silent for a moment and took a deep drag off his cigarette. "Oh, CIA," he concluded.

"That's us, the Richards and Phillips show at your service," Richards said as he did about a six step tap dance and pirouette, finishing with a deep bow.

Dolchino tilted his head and squinted at Richards' peculiar behavior.

Loking down, rubbing his eyelids with his left thumb and index finger in embarrassment, Phillips muttered, "Dammit" under his breath. He looked back up and said, "Can I call you Seve?"

"No."

"Fine. Mr. Dolchino, we were hoping you'd just answer a few questions for us. We won't take much of your time."

"You already have."

"Hey man, how about a little professional courtesy?" Richards asked loudly. "Jesus."

"Between the KGB and the CIA?" Dolchino sarcastically replied. "What are you doing that would be mutually beneficial?"

"Solving a crime."

"Crimes don't interest me. Besides, face it. You're a criminal. I'm a criminal."

Richards puckered his lips, opened his eyes wide and nodded in agreement.

"We want to talk about your old friend Carlos," Phillips said, getting right to the point.

Seve raised his eyebrows and grimaced in response. "Ah, Carlos," he said in a low voice. "Such a shame. Such a talent. I loved that boy. I'm sure your reports show that. Everybody knew it. I don't think I'll ever see him again."

"Then you shouldn't object to discussing his activities."

Dolchino's icy stare back at Richards was his answer.

"We've figured out that Carlos was responsible for destroying the U.N.," Phillips announced. "Maybe you can shed some light on that?"

"That's crap. If he'd have done that job somebody would have pinned it on him long ago. What are you really here for?" Dolchino remained completely composed, the mark of a truly accomplished liar.

Richards and Phillips knew enough to know it was an act, but it was a damn good one. "Whatever you say," Phillips replied flatly. "But we know he was in Geneva at the time of the explosion, that he stayed at the Hotel DuRhone and that the assistant manager of the hotel may have helped him."

Dolchino chuckled. "That's all you have? You fucking guys are on a fishing expedition. You think you can catch a shark with a worm? You've got shit. Now get out."

"So you were involved too, huh?" Richards concluded.

"Yeah. Right. Prove it," Dolchino sarcastically barked.

"Khalil al-Sharif," said Richards quickly. "Do you know that name?"

Seve glared at the men in a long pause, stomped out his cigarette and said, "Yeah, he's some famous actor isn't he? What about him?"

The front door suddenly flung open and the bells rattled hard as the wood hit the plaster wall. Pierre Erne stood there, red faced and breathing hard; a panicked, frightened expression stretched across his face. He didn't even notice the visitors a few feet away from him, focusing solely on the older man directly in his line of vision. "Seve, Seve, you've got to help me. I've got a big problem. An hour ago some agents..."

"I know," Dolchino interrupted, tilting his head in the direction of the Americans.

Erne did a double take at Phillips and Richards and responded with only a shocked, "What!"

Within an instant Richards was next to Erne, twisting his right arm behind his back. Erne yelped in pain. Phillips punched him in the face and blood splattered out of his nose.

Richards followed with a solid kidney chop and Erne fell to his knees. The hotel manager groaned in pain at his two American adversaries imposingly standing above him.

Dolchino shook his head at Erne in disgust. "I told Carlos a long time ago you were a piece of shit. How stupid could you be just showing up here?"

Erne was completely pale except for the blood running from his nose into his mouth. He sat down and whimpered, comprehending his new bleak destiny.

"Well Dolchino," Phillips said, "Look what the cat dragged in. We've got something to talk about now."

"Seve, please help me," Erne pleaded.

"I wouldn't piss in your ear if your brain was on fire," Dolchino sneered. He bent down on one knee to tie his shoe, but when he straigtened back up he was holding a small pistol retrieved from an ankle holster. He immediately pumped four shots into Pierre Erne's chest. The force of the bullets blew Erne back four feet into a table and lamp, which were knocked over and smashed to the ground.

Richards and Phillips stood there in shock looking at Dolchino, who stood there perfectly calm as if nothing had happened. "We have nothin' to talk about."

Erne lie on the floor spread eagled, a pool of blood flowing freely outward from around his lifeless body.

Both Richards and Phillips pulled out their weapons and aimed them at Dolchino. Richards broke the silence, "Whoa! We heard you were one crazy fuckin' guy."

Dolchino replied in a steely tone, "Don't *ever* call me crazy."

"Now we're going to have to..."

"Go rot in hell," Dolchino interrupted Phillips. "Do what you've got to do, but leave me alone." He turned around and started to trudge back to his office. "I'm not going anywhere with you."

"Freeze Dolchino," Phillips yelled, his arm extended and the trigger half pulled. "You're coming with us! Now!"

Seve stopped for a second, then spun around and fired a shot at Phillips. Barely missing him, it whizzed past his ear and shattered the front picture window. Before Dolchino could pull the trigger even a second time, Phillips and Richards both unloaded a barrage of lead into his body, sending him sprawling into a suit of armor.

Gasping, with blood rushing from his chest, he clung to the metal before gravity pulled his oversized body slowly to the floor. The armor fell on top of him and he frantically continued trying to suck down bits of air. As Richards started to remove the armor off Dolchino's torso, Seve whispered, "Fuck you," and closed his eyes.

The Americans stood in silence looking at each other. Finally Richards said, "I guess he was serious when he said he wasn't going with us."

Phillips shook his head and responded in a somber tone, "Yeah, I guess."

Richards and Phillips surveyed the bloody scene surrounding them. With nothing else left to do except call in the mess to the Swiss authorities, they simply walked out of the shop and past the crowd of local onlookers who had already started to gather.

THIRTY-THREE

"C'MON GUYS, what do you want from me? I don't have the men to keep on this detail any longer." Anthony Garber, Chief of Presidential Security for the Secret Service, folded his arms across his chest and shook his head in frustration. Staring mindlessly at the 12' by 16' map of the continental U.S. occupying a full wall of the Situation Room two stories below the White House, Garber exhaled a full breath of mentholated cigarette smoke and coughed.

Just to make sure he was understood, Garber repeated, "I don't have the men. We've got other obligations now."

"That's bullshit. You've got an army," said Edward Coston, leader of the CIA's elite Directorate of Overseas Operations.

"Don't talk to me about bullshit, Eddie. You've been on this for two weeks and you've got nothin'. What do you think? I don't read the reports? There's no way I can justify changing a well developed approved security plan at the last minute without a damn good reason. Fred, spell it out."

Deputy Director of the FBI's Foreign Counterintelligence Department, Fred Lang, grinned sarcastically at Phillips and Norman before opening a thin blue folder stamped *"Classified - Level Six."* Skimming through the pages in the file, he declared, "Here's the bottom line fellas. There is no Iraqi terrorist named Khalil al-Sharif in the United States. We've checked everywhere. No immigration record. No mailing address. No phone. No bank accounts or credit information. No registration in a university. No criminal record. Should I continue?"

"Goddamn it, Fred. You know he's got to be using an alias," Sam Phillips shot back. "Did you run other names? What other information and profile fields did you program in?"

"Jesus Christ," Lang said, slapping his forehead with the palm of his hand. "You mean I should have thought about that?" he said as snidely as possible. After a pause he continued, "We crosschecked with INS every Iraqi male in an age profile of 18 to 30 that's in the country. You know how much work that was?"

"What if he came through customs in disguise? Maybe dressed like a woman? Or an old man? Remember, Carlos was his teacher -- the master of disguise," Norman Richards emphasized.

"If that's the case, then we've missed him," Lang replied.

"You missed him," Richards said confidently. "He's probably got five fake passports with fully developed aliases for each."

"Probably," Lang agreed. "But the first place we still had to check out were the resident Iraqis. Do you have any idea how many of them are here?"

"No," Richards replied, not caring if he heard the answer.

"250,000. Do you know how many other Arabs are here?"

"Half of Detroit and a third of all cab drivers," Richards quipped.

Everyone but Lang laughed. "2.2 million. Bad odds against us. Tell me smart ass, should I have looked up every one of them?" he growled.

"Nope, just those on the Atlantic Coast," Richards replied, believing it.

Garber impatiently blurted out, "How do you know this whole thing isn't a set up by Sabar and Saddam?"

"Set up for what?"

"I don't know -- something else. Like a diversion."

"Doesn't make sense," Phillips responded. "There'd have been no reason for him to bring Norman into it on that scenario. He could have gone to see anybody."

"And besides, why would he have given up Carlos on the U.N. blast?" Coston rhetorically added.

"C'mon guys, wake up. Carlos became expendable once the French arrested him," Lang replied.

"False," Richards retorted. "Sabar knows that if the U.N. bombing was tied to Saddam, it would only lead to continued U.N. sanctions against Iraq. Something clearly not in Saddam's best interest."

"I don't give a shit," Garber concluded, ignoring the logic of the CIA's arguments. "I still don't have the men to spare."

"Don't cut us off yet," Richards said forcefully. "I'm telling you this is not some idle threat." He looked to Coston, his ex-boss, for confirmation.

Before Coston could speak up, Garber snapped, "Norman. A long time ago I took what you had to say seriously, but not now. You know why? Aside from the fact you've got no proof, you're a joke. A fucking joke."

"I've cut my drinking way back," Richards defensively replied, but not being close to truthful.

"I'm not talking about your alcoholism. I don't care that you're a drunk. You turned bad. I read up on you. You sell weapons and technology to whatever Arab's got the money. Almost all of those people, *your* clients, have interests adverse to the United States. You're a whore."

Richards bit his bottom lip and exhaled hard through his nose, holding back a smart retort. "Fine. You're right. I am a whore. But listen, Anthony, I didn't come all the way here just to go on a crazy wild goose chase after some Arab terrorist, much less to fight with you. This guy can only be here with one goal: to kill the president."

Fred Lang polished his round wire frame glasses with a handkerchief and replied, "So just what do you expect? The Bureau and the Service should do your work? Conduct your investigation?"

"Aren't you listening? We're talking about a presidential assassination," Coston replied. "This is *your* specialty and *your* jurisdiction. And this is inauguration week. Director Kelly ordered us to contact you. We've been working round the clock using all of our resources, but both of your agencies have more local manpower and different data banks than us."

"Eddie, listen to me," Garber said to the CIA man. "In the past week alone we've received over 40 death threats to the president and come hell or high water, we have to check out every single one of them. Fully. No matter what."

"This is unbelievable," Richards burst in. "Usually you fucking assholes fight about who gets to *keep* a case. Now the golden goose comes and bites you on the ass and you flick it away like a mosquito. You're a first class moron," he said looking intensely at Garber.

Sam Phillips spun around and grabbed Richards by the lapel of his blue jean jacket and hissed, "When the fuck are you gonna learn to keep your mouth shut? You're your own worst enemy. If you ever figured out how to play team ball, you'd see how things get done. And people might learn to like you. Maybe. Now shut up and behave." Phillips poked Richards in the chest with his index finger, spun on his heel and walked away. He sat down by himself at the end of a 15 foot polished mahogany table, the centerpiece of the Situation Room.

Humiliated, Richards exhaled deeply. He looked down at his feet, his flaring nostrils frantically sucking down oxygen. The room was completely silent, everyone staring at the maniac waiting for one of his infamous explosions.

Instead, Phillips words hit Richards like a lightning bolt of reality. He walked over to Anthony Garber and stuck out his hand, "I'm sorry. Sam's right. Sometimes I've got a big mouth, especially when I get emotional. And maybe I don't even blame you for not fully trusting me, but you've *got* to now. We have to find and stop this guy."

"Apology accepted," Garber replied without emotion, but only half-heartedly shaking hands.

Richards next walked over to Phillips and extended his hand. Looking his longtime friend and colleague, then hated adversary straight in the eyes, he said, "Sorry man. Peace?" He lifted his eyebrows making a sort of guilty looking face.

Phillips stared back at Richards for a few seconds contemplating their history and the apparent sincerity of the apology. Deciding that Richards had earned the benefit of the doubt just from his work in the past few weeks, he softly replied, "Yeah, peace."

"You guys kiss and make up later," Garber cracked. "I'd like to help you more but the inauguration's in two days and I just don't have the goddamn time to sit here with you talking about some unknown Arab terrorist plot, that so far doesn't even show a hint of existing."

Sam Phillips hand flew out like a projectile to seize the room's attention. "Anthony, I haven't been too crazy about this jerk off either the past few years," he said, motioning with his thumb at Richards. "But the fact is, he was the best field operative my station ever had, and I've been in the middle of this investigation with him too. Norman's right. You've got to help us and keep it open."

Lang nodded his head. "So what's the Agency's position? How much are you really behind this?" Lang asked Coston.

"Completely," the CIA executive answered. "The information Sabar gave Richards about Carlos was consistent with everything we already knew."

"What do you mean *already knew*?" demanded Richards.

"We confirmed Carlos was behind the U.N. bombing in Geneva and that he killed Brendan Richter," said Coston as if it were no big deal.

"You *did*?" Phillips asked, the shock on his face apparent.

"We have a tape. That's all I'll tell you. Carlos admitted it."

"Why didn't anybody tell me?" Richards demanded.

"Or me?" asked Phillips.

"It was on a need to know basis. Top secret." Coston advised. "Besides, Norman, who do you think you are? Why should I or anyone else have told you a damn thing?"

"Are you serious?" Richards asked with an astonished look. He lifted his shirt revealing his fake scar. "You see this? You think I asked for this? You sent me out to find who did that job and then after you found out, you didn't pull the plug. That's bullshit!"

"That's life," Coston said callously.

"Exactly what do you think I've been doing for the past few weeks with Sam since Sabar came to see me? Not anyone else. Me."

"Your civic duty, Norman. And you've got a lot of making up to do," Coston shot back.

"Yeah right," Richards sneered. "I know the way you guys think. You didn't give a shit about my business dealings because you knew it'd give you the chance to extort me to get things done you couldn't do yourselves. Just like you did," he said, cutting the air with the chop of his hand. "And then if I had a problem or even got killed, what the hell, it was only me. I quit the Agency when you tried to force me to take out Ghassan Kassem for no good reason. I played it by the book up to then. And I loved my job and I loved my country. All I did after that was play by your rules."

Again the silence in the room was deafening, this time in recognition of the truth that Richards had paid his dues. And when he really had to be counted on, such as now, he stood tall. Norman turned away from the group, facing a full wall map of the world, opposite of the U.S. map.

Phillips walked over and stood next to Richards as a show of support. After a few more seconds he broke the silence. "The Mossad reports there may be a rift between Saddam and Sabar. We think this is a real opportunity to replace Saddam with someone who has a more Western way of thinking. Norman has the best contacts of any American in the entire Mid East. The Arabs trust him. And, they don't trust just anybody."

Phillips looked at Richards and added, "Norman, that's why Ed and I sent you out to find who destroyed the U.N. If you couldn't find who did it, nobody could."

Phillips turned back toward the others. "That's also why we

attach credibility to Sabar trying to open the door to the West through Norman."

"The National Security Council and Pentagon agree with our assessment," Coston added.

Richards could hardly believe it; the tide was turning in his favor. "So what are you gonna do to help us?" he asked.

"What more do you want us to do?" Garber asked.

"Are you in, too?" Phillips asked Lang.

Begrudgingly, he nodded yes.

"Excellent, but we're almost out of time with only two days 'til the inauguration, if Khalil waits that long," Richards said, taking charge. "The odds are that he has to be located somewhere in or close to Washington. We're gonna roll the dice and focus on only a 100 mile radius of D.C. Okay?" he asked looking around.

Everyone concurred. There wasn't much choice in the matter.

"So how about this? Can you get a list of every Arabic name employed anyplace where there's an inaugural function?"

"It'll be easier to get complete employee lists and sort it out ourselves."

"I want government employees, too."

"Richards, there is no Arab terrorist working in the U.S. government," Lang sneered, although he wrote it down on a notepad anyway.

"Something else," Richards added.

"What?" Garber sighed.

"Student registration lists from the nearby Virginia, Maryland and D.C. universities."

"What else?" Lang asked.

"Let's see. ... All resident alien driver's licenses issued in those places the past two years."

Garber looked at Richards in disbelief.

"One last thing. All of the data you've collected so far. We need it to run our own analysis."

"It's yours," Garber replied, pointing to a double stack of folders piled three feet high on the table. "Knock yourself out."

"That's it," Norman said.

"For now," Phillips added.

"How long will that take?" Coston asked.

"Half a day. We probably have a lot of the data already."

"I'll send someone over to pick it up first thing tomorrow morning," Coston said.

"Eddie, that's as far as I can go until you can bring me something substantial to chew on," Garber said. "I'm spread too thin already. If my stuff falls apart because I'm dickin' around with you, my head's gonna roll. You understand?"

"We'll need access to the computers to cross check information," Phillips interjected, ignoring Garber.

Garber chuckled at Phillips moxie, "Fine, that's easy. I can't do any more though."

Richards walked back to Garber and shook his hand again. "Thanks."

"So you're actually rejoining the human race," said Coston, smiling at Richards.

Richards shrugged and replied, "I guess it's about time."

"Is that it?" Lang asked.

"Yeah. Let's go. We've all got a lot to do," Coston replied.

"What a waste of time. The president's untouchable and you guys know it," Garber mumbled under his breath.

"Don't be stupid," Richards replied. "If idiots like Squeaky Fromme and John Hinckley could take their shots at the president, a terrorist like this Khalil will have no problem at all."

Nobody else in the group commented, but in silent reflection, they each knew that while Richards was right, they hoped that Garber was more right.

As the group collectively exited the Situation Room, Coston tapped Richards on the shoulder. "Norman."

"What?" he asked, turning around.

"This is yours," Coston said, slapping something into the palm of Richards' hand. "I found it in your file and I've been holding it the past week. You might need it. You deserve it."

Richards looked down. He was holding CIA badge 4249910, the same number from his past. He smiled, nodded in satisfaction and replied, "You never know."

"YOU NEVER KNOW. LIFE IS SO STRANGE," said an unusually philosophical Saddam Hussein. Twirling a cigar in the corner of his mouth he grinned at Omar Rafsani, Rashid Sabar, Defense Minister Mustafa Hakim and Deputy Foreign Minister Sirhan Haddad. He rose from his desk and slid over to the window overlooking the lavish grounds of his palace, still paradoxically protected like a fortress by tanks, anti-aircraft guns and barbed wire. "One day you're on top of the world, the next you're banished to the depths of hell. And then somehow, there you are, back on top again." He took a deep puff off the cigar and emitted a low devilish laugh that curled out of his mouth with the smoke. Omar instinctively laughed along with his president. The others remained silent.

"Gentlemen," Saddam continued, "In less than two days Iraq rises to the height of glory once again. Our revenge against the U.S. will be complete and our victory against the Zionists will be final."

"I do not understand. What are you talking about?" Hakim asked, taken aback by the magnitude of Saddam's boasts.

"I know this is a surprise, and perhaps I should have spoken to you all about it sooner, but I didn't think it was necessary to burden you with my plans. You each had your own responsibilities."

"We have all been very busy, but we are always at your service," Sabar said. "Day and night."

"You always have been and always will be a loyal friend and compatriot, Rashid, and that's why I feel bad that I held this back from you. All of you. But, I had to."

"So what is it?" Haddad asked.

"It's simple. The Americans. They will all be dead."

"What?" Defense Minister Hakim asked incredulously. "Are we detonating an atomic device in the United States?"

"Oh no, no, no. I'm sorry," Saddam laughed. "Nothing that

dramatic. We're only killing the president. And the vice president. And their cabinet. And their entire Congress. And their Supreme Court. Everybody!" he bellowed with a big toothy smile, opening his arms in a global gesture.

"How are we going to do that?" Sabar asked.

"You remember Khalil al-Sharif, don't you?"

Only Sabar nodded yes.

"He, Omar and Ahmed al-Sharif were trained by Carlos to perform professional acts of a sensitive nature. Deadly acts. I don't know all the details, but this has been in planning for a long time. Carlos set most of it up before his arrest. There's an inauguration party that the president and everybody else will attend where Khalil's going to kill them all. I don't know where or how and I don't care to know. Just that the plan is foolproof. Nobody can escape from the room, and nothing can stop us now. And the whole event will be on worldwide T.V!" Saddam laughed again and followed with another long drag on his cigar, blowing the smoke out and upwards in a perfect long thin stream.

Hakim, Haddad and Sabar remained stonefaced. Hakim lit a cigarette pondering the ramifications of Saddam's apocalyptic disclosure. Sabar casually leaned against a wall to brace himself after his heart skipped two beats. He knew Khalil was up to trouble, but he didn't know it was this bad. Still, he smiled at Saddam as his vote of confidence. It was for self preservation.

"So what does this have to do with Israel?" Hakim asked.

"Israel? You mean Palestine," Saddam snorted. "Omar. You explain. It was mostly your responsibility."

Omar Rafsani straightened his posture before proudly announcing, "As soon as we confirm the massacre of the Americans, we have arranged for a special signal message to be broadcast on the Hamas radio station in Gaza. Three hours later, about 280 martyrs from Hamas and Islamic Jihad will blow themselves up in separate strategic Jewish occupied locations in Tel Aviv, Jerusalem and Haifa. Jewish casualties and property damage will be extensive."

A buoyant Saddam Hussein interrupted Omar's presentation with another laugh and a smack on Omar's back.

The dictator's young protege continued. "A half an hour later, when the Israeli government won't know where to turn next, and when the Americans will have their own problems, our army and air force will begin an all out assault to reclaim our Moslem land. We will be unstoppable. And, of course, we will use gas. Washington and Israel will both be destroyed. Back to back. Within hours."

He placed his arm around Omar's shoulders and squeezed. "You've done a great job. Carlos would be proud of you. I'm proud of you."

"Thank you Mr. President," Omar Rafsani replied. Then he added, "Carlos deserves a lot of the credit. I learned everything from him. And we can't forget Fathi Shkaki and Yehia Ayash. They arranged for the individual martyrs."

"How did you get Shkaki and Ayash involved?" Sabar interrupted.

"How else? We paid them well."

"Ayash is a wild man. He'll blow up anything," Sabar said.

Saddam beamed, nodding his head in approval.

Sirhan Haddad leaned forward to take the floor. "Mr. President, don't you think this exceptionally bold action may alienate the rest of the world against Iraq?"

"Who cares?" Saddam asked.

"We all should, sir. This whole plan is wrong. You can't kill the President of the United States and all those other people and expect to get away with it. Even if they are only Jews. The repercussions against Iraq will be devastating."

"Come here, son," Saddam calmly said.

The man inched towards Saddam Hussein, who put his arm around his shoulder.

"Sirhan, I know that Tariq Aziz has trained you well and respects your viewpoints," Saddam said.

"Yes sir."

"Look out the window. Everything you see is development I have brought to Iraq: the highways, the hospitals, the schools. I *am* Iraq. I know what I'm doing. The Americans tried to destroy it all.

They must pay. And, they will. Now." Saddam's voice rose and his face became flush.

"I know," Sirhan replied meekly.

"There's one thing you don't know," Saddam said acerbically.

"Yes?" Sirhad Haddad said, practically trembling.

"I don't want to hear your viewpoint!" Saddam screamed. He grabbed him by the nape of his neck and the back of his belt. In a swift motion, Saddam spun Sirhan around and shoved him out the window. The man screamed for the whole three story drop until a dull thud silenced the eerie sound. Saddam looked down at the broken corpse and yelled, "I only want you to follow my orders." He then closed the window and took another big puff off of his cigar. Nobody moved.

As if nothing happened, Saddam calmly looked at his defense minister and said, "So Mustafa, you recall the plans we developed for Operation Wolf?"

"Of course, the attack plans against Israel that we didn't get to use during the Gulf War."

"You will now," Saddam said. "They required 18 hours notice for deployment. We have given you at least 36. I presume you can have everything ready."

Hakim responded, "It will not be a problem." He knew there had better not be one.

"Good. Get the jets ready. Do not let me down. We set the table. I expect you to clear it."

Saddam then turned to the chief of his secret police. "Rashid, I'm going to send you to Jerusalem within the week. After we take over the Zionist territory you will become provisional minister, at least for a while. Congratulations." Saddam Hussein reached out and gave Rashid Sabar a hearty handshake.

Sabar returned a half hearted smile. "Thank you for the show of confidence."

"Why not? Who else could I put in this position besides you? You more than anyone else will know how to restore order among the Zionists. And how to dispose of them as well. I'm sorry that I was unable to tell you about this sooner."

"Your reasons were good."

"Of course they were," Saddam answered. After a moment's reflection he asked his staff, "Do you think I should name myself King of Palestine?" He burst out laughing once again and toked on his cigar.

THIRTY-FOUR

Inauguration Day

"I DON'T CARE IF HE'S the president of the university and I don't give a rats ass in August that it's 4:30 in the morning. Get me those goddamn records right away!" Sam Phillips bellowed at his underling, Richard Karbal. The physically imposing, but young, CIA Special Agent cowered back from the somewhat notorious Middle East bureau chief whom he had met just a day earlier.

"Run, Goddamn it! And get back here in five minutes with a report on what he says or I'll shove this pen up your ass. *Sideways!"* Phillips smacked his hands together a few times. The man turned and hurried out of the basketball court sized computer stacked Data Center, the CIA's foundation of espionage and information, situated on the second floor of its headquarters in Langley, Virginia.

"You always knew how to motivate people, Sammie," Norman Richards smiled, leaning back on an office chair and stretching his legs onto a desk. He held a fresh cup of industrial strength coffee firmly between both palms, letting the steam float up into his nose.

"Yeah, you were the only asshole I could never intimidate," Phillips shrugged.

Ed Coston suddenly appeared from behind a large bank of com-

382

puters. "You're still up? You guys really should go to the dorm and get at least a couple hours sleep."

They glanced at each other before looking back at the Director of Overseas Operations. "Yes sir," Richards politely answered, the look in his eye saying otherwise.

Coston knew it was pointless to discuss the issue further. These men had pulled all nighters before. They'd pull them again. Sleep deprivation was part of their training and a common occurrence in the field.

"Norman, I can't resist asking. Don't you ever take that disgusting blue jean jacket off?" Coston teased.

"Not if I can help it. Brings me luck," Richards replied.

"You really think so?"

"Yep. And we've been through a lot together," Richards said, sort of patting and tugging the material.

"Then keep it on. Are you at least getting any closer?"

"We'll see," Norman answered. "We've eliminated four names off the list as suspects. All students. There's one left."

"First, the ones you struck. Why?"

"They were all here on legitimate student visas. Their papers, background, phones, everything checks out."

"Were they interviewed?"

"Uh huh," Phillips replied.

"O.K. And this last guy, what's his story?"

"It's Khalil," Norman declared.

"How do you know?"

"No phone listing."

"That's it?" Coston asked. "How can you draw a conclusion like that from one isolated fact?"

"So far it ain't nobody else, at least according to the computers," Phillips said. "Tell me who doesn't have a phone? Everybody does. Or, maybe he's got a phone, but it's in a different name. Either way, that means this guy's hiding something."

"He could be dirt poor."

"Sure," Richards said. "An Arab GW student living in Washington with no money. And that's not even his cover, but I'll get to that. Eddie, except for an INS entry, there's absolutely no other data about him. Anywhere."

"Nothing?"

"Zip. Absolutely nothing with an address. No credit cards or bank accounts. No drivers license or vehicles. No tax filings. No medical insurance." He opened his arms wide. "Take my word, between Big Bertha here and the Secret Service and FBI checks, there's practically no record of this person."

"He exists, yet he doesn't," Phillips lamented.

"Where did INS say he's from?"

"Saudi Arabia."

"And you presume he came in on a forged passport?" Coston rhetorically concluded. "When did he enter the U.S?"

"Last August."

"Two months after Richter was killed," Phillips said. "If we presume Carlos was here setting the plan in June, then the timing of Khalil's arrival two months later would be logical, because the FBI gave us an enrollment register for George Washington University. Barak Hamas is listed as a student there."

"Or he could be just like six million other college kids starting school in September," Coston responded, playing devil's advocate but not really believing it. "Okay, so this is the best shot. What's next?"

"We've got that dweeb of yours Karbal waking up the president of the university right now to get us every piece of paper the school has on him."

"Norman, what was his computer cross-reference point?"

"He's an employee at the Kennedy Center. There's an inaugural ball there tonight."

"What does his employment file show?"

"Nothing. No application. No papers. They didn't even realize they don't have a local address or phone for him."

"So how'd he get hired?"

"The people at The Kennedy Center think his father's an oil sheik who made a half million dollar donation just to get his kid the job."

"That sounds strange," Phillips said. "There must have been a bribe or something."

"Who told you that?" Coston asked.

"Everybody there seems to know about it. This kid supposedly has big money but they all like him a lot. He's responsible, hard working, smart."

"Deadly," Phillips added.

"Leave it to Carlos. Brilliant plan and now Khalil's been living this alias. He must be amazing," Coston said with reluctant admiration for the plan Carlos had set.

"And the proof this is Khalil is that how can an oil sheik's son not have a phone?" Richards said. "If he was really a rich kid he'd have a phone plus a second line for a modem and fax."

Coston nodded his agreement.

Richards added, "But then again, if he had a phone number we could find, we'd be kicking down his door right now. That's called pretty damn smart planning."

"Did you talk to whoever handled the contribution and hired Khalil at the Kennedy Center?"

"It's not an option."

"Why?"

"The lady died."

"Murder?" Coston said.

"She fell in the bathtub, smacked her head and drowned. An accident." Richards shrugged.

"Where does his W-2 go?"

"Saudi Arabia address. Like I said, no IRS filings."

"A perfect plant."

"Perfect," Phillips acknowledged. Richards took a sip off his coffee and nodded as well.

"If everybody at work is so fond of Khalil, he must have friends who know where he lives."

"We can't ask too many questions without setting off the bells and chimes because we don't know if he's working with anyone.

But yes and no. He has some friends. But nobody's ever been to his place. We think he lives right in the neighborhood."

"So we'll comb the fucking streets. We've got enough now to keep the Secret Service and FBI interested. Have either of you talked to Garber or Lang lately?"

"Not in about 18 hours," Phillips said.

"All right, so what's going on at The Kennedy Center today?"

"The National Ball."

"And of course, the president attends?"

"Yeah. And the Cabinet, Supreme Court and every member of Congress."

"Don't forget the governors," Richards added.

"Everybody, huh? You don't think that Khalil is..." Coston stopped, not wanting to express his darkest fear aloud.

"Anything's possible," Richards said. "He's Carlos' boy and he's working for Hussein. You've got a madman with a motive."

"Fine. We'll just pick him up when he walks in the door at work tonight."

"No. That's a complicating factor."

"Why?"

"He's not scheduled to work tonight. And the Secret Service has torn that place apart. No bombs."

Coston instantly turned pale. "Oh Christ. Then he could be any-where and his attack doesn't necessarily have to be at The Kennedy Center. Or it could be there but his plan could be in effect already so he doesn't need to be there when it comes down."

Nobody said a word for a moment, mulling over the desperate-ness of the situation. Finally Richards said, "And that's why we've got to find him. Now! Right now!"

"What's his alias again?"

"Hamas. Barak Hamas."

"JESUS, THIS KHALIL'S one smart cookie. Look at this," Phillips said holding up Barak Hamas' George Washington Univer-sity transcript for all to view. "Straight A's. Straight fuckin' A's as an engineering major in one of the best schools in the country."

"I wouldn't expect anything less," Richards replied without looking up from the stack of papers in front of him.

"I expected more from you Mr. Karbal," Phillips said. "When I said to get me every piece of paper the school had on Barak Hamas, I meant *everything.*" He tapped his fingernails impatiently on the conference table located just down the hall from the CIA's Data Center.

"This is what they gave me," Karbal replied defensively. "I told President Matthews we needed all admissions, scholastic, bursar and student body records. What's missing?"

"The transcripts. They only show class names. I want to know who his professors are and what they have to say about him."

"Sir. I don't think that's how transcripts or college records are kept."

"I don't care. Get me that information," Phillips said tersely.

"What's it relevant to?" Ed Coston piped up, not wanting to waste critical time on potential dead ends.

"Probably nothing, but we don't have much else at this point."

Coston exhaled and thought about it for a moment. "Okay. Do it," he hesitantly agreed.

"Interview his professors from the smaller classes," Phillips added. "There's a greater likelihood they'll know their students."

"How do I know what the smaller classes are?" Karbal asked.

"Figure it out," Phillips answered, blatantly rolling his eyes for Karbal to see.

"Are you always this much of a ball buster?" Karbal asked, trying to stand his ground.

"No," Richards answered for Phillips. "He's usually worse."

Karbal sat down in the corner of the room and began pushing buttons on a multi-line telephone console, authoritatively barking out orders to whomever answered on the other end.

"Unfuckinbelievable," Richards said, shaking his head, clearly disgusted.

"What?" asked Coston.

"You wouldn't believe his internship. The Department of Defense. Shit. There had to be some major breaches in security."

"Nothing we can do about that now, except to alert them to see if he did any damage or if something's missing."

"What does Khalil's application look like?" Phillips asked Norman.

"Vague," Richards replied, thumbing through the papers. "Says he's Saudi...25...No local address, of course. Here are transcripts from Oxford and the University of Paris."

"Probably forgeries," Phillips opined.

"You never know. Straight A's there. Straight A's here..."

"Give me those," Coston said. "We'll run a check on them right now."

Richards continued reviewing the papers, "Let's see: an interview form signed by Andrew Joblove, Director of Admissions that says...Son of a bitch! This fuckin' guy met with Carlos. On June 27, 1994 he interviewed Ismael Hamas, Barak's father who made a $50,000 donation to the school to get Barak admitted."

Richards' slid the document across the table to Coston, "Here. Get copies of this made. We should all read this."

Coston barked out a slightly different order across the room to Karbal, "Richard. Track down Andrew Joblove, the Director of Admissions at GW. Wherever he is, we want to talk to him. Right now. Stop that other shit. Bring him in."

With his back to the group, Karbal raised his hand in acknowledgement, gave ten seconds of instructions into the phone, rifled through some papers and started pushing a new sequence of buttons.

Another man entered the conference room holding a cellular phone and approached Coston. "Sir, excuse me for interrupting. I have Mr. Garber of the Secret Service on the line for you. He said it was urgent."

Coston snatched the phone from the man's hand. "Tony, it's Ed." He listened on the line for 30 seconds before closing the antennae without even saying goodbye. He rubbed his closed eyelids between a thumb and index finger for a few seconds before announcing, "The Secret Service and D.C. police checked the registers on every residential property in a twelve block radius of The Kennedy Center. There's no Barak Hamas listed."

Except for the dull continuous whoosh of the heating system, the room was silent.

Richards finally spoke. "It's 10:50. The inauguration starts in an hour and ten minutes. We have to believe the Secret Service knows how to protect the president. They're on alert. He's in their hands, but we still gotta keep plugging away."

"Right," said Coston. "And every cop and agent on the street has a copy of Norman's composite sketch of Khalil."

"Yeah. Sure," Phillips dryly added, "presuming Norman's memory is good enough to remember one picture he saw for two minutes, three weeks ago, and Khalil's not out there in disguise."

Richard Karbal hung up the phone, rose from his chair, slowly shuffled over to Phillips with his head down, and said in a low voice, "Sir. President Matthews just told me Andrew Joblove is dead."

Everybody looked up.

"What do you mean dead?" Phillips snapped.

"Dead. He had a heart attack and died.... Dead."

"Are you sure?"

"That's what he said. He keeled over right in the middle of some deli. Shocked everyone because he was only 40."

Phillips put the tip of his index finger in his mouth and bit down. "When did this happen?"

He's calling back in a few minutes with a precise date, but he thought it was in June."

"Carlos killed him," Richards announced matter of factly.

"No sir. He said it was a heart attack."

Richards stood from his chair and emphatically repeated, *"Carlos killed him.* Just like he killed Richter. If you come into contact with Carlos, you die. Plain and simple. It's not always a bullet in the brain. He leaves no witnesses behind. It's one of his trademarks."

"I'll bet he gave Khalil an order to take out that woman from

The Kennedy Center," Phillips said.

Looking like a beaten man, Coston drawled, "Well, I think we're out of leads. And I know we're running out of time."

"It's not looking too good," Richards agreed softly, opening wide the manilla envelope that Barak Hamas' George Washington University application was delivered in. He stopped and extracted a folded sheet of paper that he missed because it was stuck to the inside of the envelope, and he studied it intently for a few seconds.

"Bingo!" he yelled buoyantly, punching the air with a clenched fist.

"What, what is it?" everyone asked at once.

"What did they say during Watergate? Follow the money?" said Richards.

"Yeah, right. So?" Coston said.

"Well let's follow the money." He held up a xerox copy of a check payable to George Washington University for $50,000 drawn on the account of Seltaeb, N.A.

As Phillips gave Norman a high five, Coston announced, "Norman, don't you dare take that jacket off."

"EXCUSE ME SIR. Judge Stettin just signed the search warrant for Banco de Caracas in Miami," Special Agent Karbal said, standing before Coston, reading from scribbled notes on a legal pad.

"How's it getting served?" Coston asked.

"The writ's been faxed to the federal courthouse in Miami where the Clerk will certify it. A U.S. marshall, the Miami FBI and the U.S. Attorney are all standing by to make service and assure everything goes smoothly. It's a full seizure order too, so we should have all of the Bank's records on Seltaeb shortly. Paper and computer. They'll probably start faxing us documents within 30 minutes."

"Was the Federal Reserve helpful?"

"Between the Fed and the FDIC we've got a whole slew of other reports that should be delivered here shortly."

"You know, I just remembered," Richards announced, "it could be coincidence, but Carlos was born in Caracas. Maybe there's some special tie here to this bank?"

"I want a full background check on every bank officer," Coston dictated. "Run all of their names through the National Crime Computer and every other data base you can think of. This is worth looking at. Maybe there's a direct connection to Carlos."

"We've already started that analysis, sir."

"Good," Coston replied, pleased Karbal was showing signs of living up to his lofty expectations. "What else?"

Richards put down his coffee and interrupted, "Rick, you should also get nationwide state corporate and telephone searches for any business with the name Seltaeb."

"That was the first thing I ordered." Karbal smiled in self-assurance as he checked his watch. "It's 11:55 right now. It'll be another half hour before we get the corporate information and probably an hour before the phone records come in."

"Bring me the reports on Florida, Maryland, Virginia and D.C. as soon as they come off the computer."

"Sure. Want me to pull Delaware and New York also?"

Richards nodded. "See Sammy, you're wrong," he announced loudly. "Karbal's not as stupid as you said."

Karbal uncomfortably shifted his weight and grimaced, uncertain on how to respond.

The events on the television in the corner of the room suddenly caught everyone's eye.

"I, Walter Stanley Tate, do solemnly swear that I will faithfully execute the office of President of the United States, and will to the best of my ability, preserve, protect and defend the Constitution of the United States."

SO SAID THE PRESIDENT standing behind a clear, nine foot tall bullet proof shield that enclosed the entire west front of the Capitol. Two hundred of the country's most important dignitaries sat in folding chairs in a semi-circle directly behind the president, with another few hundred statesmen and well heeled politicos in temporary grandstands immediately behind them. A sea of almost 300,000 citizens packed The Mall stretching from the Capitol all the way to the Washington Monument.

Phillips eyes remained glued to the T.V. screen where Walter Tate was resworn in as president, and was now starting his Inaugural Address. Although he was listening intently to every word of Karbal's report, his eyes remained glued to the tube, sponging up every detail of the inaugural ceremony.

"So far, everything looks fine," Phillips said, swiveling his chair to face the group. Garber told me the Service has been conducting continuous bomb sweeps all around the Capitol and every building where there's an event today. And, agents are interspersed in the crowds with metal detectors."

"That's good, but I think hitting the Capitol or some other wide open public location would be the least likely place an assassin would hit the president. Too much obvious security plus it'd be almost impossible to escape."

"You're right, unless he doesn't care if he escapes," Richards countered. "And you know that's how these Arab martyrs think."

Coston slumped back in his chair and brushed his hand through his thick black hair in bewilderment, having forgotten about the reality of that prospect.

KARBAL PRESSED the speaker phone button on the state of the art telephone console he'd just moved onto the conference table. Around him stood Phillips, Richards and Coston. "Washington here," he proclaimed into the speakerphone. "This is Richard Karbal. I've got Director Coston, Sam Phillips and Norman Richards with me."

"Norman Richards. From the Middle East?" asked the voice on the other end.

"Yeah, who's this?" Richards replied.

"It's Olesky."

"Ronnie?"

"Fuckin' a man."

Speaking softly, Richards advised his colleagues, "FBI. A real cowboy. Great fuckin' guy. Known him for 20 years." He then spoke into the squawk box, "You still got your Harley?"

"New one. How about you?"

"Sold mine a few years ago," Richards replied, slightly embarrassed by the admission. "I didn't know you were in Florida."

"Yeah, well Boomer, I didn't know you were in the states, much less back with the Agency."

"It's a long story. I'm not even sure I am." Richards looked up at Coston, "Am I?"

Coston glared and raised his eyebrows in response. Richards got the message.

"Listen man, we'll talk when this thing is over."

"Yes. Later," Coston brusquely interjected. "What do you have for us there?" he asked.

"This bank is as dirty as it gets. We found a file for Seltaeb but there aren't any account signature cards or corporate resolutions. Not even on microfiche."

"Hardly a normal procedure," Phillips observed.

"Who was helping you?" Coston asked.

"The president of the Bank. A guy named Luis Javier Ramirez. He claims to know absolutely nothing about the account. Very cool character. Supposedly well known and respected in the Miami Latin community. But check this out, not a goddamn bank employee we talked to has ever heard of Seltaeb."

"Bullshit," Richards replied.

"You got that right. Listen to this. The Seltaeb account has over $17 million in it. Seventeen fuckin' million dollars and Ramirez doesn't know his customer!"

"You said "Ramirez," right?"

"Uh huh."

"Ilich *Ramirez* Sanchez," Richards whispered.

"Here's the interesting thing about the account. It was opened over ten years ago with a $4 million wire transfer from Geneva and had no activity until last January when another $10 million came in. Only five checks have ever been written on the account, and they were all in late July."

"The money came from Geneva at the same time the U.N. bombing occurred," said Richards.

"How did you get all this information so fast?" Phillips asked, knowing that banks don't store checks by customer name or account number, but rather on microfiche by date of clearance.

"Because the only thing in the Seltaeb folder were all the monthly account statements with the actual cashed checks and wire transfer slips. The account's business address is the bank, so the statements never left the bank. We got lucky."

"It's about time," Coston said. "It also proves somebody in Banco de Caracas, maybe Ramirez, has a close connection to Carlos because there's obviously a major degree of trust there. This is not how banks do business."

"Ronnie, who were the checks written to?" Norman asked.

"Let's see, there's George Washington University for $50,000. Wow...The Kennedy Center for $500,000. Jay Friedman for $5,000. Bruno Properties for $9600 and Jesus Christ...Pluto Associates, N.A. for $1.25 million."

"Good. Hold on," Richards said, grabbing the legal pad out of Karbal's hands and reading the freshly scratched notes on it. "Anybody ever hear of Bruno Properties?"

"Sure. They're one of the largest property managers in the D.C. and Virginia area," Karbal answered. "Mostly apartments."

"Ronnie?"

"Yeah."

"Is there any legend on that Bruno Properties check? You know, an apartment number or anything?"

"Nope."

"That one's going to take a while to follow up on," Phillips said to the others.

Richards yelled out again, "Ronnie, how about on the Friedman or Pluto checks?"

"Not there either, but they were both deposited into Washington Federal the same day. That's no coincidence."

Richards pushed the mute button on the speakerphone. "That's our window guys," Richards declared. "Let's open it. Carlos washed his Seltaeb money into Pluto Associates. Pluto's the front for Khalil." He turned the speakerphone back on again.

"Hey man, I need you to fax us the front and back of all those checks right now. The wire transfers too."

"Consider it done, brother. I got your number. There's some serious shit going down right now, isn't there?"

"Later," Richards said, cutting dead the phone call. "Let's get to work. Rick, start with Washington Federal. Sammy, do the corporate searches on Pluto. I'll check for phone records. It's past 2:00. We've really got to hustle and find Khalil's home."

"What about me?" asked Ed Coston, number three man in the CIA.

"Go get us some coffee," Richards replied smiling. "We're gonna need it."

TIRES SCREECHING, KARBAL SLAMMED on the brakes of the standard CIA issue white Chevy Impala curbside at Union Station. Richards jumped out of the car before it made a full stop, with Phillips right on his heels. Dodging and weaving like halfbacks, they sprinted up the sidewalk through the flowing crowd of people, toward the Washington Federal Bank branch nestled in the entrance of the office complex and shopping mall. Four other cars, two from the FBI and two from the Secret Service pulled up seconds later and over a score of men frantically tumbled out and followed the same path as Richards and Phillips.

Norman reached the bank's front door and stopped cold. No lights were on anywhere, and although it was clear the bank was closed, he couldn't stop himself from the futile gesture of repeatedly tugging the locked front door.

"It's closed," he muttered softly, staring into the darkness, his mouth so close to the glass it fogged up. He turned and faced Phillips and the other federal agents just reaching the bank. "It's closed," he repeated a bit louder. Then slamming his fist into the door, he yelled,

"Goddamn son of a bitch bank is closed!"

Anthony Garber shook his head in disgust. "Jesus Christ, we're two blocks from the Capitol with almost every business in the vicinity closed for the inauguration. You saw the streets. You can't move."

"Then let's bust open the fuckin' doors," Richards demanded. He eyed a bronze three foot tall cylindrical ashtray, ready to shot put it through the window if need be.

Before Garber could respond, a short wiry man in a three piece suit with oval shaped glasses spoke up. "We can't do that."

"Who are you?" Phillips said antagonistically.

"Assistant United States Attorney Carlone. This is not a break order. We have no legal right to break into private property under this court order. We have very limited search and seizure rights."

"Do you think I give a flying fuck about your piece of paper?" Phillips sneered.

"Anyone who knowingly exceeds the boundaries of this order could be committing contempt of court at the least and a felony at the most. And that doesn't include the tort liability from the bank."

"If you don't bust this fuckin' door down and get us in there, then I will," Richards replied.

"Then we'll have to arrest you," the government lawyer answered.

Phillips and Norman stood side by side, Richards with his hands defensively on his hips, Phillips with arms folded across his chest.

"What kind of jerk off are you?" Richards snapped. "Don't you understand what's going on here?"

"You must be Norman Richards."

"Right."

"How did I know?" Carlone said half under his breath, but loud enough for all to hear. "I'm sure you realize that if we stop a presidential assassination and arrest this Khalil al-Sharif, that any evidence illegally obtained cannot be used at his trial, and could ultimately free the man."

"Dickhead. I'm sure you realize if we don't get in there right away and find where the fuck this guy is, we're not gonna stop the assassination."

"Gentlemen," Coston said, stepping forward. "There's a solution here and we'll find it. But there'll be no fights right now."

"Carlone, I'm Richard Karbal, the Agency liaison you've been speaking with."

Carlone nodded an acknowledgment.

"Why can't we just get Judge Stettin back on the phone and have him amend the warrant to make it a full break order. This concerns National Security. Exigent circumstances."

Carlone was silent for a moment before replying, "We can do that." He reached inside his coat to extract a cellular phone and punched in some numbers.

Half the agents standing there simultaneously pulled out walkie talkies or cellular phones and started conversations, giving updates and orders.

"I've got an even better idea," said the FBI's Fred Lang. "Tell the judge we'll pick him up and take him every place we have to go. We'll have a portable courtroom."

Three minutes and a couple of calls later Carlone closed his flipphone and announced, "He's only a few blocks away. Lang's got a driver picking him up now. He said to go ahead and break the door."

Garber clicked off his cellular and announced, "We're tracking down the branch manager right now to help us get the material even faster. This is now a Class 6 emergency."

"You better hope he knows his entire computer system," Phillips said.

Garber thought about the remark and pulled his cellular back out. "Cecil. This is Tony. Get the cashier too," he commanded into the phone.

Richards picked up the ashtray and catapulted it through the front door, sending off a shrill alarm. He kicked out the rest of the glass panel and slipped into the bank, with the others following behind.

THIRTY-FIVE

FOR THE SECOND TIME in 30 seconds Debra Klein knocked on the door and spoke into the wooden frame a few inches from her nose. "C'mon Barak, open up. I just want to talk to you for a minute." She bit her bottom lip, her patience wearing thin. "I know you're in there. I hear the T.V." After a few more seconds she crossed her arms and snorted a little louder, "If you don't open up in ten seconds I'm going to make a scene."

When she got no response she kicked the bottom of the door as hard as she could. Turning her head she yelled down the hall, "Barak, the blood test confirmed you're the father. I have a child support order with me and if you don't pay, the police will pick you up." She smiled, pleased with her ridiculous lie.

Still no response.

"Are you going to let your son starve?" she yelled again giggling, more than pleased with herself.

The door flung open, an arm reached out and grabbed her, and before Debra realized what had happened, she was standing in the familiar surroundings of Barak Hamas' living room.

"How did you get in the building?" Khalil snapped at her.

"The superintendent let me in. We're friends now and he's $5.00 richer."

Khalil puckered his lips in disgust. "Why are you here?"

"Because it's cold standing outside," she replied with a sarcastic grin while taking off her coat.

For a second he stared at her full round chest, her nipples protruding through a white skin tight body suit tucked into black jeans. She looked great, but he forced his eyes away. "Put that back on. You're leaving."

"No I'm not," she answered, tossing the coat onto a couch a few feet away. "At least not until you give me some answers."

Knowing her stubborn streak, Khalil realized it was going to be easier to give her what she wanted than to try and talk her out of it. "Okay, quickly. What?"

In a soft voice she replied, "Big night at The Kennedy Center, huh? You look very handsome in your tuxedo." She seductively brushed the back of her hand up his arm and dusted off the lapel of his jacket.

He refused to show emotion to her gesture, but couldn't stop his heart from racing. "Thank you."

"Do you think you'll get to meet the president tonight?"

"I hope so." He paused in thought, the question snapping him back to reality. "Now what do you want? I've got a lot to do."

"You're so full of shit. It's a quarter to six. You probably don't have to be at work for at least another hour."

"Debra. What is it?"

She gave him a sad puppy dog look and turned away. "I want to know why you wouldn't take my calls or see me."

"Sorry, but I don't have an answer for you," he said sharply.

"You're a liar!" she shouted, turning back around. "And not much of a man either because even as I look in your eyes right now, I can see you care for me as much as I care for you." She took a step away from him and passionately added, "The last month since I haven't seen you has been the worst month of my life. I know what I saw in your face the night we went to the Holocaust Museum. You can say what you want but I know what I saw."

Debra wiped a teardrop from her eye, a little mad at herself for allowing the physical show of emotion. Somehow Barak always pushed the buttons with her, even when he wasn't trying.

Khalil stood speechless for a moment, caught off guard and affected by the truth of her observation. Still, although he never foresaw that this sentimental moment with Debra would come, he could not discard the responsibilities he assumed years ago, which he was to carry out this evening. Hurting her feelings right now was the only answer, and he had to resolve the conflict that burned from within. "You are a Jew. I am an Arab. We were friends but that's all. Do you understand? We're nothing."

Suddenly a similar but slightly thicker accented voice announced from the unlit back bedroom, "Khalil, did you make a child with a Jewess?" Ahmed al-Sharif appeared from the shadows also dressed in a tuxedo.

"Who are you?" Debra asked, astonished at this man's striking resemblance to Khalil. Even their formalwear and haircuts were identical. In an instant she realized they were brothers.

"Was I talking to you? Did I say a word to you? You don't speak until I say so," Ahmed roared at Debra, the words shooting out of his mouth like machine gun bullets.

"No, I did not sleep with this woman," Khalil calmly answered his brother's question.

"Yes, you did," Debra lied.

"Jew girl. Don't think for a moment I believe you," Ahmed hissed at her. "Khalil would not lie to me."

"Khalil?" She looked over at Khalil and asked, "I never heard that before. What's Barak, your nickname? Your middle name?"

He looked deep into her eyes but didn't answer.

Ahmed snorted a laugh. "Didn't Khalil ever tell you he had a twin brother?"

"Barak, what's going on here?" she asked, grasping from Ahmed's tone that something was seriously wrong.

"What does she know?" Ahmed asked.

"Nothing. Absolutely nothing."

"That's where you're wrong. Now she knows about me. We

must dispose of her," Ahmed said.

"What!" Debra asked, totally baffled by the bizarre comment.

"No," Khalil shouted. "She's my problem. *I'll* deal with her."

"She is *our* problem and I say she dies. Right now. Take care of it," Ahmed demanded.

Khalil glided over to Ahmed and softly said, "I have been here for months working toward tonight. We will be gone in hours. She will not interfere, but I will *not* kill her. Understand that right now, brother."

"You have grown stupid. Did you forget the rules? Discipline. Know Your Enemy," Ahmed lectured.

"She is not my enemy," Khalil retorted.

"How can you say that? She is a Jew. If you could kill your best friend, you can kill her."

"She does not die," Khalil said emphatically, glaring at his brother.

"After all your training and planning, this is how you react about some meaningless Jewish woman?" Ahmed asked, astonished.

"I have learned as much from her as I learned from Carlos."

Ahmed's eyes opened wide at Khalil's surprising disclosure.

"Carlos?" Debra declared. "The terrorist Carlos the Jackal? You know him?"

"Shut up," Khalil snapped. He pointed his index finger at her as a warning.

Ahmed shook his head in disgust. "I will not fight with you right now. But if she opens her mouth at all, I'll kill her myself and you won't stop me." Ahmed turned to Debra, "Do you understand what I'm saying?"

Shocked, Debra was unable to find her voice. She nodded numbly.

"Sit down," Khalil ordered.

Debra dropped instantly to the floor.

"You're not going to make a sound, are you?" Khalil asked.

His cold black eyes looked different than ever before. This was not the Barak Hamas she knew and it scared her. She shook her head and mumbled "no," tears streaming down her face.

"Don't move. Even an inch," he said, then disappeared into his bedroom for a moment. He returned with a few neckties and a rolled up pair of white socks.

"Put your hands behind your back," he said to her.

"You're going to kill the president, aren't you?"

Khalil tightened the knot on her wrists and she winced. He breathed quickly and heavily through his nose.

"Barak, Khalil, whatever your name is. You don't have to do this. It's not you. I know you. You're not a murderer."

"You know nothing about me Debra. Nothing," he said coldly. "Only what I wanted you to know and hardly any of that was true."

Khalil next tied her ankles together, then picked her up in his arms and carried her to the kitchen table where he slid the knot on her arms through the table leg, ensuring she couldn't move.

"I know you're a good person. Don't do this. You can't get away with it."

"We'll see," Khalil said.

"I think we already have," Ahmed added confidently.

Just as he was about to stuff a sock into her mouth and secure it with another tie, Debra said, "Barak, you could have a life here. I love you. And no matter what you say, I know you love me. Are you ready to live? Or are you ready to die?"

Khalil dropped his eyes from hers and again her words made his heart sink. Ahmed, who was watching the exchange laughed and answered for his brother. "He is ready to die."

Khalil fastened the gag into her mouth, stood up and announced, "I *am* ready to die."

"Good," Ahmed smiled, slapping his brother on the arm. "Then let's get back to work. We've only got a few more minutes."

"Right. The pictures first," Khalil said, removing a thick set of photographs from a large manilla envelope sitting on the table. Ahmed stood next to him, and while Khalil pointed at photographs of his Kennedy Center friends and colleagues taken at basketball games and the staff Christmas party, Ahmed repeated aloud his identification of every face shown. "Shrimp... Cook... Crash...

Brumbaugh... Mehringer..." and so on until Ahmed correctly named over 60 Kennedy Center employees.

"Which entrance are you going through?" Khalil asked.

"First door on the north side of the building. I'll have my ID out."

"Next option?"

"Last door on the south side."

"How do you tell north from south?"

"The river behind the building is west."

"Third option?"

"Garage service entrance. But no sooner than 6:35. I avoid Shrimp and if I have to say anything, I tell them I went back out because I forgot my contact lenses."

"Where's the locker room?" Khalil asked, picking out an irrelevant location in the building to assure Ahmed memorized every square inch of The Kennedy Center.

"Downstairs, off the loading dock, around the corner from the employee cafeteria, right under the stage of the Concert Hall." Blow-ups of the microfiche plans to The Kennedy Center that Carlos swiped from the Washington D.C. Building and Zoning Department were spread open on the table in front of them, but Ahmed didn't have to look down to answer.

"Good. Now why didn't you play basketball yesterday?"

"Bad cold combined with emergency root canal surgery for impacted molars. Very painful. That's why my face is slightly swollen and I sound funny."

"Let me hear you sneeze."

Ahmed did. He also coughed, rubbed his eyes and sniffled.

"Excellent. What machine is the ceramic gun behind?"

"None. It's taped three feet in on the top side of the air duct in the west corner of the furnace room next to the junction box."

"Remember, it's loaded and only has two shots. There's no reason for you to touch the bullets. If you get any of that poison on you, you're dead."

"I know," Ahmed said.

"Code number on security elevator 2-E8?"

"4152."

"From where will the president enter the Grand Foyer?"

"Opera House mezzanine level, stage right."

"Prime accuracy range with the gun?"

"Thirty feet."

"Once the chandeliers in the Grand Foyer flicker, how much time do you have to get out?"

"Four minutes from the flashes. Four and a half at most."

"Excellent." Khalil smiled confidently. "It was a lot of work the last ten days, but I think you've got it."

"Khalil, tonight we make history," Ahmed announced.

"Yes, we shall. But Ahmed, are *you* ready to die?"

"I have never been more ready," Ahmed answered. "But the fact you asked the question tells me you are not. This is a night we must know no fear."

"I will die if I must," Khalil said. "But I will not go to prison and I will not talk."

"Allah may declare our deaths to be necessary."

"So he may."

"Wait, did you hear that?" Khalil asked, putting up his hand to stop the conversation.

"Hear what?"

"The T.V. They just said the president is running about a half hour behind schedule. No matter what, do not leave the boiler room until I signal you or you hear the song. Once you're in the building, you've got to stay out of sight. If he's a half hour behind now, it could be an hour by the time he makes it to The Kennedy Center."

"Do not worry about me," Ahmed said.

"Hum the song for me that tells you when the president has arrived."

Ahmed wasn't very good at keeping the tune, but he was able to demonstrate for Khalil that he knew *Hail to the Chief.*

"If you don't see those lights flash within ten minutes of the president entering the Grand Foyer I'll be dead. And after you pull the trigger, so will you."

"And we will have died as martyrs for the glory of Iraq. But Khalil, we will not die. We cannot. Because if one of us does not succeed, there will be no attack on Israel. We *must* do our jobs."

Khalil turned away from Debra, feeling some guilt for betraying her. Still, he would not relinquish his own heritage or the responsibilities of the moment. "How many Jews do you think Ayyash and Shkaki can take out during their attacks?"

Ahmed walked over to Debra, squatted down, spit in her face and said, "Thousands. Thousands of Jews will die in almost 300 bombing attacks in Israel, my little Jewish friend. Tomorrow. And that's even before Iraq's jets gas Tel Aviv and we take out the whole city. After we finish our work here tonight, the U.S. will not be in any position to come help the Zionists."

Ahmed laughed at the hate in Debra's eyes and added, "I am no fool. Now I have guaranteed your death. Even my sentimental brother knows you're too dangerous to keep alive now. We can't have any witnesses." He looked over to Khalil and asked, "Wouldn't Carlos agree?"

Khalil's heart skipped a beat as he realized Ahmed was right. Debra couldn't live. Her death was a necessary element of this military exercise. She was yelling and moaning muffled sounds that were agonizing to Khalil. He refused to look at her.

Ahmed continued to torment Debra. "If you think I am on the edge, you should learn more about your friend here. Khalil, how many people have you killed? Fifteen? Twenty?"

Khalil didn't answer.

"How many?" Ahmed demanded.

Khalil sighed heavily, walked over and put his hand on Ahmed's shoulder. "Ahmed. Carlos told us that our emotions would run high before a mission." He rested his index and forefingers to his temple. "Keep you head."

Ahmed smiled and replied, "You're right. Answer the question and I will leave it alone."

Khalil stared at Ahmed for a moment before deciding to answer.

"Fine. Thirteen to be precise."

Ahmed bent over Debra and said, "Thirteen. That is nothing. Tonight he will take out at least 1500 within seconds." He put his hands around his throat and made a gagging sound while opening his eyes in an almost comical expression. Pointing at Khalil with his thumb Ahmed added, "Do you know how much planning it took for us to kill your president and vice president, your Congress and Supreme Court? Then to destroy Israel?" Ahmed laughed and playfully patted Debra on the cheek a few times.

She started writhing, the table jerking along with her. Picking a .38 special dressed with a silencer off the table Ahmed pointed it at her forehead. "Stop it," he snapped. "If you want to go this moment I will be happy to accommodate you."

Her eyes opened wide in fright and she became mostly still except for a slight sobbing whimper.

"Good girl. But Khalil will do you in a minute anyway."

Khalil remained with his back to Debra and tried to focus on assuring that the final details of the plan were tightly choreographed.

"Where's the car?" Khalil asked.

"At 23rd & G Street."

"Keys?"

"Driver's side, underneath the seat."

"You have the money?"

"Yes."

"Passport?"

"Yes."

"Tickets."

"Yes."

"Then that's it. We're set."

"Not quite," Ahmed said. He flicked his head towards Debra. "Do her. Now."

"Right," Khalil agreed. He leaned over and put his face next to Debra's. She instantly read in his eyes the confused inner conflict of both a sad lost love and a cold blooded remorseless murderer.

"You were right," he whispered directly into her ear so that Ahmed could not hear him. "I do love you. But I must do this and you must forgive me. Goodbye."

Khalil placed his forearm across her forehead and put the back of his hand on her skull. In one quick jerk he twisted her neck and she immediately slumped over. He delicately lay her flat out on the floor, but still bound, gagged and tied to the table. "She's gone."

"Leave her," Ahmed directed, pleased with the proof that Khalil remained a soldier.

His eyes watering and chest heaving, Khalil softly instructed Ahmed, "It's time. Grab your coat and get out of here. Do not go off the route. I'll follow in five minutes."

The brothers had mapped out separate paths for each to take to the Kennedy Center. It was a busy, dark, cold night. People were festive, in a hurry and by and large, nonsuspicious. If Ahmed was polite and smiled and minded his own business, there was no reason why he shouldn't be able to slip right into The Kennedy Center as Barak Hamas at the same time that 400 other employees were coming into work for the Presidential Inauguration's most prominent ball. Even through tight security.

Just before Ahmed closed the apartment door behind him, he turned to Khalil and said, "Brother, if I do not see you in Baghdad, I will see you with Allah."

THIRTY-SIX

POISED FOR ATTACK, five members of the Secret Service's special SWAT team stood in ready position outside Barak Hamas' apartment in full protective gear, holding enough firepower to destroy a small town. Roughly 30 other agents waited inside and out of 23rd & H Street, eagle eyeing every exit, window and angle of the potential assassin's apartment building for the slightest suspicious activity. In complete silence, the entire team moved swiftly into position between the shadows of the clouded moonlight. If Khalil al-Sharif wanted a battle, they were ready to give him one.

Anthony Garber held a walkie talkie in one hand and a pistol in the other. He listened intently through an earphone for confirmation that everyone stationed below was in place. Richards, Phillips and the rest of the CIA crew stood slightly down the hall, waiting to rush in after the specialists had cleared the area.

The soldiers perched outside Khalil's apartment focused on Garber for their signal to take the room. His barely perceptible nod was enough to tell them to stand by. He stuck the walkie talkie in his coat and mouthed "on three," while raising three fingers, and forcefully slicing the air each time he eliminated a number.

The exact fraction of a second that Garber's mark hit one, an agent fired a single round into the door lock and a second man kicked it open. Three other agents bounded past them into the room, their automatic machine pistols aimed and ready to spray bullets wherever necessary to secure the apartment. In a perfectly choreographed maneuver, the first jumped straight ahead and the other two covered his opposite sides. The lock-shooter and door kicker charged in behind them. But having seized the location, when there was no sound of conflict, no gunfire, it was an ominous sign for those trying to catch an assassin.

The agents scattered through the apartment in search of Khalil, Garber signaling to the others in the hall to stay put. Richards walked right past him, drawing a dirty look, entering the terrorist's apartment with his .44 magnum out, cocked and ready to go. Phillips followed behind, giving Garber a "what the hell" shrug.

Even though the commando leader hadn't yet announced the all clear, Richards spoke up. "Forget it, we're too late. There's no one here." A half second later he clarified, "Except for her." He pointed at Debra's body.

"Who the hell is she?" Phillips said, standing over her.

"And how long has she been a prisoner?" Garber added.

"Not long," Richards concluded.

"How do you know?" Coston asked.

"Because here's her purse and coat," Richards replied, pointing at where Debra left them on the couch only two hours earlier. "If she had been here a while, I think they would have been put away," he reasoned.

"Anthony, call Judge Stettin downstairs to make sure it's okay for us to search this purse," Fred Lang said. "We're gonna catch this fuckin' guy one way or the other, and I don't want him to be able to claim any of that technicality bullshit as a defense."

"Yeah, I agree," Richards added, already having started his search of her purse.

"Dammit Norman," Coston said upon seeing what Richards was doing. "*Fingerprints.* Don't touch anything."

"You guys already have my fingerprints," he wisecracked, still rummaging through her wallet. Then he added, "Debra H. Klein, 20, D.C. resident ... ahh, George Washington University."

Coston sighed. "She obviously went to school with Khalil."

"Gimme that," Garber said, grabbing the wallet out of Richards' hand. Within seconds he was dictating orders through the walkie talkie to obtain information on the dead girl.

Simultaneously, Lang instructed his subordinates downstairs to send the forensic team up along with the coroner.

"Let's think this thing through," Richards said. "It's a quarter to eight and so far presidential security has been completely normal. Right?" he asked Garber.

"Yep."

"Now we've got a corpse, a missing terrorist and a decreasing number of locations he could hit. And *maybe* we really are on some wild goose chase."

"No, we're on to something," Phillips said. "She was killed for a reason."

"Right. And Khalil's got to be someplace where he's not supposed to be," Karbal pondered, covering Debra with her coat. He jumped back. "This girl's not dead! She's still warm."

"She's breathing?" Lang asked.

Karbal searched and found a pulse. "Strong heartbeat. Just unconscious. No visible wounds."

"Get a medic up here right now," Coston demanded.

"And untie her and take that gag out of her mouth," Lang added.

While watching the ruckus surrounding Debra, Richards clasped his fingers on top of his head in frustration and his eyes narrowed and focused in thought. "Oh shit!" he exclaimed, reaching a conclusion on Khalil's whereabouts. "He's at The Kennedy Center. He's there's right now. He's got to be."

"No. He's not working tonight. We already checked," Garber responded. "And the bomb squad has gone through that place with a fine tooth comb three times."

"That's what he would want us to believe. It's a typical Carlos plan. Hide the obvious in the truth. A diversion. Khalil gets into the building but doesn't have to work. He can do what he wants once he's inside. It's the building he knows. There's no place else he could be."

"Oh Christ," Garber replied.

"What time does the National Ball start?" Richards asked.

Karbal answered, "Normally it starts at midnight because..."

"I didn't ask normally," Richards screamed. "I asked a simple fucking question."

"8:00."

"That's less than 15 minutes from now," Coston said.

"Was his composite sketch circulated? Was anyone told to pick him up if he entered the building?" Phillips rattled off the questions to Lang and Garber.

At first there was silence, then Garber answered, "No. We didn't think this was an avenue..."

"You guys are first class morons," Phillips interjected.

Garber and Lang couldn't deny it, and nobody came to their defense.

"He's at The Kennedy Center," Richards declared. "And I'm out of here. Where is this place?"

"Only a few blocks away," Karbal said.

"Good. Drive me there."

"No way. Traffic's ridiculous. It'll take half an hour."

"Then we'll run. Let's go," Richards ordered. On his way out the door he yelled behind him, "Somebody call and clear us through security. And get your asses over there." He looked at Debra who, though groggy, was already wakened with smelling salts. "Bring her, too. Maybe she can help."

"Her? Why?" said Lang.

Richards shook his head and answered sarcastically, "She knows what he looks like." He muttered, "idiots" under his breath as he bolted out of the apartment.

Garber jumped back on his walkie talkie dictating a new alert for security at The Kennedy Center.

"Fuck the elevator. Hit the steps," Phillips said as he, Richards and Karbal ran down the hall to the stairwell. They bounded down the seven flights, holding onto the railings, skipping every two or three steps.

They hit the street and saw traffic was worse than a mess because the entire block surrounding Khalil's apartment building was sealed off. Horns blared in all directions as impatient motorists fought to make it on time to the various inaugural balls, most of which were scheduled to start within minutes.

Karbal pointed at a large modern structure a few blocks away up H Street. "That's the Watergate complex. The Kennedy Center is next door."

Richards took off up the street, his bluejean jacket flapping open in the cold and windy D.C. night, with Phillips and Karbal right behind him. At the six way intersection of New Hampshire, Virginia and 25th Streets, directly in front of the Watergate, Richards sprinted into heavy traffic, smacking square into the side of a slow moving black stretch limo. He rolled over its hood and tumbled to the ground almost to be flattened an instant later by another vehicle. Phillips and Karbal reached Richards' side and helped him to his feet. The chauffeur jumped out of the limo, but by then Richards was again standing.

"Goddamn it. Shit!" Richards ranted, dusting himself off.

"Are you okay?" Phillips asked, steadying Richards underneath his forearm.

"Fine. But look, I ripped my fucking jacket," he scowled at the shocked driver, showing that his blue jean jacket bore a new six inch tear down the side. *"Look, my jacket!"* He repeatedly kicked the front fender of the limo as hard as he could. The driver wisely cowered away.

Traffic was in a complete gridlock and automobile horns blasted symphonically. But it was the sirens of the presidential motorcade just pulling up to The Kennedy Center 150 yards away, which refocused the CIA agents' attention. Realizing it was the president and that time was short, they took off again in that direction.

All three men reached The Kennedy Center and seized the spotlight of arriving guests as they were not only doubled over gasping for air, but were dressed more for a football game rather than the premier inaugural ball. A long line of formally cloaked political bigwigs huddled together trying to fend off the chill while waiting to pass through security. The CIA agents barged to the front of the line and approached the first guard.

"Phillips, CIA," he wheezed displaying his agency badge. "Anthony Garber should have just called in an authorization to get me in here."

"No, sir. Haven't heard that."

There was no time to argue. "Look bub, let us the fuck in right now. This is a national emergency," Richards said brusquely.

"Your name sir?" the Secret Service agent politely but curtly asked, staring straight ahead.

"Richards. Norman Richards."

"Yes sir. We just received a call about you. But not him. May I see your identification please?"

Richards flashed his badge.

"These men are with you?"

"Oh for Christ sakes," Phillips said. "I'm his superior officer."

"Delusions of grandeur," Richards countered, smacking Phillips on the back. "But yes, they're with me."

"Mr. Garber said to cooperate with you fully."

"I'd hope so." Pulling a folded copy of Khalil's composite sketch from his back pocket, he handed it to the agent and whispered, "We don't have much time. Copy this and tell every one of your people to look for this guy. Orders are, shoot to kill."

"Excuse me?" the agent said, taken aback.

"This man is in here right now to kill the president," Richards said.

"When does Tate make his appearance?" Phillips asked.

He checked his watch. "In about ten minutes."

"Where?"

"Off the Grand Foyer. Go down this hall, make a left, and he'll be right off the steps in front of the Opera House."

"Give me your walkie talkie."

"If I do, I won't be able to give out your orders, sir."

"All right. What about those guys?" Richards asked, pointing at some uniformed guards helping check guests through security.

"They don't have them. They're only Park Service. I'll find you some. Give me five minutes."

Richards exhaled in frustration. "Okay. One last thing. You see how we're dressed?"

"Yes sir."

"I don't want to be stopped and I don't want interference from anyone. Get on that goddamn horn and tell everyone I want full fucking cooperation. You got it?"

"They'll know within the minute sir."

Richards, Phillips and Karbal walked ten feet away before stopping to caucus. "Now what?" Richards asked.

"We've got to split up," Phillips said. "There's too much territory here for us to cover together."

"Right," Richards agreed. "Rick. You cover this wing here. Look all over. Closets. Rooms. Everywhere. If you see him, shoot first, ask questions later."

"What if he's not doing anything wrong?"

"Need I fucking remind you he's not even supposed to be here. If he's here, it's for a reason. If you see him, kill him. If you don't, he *will* kill you. That's how terrorists think."

"Gotcha."

"And as soon as you can, take the safety off your gun. Also, if you even *see* him, fire a shot to get everyone's attention."

"Will do."

"You damn well better. This is serious fucking shit going down right now."

"I'm gonna check out that far wing down there," Phillips said.

"Fine. I'll be the rover," Richards said. "I'm gonna start with a quick search of the Grand Foyer and then work my way over to the presidential detail. Make your way back here in a few minutes to get a phone. Got it?"

They nodded.

"Good. Let's break."

The men hurried off in different directions to hunt down the assassin.

This is impossible! Richards thought as he arrived at the entrance to the Grand Foyer and saw that the dimly lit great hall was packed with people. Bands played at opposite ends of the room and every single male except him wore a tux. Somehow he would have to locate one man in the half darkness he had never seen before and that could well be in disguise. *"How? Look at the faces. Look at the faces,"* he continually repeated to himself as he zigzagged through the affluent crowd in search of Khalil.

A waiter passed by, and Richards couldn't help but snag a bubbling champagne flute off the silver tray. He emptied the glass in three quick gulps and noticed the demeaning stares of the guests around him. But he didn't care. They didn't know what he had been through. He handed the glass to another passing waiter.

Suddenly his heart shot full of adrenaline as he spotted Khalil al-Sharif standing alone 15 people deep into the crowd. Medium height and build. Dark curly hair and complexion. Young. It was him. His mind raced...what to do? *I can't start shooting in here. Too many people. I know. Put him in an armlock and drag him out of here. There's no way he's stronger than me. And even if we fight, that ends it for him.*

Richards' eyes focused directly on Khalil, everything around him a meaningless, surrealistic blur. He cautiously inched his way toward the President's killer, indiscriminately bumping into guests as his attack range narrowed to three feet. He now stood directly behind the man he had chased for three weeks from Jordan to Geneva to Washington.

Firmly poking his index finger into the middle of Khalil's back, he spoke harshly into his ear. "Khalil, I know who you are and why you're here. You can come peacefully with me right now or I'll blow a hole through you the size of a fuckin' camel hump. It's your choice."

The man spun around and yelled at Richards, "Are you threatening me? Who do you think you are? Do you know who I am? I'm Stanley Sockel. U.S. Congressman from Philadelphia. I don't know who you are, but you've got a big problem now, buddy."

Richards face went flush. "Sir, I'm sorry. I thought you were someone else. Please, I'm very sorry."

"Who are you?" the Congressman demanded.

Richards flashed his badge, leaned over and softly answered, "CIA. I'm here working. My mistake."

Sockel shook his head and muttered, "Asshole." In a louder voice he ordered, "Get out of here," and he waved Richards away.

Richards sheepishly smiled at the onlookers and backed away from the scene. The incident was quickly forgotten, however, as every guests' attention shifted to the center of the Grand Foyer and the orchestras began to play *"Hail to the Chief."* The crowd of Congressmen, Cabinet members, Supreme Court Justices, Governors and other figures of political significance started to clap to the beat of the music with accompanying rhythmic cheers of "Tate, Tate, Tate."

Less than 50 yards but many walls away, Richard Karbal was cautiously opening and closing doors, searching for anyone who was where they shouldn't be. He heard the presidential march and took a deep breath, recognizing the window of opportunity to avert a national catastrophe was continuing to rapidly close. He exited a rehearsal room adjacent to the Concert Hall, crossed through the Hall of Nations and opened a stairwell door next to the ticket office, to explore the area right above the Opera House.

He climbed the steps two at a time. Just as he reached the second level and opened the door, his peripheral vision picked up the unmistakable shadow of a person bounce off the wall a flight above him and then stop. He instantly analyzed, *Nobody should be here! The waiters aren't using these steps. Everyone else is downstairs with Tate.*

Karbal opened and closed the door but remained stone cold silent in the stairwell landing. Grateful for heeding Richards' advice by earlier removing the safety, he grasped his gun firmly in both hands and extended it in front of him, ready to fire. He felt like his heart would explode and tried to wish it silent, praying that whoever was only feet away wouldn't hear it pounding.

After a very long ten seconds the shadow flickered again and Karbal heard footsteps slowly moving down the stairs. Seconds later Ahmed stood in full view of Karbal and froze upon seeing the gun pointed up at him only a half flight of steps away.

"Don't move! Put your hands up!" Karbal commanded. He considered pulling the trigger but couldn't, for the man was clearly unarmed.

Ahmed followed the instructions, jerking his hands above his head. He opened his eyes wide and innocently said, "I didn't do anything. What did I do?"

"Shut up Khalil. You're done. Turn around and put your hands up against the wall."

"My name's not Khalil. It's Mufas Dastremi."

"I said shut up. I know exactly who you are. Now I told you once. Turn around and place your hands on the wall."

"You're wrong. I don't even know a Khalil. Check my driver's license," he said, starting to lower an arm to his inside jacket.

"Don't move your hands! Keep them up!"

"Okay, okay, don't shoot! Look, my license is in my back pocket. I'll keep my hands up and *you* take it out."

Karbal thought about it for a moment and agreed. "Back down the steps slowly. One at a time. And don't move your hands."

Ahmed did exactly as he was told, chattering on and on about what a mistake Karbal was making. He reached the platform of the second floor with his back only three feet from Karbal and his arms still held high. Karbal jammed the gun barrel into the small of Ahmed's back, and quickly removed Ahmed's wallet. Karbal reduced the pressure of the gun just slightly, in order to examine the wallet's contents with his one free hand.

In a single, fluid, lightning-fast motion, Ahmed kicked a leg back directly into Karbal's thigh, pirouetted around in the same direction and brought his forcarm down with full force, breaking Karbal's wrist and dislodging his grip on the gun, which rattled to the metal staircase floor.

Yelping from the pain, Karbal grabbed his injured hand with his good one, creating the opening for Ahmed to deliver a solid karate punch to Karbal's nose. The dazed and now bloodied CIA agent fell back against the wall but somehow instinctively assumed a martial arts fighting position. It was too late. In a brutally vicious attack, the far superior killer Ahmed dispensed a relentless series of indefensible kicks and punches to Karbal's face and body. Within seconds the American crumbled to the ground, barely conscious. Ahmed glared at Karbal and with the full weight of his body he stomped on his victim's throat, crushing everything within and causing instant suffocation. Blood flowed from Karbal's mouth and nose, and Ahmed smash kicked his face for good measure.

Ahmed picked up Karbal's gun and stuck it inside his tuxedo pant waistband. Straightening his clothes he flew down the flight of steps, exiting right into the Hall of Nations.

He walked down the red carpeted hall towards where the tune changed to *For He's A Jolly Good Fellow.* Even though Ahmed had memorized both the inner layout and the outer landscape of The Kennedy Center, it wasn't until he stood in the Grand Foyer for that first moment observing its mammoth size and spectacular decor that he was able to appreciate its magnificence, and even he was impressed.

Khalil had warned that security agents roving about would blend in with the guests, but would nevertheless be distinguishable by their earphones. They would also, presumably, not be drinking or socializing. Ahmed scanned the crowd, searching for such enemies.

Standing alone in the corner of the Grand Foyer, Richards surveyed the room, then suddenly refocused his eyes in disbelief. Standing 30 feet away from him through the crowd was Khalil. He remembered Sabar's picture and his composite sketch was actually very close. This time he was sure. This *was* the man.

Again the band broke into a rousing, jazzy *Hail to the Chief* and a famous Hollywood celebrity appeared at a microphone on a platform centered at the entrance of the Opera House. He raised his arms above his head immediately silencing all 1500 people and the orchestra, except for a continually beating snare drum. The lights dimmed almost black and a single pinpoint spotlight shined on the man's face.

"Ladies and Gentlemen. What a night! ... Here we are... The future of America...The greatest country in the world... Tonight we celebrate the inauguration of the man that will lead the U S of A ... and will lead the WHOLE..WIDE..WORLD into the 21st Century... Without further adieu, let me say it is a thrill...It is my pleasure... It is an honor to introduce to you right now... our President of the United States of America!... President and Mrs. Walter Tate and Vice President and Mrs. Randolph Mertz!"

Multi-colored lights flooded the stage, the orchestra pounded out *Stars and Stripes Forever* and in a spectacle of a fireworks boom synchronized with a blinding flash of light and smoke, the new administration was suddenly standing before the country's leadership and almost a billion people watching worldwide live on television. The crowd went wild; the noise in the room overwhelming. Moments later, a thousand red, white and blue balloons dropped from the ceiling.

"Oh shit, where'd he go!" Richards panicked, losing sight of Khalil. The combination of the balloons and smoke, red backlit spotlights on the president, white blinding television lights only feet away and barely any light from above made visibility nearly impossible. *"Go to Tate! Go to the target!"* Richards intuitively realized, barreling his way through the throng of people who pushed as close to their president as possible.

He finally made it to the front of the platform and faced the guests to again search out the assassin. His eyes roved back and forth scanning the faces. One caught his eye. *No smile. Everyone else is smiling. Khalil!* Richards' eyes locked completely onto his target.

And similarly, the cold blooded murderer's stare was fixed with purpose on his target.

As he had instructed Karbal only minutes earlier, Richards considered shooting Khalil right then, but it would have been an impossible shot in this constantly moving, not to mention high profile crowd. *I have to get closer. I have to get next to, no, on top of Khalil. It's the only way to stop him.* No more than 20 feet from where Ahmed was standing, the Secret Service started clearing a path for the president to go down onto the floor to greet his esteemed guests.

"Oh my God! Stay up there!" Richards yelled to no one in particular, realizing the opportunity for Khalil to get off a clean shot at the president was greater on the floor.

"Oh Allah!" Ahmed thought, astonished that an unexpected opportunity for a point blank shot at the president was only moments away. It was not part of the plan, but Carlos taught him well that improvisation was a critical element to assure success of any mission. Khalil would finish off the rest of the room in a few minutes anyway. *I might die. I will die. But death with honor is the quest of life. I will not see Khalil two days from now in Baghdad, but at some unknown point down the road with Allah.*

President Walter Tate stood ten feet from his assassin, grinning, laughing, shaking hands, draping his arm around an old colleague's shoulder, playing it up for the T.V. cameras recording his every twitch. A Secret Service agent flanked him on each side. The lighting, the mix of aggressive people and Ahmed's subtle movements prevented the president's guards from observing that a handsome young man no more than four feet from the president was holding a pistol in his hand.

But Norman Richards had seen it. Before Ahmed's arm could even reach waist level, Richards landed a smashing punch to the back of Ahmed's neck, sending him into a woman in front of him who in turn fell into one of the president's guards who tumbled into someone else. Instant chaos resulted. The other Secret Service agent jumped in front of the president, shielding him from whatever might be next. Within seconds, three male guests held Richards firmly in their grasp and the other Secret Service agent bounded back onto his feet and aimed his 9 mm. pistol two inches from Richards nose.

"Don't move," he warned, also yelling a security alert into a communicator.

Ahmed, dazed from Richards' powerful blow was helped to his feet by other sympathetic guests. He'd lost his ceramic gun during the melee, dismayed that it was on the carpet somewhere nearby.

"I want this man arrested," Ahmed yelled, poking his index finger into Richards' chest.

"Get this jerk out of here," a voice agreed.

"Lock him up," the woman concurred, still sitting on the floor.

Three other agents appeared and started questioning the witnesses.

"Goddammit, I'm a government agent," Richards snarled. But because he was tightly bound he could only point with the nod of his head and insist, "He's Khalil al-Sharif, an Iraqi terrorist here to kill the president."

"You're a lunatic," Ahmed screamed at Richards. "My name is Mufas Dastremi. I'm the ambassador from Pakistan and I'm going to lodge a formal complaint with my embassy over this incident." He flashed his wallet as if to prove it contained official papers. Ahmed looked and sounded more convincing than Richards.

One of Richards' captors noticed his .44 magnum holstered inside his jean jacket. "Look, he's got a gun!"

"I'm telling you I'm with the CIA," Richards snapped. "Check my ID," he insisted. "It's in my back pocket. And call Tony Garber and get him over here. He'll tell you."

Richards gained instant credibility with the Secret Service agent -- no civilian would ever know who Anthony Garber was.

The Secret Service agent studied Richards' badge and the contents of his wallet before looking up disgusted at his CIA colleague. "You? You're Norman Richards?" He shook his head and said to his colleagues. "Let him go."

"I've been trying to tell you that," Richards replied. "Didn't you see the composite sketch that we circulated?" Richards pointed at Ahmed. "Go get it. That's him."

Ahmed had heard enough. It was now or never. He pulled Richard Karbal's gun from his back waistband and fired two shots into the Secret Service agent's back, spun around and quickly fired two more into the other agent protecting the president. He next aimed his gun directly at Tate, who was frozen still only 12 feet away as people dove for the ground screaming. Five more shots echoed through the hall. The first three from Richards' .44 magnum ripping into Ahmed's back, and then two errant shots from Ahmed wounding people around the president.

Ahmed fell to his knees where he stayed for at least ten seconds, blood gushing out of his back and chest, which heaved as he gasped large breaths in vain. He finally fell face down.

Pointing his gun at Ahmed's head, Richards squatted down and turned Ahmed over. He was surprised Ahmed's eyes were still bright and that he appeared alert. Ahmed smiled at Richards, whispered "Allah" and slowly closed his eyes.

The unambiguous reverberating gunshot explosions stopped not only both orchestras midsong but every conversation midsentence. The Grand Foyer suddenly became as silent as if it was completely empty in the middle of night. People didn't have to see what happened to know something with a gun did, and that there could only be one target. Those in the vicinity of Norman Richards had their eyes transfixed on him.

Displaying the leadership for which he was elected, President Tate climbed back up to the platform, took the microphone and raised a clenched fist high in the air. "Everything's okay people. We had a little problem but things are under control now. I guess you just can't put Democrats and Republicans in the same room."

The crowd laughed uncomfortably.

Tate pointed to the band at one end of the great hall and majestically commanded, "Maestro."

The room broke into applause, at first soft and sporadic and then to a thunderous ovation with more cheers of "Tate, Tate, Tate." The orchestra started playing and guests at the end of the hall who didn't know what happened, restarted their conversation. An army of government agents and D.C. police suddenly swarmed into the room from all directions.

The president walked back down the platform and headed straight for Richards. He grabbed his hand and asked, "What's your name?"

"Richards, sir. Norman Richards."

"Mr. Richards, I don't know who you are, but you're a friend of mine now. And, I take good care of my friends. Think of a favor you need. I'll be in touch."

The president shook his hand again and smacked him on the arm.

Tate turned and motioned another agent over. "Young man, what's your name?"

"Clark."

"Mr. Clark, do me a favor. First, make sure you get those cameras off of those bodies, and second, get those bodies out of here. Now! You understand?"

"Sir, with all due respect, this is a crime scene." He pointed at Ahmed's body and added, "This guy just tried to kill you. We need to shut down here, take statements and figure out what went wrong."

"Nothing went wrong. I'm here. He's gone. We'll sort this out later. Go ahead and get some names and take a few pictures but try and be subtle. I don't want this inauguration ruined."

"But sir, I think..."

"I hear Alaska's very nice this time of year. You ever been there?" the president interrupted.

"I understand exactly how you want this handled sir."

"Good, Mr. Clark." Tate turned on his heels and disappeared into the crowd as if nothing had happened.

Out of breath, Sam Phillips materialized next to Richards, his eyes darting about. "What the hell happened here?"

Agents, cops, medics and photographers were already attacking the bodies.

"Look," Richards said, pulling him over to Ahmed. "The party's over."

"Khalil! You got him! It's a Kodak moment."

Physically and mentally drained, Richards merely nodded assent.

Phillips smiled and wrapped his arm around Richards' shoulder. "Great job Norman! Great job."

"Thanks man."

"How close did he get?"

"Close."

"I can't believe I missed it."

"Don't worry. You'll have instant replay," Richards said, pointing at a CNN crew who recorded the entire incident.

A reporter approached Norman with his microphone out and the camera rolling. Thrusting the mike an inch from Richards' nose, the reporter said, "Excuse me. I understand your name is Norman Richards and you're a CIA agent. You just saved the president's life. How does it feel to..."

"Get the fuck out of my face," Richards said live to half the world, before walking away.

"Have you seen Karbal?" Phillips asked.

"No, he's probably still crawling around somewhere looking for Khalil."

"Hmm. Yeah. We'll find him later. Right now I need a drink," Richards said, signaling a waiter over. "I've earned it."

"I can't begrudge you this one, buddy."

He downed a glass of champagne like it was water after a workout, and handed the empty flute back to the waiter who smirked.

"Screw him," Richards said after the waiter walked away. "What I need now is some sleep. I'm wasted."

"Yeah, me too," said Phillips. "So let's get out of here before we have to spend the rest of the night answering questions. This mess'll be here tomorrow."

They turned around only to find Coston, Garber, Lang and Debra Klein rushing towards them.

"Too bad you guys missed the show. Khalil's dead. He's over there." He pointed behind him with his thumb.

"You think so. Come here," Coston ordered. Everyone followed him to Ahmed's body, though Richards and Phillips did so begrudgingly. Debra gasped when she saw the smiling bloody corpse.

"Is that him?" Lang asked Debra.

"That's not Barak. That's his brother. I think his name was Achmad or something like that."

"Are you sure?"

"I'm positive. Barak's face is a little thinner."

"You're sure?"

"I *said* yes."

"Wait a second," Phillips intervened. "You mean this dead motherfucker isn't Khalil? It's his brother Ahmed?"

"Right."

Richards jaw dropped and his posture slumped.

"If you assholes would have picked up your walkie talkies at the front like you were supposed to, you would have known Khalil is still in the building," Garber said.

"Yeah, like I wasn't doin' nothin' else," Richards snapped.

"Well something else is going down." Garber said.

"Like what?" Phillips asked.

"How about this?" Coston answered, handing him a piece of paper.

"He didn't have much in the apartment, but this was folded up in a coat pocket." Garber added.

"A label?" Phillips read it aloud, "Hoosier Chemicals. So what?"

"Carbonyl chloride," Coston said.

Richards and Phillips looked at each other blankly.

"It's the primary ingredient to make phosgene," Coston added.

"Holy shit!" Richards exclaimed. "He's got phosgene in here somewhere?"

"What the hell is phosgene?" Phillips asked.

"Poison gas. Used first by the Germans in World War One," Richards answered. "It would take very little to wipe out this whole building. Very little."

"Debra, tell us again. What exactly did Ahmed say Khalil was going to do?"

"That Barak would take out 1500 people within seconds, and then he grabbed his throat and made a gagging sound."

Richards looked up at the ceiling and then at his colleagues. "The only way to kill the whole room quickly would be to pipe it in through the ventilation system."

"Exactly what we figured," Garber said. "Code Red?"

Coston and Lang nodded affirmatively.

Garber waved Agent Clark over. "Clark, we've got an emergency. Evacuate the building. Now."

"But the president just gave me explicit instructions to --"

"Screw the president. Do it!"

"But sir, only the front Hall of States doors are open. There'll be a stampede. There's over 2000 people spread out in the building. I'll need at least five minutes just to get something organized."

"Do it!"

Debra impatiently tugged on Coston's overcoat sleeve. "Mr. Coston."

"Yes Debra."

"Barak also told Ahmed that once the lights flickered in the room, he had four minutes to get out of the building."

"Annnnd," Coston said, prodding her along waving his hand.

"Those chandeliers up there just flashed."

Everyone was so preoccupied that nobody noticed.

"They did?"

Her eyes drew taut and biting her bottom lip, totally petrified, she nodded yes.

Richards grasped her hand and held it tight. "Debra you have to help us. You might be able to stop him."

"No. I want to get out of here. I don't want to die."

"Debra please. We need you. You may be our only hope."

"No."

"C'mon. We're running out of time," Richards pleaded. "You'll be with me. You won't get hurt. I promise."

She closed her eyes for a few seconds and took a deep breath. In a low sad voice she said, "Okay, I'll go."

"You must be the building superintendent we called for, right?" Lang yelled at John Brumbaugh who was now standing a few feet away.

"Yes sir."

"Where's the ventilation system for the building? Quick!"

"Fourth floor. Above the restaurants."

"We need you to get us up there right now! The fastest way possible!"

"There's a service elevator over around the corner."

They all instantly took off running.

Four stories above them, Khalil was triple checking his preparations in a very dark and narrow work space behind a massive generator. The past hour had been spent drilling and boring a perfectly measured one inch hole into the primary ventilation tin ductwork that served as the source of origin for circulating all heated air through The Kennedy Center. From there he fit a rubber stopper with a long tube into the hole, and caulked it tightly into place with a fast drying silicon gel. The hose ran down from the duct directly into another rubber stopper lodged into one of two side by side five gallon containers filled with carbonyl chloride.

Khalil realized that it would take slightly longer for the gas to travel down four floors into the Grand Foyer, and some areas, such as the nearby kitchen, might receive a slightly higher concentration of poison. But who cared? The likelihood of success, of reaching downstairs and killing everyone, was 100%. Victory was at hand.

The elevator door opened and Brumbaugh led the group into The Kennedy Center's cavernous boiler room. It was dimly lit and rows of various machines in all directions hummed a low, nonstop roar. Parallel white and gray pipes lined the ceiling, and interspersed among them was boxy tin ductwork that ran across and around the room as far as the eye could see.

"The furnace. The ventilation system. Where is it?" Coston demanded.

"We have a few furnaces. They're spread out."

"I want the primary system that circulates the air through the building."

"Could be one of two. There's one about fifty yards down this aisle next to a generator, and there's another all the way at the other end of the building, sort of above the Hall of Nations."

Richards took charge. "Sam, Debra and I will find the one down here. You take these guys to the other one," he said to Brumbaugh. "We only have about a minute left."

As the two groups ran in opposite directions, this time Garber shouted, "Shoot to kill!"

Downstairs the Grand Foyer broke into total pandemonium. Agent Clark finally realized there was no other option but to commandeer the center stage microphone and order the room to evacuate immediately. He didn't even know why. Within seconds, president Tate was in his face banishing him to Alaska.

For security purposes, the Secret Service had chain locked the numerous double glass doors located throughout the entire Grand Foyer opening up to the River Terrace in the back of The Kennedy Center. Though nobody knew what the problem was, most guests realized the seriousness of the threat because of the shootings only minutes earlier. As Agent Clark predicted, a horrifying rush occurred with over a thousand government leaders panicked, fighting their way down the long length of the Grand Foyer and the Hall of States to try and escape through the only open doors. About a third of the guests ignored the warning figuring that if the president, vice president and half the Cabinet hadn't even moved from the Grand Foyer, why should they?

At the same time, Khalil sat cross-legged resting his back against the wall, a flashlight lantern strategically illuminating the mechanism inserted in the first glistening bottle at his feet. He checked his Rolex and calculated that Ahmed had to be out of the building by now.

He symbolically kissed his gas mask before carefully placing it over his head and tightening the rubber straps. His heart raced, knowing that years of hard training, planning and work was about to result in achieving the greatest terrorist feat in history. Perhaps Saddam would rename a city after him.

Khalil inserted a funnel into the rubber stopper on the bottle of carbonyl chloride, and held a sewing thimble in his hand ready to insert it into the funnel hole once he poured the water in the bottle and the lethal chemical reaction started. Checking his watch he picked up the pitcher of water, and thought, *Praised be Allah.* He focused on the funnel and raised the pitcher over it.

"Freeze!" Norman Richards screamed.

Khalil turned and stared at Richards and Debra in disbelief.

"If you move a fucking muscle, I'll shoot you in the head!" Richards added.

Khalil froze, then rebounded quickly. "If you shoot me in the head, then I drop this water in the bottle and you die too. This is a very deadly gas."

"I know what it is," Phillips said.

"Put down your gun," Khalil yelled, his voice muffled through the mask.

"Sorry asshole. That only happens in the movies," Richards said calmly. "You know you can't get away with this."

"I already have," Khalil said, subtlely allowing drops of water to run into the funnel.

"Don't do this, Khalil," Debra begged, calling him by his real name for the first time. "You're not a murderer. You couldn't kill me before. Don't kill me now. Please."

"I gave you a chance to live," he answered. "I love you, but it's not my fault you're here. The worst that happens now is we die together."

"You don't kill someone you love. And I don't want to die."

"Well I'm prepared to. This is my destiny. And I've come too far for you to stop me now."

Noticing that the angle of Khalil's hand had just turned slightly downwards, Richards emptied four shots into Khalil's chest, which exploded in red through the eerie light shining on him.

"No!" Debra screamed, collapsing to her knees.

As the bullets ripped open Khalil's body, the natural movement of his hand spilled even more of the water into the funnel, and with the course of gravity, it ran into the bottle.

"Run! Get the hell out of here!" Richards yelled, gulping in the largest breath of air he could.

Phillips grabbed Debra by the hand, pulled her up and they sprinted down the aisle towards the exit.

The water and carbonyl chloride were already reacting together forming a mist within the bottle. Richards knew that even the smallest amount of this phosgene allowed to circulate into the building's atmosphere was enough to kill anyone who breathed the polluted air.

Reacting instinctively, he yanked the hose out of the rubber stopper running into the air duct and covered its little plastic opening with his thumb. Then, realizing the hole from the funnel into the bottle was still open, he covered that with the middle finger of the same hand.

He fought with Khalil's dead body to remove the gas mask, struggling to keep his breath, fearful some of the poison gas had already infiltrated his lungs. Just as he thought his wind would give out, he manipulated the mask over his mouth and nose, and took grateful repeated deep breaths. He considered his next step; one hand was keeping the deadly gas from contaminating the air, and the other was barely holding the gas mask in place.

Garber, Lang, Coston and Brumbaugh suddenly appeared and quickly surmised what happened. "Go," he ordered in a muted voice through the mask, realizing it might already be too late for them.

All but Coston left instantly. Coston took a deep breath, slid in next to Richards and fit the gas mask firmly onto Richards' face. He then placed his thumb on top of Richards', who moved his thumb away and Coston's immediately covered the hole as the fog in the bottle grew more pronounced. Richards crimped the latex tube and then tied it into a series of tight knots to seal off one means of the gas's escape.

Seeing that Coston couldn't hold out much longer without breathing, Richards took a deep breath, ripped the mask off his face and pushed it against Coston's. He allowed Coston to breathe for a minute then signaled he was putting the mask back on himself. After getting the all clear from Coston, he quickly replaced the contraption on his head and put his thumb back over Coston's.

"Now go. I'm okay," Richards commanded, and Coston obeyed.

Norman still had one hole to plug and one hand to do it with. He didn't see the thimble at his feet or any other material within arm's reach that could be used. Grabbing the ripped edge of his blue jean jacket, he freed a swath of material from its binding. He twisted it around the tip of his index finger and shoved it into place inside the rubber cap, filling in as much material as it would hold.

This time it was over. Khalil was dead and his poison gas contraption disabled and ready for disposal by professionals.

Richards trudged down the entire stairwell uncertain what he would find below, praying it wouldn't be a site of mass death. When he finally exited at the ground floor into the Hall of States he witnessed not only total chaos, but that only a small minority of the guests made it outside and were shivering in the freezing cold. But there was no genocide. The gas died with Khalil.

His mind and body felt totally beaten but he was alive. *God I wish I had a drink.* Then for the first time something about the alcohol overcame him. *No, maybe not. Just some ice water.* It *was* finally all over.

Hundreds of focused stares tuned onto this raggedy man wearing a gas mask and beat up torn clothes. After a minute of him watching the crowd and the crowd watching him, which grew more silent by the moment as more people noticed Richards, he took off the mask and dropped it at his feet. Somehow the people all knew he had just saved their lives, and as Norman Richards walked past senators and Supreme Court Justices into the Grand Foyer, they cleared a path for him, some patting him on the back, some applauding.

He stopped and looked back at the herd of people still fighting to escape through the front of the Hall of States, oblivious that the threat was over, much less what it was even about. He walked up to one of the Grand Foyer's locked double glass doors, pulled out his .44 and fired twice, shattering it. Screams rose through the building at yet more gunshots. Richards didn't even turn around. He kicked out a portion big enough to scoot through and stepped outside onto the River Terrace overlooking the Potomac River. Everyone he had worked with and countless others from the government and press ran after him.

Trying to grasp the significance of the events as they unfolded this day, his eyes began to water. A barrage of questions and congratulations enveloped him. Everyone wanted a piece of Norman Richards. But they wouldn't get it right now. He put up his hand for silence and refused to acknowledge the presence of anyone. Instead, he took off his blue jean jacket, rolled it into a bundle and threw it over the balcony and into the river where it disappeared into the darkness. Then, finally, he had silence. He leaned against the rail, staring out into the nothingness of the black Washington night, oblivious to the cold.